Going Solo

The Brent Boys Series - Book II

D.P. Clarence

First paperback edition May 2025

Book design by Bailey McGinn

ISBN 978-1-7395509-5-0 (paperback)

ISBN 978-1-7395509-6-7 (Kindle ebook)

ISBN 978-1-7395509-7-4 (ebook)

www.dpclarence.com

Also by D.P. Clarence

The Paper Boys

The Silly Season (free novella)

For my aunts.
They know what they did.
Luckily, the cops don't.

Content Warnings

This book does not contain explicit sex on page (it's fade to black) but it does contain sexualised content, including characters making out and quite a few fairly ribald jokes.

This book also contains:

- Mentions and depictions of drug and alcohol addiction
- The off-page death of a minor/parental character
- A character coming out and concerns about family reactions
- A gay character being forced back into the closet
- The use of a trans character's dead name
- Mentions and depictions of a controlling and manipulative boss
- Mentions and depictions of a controlling and manipulative ex
- Mentions and depictions of invasive media practices
- Cows
- A happily ever after.

Glossary

Apparently some US readers felt a bit whopped by the Britishness of The Paper Boys, *so this is here to help you out!*

Cans – headphones

Well – used to mean 'very'

Innit – Essex-speak for 'isn't it?'

Nut – Essex-speak for 'head'. "Doing my nut" means someone is driving you crazy

Mug or muggy – to be 'muggy' or to 'mug off' someone is to make them look/feel stupid, deceive them or treat them badly

Melt – pathetic. A wimp or a loser

Tesco – a British supermarket chain

Scouser – a person from Liverpool

Fanny – lady parts (and not the bottom, as in the US)

Gaff – a house, a place to stay

Lorry – a truck

Aggie – short for aggravated, meaning 'angry'

Glastonbury – a big music festival, like Coachella

Haribos – a brand of soft gumdrop or jelly type candies

Wetherspoons – a chain of pubs, taverns and bars.

You lit a fire inside me
That burned like the sun.
You lit the way forward.
You were the one.
How did it burn out?
Please, baby, explain
Why the fire died inside you.
And I'm still holding the flame.
It burns and it burns and it burns.
You turn and I yearn and you burn—me.
"The Flame," lyrics and music by Cole Kennedy

Prologue

Tap. My microphone was live. The On Air sign bathed the studio in the soft red glow that made my heart race every time. The moment the song ended, I'd be talking to the entire United Kingdom. Well, the part of it obsessed enough with pop music to still listen to the radio. OK, mostly I'd be talking to people trapped in motorway traffic jams in cars without USB cables, but my show, *Pop Review*, did also have a loyal audience of dedicated music fans. My listeners were the Swifties, the Arianators, the Mendes Army, and they tuned into my radio show like they turned up to Glastonbury—strapped into a pair of cheap hardware store rubber boots and prepared to wade through a lot of shit to hear some great music. *Pop Review* was the place the UK's pop music conversation took place— every Saturday afternoon, between midday and four o'clock. And, for the past four years, I had been its host.

The final notes of the song faded out.

"This is *Pop Review*. I'm Tobias Lyngstad. That's the new one from Norwegian wunderkind Metteson. Not gonna lie, I love it! What do we think, pop tarts? Bothered or not bothered? Let me know. Hit me up on the chatline."

Tap. I fired off the five-second "sweeper" promo giving the chat-line number. Through the studio glass, I saw the heavy door to the news booth swing open on its automatic hinges and Nick steer his wheelchair in. He nodded at me. I gave him a thumbs up. The door closed behind him, and he slipped his headphones on. I loved working with Nick. Not just because he was my absolute best mate—a guy who spoke with an honesty as raw as my penis that time I caught syphilis from a hot tub hook-up on a package holiday to Magaluf—but because he was, to be fair, the best in the business. When you made radio with Nick, everything ran like clockwork.

The sweeper ended.

"Don't forget to use the hashtag *Metteson*. I'll share all your hot takes after the news. Also, next hour, we've got Manu Fernandez coming into the studio." I dragged out the vowels of the Spanish pop star's name, helping build the excitement. *Tap.* I faded up a clip of the chorus from Manu's big hit of the summer, "Te Encontré," then faded it back down as the clock on my screen told me I had five seconds to go. "Gets right in your nut, don't it?" I said, letting a little bit of the Essex accent out to play, because PureFM's focus groups said listeners loved it when I did. "You'll be singing it for days. Manu's here after the news at three. Don't miss it."

Tap. I fired off the commercial break. A highly produced station promo reminded the audience they were listening to "Pop. Pop. *Pop Review.* The UK's top pop music review show. On PureFM. Taking. Pop. *Seriously.* PuuuuureFM."

Tap. I turned off the mic, and the on-air light flicked off. Nick's smooth, lilting Aberdonian accent rumbled through my headphones. "Have you checked your socials in the last hour, Tobes?"

His voice had a tone my Aunty Cheryl called "a real panty dropper." And she was right. Although I'd have preferred it if she hadn't said so to his face.

I pressed the button that allowed me to talk directly into Nick's headphones. "Haven't had time, babes. I've been prepping for Manu. What's up?"

He was staring at me through the glass, giving me that look people give each other in disaster movies when the meteor is about to hit or the plane is about to crash and they realise their only hope for survival is Nicolas Cage.

"OK, pal," he said, his voice calm, "I need to issue a personalised trigger warning for this bulletin."

I sensed what was coming instantly. There was only one thing it could be.

The news theme jolted me out of my head.

"It's three o'clock. This is Nick Ross in the PureFM newsroom." I steadied myself against the studio desk. "Cole Kennedy has announced he's leaving the Go Tos—"

Cole. The four-letter word that had been haunting me for a decade, like a poltergeist with clinical attachment issues. The temperature in the room seemed to plummet. I shivered. Nick was still talking, but my brain couldn't process a word he was saying. The name Cole was echoing around my head like Nick had hollered it across a canyon. Through the glass to the left of the news booth I could see my producer, Tarneesha, laughing and joking with Manu Fernandez. I felt like I was watching it all on TV. I tried to tune back into Nick's voice.

"After ten years with the world's biggest boy band, the twenty-six-year-old pop star said he wanted to take his music in a new direction—one that, in his words, better reflects his artistry."

"No, no, no, no, NO!" I said, feeling my blood pressure skyrocket.

"The Go Tos came together a decade ago on season six of the reality TV show *Make Me a Pop Star* and went on to become the world's most successful pop band, regularly topping the charts with multiplatinum albums and selling out stadiums over multiple world tours. Kennedy, a talented songwriter, wrote the band's biggest hit, 'Genevieve.' There's no word yet from Kennedy's bandmates, but *Make Me a Pop Star* executive producer and Totally Records chief executive Felicity Quant said she wished Kennedy well, and the Go Tos would go on without him.”

This was *huge*. Cole's fan base, the Kenneddicts, were going to lose their minds. On my screen, the PureFM chatline was spinning like a Las Vegas poker machine, with dozens of new messages loading every second. Cole Kennedy had completely ruined my carefully planned show. But what was new? Ten years earlier, Cole Kennedy had ruined my entire life.

Part One
TEN YEARS EARLIER

Are you the U.K.'s next pop superstar?

Filming for the new season of "Make Me a Pop Star," the hit reality TV show that made Jocasta Rose and Boy Treble household names, begins in Colchester this weekend.

Thousands of hopefuls from across Essex, Suffolk, Norfolk and Cambridgeshire are expected to descend on the Lion Walk Shopping Centre on Saturday to audition in front of celebrity judges Felicity Quant, Robbie Johnswagger and Johanna Thorsdóttir.

Quant told the Chronicle: "As a long-time resident of Suffolk myself I'm well aware of the incredible musical talent we have here in East Anglia. I can't wait to see what our contestants have in store for us and to make their dreams of pop stardom come true."

Jocasta Rose, who won the first season of "Make Me a Pop Star" six years ago, is currently topping the U.K. music charts with her song "Say It to My Face." Last year she was the country's top-earning musical act—helping Quant's label, Totally Records, become the U.K.'s biggest domestically owned record company.

Registrations for the "Make Me a Pop Star" auditions open at 8 a.m. on Saturday at Shop 9 (the old WHSmith) in the Lion Walk Shopping Centre, Colchester.

Chapter One

Colchester was absolutely heaving. There hadn't been a free car-parking space anywhere. By the time Mum and I had circled the town centre for forty minutes trying to find a spot, stopped to let Gaston (our bichon frise) have a comfort stop against the wheel of a Range Rover, and dashed the half mile back into town, we were well late for the auditions.

"I don't understand why we couldn't park around the back of the salon," I moaned as we trotted along the footpath.

"Because a rough sleeper's set up his tent in my spot and I ain't moving him on so you can get your face on the telly, Tobias Lyngstad," Mum said.

The day was a scorcher. Not exactly Alicante, but hot for England in July—and way too hot to be running up the high street. I was regretting falling out of an exercise habit during school exams, and I was certainly regretting wearing spray-on super skinny jeans. My thighs were on fire from the chafing, and a bead of sweat was racing down my back towards my bum crack with the single-minded determination of a teenage boy on a mission to lose his virginity. (Which, given at this time I was literally a teenage boy on a mission to lose his virginity, was something I understood, one hundred per cent. To be honest with you, I'd have settled for a light fingering from one of the school's rugby sevens in the back of their mum's old Hyundai. Despite my best efforts, I hadn't even got as close as that. I was too awkward, too queer, and too *Toby*.) As we dashed past Costa Coffee, I caught sight of my reflection in the window. I was a mess.

"What do I look like? I spent three hours doing my hair and make-up, and it's already ruined."

"Stop moaning, Tobes," Mum said, "I've got half the salon in me bag. We can fix it."

By the time we finally found the queue for the auditions, the line snaked all the way out of the shopping centre and around the church-yard. Half of Essex had shown up, scrambling for their chance at fame. (The other half of Essex was already famous and probably avoiding town in case the stench of middle-class ambition triggered their PTSD.)

A woman in a plaid shirt and a fit lad in a black leather jacket and with a guitar slung over his shoulder joined the end of the queue. Mum and I slipped in behind them.

"Is this the line for *Make Me a Pop Star*?" Mum asked breathlessly. The woman turned to face us, her shoulder-length brown hair catching the breeze.

"I sure hope so," she said in a thick Irish accent. She flicked a thumb towards the church. "If I get to the front and discover I've queued for some bastard's funeral, I'll be fuming."

Mum laughed so hard she snorted. She slapped her hand over her mouth in embarrassment. The woman giggled. Gaston, upset at being left out, popped his fluffy little head out of Mum's Hermès Birkin handbag and barked. And that's when it happened. The lad in the leather jacket turned around. I remember it in slow motion, like he was in a hair care commercial. For the first time, I saw those sultry chestnut eyes and their soulful intensity. The lad was well fit: Dark olive skin. A strong Roman nose. Thick eyebrows. A voluminous swoopy mop of raven hair. A strand of rock star fringe that fell across his face, like he was Elvis or James Dean or pre-creepy Johnny Depp. I was mesmerised. He was tall, broad-shouldered, and upright and exuded the kind of confidence the advertising industry would have us believe can only be achieved by the right deodorant or an incontinence pad. He wasn't just fit; he was, as we say in Essex, *reem*.

"And who is this?" the fittie said, crouching and offering the back of his hand to Gaston. His voice was deep and smooth and velvety. His accent wasn't Irish, though. He sounded Suffolk born and bred. That surprised me, as I'd assumed the Irish woman was his mum.

"This is Gaston," Mum said. The dog sniffed for a moment, then, rather regally, granted the boy in the leather jacket an audience.

"Hey, Gaston, I'm Cole," he said. "And this is my mum, Orla."

That answered that. Cole and Orla patted Gaston while Mum introduced us both, not passing up an opportunity to clarify she was *the* Chloe of Chloe's Hair and Beauty on the high street.

Cole's eyes drifted in my direction, taking in my super skinny jeans and sending me into a micro-panic that the sweat was showing through the fabric of my T-shirt. I shifted my weight so my thighs were side-on, which was angle enough to hide any lower-back sweat while letting him clock the goods round the back. I was sixteen and horny and I'd never been kissed, so if he wanted to look, I'd go full peacock. I was one flirty wink away from flipping my top up behind my head and shimmying my tail feathers. As he stood up straight, Cole's eyes locked on to mine. One corner of his mouth turned up slightly, and my heart fluttered. Within months that smirk would grace everything from magazine covers and T-shirts to billboards and bed linen. But in that moment, that unconsciously sexy half smile wasn't for the cameras, it wasn't for millions of screaming fans, it was for me—awkward, queer, uncomfortable-in-his-skin Toby Lyngstad. It stirred something in my loins that neither my brain nor my jeans had the capacity to handle.

"Lovely to meet you, Toby," Cole said. The sound of my name

rolling off his tongue vibrated through my groin, and I nearly pissed my knickers right there on the footpath outside the Trinity Church. A charge of heat surged through my body as Cole's hand slipped around mine. The tips of his fingers were hard—calloused, I guessed, from hours of guitar practice—but his hand was soft and his grip firm. The way he looked me up and down was well intimate. It was like he was undressing me. Sweat burst from my palm. It couldn't have been more obvious I was into him if I'd slipped him a fistful of lube and a note with my opening hours.

"You too," I said. The words squeaked out of me like my voice was still breaking. I coughed to clear my throat. Cole smirked again and let go of my hand. I was still lost in the deep mahogany pools of his eyes and noticed how they sparkled with flecks of amber.

Mum nudged me with her elbow. "Orla asked you a question, Tobes."

I felt like I was emerging from a general anaesthetic. How long had I been under?

"Huh?"

"Orla asked what song you're singing for your audition," Mum said, voice slightly impatient.

"'Firework,'" I said, suddenly super embarrassed by my song choice. Don't get me wrong, I loved the song. But with his leather jacket and his guitar, I was willing to bet Cole's song choice would be something much cooler than Katy Perry.

"Toby loves *Make Me a Pop Star*," Mum said. "He's never missed an episode. We've been up to London every year to be in the audience for the live shows. He knows everything there is to know about the show. I told him he should start a YouTube channel or a podcast or something. He's so smart, he's like the Stephen Fry of pop stars."

"Mum!" I felt sweat prickling on my face, my hands, my back. My pores were opening like fire hydrants.

"Cole's doing 'Hallelujah,'" Orla said, and I was sucking air through my teeth before I could stop myself. Cole frowned. "The Jeff Buckley song," she added.

"Leonard Cohen, actually," Cole said. His eyes seemed to question me, as if this bit of information might allay my fears.

"It'll always be Jeff Buckley to our generation, ain't that right?" Mum said, nudging Orla with her elbow.

"What's wrong with the song?" Cole asked, serious.

"Everything," I said. "If you go in there and sing Leonard Cohen, Felicity Quant is going to stop you before you're two bars in, and she's going to ask you to sing something else."

"How do you know that?"

"Didn't you watch season four?"

Cole and Orla looked at each other meaningfully.

"Oh my God, do you not know what happened in season four?"

Cole shook his head.

"You've never heard of Jamie Struff?"

He shook his head again. How did Cole not know this? This was *Make Me a Pop Star* folklore. This was British cultural history—like Shakespeare's plays, the Beatles' music, and that bit in *Love Actually* where Alan Rickman gives Emma Thompson a CD for Christmas.

"At the Manchester auditions, Jamie Struff starts singing 'Hallelujah.' Felicity Quant raises her hand, and the music stops. Jamie's thrown completely. He looks shattered. Felicity says, 'Save it for your nan's funeral, mate. What else have you got?'"

"She did not!" Orla said.

"One hundred per cent. In short, you need to pick another song."

Cole looked crestfallen.

Mum rallied. "Well, if anyone can help you pick the right song, it's my Toby. Tell you what, why don't Orla and I pop down to Costa and get us all a nice cup of cino, while you two put your minds together?"

"Great plan," Orla said. She put a hand around Cole's neck, pulled him down to her height, and kissed him on the forehead. "Do you want a water, darling?"

He nodded. "Still, please." She released him, and he flicked his hair back, running his fingers through it so it bounced back into place with the perfect swoopiness. It was the sexiest thing I'd ever seen—and I'd been in the front row of the Jonas Brothers at Wembley Arena. Both nights. I'd been so close I could actually smell Joe's eyebrows. But Cole Kennedy was somehow even sexier than that.

"Did you seriously not watch *Make Me a Pop Star* season four?" I asked as Mum and Orla disappeared around the corner.

Cole leaned into me and whispered in my ear. "Will you think less of me if I confess that I've never watched a single episode?"

I stepped back, literally clutching my imaginary pearls.

"Sorry. I'm not much of a reality TV person."

I shook my head. "Babes, you need to sort your priorities out. This is a life-or-death situation."

"I'm... not sure it is." He giggled, studying my face with amusement.

"If you don't like reality TV, what are you even doing here?"

"Well, I'm not supposed to say anything, but a producer called up and asked me to audition."

"Shut up, they never!"

Cole nodded. "No, really. They saw a YouTube video of me singing at my local pub, tracked me down to the farm, and got in touch. I didn't particularly want to audition, but Mum and Fiona were dead keen."

The mention of a girl's name cut through my consciousness like a record scratch. "Is Fiona your girlfriend?" I asked, poised for heartbreak.

"My sister," Cole said, to my relief. "Anyway, they insisted, so here I am."

"You're a shoo-in, then."

"I'm not expecting anything," Cole said, as cool as a cucumber that's jumped into an ice bath to recover from a long weekend at home with a lonely homosexual.

"You must be good," I said, dialling up the flirting a notch.

Cole blushed. A coy side-smile widened into a sexy grin. It was infectious. I smiled and blushed in return. Our eyes met, and I held his gaze. For all that outward confidence, my legs turned to jelly. Cole laughed awkwardly, and in that moment, I felt the instant, undeniable spark of something between us—like a magnetic force was pulling us towards each other.

The silence had gone on for too long.

"Isn't it warm in that?" I pointed at his leather jacket, hoping he'd agree and take it off. He was only wearing a tiny vest underneath. The scooped neckline showed the valley of lean muscle that divided his chest, with its olive skin and light smattering of clipped dark hair. It was almost too much to bear, but obviously, I wanted to see more.

"It's my look," Cole said. "For the audition."

I nodded, disappointed. "Fashion is pain, right? To be honest, these skinny jeans chafe around my thighs something shocking, but it's the classic look, innit?"

"So, you're planning to keep them on, then?" Cole winked, and my heart burst out of my chest and punched him in the face. "Fair enough. It's a good look on you."

I felt my cheeks flush. "Shu'up! Thank you."

"You're welcome," he said, flicking his gaze to the ground. I couldn't believe it. As if a lad as fit as Cole was flirting with me? Mum always said the blond hair and blue eyes of my Swedish heritage would make me irresistible to the right lad one day, but to be fair, I thought that day was years away. I had acne. I was carrying around so much teenage puppy fat that if you harvested it and rendered it down to make candles, you could light up Colchester town centre for Christmas. Silence hung between us for a minute. Cole's foot moved back and forth across the pavement. I let my eyes trace the line of his jeans, up his calves and thighs, across his torso. Our eyes met, and we giggled and looked away. Had we both been checking the other out? Cole flicked his hair back, refreshing the swoosh.

"So, what happened?" Cole asked, his head tilted to reveal a sexy vein in his neck.

"Huh?"

"To Jamie Struff. You never told me."

"Oh! He panicked, sang Cheryl Cole's 'Promise This,' and was never heard of again."

Cole frowned. "How come you remember his name, then?"

"Because the poor lad became an internet meme! People have been openly laughing about him for two years. His face is shorthand for making a terrible panicked decision."

"That's... awful."

"I know. It weren't right."

Cole let his guitar case slip from his shoulder and swung it around to rest the base gently on the ground.

"You think I should change my song?"

"Definitely."

"Maybe I could sing one of my own compositions?"

Of course Cole wrote music. He oozed proto–Bob Dylan.

"Whatever you do, do not sing one of your own songs." Cole looked surprised. "Not only will the audience think you're full of yourself, but you're robbing them of familiarity, which is important because that's how they connect with you. And the judges will think you believe you're better than the last sixty years of pop music. Which, given they're all music-industry legends, they're likely to take personally."

Cole was visibly starting to panic. A bead of sweat dripped from his neck and ran down his chest. I wanted to collect it in a bottle to stick up my bum later.

"What should I sing?"

"Pick something upbeat that shows off your vocal range."

Cole tapped two fingers against his forehead, as if he were scrolling through a mental list.

"What about Queen? 'Somebody to Love,' maybe?"

"It gets done every year, babes."

"'Feeling Good' by Nina Simone?"

I shook my head. "Tommy Baldock did it three years ago and went on to win."

"Vocal range..." Cole was muttering to himself now. I'd sent him into a tailspin, and I would have felt bad but my advice was solid. One hundred per cent.

"I Will Always Love You!" he said, inspired.

"I appreciate the sentiment, but you ain't even taken me for a test drive yet."

Cole didn't laugh.

"If you can't do it better than Whitney, don't do it," I said.

"Livin' on a Prayer?"

"Not being muggy, but why is that song even in your repertoire?"

"I play it at the pub sometimes. It goes down well."

This was an idea I could work with. "When you're singing down the pub, is there a song the crowd goes absolutely batshit for?"

"I'm not doing 'Five Hundred Miles.'"

I laughed.

Cole roared in what I guessed was frustration. "I was so prepared!" The vein pulsed in his neck. Another bead of sweat rolled down his chest, and I wondered if there was a discreet way to lick it off him. His intensity was dead sexy.

"Don't worry about it," I said, touching his elbow, "you'll find the perfect song. Trust me, you got it."

Cole seemed to grow two inches taller. His confidence had returned. "You're a genius."

"Who's a genius?" Orla asked. She thrust a bottle of water between us, and I let my hand drop from her son's elbow.

"There's been a change of plan," Cole said.

"Hallelujah!" Mum said.

Gaston barked.

Chapter Two

The first time I ever heard Cole Kennedy sing, he was standing on the other side of a closed door. Even then, it was obvious he was good. Like, *really* good. He was a natural baritone and had serious range. His voice had a smooth, silky quality. He sang with real emotion and incredible power. He'd chosen to sing Roy Orbison's "You Got It," and when he finished, there was clapping in the room. This was only the producer audition (the audition you did before you auditioned for the TV judges), but we'd probably listened to the last twenty acts performing through that door, and we'd never heard clapping before. How was I going to follow that?

The door opened, and Cole emerged with a massive grin on his face. "I'm through to the judges."

Orla threw her arms around him. "I'm so proud of you!"

Cole, still holding his guitar, wound his free arm around her. Then he looked directly at me and dipped his head in a small bow. "It's all thanks to Toby. Changing song was absolutely the right call."

When Orla finally released him, Cole hugged me. My heart was thumping like it had joined a stampede. I hugged him back, tucking my head into his shoulder, breathing in the smell of him—the shampoo, the leather, the Lynx Africa. A bead of sweat was within licking distance. I nearly went for it.

A Scottish voice boomed throughout the room. "One hundred and forty-six!"

Mum whacked me in my ribs. "That's you, Tobes. You're up, bubby."

"One hundred and forty-six!" the voice called again.

"I better go," I said, pulling free of the hug.

Cole put his hand on my shoulder and looked me square in the eye. "You got it."

"Do you two know each other?" It was one of the *Make Me a Pop Star* producers, the same one who had been calling out my number.

Cole turned to the woman and grinned. "We met in the line earlier." He let his arm slip around my shoulder and pulled me into him. Then, like a gentleman in a regency romance, he introduced us. "Indira, this is Toby. Toby, this is Indira—she's an assistant producer on the show."

Indira looked at Cole. Indira looked at me. She looked back at Cole. She looked back to me. Then she raised a hand, pointed a finger at Cole, and then pointed it at me.

"You're not a"—she waggled the finger back and forth—"*thing*, are you?"

"Oh!" Cole said, letting his arm fall from my shoulder. "No, no. Nothing like that."

Indira smiled. I wasn't sure if she was relieved or if she didn't believe him. "Well, come on, Toby. You're up."

* * *

There was no round of applause for me. My heart was pounding in my throat as I waited for the producers' verdict on my "Firework." Indira leaned over to another producer and whispered something in his ear. He nodded. He looked up at me, smiled, and kept nodding.

Indira pointed at something she'd written on her clipboard. The other producer stared at me. My fight-or-fart mechanism was triggered, and my bumhole clenched like it was tightening a nut.

"Toby," Indira said, finally, "we'd like you to sing for the judges this afternoon."

Tears sprung from my eyes with the relief. It was like someone had loosened my corset and suddenly I could breathe again.

"Thank you! Thank you so much!" I squealed. Then, for some reason, I curtsied. "What am I like?" I said. Indira and the other producer laughed. That was encouraging. At least I would be good telly. I skipped out of the room, feeling as high as my Aunt Cheryl that time she did ketamine on an easyJet flight to Las Palmas de Gran Canaria. I was in with a shot. There was a chance all my dreams would come true, and I could be a pop star.

Chapter Three

ake Me a Pop Star host Dorinda Carter and a camera crew found us in the area where the producers had corralled the contestants who were going to perform for the TV judges onstage at Colchester's Mercury Theatre later that evening. This was either really good news or really bad news. If the camera crew followed you through the auditions, you were going to be on the show. It meant you were either good and they expected you to get through, or they thought you were well delusional and were about to become a laughing stock on national television. No one wanted to be this season's Jamie Struff.

"Hello, boys," Dorinda said in her thick Birmingham accent. I couldn't believe it. I was meeting TV royalty. My heart raced like it was in the three o'clock at Newmarket and the stable boy had given it a sneaky injection of something spicy.

Dorinda was big and Black and had a laugh that cackled out of her like one of those wheezing cartoon hyenas. I was fangirling.

"Now, which one of you is Cole Kennedy?"

Cole raised his hand shyly.

"Fab! So, you must be Toby, are you, darlin'?"

I nodded.

"Right, boys, so what we're gonna do is, you'll both be in the same shot, yeah? Then, one at a time, you're going to introduce yourselves. Say your name and where you're from, how old you are, and a fact about yourself. OK?"

We nodded. The camera guy framed us both up and said he was rolling. Neither of us said anything. We stared at the camera, frozen—like its sight relied on movement and if we flinched it'd rip us apart.

"Cole, why don't you go first?" Dorinda said.

Cole cleared his throat and ran his hand through his hair so it swooshed.

"Still rolling," the cameraman said.

"Hi, I'm Cole Kennedy, I'm from Polstead in Suffolk. I'm sixteen, and I love classic rock and roll."

Dorinda nodded and pointed to me.

"Hi, I'm Toby Lyngstad, I'm sixteen, and I'm from Colchester in Essex. And I am obsessed with pop music. Like, honestly, I love all the divas. Beyoncé. Kylie. H from Steps. My audition song today is 'Firework.'"

I looked at Dorinda for confirmation I'd done a good job. Her expression was grim.

"Tell you what, boys, let's try something different. I'm going to record a quick intro, and then I'll ask you some questions. Make it feel a bit less formal."

The camera swung around, and Dorinda was instantly *on*. No wonder she'd won so many National TV Awards.

"I'm with Cole Kennedy from Suffolk and Toby Lyngstad from right here in Colchester. They're sixteen." As the camera panned across to us, Cole threw an arm around my shoulder, stuck a tongue out, and gave the camera bunny ears. This lad was a freaking natural. A real superstar. I smiled like a red squirrel with a nut in each cheek.

"You boys seem pretty chummy, are you schoolmates?" Dorinda asked, shoving the microphone under Cole's chin.

"No, we met in the queue this morning."

"Firm friends already?"

"Exactly," Cole said. "Forged in the fire."

My legs were tingling. I could feel my pulse in my ears. Cole was being Mr Personality on camera, and my face was frozen like a Tesco pizza.

"Toby's the whole reason I got a chance to audition tonight," Cole continued.

"How so?" Dorinda asked.

"I'm embarrassed to say, I came here today intending to sing 'Hallelujah.'"

Dorinda grimaced in mock horror. "You never heard of the Hallelujah Curse?"

"Afraid not. But Toby here did me a solid and set me straight."

"Toby, you could have let him sing 'Hallelujah' and seen off the competition! Why did you help him?"

The microphone was suddenly under my chin. Panic gripped me. I could have said anything in that moment. I could have said the truth —that it was the obvious thing to do, that of course I wouldn't let someone ruin their shot at achieving their dreams. But I didn't say any of that. Instead, I blurted the words, "Why wouldn't I? He's marriage material!"

Dorinda's face morphed into a broad grin, and that famous laugh exploded from her mouth, filling the room. I felt Cole's arm unwind from around my back, the warmth of him retreating.

"What do you say to that, Cole?"

Cole's eyebrows were raised, his forehead frowning. "Yeah, um, that's... a bit intense," he spluttered.

"Not keen on marriage?"

"Someday, sure," he said, one hand rubbing his face. "When I meet the right person. And maybe when I've known them more than, like, four hours."

In those five seconds, I died a million tiny deaths. Without even thinking, I'd said something stupid. On camera. Understandably, Cole had mugged me off. I was going to look like an absolute melt on national television.

Chapter Four

A few hours later, I stood in the wings of the stage at Colchester's Mercury Theatre, watching Cole sing "You Got It." The judges lapped it up. Cole played guitar along with the backing track and rocked around the stage in his leather jacket like he owned the place. He was effortlessly cool and sexy, with a voice so full of flavour it was like popping one of each colour Starburst in your mouth at the same time. A few steps in front of me, Dorinda Carter hammed up her reactions for the camera.

"That voice!" she mouthed, fanning herself.

The song ended, and the audience erupted into applause. On the monitor I could see them on their feet. The judges swivelled in their chairs to look at the crowd. Robbie Johnswagger—an old-school rocker from the 1980s—slowly got to his feet, joining the standing ovation. The crowd went wild. Cole slapped his hand to his heart in thanks. A moment later Johanna Thorsdóttir—an Icelandic songstress who had a string of hits in the early 2000s after a spectacular Eurovision appearance—also stood. That left Felicity Quant—the multimillionaire music-industry mogul and *Make Me a Pop Star* executive producer—sitting down. The audience wasn't having it.

They began stamping their feet, making the theatre vibrate. Felicity played it cool, looking around at them, looking down at her notes, looking at her fingernails. The crowd's outrage was deafening. Finally, Felicity leaned forward in her seat and stood. The audience lost its collective shit. Literally.

Cole held his hands up as if in prayer, humbly accepting the applause. When the noise finally died down and everyone had taken their seats, it was time to film the judges' comments.

"From one old rocker to another," Robbie Johnswagger said in his broad Leeds accent, "thank you for bringing this performance to this stage. It gladdens my heart to see the younger generation paying respect to a legend like Roy Orbison and doing such credit to his artistry in this way. You're an incredible performer already, and I can't wait to see what you can achieve on this stage."

Robbie hit his button, and a big green tick lit up over his head. The crowd erupted. Felicity Quant put up her hand, the accepted symbol on the show for "That's enough, shut up, you plebs, the adults are speaking."

"I agree with Robbie," Johanna Thorsdóttir began, "it was an incredible performance. You have a beautiful tone. But your voice is in the lower register, and we're trying to find a pop star here, not—"

"Whoa, whoa, whoa," Robbie leapt in, "you think baritones can't be pop stars? What about Elvis, Hendrix, Tom Jones, Neil Diamond—"

"Got anyone this century?" Johanna hit back.

Everyone in the audience *ooo*ed in unison.

"I can't believe we're even having this conversation." Robbie looked exasperated. "Chris Martin. Will that do you? The front man of the biggest band in the world."

The audience booed and laughed and cheered. Felicity's hand went up. They shushed. This was amazing telly. There was no way someone of Johanna Thorsdóttir's experience thought a baritone couldn't have a fantastic pop career. They were creating tension to milk Cole's moment onstage.

"But I think you're incredible," Johanna said. "And you deserve to go through to London."

A big green tick appeared above her head, and the audience burst into rapturous applause. Felicity Quant raised her hand, and a hush descended over the room. It all came down to this moment. Everyone knew the other two judges had no real say. Felicity's word was final.

"You're a good-looking young man," she said. "You're confident. You can sing. You can move. You can clearly play guitar. Do you play anything else?"

"Piano," Cole said. "Most instruments, I guess. With time." Felicity nodded. "And I write my own songs as well," Cole added.

Felicity raised an eyebrow. "Who are you here with today?"

Cole pointed to the wings, where Dorinda was standing with Orla. The camera beside me swung around to focus on them.

"My mum," Cole said.

Dorinda and Orla waved into the camera.

"And you come from Suffolk, I believe?" Felicity Quant said.

"My family have a dairy farm," Cole offered.

Felicity's eyebrows were on the move again. "I come from Suffolk," she said. "Do you know Long Melford?"

"Of course! We're only over in Polstead."

This was more than small talk. This was Felicity Quant establishing a personal connection with Cole. She only did this when she knew she was sitting on a superstar. This was a moment that would be cut up and reused all over YouTube for "humble beginnings" videos for years to come.

"In the Dedham Vale!" she said. "I know it. Do you ever go to the Crown at Stoke-by-Nayland?"

"I perform there sometimes!"

The penny dropped. Felicity already knew that. It was obvious to me in that moment that Cole was going through. Heck, he was a real contender to win.

"They do a great Sunday roast," Felicity said.

Cole nodded.

"And what's your heritage?" she asked. The question was the elephant in the room. Where *did* those smouldering dark good looks come from? Because they weren't from Orla, and they certainly weren't from a sunbed.

"My father is Polstead born and bred," Cole said. "My mum is from County Wicklow in Ireland. But if you mean why am I so brown when my parents are so white, I'm adopted."

That made sense.

"I don't know the full story, but I know my birth mother was white British. I don't know where my father was from. Greece, maybe. Perhaps somewhere in the Middle East. All I know is I was fostered out to my parents as a baby... and they must have taken a shine to me, because they adopted me."

The audience applauded. Johanna Thorsdóttir managed to weep —something she did so often I was pretty sure her contract insisted she was paid by the tear. It was a weird vibe, and I thought Cole looked uncomfortable.

"To be fair, I think I was too good at milking cows, and they couldn't afford to let me go."

Laughter rippled through the audience.

"But my parents are amazing people. As are my sister, Fiona, and my brother, Tully. We're a close family. I'm doing this for them. To make them proud."

The audience clapped uproariously. Cole smiled. Felicity raised a hand. She'd got all the narrative and all the footage she needed for now.

"Well, I look forward to meeting them all in London," she said, and pressed the button for the big green tick.

Chapter Five

If there was applause as I walked onto the stage, I couldn't hear it over the sound of my heart pounding out a drum solo in my ears. Felicity Quant spoke, but I didn't hear that either. I felt my hands start to shake and stuck them in my back pockets. I saw myself on a screen. I couldn't have looked more terrified if the clown from *IT* was staring back up at me from the orchestra pit.

"Name?" Felicity sounded impatient. I'd made her repeat herself. This was off to a terrible start.

My voice squeaked out of me like I'd swallowed an accordion. I cleared my throat and tried again.

"And where are you from, Toby?"

I said Colchester, and the home crowd cheered.

"You seem nervous, ástin min." That was Johanna Thorsdóttir—the compassionate voice on the panel—throwing out her much-loved Icelandic catchphrase to please the fans. "Ástin Min" was the name of her hit Eurovision song. Apparently, it was a term of endearment that meant "my love," but it could have been an Icelandic brand of tinned herring for all I knew. "Deep breaths," she said, her piercing blue eyes offering reassurance. "Everyone in this room wants you to succeed."

The crowd clapped. I took a deep breath, pulled my hands from my back pockets, and shook them out. In the corner of my eye, I saw Cole standing at the side of the stage. He gave me a thumbs up. God, even his thumbs were fit.

The music started. My voice croaked on the first note, and I felt my throat close over. I only had one shot at this, so I coughed, found my voice, and gave it my all. The next ninety seconds were a complete blur. When I was done, Johanna responded first.

"We could hear the nerves at the start, but once you hit your stride, you delivered an anthem. Why did you choose 'Firework'?"

"It's about personal acceptance, innit, and I find that empowering," I said, exactly as I'd rehearsed in my bedroom mirror. "Katy Perry dedicated it to the It Gets Better campaign, which is all about supporting the LGBTQ-plus community."

"Are you a member of the LGBTQ-plus community yourself, Toby?" Johanna asked.

"Non-practising, babes, but yes," I said. The audience laughed.

"Well, you did them proud, ástin mín." She hit the button for the big green tick, and I dared to hope.

Robbie criticised my ropey start, my vocal range, and my "lack of broad appeal"—which was *Make Me a Pop Star* code for too gay, too brown, too fat, or too ugly. With my Ultra Rich Sunny Honey Bali Bronze Spray Tan, I was arguably a full house.

"You're not a pop star, mate." He pressed his button, and a big red cross appeared above his head. "That's just how it is."

I felt my dream slipping, and my heart rate doubled. The crowd booed. At least they were on my side. Sometimes the judges kept you in if you were a crowd-pleaser. But had I done enough? My nerves couldn't have been more wrung out if a nineteenth-century laundry maid had fed them through a mangle.

"You're a real entertainer, there's no doubt you've got charisma," Felicity said. That was worryingly non-committal. There was a long pause while she riffled through some papers. "I want to see what else you can do," she said, looking up, as a big green tick appeared above her head. "Congratulations, you're coming to London."

EXCLUSIVE: Pop star pub brawl!
Johnswagger's big Essex night out

In Colchester for "Make Me a Pop Star," the show that rehabilitated his career, Robbie Johnswagger wasted no time getting rock and roll royally smashed the minute the cameras were off.

Luckily, The Bulletin's cameras were still turned on, so our snappers captured the moment the ageing rocker was chucked out of the Quickly Whippet Inn on Colchester High Street. (See pictures.)

The Bulletin understands Johnswagger got into a heated discussion with members of the pub's house band over the artistic merits of "Junkyard Mongrel," Johnswagger's first solo album after he split from iconic '80s rock band Buzzsaw. A pub regular told us that an "utterly wankered" Johnswagger—apparently not a fan of constructive criticism—threw the first punch.

"The whole band piled in to support their mate," our witness said. "The drummer whacked Johnswagger around the side of the head with an ice bucket. Old Robbie looked like it didn't even register. He's hard, I'll give him that."

The fight only stopped because Johnswagger stepped back to line up a punch and slipped on a cube of ice. He was knocked out cold for a few seconds, which gave the bouncers time to shirtfront him and throw him out into the street!

Chapter Six

On the Tuesday afternoon after the audition, as my summer vacation got off to an early start, I was helping out at the salon. I was sat at the reception counter, bored out of my mind, amusing myself by watching to see what a little kid in the street did with the enormous booger he'd just picked out of his nose, when my phone pinged.

Cole: *Hey, can I run my song choices for London by you?*

Heat flushed through my body, and I jumped up to open the salon door and let the breeze in. The little kid looked up at me, spooked by the sudden movement. The booger was gone, the offending finger now firmly gripped in his mother's hand. Parenthood was *not* for me. Cole and I had swapped numbers after the auditions, but I hadn't expected to hear from him. I mean, I'd hoped I'd hear from him. I'd visualised it, prayed to Madonna about it, and sent two pairs of underpants to the laundry basket trying to manifest his presence in my bedroom at night. But I hadn't expected it to work. Spending last summer sitting by the pool in Benidorm reading *The Secret* had really paid off. My hands were shaking so much, I could barely type.

Toby: *Course babes!*

"Shut the door, Toby!" Aunty Cheryl called across the salon. "I've spent twenty minutes gluing tiny gel penises onto Gemma's nails for her hen do, and you're letting dust in."

Aunty Cheryl was nursing a three-day hangover. Along with half the other mature-aged single women in Essex, she'd spent the weekend scouring the pubs of Colchester, unsuccessfully trying to land a shag with Robbie Johnswagger—something that apparently had been on her bucket list for some time.

"Sorry, girls!"

"You're right, babes," Gemma called back.

As I shut the door, my phone pinged again.

Cole: *Did you just call me "babes"?*

Uh-oh, had I screwed this up already? I sank back into the reception chair and crafted a cautious reply.

Toby: *I'm from Essex, everyone calls everyone babes. Soz do u not like it?*

Cole: *No, it's cool. I liked it ;) Don't think anyone has ever called me babes before.*

Toby: *Tell me ur not from Essex without telling me ur not from Essex!*

Cole: *Guilty as charged.*

Cole said he needed my help deciding between two songs for our first London TV audition. One was by Patti Smith, who I'd sort of heard of but never listened to, and another by a band called Nirvana, who I'd heard of but only because you see the word written across T-shirts worn by the kind of guys who look and smell like a debilitating water allergy has devastated their personal hygiene routine.

Toby: *Let me bring them up on Spotify. BRB.*

"I'm changing up the music for a minute," I called across the salon. No one replied. Patti Smith's "Because the Night" filled the air.

"What's this shit, bubby?" Mum said, after a minute. "Are you trying to put me out of business?"

I explained what I was doing and—when Mum had finally finished telling the entire salon how lovely Cole was—took a straw poll of the room. Patti Smith was a unanimous no. I lined up Nirvana's "Smells Like Teen Spirit." This time, the salon went wild.

"Tune!" Gemma shouted. Mum and Aunty Cheryl were singing along. Mum danced around the salon with scissors in her hand. She was an occupational health and safety nightmare, but if you tried telling her she was an accident waiting to happen, she'd stab you with them on purpose instead. I thought the Nirvana singer sounded like his voice was battling its way through a throat full of barnacles, but everyone else seemed to love it.

Toby: *Totes scientific poll of salon says 2 go w Nirvana babes. I think it's a winner.*

Cole: *Really?*

Toby: *Defs. 1. U get to play ur guitar n impress the hell out of everyone. 2. It fits ur rock vibe. The audience will go mad. 3. It'll stand out from all the poxy ballads. 4. Ur guaranteed pts from Johnswagger, who'll b as rigid as the Southend Pier.*

Toby: *And so will most of the audience, tbf.*

Toby: *Including me babes.*

My fingers had typed and sent the final message before my brain gave consent. I had no idea how to flirt. The adrenaline dam in my body burst like it had been bombed by the Luftwaffe. What had I been thinking? My phone pinged immediately. I nearly jumped out of my skin. No words, just a devil emoji. Internally, I was screaming. My phone went off twice more.

Cole: *Dad's getting the cows in. G2G get the dairy ready.*

Cole: *x*

I stared at that little *x* for the rest of the afternoon, willing it to jump out of the screen and stick its tongue down my throat. What did it mean? Whatever it was, there was only one correct response.

Toby: *x.*

* * *

That evening, my phone pinged again.

Cole: *I never asked what you're planning to sing. That was rude.*

It was half past ten and I was lying on my bed in my jimmy jams, next to Gaston, watching *Madonna: Truth or Dare* and working my way through a packet of Wotsits with the diligence of a convert to the Church of Our Lady of Coronary Heart Disease.

Toby: *Surefire banger!!! Robyn's Dancing on My Own.*

When my phone went off again, it wasn't a text. It was a photo of a shirtless, damp Cole, towel tied loosely around his waist, foggy bathroom mirror behind him, and one hand raised, with his fingers giving the "rock on" horns. His tongue was sticking out. Underneath the picture was a one-word caption.

Cole: *Tune!*

A Wotsit fell from my mouth and onto the bed sheet. Gaston leapt on it. I stared at Cole's stunning, lean body. The tight musculature, the brown-pink nipples, the light rash of hair on his chest, and the treasure trail of short curls that disappeared under the towel. What was happening? What had I done to deserve this? How the hell was I meant to reply? Should I tell him he was beautiful? That his body was perfection? No one had ever sent me a flirty message before, let alone a picture. Wait, this was flirting, wasn't it? How I replied seemed super important. It had to let him know I was interested.

Toby: *Ur up late. Don't u have 2 b up early 2 milk cows or something?*

What can I say? I panicked.

Cole: *Not tomorrow.*

Three little dots danced on my screen. I licked the Wotsit dust from my lips.

Cole: *Hey, um, sorry for the unsolicited pic. That wasn't cool. My bad.*

I was such an idiot. Now he thought I wasn't into him when, in reality, I'd have hacked his phone for that kind of content. I hit pause on Madonna, threw the bed sheet off, and put an unimpressed Gaston out into the hallway. This conversation needed my full attention. I had to get better at this.

Toby: *Don't be silly babes.*

How did I fix this? Should I send Cole a picture? I didn't have a body like his. There was no way I was taking my top off. A cute face pic? A quick look in the mirror revealed Wotsit dust everywhere and a giant spot on my left cheek. I was beginning to spiral.

Cole: *Are you sure? My sister is always going on about how consent is important. I got carried away. I'm sorry.*

This was spinning out of my control. Now not only did Cole think I wasn't into him, he was worried he might be a sex pest. My heart was thumping in my chest like an angry Karen demanding to speak to the manager. I had to get this back on track.

Toby: *I absolutely consent. Ur well fit babes.*

Cole: *Thanks, Mr! So are you. ;)*

So. Are. You? I threw the phone down on the bed and jumped up and down on the spot, silently screaming. It was more than I could take. My hands started to shake, and as my brain was now completely unable to function, it let my insecurities write back.

Toby: *I'm really not babes.*

My phone pinged.

Cole: *Sorry, do I have the wrong number? This is Toby, right?*

The message was followed by a photo of Cole scratching his head —his hair still wet and unbrushed from the shower, his shoulders bare —with a confused look on his face. He was so gorgeous. This was it. This was my cue to send Cole a photo in reply. If I didn't, I was convinced he wouldn't send me another one, and I wanted to see where this ended up—because I was sixteen and never been kissed and no boy had ever been interested in me before. He was interested in me, right?

I ripped my top off, looked in the bedroom mirror, and pulled it straight back on. Flesh was not the solution. I spotted a tub of mud mask on my chest of drawers. Thirty seconds later I had a face like I'd sneezed into a chocolate fountain, but my gigantic zit was hidden. I sucked my tummy in, tensed my non-existent muscles, framed myself up with my mirror in the background so it caught the round of my butt, and snapped the pic. *Send*. Ten seconds later my phone vibrated.

Cole: *Are those Strawberry Shortcake pyjama bottoms?*

Balls.

* * *

I thought I'd massively blown it. Over the next few days, the messages I got from Cole were less flirty. At least, I thought so. My phone would ping and my stomach would drop out my butt and I'd check my phone to see Cole had sent me a funny meme or a cat video. There were no more shirtless photos. I'd reply with an emoji or a short message, but there wasn't much back and forth or banter. Then, on the Saturday night, I was sitting on my bed watching old *Sonny & Cher Show* clips on YouTube when a video call came through. It was Cole. I hadn't jumped out of my skin like that since Aunty Cheryl quit experimenting with black market chemical peel treatments.

"There he is," Cole said, a broad grin lighting up his face. He was lying back on what I guessed was his bed, shirtless, propped up against the bedhead with pillows.

"Hi," I said. "This is a surprise."

"A good one, I hope?"

"Of course." I'm sure I blushed because my face felt exactly like it did about thirty seconds after Aunty Cheryl applied the black market chemical peel.

"I'm not interrupting, am I?"

"Literally, I'm watching Dolly Parton and Cher on YouTube. From, like, the seventies."

Cole didn't even bat an eyelid.

"Icons," he said. "Dolly's an amazing songwriter. Have you ever listened to 'Jolene'?"

"Duh, does the pope shit in the woods?"

"Like, it's unmistakably a country song but, I'm telling you, if you isolated the bass and the drums—"

I couldn't even wait for Cole to finish. "It's a funk beat! I know!"

"It could absolutely be a funk song," Cole said. "I'd like to try that someday."

Before I knew it, three hours had flown by. Cole and I spent the whole time chatting about music, dissecting songs we liked, trashing the ones we didn't, defending our favourites where the other disagreed. I'd never met anyone I could talk to about music like this before—someone who understood music and loved it the way I did, even if our tastes were different. I was already imagining our perfect life together as fabulous, famous pop stars and gay icons.

There was a knock on Cole's bedroom door, and he startled. I heard the door open.

"Lights out, kiddo," a man's voice said. "You're on for milking in the morning. Get some sleep."

"Ten more minutes, Dad. Please?"

"Now! Whoever she is, you can talk to her tomorrow. Sleep."

Pardon?

Cole was plunged into darkness, his face lit only by his phone screen. I guessed his dad had turned off the big light. I heard the click of his bedroom door close.

"Are you not out?" I said. "Or are you... straight?" This particular horror had never even occurred to me until this moment.

"I'm not out to my dad yet," Cole confessed. "Not yet. Mum and Fiona know. And Tully. I only came out to them a few months ago. I'm... still finding my way, you know? Mum wanted me to be sure before I told him."

"Sure about what?"

"Sure I'm gay."

"You're not sure?"

"I might be bi, maybe? I don't know." Cole grimaced. "Does... it make a difference?"

"To what?"

"To you."

"Why would it make a difference to me?"

"Dunno. I'm new to all this. I'm not sure how it all works."

"Me neither, babes, and I've been out since I was thirteen."

Cole's eyes widened. "That's amazing. And your family were cool with it?"

I nodded. "Mum reckoned she'd known for years. Said she'd had her suspicions when aged five I asked if she would help me blow wave my Barbie's hair. But it was demanding an ABBA-themed ninth birthday party that finally clinched it. She said no child was *that* Swedish, and I'm only half Swedish. Dad was cool with it. Barely looked up from his golf putter. Aunty Cheryl was thrilled and immediately started listing off the gay bars she wanted to sneak me into."

Cole laughed. "I'm in awe."

"Of Aunty Cheryl?"

"Of you. Your confidence. You are who you are. I love that about you. I wish I could—"

There was a loud bang on Cole's bedroom door, followed by the boom of his dad's voice. "Sleep!"

"I have to go," Cole mouthed silently. "Talk tomorrow?" I nodded, and we quietly said goodnight.

* * *

We spoke again the next night, and the night after that, until it had become our routine. We'd text during the day, while I was working at the salon. Then, after dinner, I'd bound upstairs to my room, check my hair, apply a little lip gloss, and wait for Cole to call. We'd chat for hours, until it was time for sleep, learning each other's innermost thoughts and secrets, all the while wishing we lived close enough to hang out in person. I was feeling more and more confident that this was a *thing*. The instant crush I'd had was developing into something much deeper. We told each other everything. One evening, as I was telling all my business, I confessed to Cole how desperately I wanted to be famous.

"When you're famous, you can leverage it," I said. "There's always a way to make money, always a product to endorse, always a guest list to get your name on, you know? We have some celeb clients at the salon. Do you know Priti from *Dress for Successex*? She says if you treat your fame like a business, you'll never be poor."

"Is that what this is about for you?" Cole asked.

"Of course, babes. Isn't it why we're all there? Don't you want to be famous?"

Cole didn't answer right away. "I just want to make good music, you know?"

"But you're already making good music. What you want is for a bigger audience to hear it."

"True, I guess."

"Exactly, babes, it's a platform. The show is how we get from where we are today to where we want to be tomorrow."

There was another thoughtful silence from the other end of the phone. Cole was a deep thinker. I waited for him to speak.

"Right now, I want to be where you are," he said, and all my limbs tingled. "I want to see you. For real. Not on camera."

"The London auditions are still two weeks away."

"I don't want to wait two weeks," he said.

I'd forgotten to breathe by this point. If a paramedic had checked my vital signs, they'd have pronounced me dead at the scene and would've been calling my next of kin. "I can't wait two weeks either."

"So, I had an idea," Cole said. "Mum and Fiona have appointments booked at your salon this Saturday."

"Do they?" Who'd put that in the diary? Mum must have taken the booking from Orla directly.

"Mum's taking Fiona in to get her hair coloured for her birthday. It's a girls' day out. I was thinking... I could come down with them."

"For a girls' day out?"

"Keep up, *babes*. While they're having a girls' day out, maybe we could... hang out. You know. In person."

My squeal of delight was so high-pitched, it rerouted migratory birds and interfered with aircraft landing at Stansted Airport. Saturday was only four days away. I was going to need a top-up spray tan in the morning.

* * *

The next night our conversation got deep and meaningful. When it was too late to talk without Cole getting in trouble, we switched to text messages.

Toby: *What's ur biggest secret?*

Cole: *You know I'm only out to a few people.*

Toby: *Not that. There must b sumthing else. U tell me urs & i'll tell u mine!*

Three dots appeared in the chat, then disappeared again.

Toby: *I'm serious. Cum on, u can trust me. i trust u!*

The three dots returned, bouncing up and down on the screen. It took a while for Cole's reply to come through. I could imagine him lying back in his bed, shirt off, tongue poking deep into his cheek.

Cole: *People think I'm this super confident guy but in reality I feel like a lost little boy.*

That took me by surprise.

Cole: *I've always been the kid of slightly the wrong colour. Now I'm the wrong sexuality, too. I can't shake the feeling I'm living in the wrong country, maybe growing up in the wrong religion, and certainly in the wrong culture. I'm forever grateful for the life Mum and Dad have* *given me but I can't escape the thought I don't belong here. That I might have another family out there. I don't know who I am. And they might not even know I exist.*

I swallowed, unsure how to reply. I had been expecting him to say "sometimes I take a piss in the garden" or "I like to jerk off in the barn."

Toby: *Thats so sad, babes. Im sorry. So u no, n this is me bein honest with u, I think ur amazing as u r.*

Cole: *Thanks Mr. I just feel like I need to know more about where I come from. A few years ago I asked mum about my birth parents but she didn't know much. Apparently, the agency they fostered me through didn't have any information about my father at all. It seemed to upset her so I never asked again. So, here I am. A lost little Cole.*

Toby: *Wld u ever try 2 find ur birth parents?*

Cole: *Nah. It'd kill mum and dad. I don't want them to think they're not enough. I'd hate that. They're the best.*

I started to type something reassuring, but Cole messaged again, clearly ready to change the subject.

Cole: *Anyway, what's YOUR big secret?*

Toby: *Was gonna say I piss in the garden sumtimes but i'll have 2 cum up w sumthing else now.*

Cole: *Everyone does that. Come on. You can do better.*

I could. I had no shortage of shortcomings to share.

Toby: *Just gonna say it as is. I hate the way i look. Face is 2 chubby. Skin is see-thru. Teeth are crooked. Hate everything abt the reflection in the mirror. When i walk up the street, i worry ppl r laughing at me. Any 'confidence' you see is a lie.*

It took a minute before three little dots began to ripple across my screen.

Cole: *You're beautiful exactly as you are.*

Cole: *And your face is NOT chubby.*

Cole: *And your arse is deliciously round and I can't stop thinking* *about it. That's probably what people are noticing when you walk up the street.*

I cringed. I'd spent so long wanting a boy to see me the way Cole said he saw me. But in a couple of days Cole would be standing in front of the real me, in person, instead of staring at an image of me on a screen. And for all we'd been friendly and flirty and even occasionally quite a bit sexty on the phone, there was no guarantee that chemistry would translate when we were stood in front of each other. Our online banter was comfortable, familiar. In person was a new ball game altogether. What if he saw me and realised I was disgusting?

Cole: *And I KNOW you don't believe me, Toby, but when I see you on Saturday, I'll prove it to you. I won't leave a single doubt in your pretty little head. :P xxx*

Cole: *PS. I have a surprise for you when I see you!*

Chapter Seven

The little bell above the salon door tinkled, and adrenaline flooded my body like rosé floods Aunty Cheryl's bloodstream every night from half past five. I looked up from my phone to see Orla Kennedy stride in. She was followed by a shorter, rounder version of herself—Fiona—who was followed by Cole. No leather jacket today, but he was carrying his guitar like he never left home without it. He was in a vest and a zip-up hoodie open to the waist. The sleeves weren't wide enough for his biceps. He looked well fit.

"You orright?" I said, leaning over the counter to kiss Orla on the cheek.

Mum shouted hello from across the salon, and Orla waved back.

"This is Cole's big sister, Fiona," Orla said, turning her attention back to me. "She's home from Cambridge for the summer. She's studying law."

Fiona blushed with embarrassment. Orla probably bragged about that at every opportunity. I leaned over for an air kiss and wished her a happy birthday.

"And you know Cole, of course."

Cole offered me a hand to shake, as if we'd just played ninety minutes of heterosexual football and were off to heterosexually shower with our heterosexual teammates. I grabbed his hand, pulled him into me, and pecked him on the cheek. The smell of him, his hand in mine, sent a charge through my body.

The whole salon had gone quiet, as if everyone knew exactly what was going on. Cole blushed. I looked down at the booking ledger, trying to appear charming and professional, but my nerves had kicked in.

"So, it's two of Chloe's Deluxe Pamper Packages, including facials, nails, and a cut and colour for you today, ladies. Orla, you'll be with Mum. She'll be with you in a minute. Fiona, you'll be with Cheryl. Apologies in advance if you can smell booze on her breath. That'll be, well, the booze on her breath." I lowered my voice. "She went to three different hen dos last night. Occupational hazard, innit?"

Fiona looked alarmed.

"Don't worry, it'll be fine," I said, reassuringly. "Her hands have stopped shaking now. Be grateful you weren't her nine o'clock. Mrs Fitzpatrick went home looking like she'd been mugged by a gang of amateur wig makers."

Fiona gripped her lustrous auburn locks like she was farewelling them at an airport. I realised I'd overdone the charming and failed at the professional.

"I'm only winding you up!" I said. "You two take a seat. Mum and Aunty Cheryl will be with you in a minute." Fiona laughed nervously and let her shoulders drop. "And what about you, Cole?" I said, looking at his floppy mop of thick black hair. "Fancy a trim while you're here?"

"I'm going down to 78s," he said. This part of the conversation was entirely planned. 78s was the record store up the far end of the high street. No one ever went in there except old dudes and hardcore musos because, let's be honest, Spotify existed. Cole ran a hand through his hair, and it swooshed back into place. His eyes locked on to mine again, and he smirked, which made me smirk. Surely everyone knew what was up? The air between us was so pregnant with expectation, I should probably have pissed on a stick.

"I get off in half an hour," I said. "What if I come find you at 78s? We can get some lunch and maybe find a bench in Castle Park?"

He nodded. "Sounds good." He seemed so calm. I was drenched in sweat.

Cole winked, said goodbye to the women in his life, and disappeared up the street.

Thirty minutes later I was rushing out the door when Aunty Cheryl summoned me to the back of the salon, pulling the red velvet curtains closed behind us.

"I've got somewhere to be, babes, what is it?"

She held a finger to her lips, hushing me—the perfectly painted watermelon-pink acrylic nail matching her lip gloss to perfection.

"Fine, but why are we whispering?"

Aunty Cheryl's watermelon-pink nail disappeared into the pocket of her spray-on super skinny three-quarter-length jeans, and she plucked out two shiny gold packets.

"Safety first, babes, OK? Always."

I screeched, put my fingers in my ears, closed my eyes, and jogged up and down.

"No, no, no, no!" I said. I could have died right then and there. Here lies Tobias Lyngstad, sixteen, killed by the world's most embarrassing aunt. She snatched my hand from my ear, prised my fingers open, and shoved the condoms into my palm.

"This ain't a joke, Tobes. This is your health."

I opened my eyes. "Are you kidding me?" I growled through gritted teeth, jamming the packets in my pocket to hide them before anyone burst through the curtains. "Cole's mum is three metres away!"

"And hopefully she's been responsible too."

"I'm not going to... we're just... we're not... we've haven't even—"

"It's better to be safe than sorry, Tobes."

The perfectly painted watermelon-pink acrylic was now tapping at my chest.

"I was a teenager once, Tobes. I remember what teenage boys are like."

"You're so embarrassing!"

"Listen up, it's your body, your rules. Don't do anything you don't want to do. This is in case you decide you *do* want to do something, orright?"

"You're literally killing me," I said.

Aunty Cheryl grabbed my shoulders and pulled me in for a hug.

"You're welcome, babes."

* * *

Cole was waiting outside the record store, leaning back against the shop wall with his guitar case slung across his front and a couple of vinyl albums under his arm. He looked like an album cover. Effortlessly cool. I trotted up the street towards him like a hog after its breakfast, cursing myself as I felt a trickle of sweat roll down my back. Cole turned and saw me, his face cracking into a big smile.

"Hey, you made it."

He wrapped an arm around my shoulder, and I worried he might feel dampness. I twisted into him to try to hug him properly and kiss his cheek, but the guitar between us made it awkward.

"Watch the new vinyl! This is the Velvet Underground anniversary edition."

"Sorry!" I jumped back, abandoning my attempt to kiss him and cursing my clumsiness.

"I'm starving. Do you still want to grab some lunch and sit in the park?" Cole asked.

"Absolutely. I've booked us a table at the finest restaurant I could afford. It's on the way."

Twenty minutes later, unable to find a free bench in Castle Park, we were sitting on the grass, shoving Big Macs into our mouths and admiring the thousand-year-old castle the Normans had built on the site of some old Roman ruins.

"Have you ever been in?" I asked.

Cole nodded. "School trip. I love ancient history. I was *obsessed* with Queen Boudica."

"I've always vibed with Boudica," I said, slurping on my Coke. "Probably because she burnt Colchester to the ground, which is an idea I can really get behind."

Cole laughed.

It was a glorious day, and the midday sun was beating down on us. The park was bustling with people enjoying their lunch breaks. A couple of fit lads had taken their shirts off. I felt a bead of armpit sweat roll down my side.

"It's a hot one today," Cole said, stripping off his hoodie to reveal the vest underneath. "Aren't you hot?" As he sank his teeth into his Big Mac, I tried not to stare at the lean, firm muscles of his arms, pretended not to notice the way his shoulders were more heavily tanned than his biceps, tried not to imagine whatever shirtless agricultural labours had created this body. I wanted to lean over and kiss him, but he had a mouth full of hamburger. Sweat trickled from my other armpit. Cole pointed at my chest, apparently suggesting I take off my top.

"In the middle of Colchester? No way. You must be mental."

Cole shook his head and pointed again. I looked down to see I'd spilt tomato sauce and mayo all down my T-shirt.

"Bollocks!"

Already dying of embarrassment, I grabbed for a napkin to wipe it up, knocking over my Coke and sending black sugary liquid and half-melted ice across the lawn towards Cole's hoodie and guitar.

"Sorry!"

"It's OK, don't worry about it." Cole laughed, plucking his belongings out of harm's way.

I dragged the napkin up my white T-shirt, trying to scoop up the bulk of the sauce and succeeding in smearing it everywhere. Why was this all going wrong? My hand started to shake, and I hesitated.

"Here, let me do it."

Suddenly Cole was on his knees on the grass in front of me, a napkin in his hand, dabbing at the tomato sauce. His face was inches from mine. The swoosh of his hair brushed my face, tickling my skin, making the hair on my arms stand on end. Cole's face was set in concentration, his eyes determined, his brow furrowed. It was so sexy. I couldn't look away, even as he dabbed gently at my chest. He looked up. Our eyes met.

"It's a goner, I'm afraid," he said. "This needs stain remover and a washing machine."

Cole's eyes were burning with intensity. His lips were so close. Was this the moment? Was I about to have my first kiss? My mouth felt dry. I swallowed, ran my tongue across my lips—and found a sesame seed in the corner of my mouth. And my butt felt wet. The Coke had found my jeans. I wanted to cry. This whole stupid day was a write-off. I'd humiliated myself in front of a lad I had a massive crush on—the only guy who'd ever been interested in me. I'd ruined it.

"Sorry. I think I want to go home."

"We can do that."

"No, I mean, I have to go." I stood up, brushing my greasy hands on my jeans. I felt crushed, empty. Cole was never going to want to see me again after this. I had to get out of there.

Cole stood. "Whatever you need. We can hang out another time."

I froze, letting the words sink in. He still wanted to see me again?

"Can I walk you home, maybe? Is it far?"

"I'll probably get an Uber."

Cole rolled his bottom lip between his teeth and ran his hand through his swooshy hair.

"You know, it's a shame because I didn't give you your surprise yet."

I'd forgotten he'd promised one, and I'm not going to lie, I was intrigued.

"I worked hard on it. And I have, like, at least three more hours to kill before Mum and Fi will be ready. I should get this vinyl out of the sun, anyway. And, frankly, I wouldn't mind some air con either."

I laughed. "OK then."

"There we go. There's that cute smile." Cole put one hand lightly on my shoulder. "Come here, you saucy minx," he said, pulling me into a hug. My breath caught in my throat. My heart pounded. This was our first proper hug. It felt so real. So right. So romantic. It felt... so incredibly sweaty.

"Plus, I want to see those Strawberry Shortcake pyjamas in the flesh," he said.

* * *

Everything in my bedroom was embarrassing. The dresser covered in bottles of hair product, make-up, scent, and spray tan. The old Jonas Brothers posters on the wall. The Lady Gaga *ARTPOP* duvet cover. This was my inner sanctum. This was who I was—the stuff that made me happy. But, to my mind, it wasn't cool enough for Cole.

Cole leaned his guitar against the wall, put his precious vinyl down on my desk, and headed straight for a picture frame containing the historical record of one of the best nights of my life.

"Is this you?"

"*That* is Girls Aloud," I said, digging through my wardrobe for fresh clothes.

Cole tapped on the glass.

"And yes," I said, "the fat little kid clinging to Nadine Coyle's neck like he plans to make a souvenir trophy of her head is me."

"When was this?"

"When they played the Millennium Dome. Maybe five years ago. Mum got me tickets to the meet-and-greet. I'm going for a quick shower. Do *not* snoop while I'm gone."

Cole put up his hand like he was swearing on a Bible.

"Scout's honour."

When I came back ten minutes later, dirty clothes rolled up in my arms, Cole was sitting on the edge of my bed, plucking away at his guitar. His eyes lit up.

"Strawberry Shortcake!"

I curtsied. "As requested."

Cole put his guitar behind him on the bed.

"You look super cute," he said, smiling, and I felt a blush that started at my toes and roasted its way up through my whole body to my face like I was being burnt at the stake.

Cole stood. He stepped towards me, looking sexy, sweet, determined. This was it. *This* was the moment. I closed my eyes, waiting for the soft touch of Cole's lips on mine. Instead, I felt him grab the dirty clothes from my hands.

"We should put that T-shirt in to soak," he said.

Instinctively, I reached for them. "I can do it later."

"Mum always says the earlier the better when it comes to stains."

Now we were having this weird tussle, both grappling for my pile of clothes.

"It won't take a minute," Cole said.

"I'll do it later!" I yanked the clothes out of his hands—but Cole didn't release them, and as the bundle spilt open, Aunty Cheryl's condoms fell out of my jeans and onto the floor between us. I wanted the ground to open up and swallow me whole. My mouth went dry, and I completely lost the ability to speak.

"They're not mine!"

"Oh." Cole bent down and picked them up, the gold packets shimmering between his fingers. He bit his lip. "Were you expecting..."

"No! God no!"

Cole's eyes sparkled. "Because, I mean, if you want to—"

"Gosh, no! I don't want to put you to any trouble."

Cole burst out laughing. It came from deep inside his belly and lit up his whole face. I closed my eyes, willing an assassin's bullet to end my humiliation with a clean kill.

I felt Cole's hand rest gently on my shoulder. "Toby, it's OK."

I shook my head.

"It really is," he said.

I felt his other hand hold my hip, felt him gently step towards me, pull my body towards his, felt his soft lips against mine. That's when it finally happened. Tobias Lyngstad. Sixteen and finally been kissed. It was gentle, sweet, perfect. It was the first kiss I had always dreamt of, and I knew for certain, this was more than a crush. I opened my eyes to find Cole smiling, looking at me like it was the first time he'd ever even seen me.

"Hello, you," he said.

I giggled. "Hi."

"You're shaking."

"I'm nervous. Aren't you nervous?"

"Bricking it."

"You're not shaking, though."

"I am. I think our shakes have probably synchronised so we can no longer feel it."

I laughed. Cole grabbed my hands and sat down on the bed, pulling me down to sit beside him.

"Do you want your surprise?" Cole said.

I wanted another kiss, but I nodded.

"I wrote this song for you." Cole reached behind us, plucked his guitar from the bed, and began strumming the chords. As he started to sing, his eyes found mine.

. . .

"I'm sitting on this tractor, going round and round this field. Slowly getting nowhere, when I want to get to you."

I nearly choked on a giggle and had to pretend I was clearing my throat. I put a hand against Cole's back, partly to encourage him and partly to smother my guilt at finding this so cringey.

"Got up before dawn, to sit behind this wheel. Going round in circles. Driven mad for want of you."

For the next two minutes or so, Cole sang his heart out. He'd put so much work into this song, and the musicality was genuinely great, but the lyrics were, shall we say, clunky. When he was done, I leaned in and kissed him.

"Thank you. That was beautiful."

"You're beautiful."

I snorted.

"I think you're beautiful." Cole stood and put his guitar down against the wall. "If the song didn't give it to you, I think you're the most amazing boy I ever met."

I felt my face burn red and my heart thump harder. "What are you like?"

He picked up his vinyl. "You don't have a player, do you?"

I shook my head. Cole took his phone out of his pocket.

"Have you ever heard the Velvet Underground before?"

I shook my head again. As the tinkling music started to play, Cole moved slowly towards me, his eyes never leaving mine. He rested his hand on my shoulder, the back of his fingers gently tracing their way up my neck and along my jaw until his thumb found my chin. I gripped Cole's waist. He leaned in and kissed me. Short and sweet. Then he pulled off his vest—his flat stomach and bare torso filling my whole field of vision like the world's sexiest IMAX cinema screen. I could barely breathe. My entire body was tingling. My pyjama bottoms were hiding nothing. Cole straddled me, his knees sinking into the mattress. His lips found mine. As we leaned back, his body found mine. Finally, my head found the wall.

"Ouch!"

"Sorry!"

After a pause to confirm there was no damage, we lay down the correct way along the bed. I closed my eyes to move in for a kiss, misjudged, and we smacked our teeth together.

"Ouch!"

"Sorry!"

After about half an hour, we'd got the hang of making out. Our hands were exploring each other's bodies—hungrily, urgently—and, eventually, unable to resist any more, I reached down and grabbed the little gold packets Aunty Cheryl had given me.

"Are you sure?" Cole said. I was well beyond the point of no return, but Cole had clearly internalised Fiona's lectures about consent, and I rated that.

"Yes," I said, breathlessly, having never wanted anything so much in my entire life.

In that moment, I would have given Cole Kennedy the world. It felt like he was giving *me* the world. As the Velvet Underground sang softly about pale blue eyes—perfect, somehow, for the moment—we pressed our naked bodies together, and poked and probed and winced and laughed and fumbled our way towards our urgent, ultimate, cataclysmic goal. And I felt more whole, more complete, more *full*, than I had ever felt in my entire life.

Local lads advance in TV talent quest

Twelve East Anglian residents are among the 107 hopefuls currently in London for filming of the group stage of hit reality TV show "Make Me a Pop Star."

Among them are sixteen-year-olds Tobias Lyngstad of Colchester and Cole Kennedy of Polstead.

Kennedy, who attends the June Brown Performing Arts College in Sudbury, is the son of dairy farmers Andy and Orla Kennedy of Dollops Wood Farm.

"Music is my life, and I want to share that passion with the world," Kennedy said.

Lyngstad's father, Bjorn, is a project manager for construction giant EssBuild. His mother, Chloe, owns a salon in the Colchester high street.

"This is a life-changing opportunity," the Hawthorn Academy and Sixth Form College student said.

The boys have struck up a friendship and travelled down to London together with their mums for filming. Famously, the show's contestants all bunk together in the same hotel during the competition.

"I'm treating it like a great big adventure," Kennedy said.

In the group stage, contestants must perform a specially prepared song for the judges. They are then sorted into three groups. Each group is mentored by a different celebrity judge over the course of ten days, during which time they compete and collaborate through a workshop process designed to see talent rise to the top—either in groups or as solo artists. At the end of the group stage, twenty-one acts go through to the televised live shows, when one act is eliminated by public vote each week until the final.

The first chance the show's fans will have to see Cole and Tobias on television is in three weeks' time, when the East Anglian auditions episode (filmed in July) goes to air. Once the pre-recorded audition and group stage episodes have been shown, the live shows—featuring the final twenty-one contestants—will air on Saturday and Sunday nights from late September until Christmas.

Chapter Eight

Robbie Johnswagger shot me daggers and held up a hand. "Stop, stop. All of you."

Seven male voices petered out.

"What the hell was that, Toby?"

I'd added a vocal flourish to Bill Withers's "Lean on Me." It was not my first mistake of the day.

"I thought—"

"You're not here to think, mate."

No, I was here to win, and I needed to do something to stand out. Bafflingly, my prepared song, Robyn's "Dancing on My Own," had landed me in Johnswagger's group. It meant I got to hang out with Cole all day, which was lush, but Robbie and I were not a good fit. We were three days into our ten-day-long group stage boot camp, and so far, I had managed to do nothing to impress him, nothing to stand out, and nothing to earn me a place in the live shows. I needed to do better.

"Never steal focus, it's a golden rule," Robbie said. "Cole is singing this part. You're background, mate. Don't get in the way."

"Sorry, I—"

"Never mind." He rubbed his fingers over his forehead in what I took to be frustration. "Let's all take a break for an hour, yeah?"

Indira, the producer I'd met on the day of the auditions, raised her clipboard.

"Before you all disappear, I have some exciting news—Dorinda is here!" A cheer from the boys. "She'll be doing one-on-one interviews with you all, just to ask how you're enjoying the group stage. She's in the courtyard garden with crew number two." Indira pointed at me. "Toby, you're up first."

I nodded, then looked over at Cole. Partly to apologise for standing on his solo, partly to check in. He smiled, flicking a hand over and linking his pinkie finger in mine for a nanosecond before letting it drop again.

"Cole, can I borrow you for a minute, son?" Robbie said.

* * *

In the courtyard garden, Dorinda Carter was all smiles. I was genuinely pleased to see her. She swallowed me up in a bosomy hug, then stood me on my mark. The cameraman called, "Rolling."

"Toby, how are you enjoying the groups so far?"

"It's intense, innit?" I said.

"But are you loving it?"

"They're a great group of lads. It's a lot of fun."

"You looked pretty surprised to be chosen for Robbie's group, why was that?"

"Obviously Robbie is amazing, and it's a privilege to get to work with a rock legend."

"Uh-oh, I can hear a but coming!"

It was clear the "but" was *exactly* what Dorinda wanted to hear.

"I'm not going to lie, I'm a more natural fit for Johanna's group. You know I love my girly pop, my Scandi-pop. I'm not exactly a rock and roller. But I'm in Robbie's group? I can't get my head around it."

Dorinda's eyes sparkled.

"It means you get to spend more time with Cole, though. You boys have become close, haven't you?"

This alarm bell could not have rung louder in my head if I'd swallowed the clock on my bedside table. Although it was common knowledge Cole and I were friends, we didn't want anyone on the production to know we were shagging like rabbits every opportunity we got in case they split us up or sent us home. We were a duty of care nightmare. But, more than that, Cole was still not out to his dad, so we couldn't risk it becoming a narrative for the show.

"We've hung out a bit," I said.

"Do you think he's going all the way?"

Ideally, you want the presenter of a television show on which you are a contestant to ask you if *you're* going all the way, not if another contestant is going all the way. It was becoming abundantly clear to me Cole was the big favourite back in the Totally Television production studio. Felicity Quant had recognised his talent; she was going to make him a star.

"He's extremely gifted," I said. "He'll be huge someday."

"What would it mean to you to be in a group with Cole for the live shows?"

OK, this was definitely a narrative for the show, and it made me super nervous. I had to protect Cole.

"It'd be an honour," I said. And left it. Dorinda's eyebrows went up. I kept my face blank. After an awkward pause, she moved on.

"How are you finding living in the house? You're rooming with Chase French, aren't you? What's that like?"

"Chase is great!" I said, meaning it. Chase was a rugby-fit lad with a voice straight from the Welsh valleys. What I didn't say was I'd hardly spent any time with him, despite bunking with him. The producers had allocated our rooms, and Cole was up the hall with Yoshi Kawaguchi—a Japanese exchange student with an extraordinary voice who had auditioned on a dare by his host sister.

Cole and I had tried to hide things, but Yoshi and Chase soon clocked what was going on between us and had been politely going to hang out in one room so Cole and me could make out in the other.

"What's the best thing about living with Chase?" Dorinda asked.

The interview went on like this for another five minutes, asking about various contestants. Had I been reading too much into all the questions about Cole? I couldn't shake the fear we were becoming a narrative for the show, and I had to warn Cole before he was outed on national television.

* * *

When I finally found him, Cole was sitting in the hotel dining room with Yoshi and Chase. I slid in beside him and stole a chip from his plate.

"Oi!"

"Ow, isshh hot."

"A seagull doesn't get to complain when he burns his tongue on the chips."

I rolled the steaming-hot chunk of deep-fried potato around in my mouth, trying to cool it down.

"We'll give you boys some space," Chase said. He and Yoshi stood, picked up their plates, and moved to another table. Cole's thigh pressed against mine.

"Hab you dub... your interbew... wib... Dorimba," I said, forming the words as best I could around the hot chip.

"Yeah."

"Dib she ars you a lob ob..." This was ridiculous. I swallowed the chip. It burnt all the way down. "Did she ask you a lot of questions about me?"

"About you?"

I nodded, stealing a sip of Cole's water.

Cole shook his head. "No. She asked me about working with Robbie. Why?"

"I think they know we're a thing," I said.

Cole didn't even blink. "They definitely know we're a thing."

"Oh."

"That's what Robbie wanted to speak to me about earlier."

"What did he say?" I reached for another chip. Cole slapped my hand and I retracted it, shoving it inside the pocket of my hoodie.

"It was a warning. He said the producers have some storyline about us, he didn't say what, but they're trying to catch us on camera together whenever they can. Based on what he said, I'm surprised they're not filming us right now."

My eyes flicked subconsciously up to the CCTV cameras. "Why?"

"He didn't know. Or, at least, he didn't tell me. But he's worried they're going to turn me into part of reality TV's first gay couple."

"But you're not out!"

"I know." Cole looked down at his plate and began rubbing a chip through the sauce, making patterns. "But it's not my dad I'm worried about. Robbie pointed out if they tell that story, that's all I'll ever be —a novelty. I won't be known for my music, I'll be the guy who had a teenage romance on television. Forever."

I felt the crush of Cole's words. He blew on his chip and bit it in half. As I watched him chew, the full potential of the opportunity we had in front of us dawned on me. My pulse quickened.

"If we lean into it, though—if you come out to your dad and then we let them tell this story—we could be famous forever. We'd have something to leverage a career out of. Forever. This could be our big shot."

Cole met my eyes. "I can't risk that, Tobes. I want a career as an artist and songwriter. I want to be a serious musician."

What he meant was *A novelty narrative might be your big shot, Toby, but it won't be mine.* And he was right. Deep down I knew I wasn't going all the way in the competition, not in Robbie's group, anyway. But Cole had a real shot. It wasn't fair for me to ask him to risk that for me, let alone force him to come out to his dad so I could get what I wanted. I would have to use my charms and guile to stand out on telly instead.

"I know," I said, sliding my hand onto his thigh under the table. "And you will be. I can feel it in me bones."

Cole smiled. It lit up his face. He was so beautiful.

"Thank you for understanding, Tobes. I know how much your dreams mean to you too."

"Of course." I squeezed his leg. "I care about you *so much*."

It was a masterful understatement. Care about him? This was love. Young love. First love. Body-engulfing, brain-soaking, intense-as-Shakespeare teenage love. I ached for Cole. I hated every minute I wasn't with him. I would have done anything for him. I'd have opened my own chest and carved his initials into my heart with a rusty compass if he asked me to.

"I know." His hand found mine under the table and squeezed it. "You know I care about you, too, right? Like, *a lot*."

I nodded.

"I'm worried they're not taking you seriously, Tobes. The way Robbie was talking, I feel like they're disrespecting you."

I pulled my hand away. "Did Robbie say something?"

"Nothing specific, but... why are you in Robbie's group? It doesn't make any sense."

Clarity dawned. "It's part of this romance narrative?"

It made sense. They needed us in the same group so we'd be around each other all the time so they could get us on camera together.

"Exactly." Cole wiped his hands on a napkin. "You would have shone in Johanna's group. Everyone knows it's where you belong. I think you might be in Robbie's group because of me. And I'm worried that's ruined your shot. I'm sorry."

I was fuming. Not at Cole. Not even at the show. I was angry with myself. I'd watched every single episode of *Make Me a Pop Star*. Reality TV was my religion. I had an honorary degree in trash telly. And I'd fallen right into the oldest trap there was. Well, two could play at that game. I would not be turned into this season's Jamie Struff. I felt a plan starting to form.

"This show lives and dies on manufactured narratives," I said.

Cole's eyebrows went up. "I'm listening."

"Every storyline costs time and money to film and edit. If Robbie says they've decided to tell our story, they know how they want it to end. And I think *we* should get to decide how our story ends—if it ends. We need to take charge of our narrative, babes."

Cole's thigh pressed into mine. "You're very sexy when you're worked up, do you know that?"

"They need us on camera together for this story to work. What if we refuse to give that to them?"

Cole nodded. "You mean if they don't have the footage, they can't tell the story?"

The best strategy, I suggested, was to keep our distance from each other on camera—to be aloof from one another. We could still hang out when the cameras weren't around—I wasn't going to give up our nights together after the crew had gone home and our overworked chaperones had passed out from exhaustion. But anytime we were on camera, or in a situation where a camera could easily turn up, we'd put a few good metres between us. If we were asked about each other, we'd be polite but evasive. No details. Absolutely nothing to indicate we knew each other so intimately that we'd permanently altered each other's gut biomes.

"Are we agreed?"

Cole smiled. "Agreed."

Chapter Nine

Indira passed around the lyric sheets for the Bruno Mars hit "Marry You" to the fifteen boys in Robbie Johnswagger's group. It was a sunny day, and we were rehearsing outside on the lawn. For the past few days, Cole and I had successfully given the producers the runaround. They'd try to get us into the same interview, and one of us would need the toilet. Whenever all the contestants were together, Cole would stand at one end of the group, and I'd stand at the other. When the cameras were around, Cole and I stayed at least ten feet apart. When they weren't, we shagged until the skin shed from our knobs like potato peelings.

It was day six of the group stage, and I'd already clocked the producers wanted to put together a boy band. They had tried us in every variation imaginable—in combinations of threes, fours, fives, and sixes—testing how we looked and sounded together.

"When I call your name, come and line up over here," Indira said, pointing to a patch of lawn by a tropical flower bed. "Yoshi. Chase. Duncan. Paul. Cole. Toby."

I didn't even glance at Cole as we silently crossed the lawn. I stood at one end, Cole the other.

"No, I gave you the order," Indira barked. "Toby, move around next to Cole, please. Everyone shuffle up."

I moved, my heart sinking. Everyone shuffled. Cole's shoulder gently brushed mine—the briefest connection sending a charge of electricity through my body. Robbie Johnswagger walked onto set and sat down in his director's chair. A camera was trained on him. Two more were trained on the six of us, and a fourth on the remaining group of nine boys. Robbie announced which of us would be doing which parts, and we started singing. Two verses in, Robbie cried for us to stop.

"Boys, this is a song about being so madly in love you want to do something crazy. Run off and get married. Haven't any of you been in love before?"

My arms went rigid at my sides. Cole didn't move. Duncan raised his hand.

"Duncan, what does being in love feel like?"

Duncan was a Scouser in his mid-twenties and had a steady girl-friend at home in Liverpool.

"You know the film *28 Days Later*?"

Robbie frowned. "The zombie film?"

"They're not proper zombies," Duncan said. "The people aren't dead, they've caught this terrible virus that, like, takes over their brain and makes them insane and, like, incredibly violent and stuff."

Robbie was shaking his head.

"Like, imagine Friday night in a really rough Wetherspoons, but a thousand times worse. Blood and guts everywhere. But it's the virus doing it. It controls the people's minds and their bodies and, like, every action and thought and reaction."

Cole's shoulder jerked against mine, and I realised he was trying not to laugh.

Robbie had his head on his hands. "Where are you going with this?"

"Love," Duncan said, as if it were obvious. "The virus is love.

Once you catch it, it's like your brain and your whole body have been hijacked. You're not in control anymore. You'd do anything for the person you love. They're all you can think about, every waking moment. Everything you do, you do for them."

I recognised that kind of love. My heart pounded in my chest.

"Only, generally, when you're in love, the army doesn't round you up and shoot you," Duncan said. "I'd hope."

"Jesus Christ," Robbie Johnswagger said, knocking back his drink in a way that suggested it definitely wasn't water.

Cole's shoulder rested briefly against mine. I desperately wanted to look up at him, to catch his eye, to tell him that's how I felt about him—like I'd lost control of my mind and body. But the cameras were trained on us, so I stood still.

"OK, reset," Indira said. "Guys, can you all turn towards each other in pairs. Yoshi and Chase, you're singing together. Then Duncan and Paul. And Cole and Toby."

Shit. My stomach sank. The producers were taking the piss. Cole and I turned to face each other. He looked terrified. The music started, and we began to sing in our pairs. I'd been such a melt. Everything we'd done had been completely pointless. The producers had us over a barrel. They could make us do whatever they wanted. This was a game, and they made the rules. Now they had footage of Cole and me together, singing a song about being madly in love—and there was nothing we could do about it except sing our hearts out like the virus made us do it.

* * *

By the eighth day, the producers were clearly ready to lock in their decision. I knew for sure because Felicity Quant had turned up. We were by the swimming pool in the back garden of the enormous house where we rehearsed during the day. Felicity and Robbie John-swagger were sitting in garden chairs in front of us as Cole, Joey,

Chase, Yoshi, and I sang an a capella version of "Dream Fantasia"—a song that had been a hit for Robbie in the eighties, after he'd split from Buzzsaw. My heart was pounding. With Quant here, everything rode on this performance. Our group felt solid. A good mix of voices that harmonised well. A pick-and-mix collection of non-threatening, cookie-cutter-gorgeous teenage boys. And me. The ten lads not in our group were standing off to the side with a separate camera trained on their every reaction. Cole, of course, had been given the opener and took the lead on the chorus. He was by far the best vocalist and the most musically talented. If this boy band was going to be a cultural Christmas present to Britain, Cole was the big gift tied with ribbon, while the rest of us were stocking filler. But the third verse was mine, and I had rehearsed the hell out of it. I thought it went well. As Cole's last note left his lips, everyone around us erupted into applause. I felt both relief and exhilaration. I was standing on the precipice of all my dreams coming true. Keeping to the plan as far as we could, Cole and I refused to look at each other. Silence fell over the garden.

"What do you think?" Robbie said, turning to face Felicity. He sipped his cola.

With her sunglasses on, Felicity's face was unreadable. She sat back in her chair and put a finger to her mouth, one long fuchsia-pink nail tapping at her lips. She looked at the five of us. She looked over at the leftovers group. She looked back to us. After the longest thirty seconds of my life, she finally spoke.

"Taylor," she said, plucking the name of a lad in the other group as if from the air. She didn't even look at him. "Swap with Toby." She pointed her fuchsia fingernail in my direction. "Toby, you go stand with the others."

My heart fell out of my arse, skittered across the paving, and rolled into the pool, where it was dragged under by the weight of my despair. Barring some miracle, this was the end of the ride for me. Felicity was mugging me off. I had no idea what I'd done wrong. I left the line-up, circling around the back of the boys and taking a place with the other lads beside the pool.

My face was burning, and I knew it would look blotchy and red on camera. As I looked over at Cole, hoping for reassurance—knowing a moment's eye contact would give me the strength I needed to hold it together—I felt a camera right in my face. Cole blanked me. In the line-up, Taylor Knight had slipped seamlessly into my spot.

"Taylor, do you know the words?" Felicity asked.

"To the greatest rock ballad of all time? I think I can manage it." Taylor winked at Robbie. The creep.

"You're on verse three," Felicity said. "Take it from the top."

Ninety seconds later, it was over for me. Taylor's voice was rich and mellifluous. It slipped into the group even more seamlessly than Taylor had himself. The five of them already looked bedroom-poster-ready. Taylor was the last piece of the boy band jigsaw puzzle. When the song ended it was obvious to every single person around that pool that we'd witnessed a moment of musical history.

Chapter Ten

That evening, I was lying on my bed back at the hotel, bawling my eyes out, when Cole slunk in through the door. He locked it behind him, crawled up the bed towards me, and folded his arms around me. I felt the warmth and weight of him.

"Are you OK?"

That made me wail like a grieving widow on the TV news. I couldn't help it.

"Is that a no?"

He combed his fingers through my hair. His big brown eyes looked so sad. He kissed my forehead, my nose, my chin, my lips.

"I'm a bit snotty, babes," I said.

"I'm a farm boy, Toby. It takes a lot more than snot to gross me out."

I laughed, and a snot bubble formed on my nostril and popped. I sniffed heavily and wiped my nose on my sleeve.

"But congratulations, you found a way to do it," Cole said. "I am absolutely grossed out."

I snorted. "If you can't handle me at my nose-bubbliest, you don't deserve me at my butt-bubbliest."

"It's going to be OK. You know that, right?" Cole said. "You're doing a duet with one of the girls now, right?"

I was singing "Islands in the Stream" with Emily, whom I'd only met that night. It was Felicity's choice. All of it. My voice was all wrong for the song. "We're the leftovers they didn't know what to do with." I sniffed. "It's going to be a disaster."

There would be three elimination shows—one for each judge's group—pre-recorded in front of a studio audience. Our group was going first. We'd have all tomorrow to rehearse our songs in our final arrangements, before performing onstage in front of the judges and our first live studio audience tomorrow night.

"Everyone loves a bit of Dolly and Kenny," Cole said. "It's a classic. You'll be great."

"We're a novelty act, babes. We're being sent home."

"You don't know that."

"I do know that."

Cole put his arms around me, pulling me into him. He nuzzled his head down into the pillow beside mine, his warm breath on my neck.

"Someone smart once told me that we should get to decide how our story ends," he said.

I rolled my eyes. "I know how these shows work. It's over for me, Cole."

"Don't go down without a fight, Tobes."

An hour later, when I'd cried out all my tears and felt comforted by his cuddles, Cole casually mentioned that he had some news.

"I came out to my dad."

I sat upright. "What? When? Why didn't you tell me?"

"You had stuff on your mind."

"You let me bleat on like that for hours, and all this time—" I shook my head. "How'd it go, babes? What did he say?"

Cole smiled, and his eyes sparkled.

"It went fine. He's happy for me. Said he'd love me no matter what. These old Catholics can surprise you sometimes."

"That's brilliant. How do you feel?"

"Amazing. I feel free. Genuinely free. Like nothing can hurt me now. Like I could take on the world. I didn't realise how much stress I'd been carrying around."

I squeezed Cole tighter than I'd ever squeezed him before, sharing in his relief.

"Congratulations, babes. I'm so proud of you." My lips found his. Tenderly at first, then more hungrily. I kissed him and held him and loved him like I *knew* he was my forever. A little while later—exhausted, spent—we fell asleep in each other's arms. I had no idea it would be our last night together.

* * *

The next night, as I'd predicted, Emily and I were knocked out of the competition. We gave it our best shot, but neither of us was surprised. To be honest, it was all a bit of a blur. I remember Mum and Dad hugging me in the wings when I came offstage. I remember Dorinda Carter asking me a few questions, the camera right up in my face. I don't remember any of them except the one where she asked, "Everyone wants to know what happened between you and Cole. Did you fall out or something?"

"I have no idea what you're talking about?" I said, in a daze.

From the green room I watched the other contestants perform. Only seven of the sixteen acts would go through. In a shock to precisely no one, Cole's group sailed right through to the live shows. My heart ached as I watched Joey, Yoshi, Chase, Taylor, and Cole jumping up and down onstage, hugging each other, tears streaming down their excited faces. They deserved their success, but envy boiled inside me. It had so nearly been me. I'd been one fuchsia fingernail away from all my dreams coming true.

The producers hauled the failed contestants and our parents off to somewhere deep in the bowels of the hotel to sign paperwork. There was always so much paperwork, so many things to sign. I didn't care what the contract said, the disclaimer said, the non-disclosure agreement said; I wanted to go home. I didn't bother reading any of it. I left that to Dad, while Mum came with me to collect my stuff from my room. I opened the door, hoping Cole might be there. He wasn't. I was so heartbroken and *so* tired. I'd finished packing when Mum's phone rang.

"Orla! Where are you, babes?... Uh-huh... You're joking?... Are you winding me up?... The bloody cheek!"

I looked at Mum. She put her hand over her phone, like it was the 1980s and she was covering an old-fashioned receiver. "They're mugging you off, bubby." Mum had the same look she gets on her face when the Salons Direct rep comes around and tells her the price of dry shampoo has gone up again. She uncovered her imaginary receiver.

"Well, I ain't having it, babes... No, that sounds like a plan... We'll see you there in five."

"What's going on?"

Five minutes later we burst through a heavy fire door and marched across an underground car park towards Orla and Cole. Cole lifted his head, our eyes met, and he ran across the car park towards me. I ran to him. He threw his arms around me.

"They wouldn't let me see you," he said.

"What's that about?"

"They don't want us to see the eliminated contestants. I don't know why. They won't let us go back into our rooms until you're all gone. I'm only here cos Mum told them she was taking me out for a hot chocolate before she heads back to Suffolk."

It was unbelievable, yet I wasn't surprised. I buried my nose in Cole's armpit, breathing in the smell of him. The leather, the sweat, the Lynx Africa. In the corner of my eye, I saw Mum giving Orla a hug

—these two amazing women who had conspired to give their sons a few precious minutes together to say goodbye.

"Congratulations," I said. "I'm so proud of you. You're going to be a pop star."

Cole leaned back, loosening his grip. He raised his eyebrows. "You mean a rock star."

"I think you've misunderstood the point of the show, babes. The clue's in the name."

Cole shrugged. "I plan to leverage it."

"I knew you were smart."

He kissed me on the forehead, rubbing a hand up and down my back. "You were great tonight. Are you OK?"

I felt a lump in my throat that I couldn't swallow. I tried to clear it. "When will I get to see you again?"

"I have no idea. It looks like they're going to keep us locked down during the show. We'll figure something out. I promise, I will message you every day."

"You promise?"

"I absolutely promise. I will message you every single day."

Cole hugged me tightly. I hugged him tighter still.

Chapter Eleven

That weekend, the *Make Me a Pop Star* theme burst from the speakers of the huge ninety-inch TV on our living room wall. It was the Colchester audition episode, and my heart was pounding with excitement, fear, and dread. My face would be on the TV for the next month, as the pre-recorded audition and group stage episodes went out. I should have been on cloud nine. I wasn't.

The house was overflowing with relatives, family friends, and assorted hangers-on. I'd been crying most of the day, hiding in my room. Aunty Cheryl had arrived late, wearing a silk neck scarf to hide her hickeys and pulling one of those shopping baskets you see old ladies dragging around the supermarket, stocked with gin. She looked like a Ryanair hostess who'd nicked the passengers' duty-free. Mum plonked herself down beside me on the couch, sending bubbles swirling over the top of her champagne flute.

"Have a sniff, Tobes." She offered me her glass. "Go on, bubby. You've earned it. You're famous!"

As I knocked back a large gulp of Mum's fizz, Dorinda Carter's beaming face appeared on the screen.

"Here we go!" Dad said.

A dozen kids were running around our back garden, screaming, ignoring the main event. The trampoline was seeing its first use in years. It was holding together better than I was, but either of us could have randomly flung a child over the fence at any moment. Dad barked at my sister.

"Elsa, shut the patio doors."

Elsa groaned. "Why do I have to do it?"

"You're the closest."

She got up with a huff.

The noise outside muffled as the latch clicked into place. The house stank of barbecued sausage fat and J'adore by Dior. Dad turned the TV volume up a couple of notches. A roar went up around the room as my face appeared on the screen in a crowd shot.

"There he is!" Mum shouted in my ear. "There's my boy." Random hands slapped my shoulders, my legs, the top of my head.

On the TV, Dorinda Carter walked through the crowd of audition hopefuls, asking people who they were and where they came from. Cole and I appeared on-screen again. The house erupted into screams of delight. Mum hushed everyone in time to hear Cole and me say our names and where we were from. The package moved on to a couple of girls who'd obviously been asked to do the same.

"I'm super proud of you, bubby," Mum said.

"You remember that I didn't get through, right?"

"You get through in this episode, bubby. Anyway, you did your best. I can't ask for more than that. There's always next year. Did Cole message to wish you luck?"

I shook my head. Despite Cole's promise, it had been three days since I'd been kicked off the show, and I hadn't heard from him once. It was the longest we hadn't spoken since the night we started texting.

"He's probably busy with the show, bubby."

"Did you hear from Orla?" I asked. Mum had invited the Kennedys down to our watch party.

"They couldn't make it. It turns out milking cows twice a day really interferes with your social life—even on the weekends."

"Did she say anything about Cole?"

Mum frowned. "Sorry, love."

Forty-five minutes later, Cole appeared on-screen again, strumming the opening chords to "You Got It."

"Cheryl, this is Orla's boy," Mum said. "You remember. He came into the salon."

Aunty Cheryl looked up from her phone. "Tall bloke. Boy band–issue swoopy fringe. Carries broken hearts around in his pocket. That the one?"

My phone pinged.

Aunty Cheryl: *Stay strong. I love you. xxx*

We watched as the song ended and the argument between Johanna Thorsdóttir and Robbie Johnswagger played out. Erik, Dad's workmate and weekend sporting buddy, couldn't believe his ears.

"They can't be serious. The kid was incredible."

"Shu'up babes, I wanna hear this," his wife, Delice, said.

Next, Felicity Quant asked Cole about Suffolk and their mutual haunts.

"Is old FQ *flirting* with a teenage boy?" Dad said. I felt bile in the back of my throat.

Felicity asked Cole about his heritage, and he explained that he was adopted and didn't know where his birth father was from.

"Oh, that's well sad," Delice said. "He should do one of them NDA tests and find his real family."

"It's DNA, you melt," Erik said.

"All right, Albert Epstein. Do y' mind, I'm trying to watch this."

Cole walked offstage to a roar of applause from the crowd, and the camera cut to Dorinda slapping me on the back and wishing me luck. The living room erupted into squeals. Dad and Erik shouted "Come on" in the same way they did when they were flogging each other on the tennis court. The shaky first notes of "Firework" quivered their way past my vocal cords. I sounded like a cat trying to claw its way out of a set of bagpipes. I felt everyone in the room wince and knew they were already trying to work out what consolatory things to say. I sank into the sofa. But, on-screen, I warmed up—and soon I was belting out the chorus and dominating the stage. Mum's hand gripped my knee, and I couldn't tell whether the wet patch forming was her sweat or mine. The song ended, and the room erupted into cheers and cries of "well done" and "congratulations." In the relief, I cried.

"Shush, it's the judges' comments," Mum said. I closed my eyes, not wanting to watch as the inevitable played out. When Felicity Quant finally said yes, the room went wild. I opened my eyes to see myself crying on the screen. I bowed. I clasped my hands in front of my chest and minced offstage into the waiting arms of Mum and Dorinda Carter. Then they showed the moment where I spotted Cole and threw my arms around him. Cole looked... shocked. Which was not how I remembered that moment. They cut to an interview with us, filmed earlier that day. Dorinda asked Cole about us forging a friendship in the queue, about his song choice, and about the Hallelujah Curse. Then the microphone moved to me, and Dorinda asked why I'd helped Cole. And that's when it happened. That's the moment my life changed forever. That's when I opened my stupid mouth and said, "Why wouldn't I? He's marriage material!"

Everyone in the living room cringed.

Worse, on the TV, Cole cringed.

The sound of a record scratch blasted from the television speaker. The footage rewound. The microphone reappeared under my chin. Dorinda asked her question again. I said, "Why wouldn't I? He's marriage material!" again. And the camera punched in on Cole's reaction. They froze the frame on him, his eyes bulging. Closer. *Closer.* *CLOSER.* I watched in horror as, in slow motion, Cole unwound his arm from around my shoulder.

Finally, Dorinda went on with her interview. "What do you say to that, Cole?"

"Yeah, um, that's... a bit intense," he replied.

"Not keen on marriage?"

"Someday, sure," Cole said. "When I meet the right person. And maybe when I've known them more than, like, four hours."

Another record scratch. Rewind. The editors had enjoyed themselves.

"Maybe when I've known them more than, like, four hours!"

The camera focused on me, and the image on screen burst into flames, and my face melted away. The show cut to an ad break. My utter humiliation was complete. Hot tears scalded their way down my cheeks.

The room fell into silence.

"What were you thinking, mate?" Dad said.

Mum enveloped me in a hug. "Oh, Tobes."

My sister chimed in triumphantly. "Oh my God, social media is *not* being kind."

"Already?" Mum said.

Elsa burst into laughter and held up her phone for everyone to see. "You're already a meme! How are people so fast?"

I ran up the stairs to my bedroom, slammed the door behind me, and threw myself onto the bed—screaming into my pillow, drenching it with tears. My phone was pinging with text messages. I switched it off.

A few minutes later, there was a light tap on my door.

"Tobes?"

"Go away!"

I heard the door click open and close again, smelt the telltale cloud of J'adore, and felt Aunty Cheryl sit on the edge of the bed.

"You OK, Tobes?" She rubbed my back with her hand.

"Leave me alone."

"I can't do that, babes. Not till I know you're OK."

"I'm not OK. I'll never be OK again!"

She held my shoulder and tried to roll me over. I buried my face deeper in the pillow.

"Look at me."

"No!"

"Look at me."

She sunk her nails in, deep enough to show she was serious. I rolled over.

"Sit up. Come on."

I did as I was told, and my aunt folded me up in a hug.

"I love the bones of you, Toby. You know that?"

I nodded.

"And I'm so bloody proud of you. That was a brave thing you done."

"Everyone's laughing at me."

My aunt pulled back, one hand gripping my shoulder, her piercing blue eyes staring fiercely into mine.

"I'm not being funny, but fuck 'em, babes. You spoke your truth."

"It's a stupid saying! It was a joke, and it's ruined my life."

"Only if you let it, Toby Lyngstad." A fierce watermelon-pink nail sliced the air, millimetres from my face. "What you done, going to that audition, getting as far as you did on that show—and doing it all as your true self, not hiding anything, putting your heart and soul out there. I've never been so proud of you in my whole life. And I was so proud of you the first time you did a poop on the potty, I kept the photo on my fridge until you were five."

"A photo of... my poop?"

"No, you melt, a picture of you on the potty. What are you like?"

"I do not remember this."

Aunty Cheryl's arm wrapped around my shoulders. She squeezed me, rocking me from side to side. I buried my face in her hair extensions. "I've got a scrapbook of everything you ever done, Sonny Jim. Did you know that?"

I sniffed. "No."

"I do. I've got all the programmes from your school nativities. That get-well card you drew for me when I got my boobs done. And I've been keeping all the articles about *Make Me a Pop Star* too."

"You can chuck those out."

"I know you're hurting right now, babes. But one day you'll want to look back on this experience, and you'll be glad someone kept a record. Who knows what this might all lead to."

"Public humiliation and heartbreak?"

"That's the risk we take when we dare to dream. What matters, Tobes, is that we continue to dream."

That was too much. I choked on my sobs. Aunty Cheryl gently rubbed my back, listening to me cry.

"God, I need a spliff," she said.

Over the next few days, I got hundreds more texts and calls. Some supportive. Some vicious. Some from the press. What absolutely killed me was not one of them was from Cole.

The internet's 10 best jokes about "marriage material guy"

Move over, Jamie Struff, a new "Make Me a Meme Star" is born! Enter stage left, our freshest national embarrassment, Toby Lyngstad.

@antsypantsy92: *Ladies, if a 16-year-old chav from Essex can have the church booked and the dress ready to go four hours after meeting a smokin' hot dish in the street, then your man has no excuse for his commitment issues. #respectyourself #marriagematerial*

@247aggression: *The only place he gettin laid is his damned sunbed. #marriagematerial*

@maddiethegreat: *That sound you heard was the entire nation sucking air in through its teeth. If we could have harnessed that energy, we could have powered a JCB earthmover long enough for Toby to dig a hole and bury his deceased arse. #marriagematerial*

@charliee2thef: *Cole rejecting him may have saved Toby's life. NOTHING is more powerful, terrifying or ruthless than a mob of teenage girls obsessed with a popstar and Cole Kennedy is 100% a*

STAR. They'd have killed him. #lambtotheslaughter #isurvivedbeiber-fever #deadonarrival

@makemeapoostar: *Do you ever feel, like a tragic chav/who's now a laughing stock, wanting to start again?/Did you ever go, on a TV show/and ask a random boy, if he will marry you? #makemealaughing-stock #firework #katyperry*

@princess_jen: *Cole: *sings You Got It**
    Toby: I want it.
    Cole: Not you.

@AbsolutelyDrakulous: *To be fair, that's unlikely to be the only proposal Cole gets during this season of Pop Star. Johnswagger's so hard for him the judges' desk is on a weird angle. #makemeapopstar*

@born2switch: *As someone who NEVER knows what's going to come out of my mouth when I start speaking, I find Toby so relatable!!! Did you see Cole's FACE? I'd be like, "if you want to stop the stupid shit coming out of my mouth, put something in it!" #marriagematerial*

@ennameenashinymo: *Toby's skin is so orange he must have thought Cole was giving him an amber light but that signal was fully red! This is what happens when you do not proceed with caution. #LearnYour-HighwayCode #marriagematerial*

@minesafryup: *Cole's marriage material must be Kevlar cos ain't nothing getting through it! #makemeapopstar*

Chapter Twelve

An empty shampoo bottle glanced off the side of my face, hit the computer screen, and skittered across the salon counter, burying itself among the stationery.

"Ouch!"

"Didn't you hear me?" Aunty Cheryl said. "The towels are finished in the dryer. Can you fold them please." She turned to Mrs Fitzpatrick, who was having her freshly blue-rinsed perm set. "Love the bones of him, but honestly, who'd have kids?"

"I had twelve," Mrs Fitzpatrick replied.

"Jesus, love."

I got up and walked to the back of the salon in a stupor. I'd been in a daze since Saturday night. It was now Thursday lunchtime, and I still hadn't heard from Cole. I wanted to be at home in bed, but Mum had insisted I come into the salon to help out.

"How'd your fanny hold up with all them kids?" Aunty Cheryl asked.

"By the fifth one I didn't even put down my knitting. She shot out of me like a Nissan Micra out of the Blackwall Tunnel. I haven't sneezed with confidence since 1972."

I'd just opened the dryer when I heard the doorbell tinkle. I craned my head to see if I was needed at the counter, but it was only Mum and Gaston coming back with lunch. I squatted to pull the towels out of the dryer, the heat of them radiating through my leg and the fresh smell of laundry powder filling the air. Gaston nuzzled against my bum, his nose cold and wet against the exposed skin where my jeans had pulled down.

"They didn't have any chicken and avocado left, bubby, so I got you the Caesar," Mum said, plonking the salad bowls down on the benchtop. "Thanks for doing that, Tobes." She leaned down to kiss me on the head. "Any news from Cole yet?"

I shook my head.

"Look, I been thinking. Why don't you give Orla a call? Find out whether something serious has happened or if he's mugging you off. Cos all this moping ain't healthy, Tobes."

"Can you do it?" I said, standing to dump the pile of towels on the benchtop.

"And be the go-between between you and the other go-between?" Mum opened her salad bowl and shoved her fork into a piece of boiled egg. "No thank you. Besides, I've got Priti from *Dress for Successex* coming in for a cut and colour in fifteen minutes. You're a big boy. You know how to use the phone."

I rolled my eyes.

"And you can't keep sitting at the front counter with a face like that. Mrs Fitz come in this morning, said she nearly turned around and walked back out again. Said she thought she'd walked into the funeral home by mistake."

She shoved the egg into her mouth.

I put the towel I'd been folding down on the benchtop. "I'm scared, Mum. What if he doesn't want to see me because of all this 'marriage material' stuff?"

"It's better to know, bubby. We're all here for you, whatever happens."

* * *

There was silence on the other end of the phone, followed by a deep sigh.

"They said they were going to call you," Orla said, frustration obvious in her voice. "I asked them specifically, and they promised me someone from the show would be in touch with you."

"Is Cole upset with me? Have I embarrassed him? Because I promise whatever he's been going through, it's been so much worse for—"

"What? No, sweetheart. They took his phone off him."

"Are you joking me?"

"They took their phones off all the boys. For filming reasons, supposedly. And to keep them from seeing coverage and socials and so on. Then they made them all sign new contracts—at two in the morning, mind you, after a full day of rehearsals—stipulating who they could have contact with. They gave them new phones with new numbers. I only found out yesterday. I'm fuming. Fiona says the contracts are probably not legally binding, because they're minors and they signed under duress with only a Totally Records lawyer present. But Cole is worried if we kick up a stink, they'll boot him from the show."

"So, he's not angry with me?"

"No, darling, he's not angry with you."

"Do you have his new number? I need to speak to him."

More silence.

"Listen, I'm not sure, darling. This contract they made him sign. If any information about the show or what they're filming gets out, he'll be kicked out of the competition."

"I won't ask about the show. I ain't bothered about that. I need to hear his voice. I miss him."

"I know. He misses you too," Orla said. "When I spoke to him yesterday, he asked after you."

"Did he?"

"He did."

"What did he say? Did he have a message for me or anything?"

"He asked how you were doing and whether I'd spoken to you."

"Is that all?"

More silence. This time it felt loaded.

"Look, I shouldn't have to tell you this. I can't believe those arseholes are making me do this. They've told Cole he can't have contact with you during the competition."

"What?"

"Apparently, it doesn't 'fit the narrative,' whatever that means."

I knew what it meant. The narrative was that I was Cole's love-crazed stalker and he wasn't interested in me. That's what the editing of the audition episode showed. That's what the internet thought. If anyone knew we were boyfriends, it'd ruin their storyline. Our strategy of avoiding one another on camera had played right into their hands.

"When I spoke to them," Orla continued, "I told them they had to call you and tell you that because I wasn't going to. They should have called you by now."

"No one's called me."

"I'm sorry, Toby. Look, when this is all over, we'll have you up to the farm and you can stay for the weekend, longer if you like, as long as it doesn't interfere with school, and you boys can hang out. We'd love to have you. It'll only be a few months."

"It won't be a few months," I said. And I knew it was true. "Cole is going to win this thing. You realise that, don't you? By Christmas he's going to be a big celebrity, and I'm never going to see him again."

More silence.

"Listen, I'm going to text you his new number so you can message him," Orla said. "Please, for the love of God, be careful with it. This opportunity means the world to Cole, and he'd never forgive either of us if he lost it because of something we did."

I started to cry. I was thrilled I was going to be able to speak to Cole, but I also could not be the reason Cole got kicked off *Make Me a Pop Star*—not when it was clearly going to change his life and help him share his music with the world. I took a deep breath.

"No," I said. "It's OK. Tell him I miss him, and that I'm rooting for him, and that... and that... you know. He knows. I just... miss him."

"Are you sure?"

"Yes."

I hung up the phone and crumpled onto the salon front counter for all the world to see. Ugly tears streamed down my face, staining my clothes. My phone pinged.

Orla: *In case you change your mind x*

She'd sent me Cole's new number. I felt like I was choking. I needed air. I scrambled around the counter and out the salon door. My hands on my knees, bent over in the street, I cried and cried and cried until I thought I'd be sick. I cried because it was all so unfair. I cried because I hated myself. I cried because my situation was hopeless. I cried because Orla had given me the means to blow everything up. I cried because I knew I couldn't do it. I had enough sense to realise I could never, *would* never, call that number. Cole's future wasn't mine to risk. If the situations had been reversed and he'd put my place in the competition at risk, I'd have been fuming. What I didn't have enough brains to realise was that if you're going to cry like your life is ending, do not do it in a public place. Not if your face is going viral all over the internet.

"Marriage material" boy's manic meltdown over TV heartbreak

An eagle-eyed Bulletin reader snapped these exclusive pictures of 16-year-old Toby Lyngstad having a full-on breakdown in the Colchester high street, days after "Make Me a Pop Star" aired the awkward moment he called Suffolk's Cole Kennedy "marriage material."

Lyngstad was apparently inconsolable as his mother Chloe, 39, tried to get him back inside the shop. Lyngstad collapsed to the ground, repeatedly hitting a fist into the pavement, shouting "This is bulls**t, this is bulls**t." Another woman then emerged from the salon with a glass of what appeared to be rosé in her hand and tried to help. Lyngstad was heard to shout, "F*** off, Aunty Cheryl."

Chapter Thirteen

The editing of the group stage of *Make Me a Pop Star* was as brutal as the auditions. You know how in a nature documentary, when the killer whales are stalking the seal and it's clear the poor bastard is done for, the whales play with him for a bit, flinging him into the air and catching him again, but then before the actual kill the editors cut away to some adorable lion cubs or something? There was none of that mercy for me. They showed the capture, the torture, and the kill in high-definition Technicolor CinemaScope and Dolby Digital surround sound. At every turn, I was shown pining after Cole like a lovesick puppy, and he was shown blanking me. In that final moment by the swimming pool, when Felicity Quant plucked Taylor from the reserves and sent me off into obscurity, the audience saw me looking longingly over at Cole with my bottom lip quivering, and Cole looking directly forwards with all the emotion of an Easter Island statue. It was total and utter humiliation. The next morning, someone had sprayed the words *SAD FAG* across the front of the salon. We filed a police report. Aunty Cheryl cleaned it off herself. The next day it was back. The council's CCTV showed two teenage girls were responsible. It was the first warning of how obsessed and how evil Cole's fandom would become. No one was ever caught or charged. Mum put up new security cameras around the salon and the house. I deleted all my social media accounts. I dreaded the show going to air. Each week, the memes and the jokes and the calls from the newspapers and the "funny" FM radio breakfast hosts got worse. My only consolation was the occasional titbit from Orla, via Mum, saying Cole was doing well.

If I'd thought my summer holidays had been a nightmare, returning to college was an unimaginable horror show. A first-year I'd never even seen before pointed and shouted down the corridor, "Hey, Toby, am I marriage material?" Everyone laughed. When I ignored him, he shouted, "What's the matter, am I not good enough for you?" Then his chinless mate chimed in with "I'd marry you, Toby... if you weren't so pathetic." A couple of girls walked into my media studies class side by side, humming the bridal march and pretending to carry bouquets. Then, while waiting for Mr Bourgault to turn up for our music tech class, Tamillah Fayet, who I'd always got along with, yelled across the room, "Hey, Toby, is it true even your dildo has now turned you down?" Everyone was in fits. This room had always been my safe space in the school.

"I hear you like your sex like Cole Kennedy likes his knock-backs," Tamillah continued, "rough and public."

The whole class descended into uncontrollable laughter. My fight or flight response was speeding down the runway in sensible shoes, shouting, *Cabin crew, please arm doors and cross-check.* I started to shake uncontrollably. My chest tightened. I couldn't breathe. The fear was total. I grabbed my bag and dashed out of the room. I ran, gasping for air, until I was well clear of the school, then slowed to a walk, sat in a bus stop about a mile from home, and cried until the district qualified for flood relief. Two, maybe three, buses went past. The next bus that rolled in had an ad for *Make Me a Pop Star* on the side. Cole Kennedy's dark, chiselled face stared back at me from a group photo with Chase and the boys. It stretched the whole length of the bus.

"You getting on, bruv?" the driver asked.

I shook my head. "Thanks. I'll walk."

The driver shrugged, the door closed, and the bus drove off. Another image of the boys was on the back of the bus, with the *Make Me a Pop Star* glitter ball logo and "7.30pm every Saturday and Sunday." As Cole's face disappeared into the distance, it felt like Cole himself was getting further and further away from me. If it hadn't been for the relentless taunting and misery I was enduring, the whole thing could have been a dream. I felt empty, lonely, shattered. Cole was slipping away from me, and I wanted him back. I couldn't lose him. I had to fight for him—fight like that poor bloody seal—or die trying.

I got out my phone and dialled the number Orla had given me.

"Hello?" It was one word, but it was unmistakably Cole's smooth, sexy voice.

I couldn't speak. Every word I needed to say got caught in my throat, unable to reach my tongue.

"It's Toby."

"Oh my God!" Cole changed his voice to a whisper. "It's so good to hear from you. I've missed you *so* much."

Tears burst from my eyes. If my face stayed wet any longer, my eyelashes would turn into peat.

"I've missed you!" I said.

"You shouldn't be calling me on this number."

There were footsteps and rustling, as Cole moved from wherever he was to someplace safe to talk.

"I know. Your mum gave it to me."

"She shouldn't have done that. I could get in *sooo* much trouble."

"I'm sorry, I wanted to hear your voice."

A heavy door creaked open. Cole cleared his throat. "I'm glad you called." The acoustics had changed, Cole's voice no longer echoing off walls. He was outside. "I was hoping maybe I'd see you at one of the live shows. I know you never miss them. Are you coming along?"

"Are you serious?" I said. "Do you know what it's been like for me? Cole, I'm a laughing stock."

A moment of silence on the other end of the phone.

"Is this the marriage material thing?"

"Are you winding me up?" Anger rose inside me. "I can't leave the house without an armed escort, babes. I've got the paparazzi hounding me. Have you seen what they're saying about me on social media?"

"To be honest, no," he said. "They don't let us go on the apps. We see a rundown of important media stuff at breakfast each morning. I know a heap of rock fans have started a 'let Cole be Cole' campaign because they think I'm better than pop songs, which is awesome, but—"

"My life is a living nightmare."

"I'm so sorry, Toby. I had no idea."

"Have you even thought of me at all?"

"Of course I have! The other day I was doing an interview, and this girl outside the radio station had a sign that said 'I'm marriage material,' and I thought of you."

My piss had officially boiled.

"Are you having a laugh?" I was in utter disbelief. "Your fans are pure, unrefined evil. This whole situation has ruined my life."

There was a long pause, then a sigh. "I'm sorry. I didn't think that through. Hey, listen, like I said, I'm glad you called. I needed to speak to you."

"You could have called at any time. I was waiting."

"I didn't have your number in this phone."

"Seriously?"

Cole yawned. "Sorry. Incredibly long days. So, listen, um... about... us..."

"I don't believe this," I said, sensing what was coming in the same way a rabbit senses that the oncoming headlights are probably not good for their health: dazzled, frozen, about to be flattened by the inevitable. "You're fucking kidding me."

"I'm sorry, look... they... they don't want me to be... *out*... on the show."

"What are you saying?"

"It's the fans, apparently," Cole said. "It's the girls with 'marriage material' signs. Felicity said they need to believe I'm 'achievable.' That's the word she used."

"You're going back into the closet for a TV show?"

"I guess. But it's not like I was ever very far out of the closet, anyway."

"You're breaking up with me."

"I don't want to! I'm sorry. I tried to reason with them. They didn't give me a choice. It's only until this is all over, then we can be together."

I scoffed my disbelief and disdain. My whole body was numb, but at least I finally knew where I stood.

"Listen," Cole said, "a Totally Television lawyer is going to contact you about signing a non-disclosure agreement." Nothing would have surprised me by this point. The rabbit was already dead, why not reverse over it? "It's to protect us both, you know?"

"*Both* of us?" I laughed.

There was silence on the other end of the phone.

"I'm sorry," Cole said. He sounded like he meant it, but I wanted to hurt him for epically disrespecting me.

"I'm not signing an NDA."

"Please, you have to," Cole said, a little too quickly. "Felicity said otherwise I'll be walking around with a loaded gun pointed at my head and you could pull the trigger at any time."

"You think I would *out* you, Cole? Really?" My voice was fizzing with anger. "Do you seriously think so little of me?"

"People do crazy things, Toby," he said, then added, meekly, "Especially when they're angry."

"I would never 'out' you, *Cole*." I spewed as much venom as possible into his name. "That's Queer Code 101. So, no. Respectfully, you can take your NDA, roll it up into a ball, and shove it up your arse."

"Toby, please. I need you to sign it."

I was so angry I was shaking. "You think you need me to sign it because they're dangling fame and fortune in front of you. You might feel like you're walking around with a loaded gun at your head, but one day you'll be begging me to pull that trigger—because one day, Cole, you're going to be sick of not living your truth."

"Please, Toby. Don't do this to me."

"I'm not doing this to you, you're doing this to me, and I can't get my head round it. Like an idiot, I loved you. I can't believe you're mugging me off. It's bang out of order!"

"You... love me?"

"I *hate* you."

"You don't mean that."

"I do." And I did. I meant it.

"I'm so sorry." Cole was pleading now. I could hear him crying on the other end of the phone. I imagined his eyes all puffy and red, his swooshy hair getting stuck in his tears.

"Well, you should have thought of that before. How did you think this was gonna play out?"

"I thought you would understand!" Cole's voice was scratchy. "You would do the same. You know you would. Felicity—"

"Fuck Felicity. I made one stupid joke, and she's literally ruined my life."

"She made you famous. Isn't that what you wanted?"

"Famous for doing something worthwhile, not for being a melt!"

"But you can still leverage it, right?"

"Piss off, Cole." I'd had enough. I wanted out of this call. "I'm not signing your NDA. I'm going to say it as it is: You do *not* have a gun pointed at your head. But I'll gladly let Felicity think she has a gun pointed at hers."

"Why are you being so petty? Is revenge more important to you than I am?"

"Is fame more important to you than I am?"

"You mean sharing my music with the world?" Cole said. "Toby, this is my dream."

"Well, you can sod right off, then."

"Please, Toby, I love y—"

I hung up the phone.

Two days later, a lawyer from Totally Television turned up on the doorstep. I refused to sign the NDA. I'd doubtless made a powerful enemy. But then, how could they possibly make my life worse? I called Cole to give him a piece of my mind, but his new number was disconnected.

Cole and the gang the "Go Tos" for Quant

With the first of the "Make Me a Pop Star" live shows starting this weekend, Felicity Quant's Totally Television has revealed the names of the acts formed during the show's gruelling group stage.

The five-piece boy band starring this season's heart-throb and certified "marriage material" farm boy, Cole Kennedy, will be called "the Go Tos." Kennedy and bandmates Joey Demasi, Chase French, Yoshi Kawaguchi and Taylor Knight released a short promo video on social media showing off the band's new branding and an accompanying hand gesture that has already taken social media by storm.

As one internet wag pointed out: "They've got a logo, they've their own sign language, and they're already the biggest boy band in the country. Imagine what'll happen if they actually release a song?"

Announcing the name on the social media accounts of Totally Television and Totally Records, Quant said the name "the Go Tos" alluded to the fact that "throughout the auditions, these five boys were the ones we kept going back to, time and time again."

Other acts include a four-piece girl group called Crush, the duo Bernie and Audrey, and "alternative" trio BatSkink.

Chapter Fourteen

I didn't watch any of the *Make Me a Pop Star* live shows go out. I couldn't. It hurt too much. The bullying at school was relentless. I struggled to leave my bedroom. Even Elsa had realised something was seriously wrong and stopped making fun of me. And while my life went to hell, Cole and "the Go Tos" were becoming more famous by the day—and harder to avoid. They were everywhere: TV, radio, billboards, social media. In November, I started skipping school. The school called my parents, obviously, which led to a blazing row that ended with me running out of the house in floods of tears. I went to the only place I could think to go.

"Don't eat the brownies, they're hash." Aunty Cheryl had her back to me while she made me a cup of tea. "They're for my book club."

"You belong to a book club?"

"I can read, you know."

"Yeah, but, like... *do* you read?"

She waved a hand in the air. "I usually read the synopsis on Wikipedia, to get the gist. In case the topic comes up."

"Isn't talking about the book the whole point of a book club?"

She plonked my tea down in front of me.

"Sometimes I forget how young you are, Tobes. The point of a book club is so the girls can get together to drink rosé midweek and slag off their nearest and dearest." She opened a kitchen drawer and pulled out a bottle of whiskey. "Irish?"

"I think you've forgotten how young I am, again."

She shrugged and emptied a slug of Jameson's into her mug.

"How you coping, babes?"

Suddenly there was a lump in my throat, and I couldn't find the right words.

"We need to toughen you up, babes. What have I told you a thousand times?"

I knew what was coming. My aunt held a hand up in front of her face and waggled her now raspberry nails.

"These nails are my sword," I recited dutifully.

"That's right." She grabbed a handful of her hair. "And these extensions are my shield." She circled her face with her finger. "*This* is my battle dress. When I've got my eyelashes on and a face full of slap, no one can get through me."

I sighed. Aunty Cheryl reached over and twisted a piece of my fringe, combing it back into place with her acrylics.

"You're a special boy, Tobes. We need to build your armour up."

"I'm not going back to school."

Aunty Cheryl took a sip of her tea.

"Why don't you come work at the salon full-time?"

I shook my head. "Mum and Dad want me to finish my exams."

"Ain't either of them got any A levels, and they done all right. Come work at the salon. You did great over summer. When you weren't mooning like a lovesick puppy, at least. Or off rutting. Seriously, though, we could get you on the apprenticeship scheme as soon as tomorrow morning."

For the first time in months, I felt something like hope.

"Really?"

"Course." She winked and picked up a brownie. "You leave your mum and dad to me," she said, popping it in her mouth.

* * *

In December, as I got into the swing of my apprenticeship, the Go Tos won the sixth season of *Make Me a Pop Star* with seventy-one per cent of the total audience vote. It was the widest margin seen in the show's history. The fan base already had its own name, the Extremes. The coverage was inescapable, as the Totally Records publicity machine switched into top gear and the boys did a victory lap of commercial radio stations and regional shopping malls. Two days later, the band's debut single came out. Called "My Daydream Girl," about a teenage boy yearning for a girl no one else seems to notice, it rocketed straight to number one. It was the UK's Christmas number one. I banned it being played in the salon. When tickets went on sale for the Go Tos' first tour a few weeks later, they sold out in less than a day.

I was angry, empty, and jealous. I hated Cole for abandoning me, for getting to live my dream, for his success. I hated myself for auditioning for the show, for saying something so stupid on camera, for not being strong enough to handle the fallout. Aunty Cheryl was right: I needed armour. I spent most of my first pay cheque on a down payment for tooth veneers. A month after I started my apprenticeship, I stepped into a gym for the first time in my life.

EXCLUSIVE! "I don't belong here"!

Cole's anguish over long-lost family

Pop's newest superstar, the Go Tos' Cole Kennedy, fears he doesn't belong in Britain and is desperate to find his long-lost family.

The 16-year-old has spoken openly about his adoption by Suffolk dairy farmers Andy and Orla Kennedy, who fostered Cole after he was given up for adoption by his birth parents.

But now The Bulletin can exclusively reveal Cole's private anguish at the family and future he lost when his birth parents abandoned him, and the mystery surrounding his mixed-race heritage.

Cole told a friend he felt he couldn't "shake the feeling I'm living in the wrong country, maybe growing up in the wrong religion, and certainly in the wrong culture."

The teenage heart-throb was also haunted by the fact he might still have blood relatives alive who "might not even know I exist." Tragically, Cole told friends he feared tracing his birth family would "kill" his adoptive parents, who might "think they're not enough"...

***A month after winning* Make Me a Pop Star**

Chapter Fifteen

The salon phone rang. It was a busy Saturday morning in January, and I was folding towels out the back.

"Can someone get that, please?" I called out. "I'm in the dryer."

Not two minutes later I stepped out into the salon with a pile of toasty warm towels, ready to put them away under the sinks, to find everyone staring at me. Aunty Cheryl switched off the hairdryer she was using on Mrs Fitz.

"What? What is it?" I said.

Mum set her comb and scissors down and walked towards me. You could have heard a pin drop. Every person in the room was watching me intently. Mum put her hands on my arms, rubbing my biceps with her thumbs—the pile of towels between us. She had a look on her face I'd last seen when she went to place an order on the Séance Beauty Products website and the browser auto-filled with SeanCody and the house rang with the sounds of gay porn. This was her Mum's-very-disappointed-in-you face.

"What have you done, bubby?" she said.

I was genuinely baffled, and I said so.

"Well, Orla Kennedy has cancelled her three o'clock and said she won't be coming into the salon anymore."

"What, why?"

"I dunno, Tobes, you tell me." Mum folded her arms. She meant business.

"Why does it have to be something I've done?"

"Why would Orla Kennedy say 'After what Toby's done, I think it's best if I get my hair done elsewhere' if you ain't done something?"

The salon was so quiet you could hear the steam coming off the towels. I put them down on the sink. Every pair of eyes was on me.

"Has he got a bird pregnant, then?" Mrs Fitz said.

Aunty Cheryl laughed, swallowed it, and pretended to clear her throat.

My phone started vibrating in my pocket. It was a withheld number. I had a dreadful feeling that whatever I'd done, I was about to find out about it. I answered it.

"I can't believe you would do that to me." Cole's voice was cold, angry.

"Do what? I don't know what I'm supposed—"

"Argh! Shut up, Toby! I don't even want to hear it. I don't want to hear your excuses. You know what you did."

"I genuinely don't." I stepped through the curtain and into the back room. It offered no soundproofing, but at least I was out of sight.

"You're so full of shit," Cole said. "Our private text messages are all over today's *Bulletin*. No one else had them. I know it was you."

Injustice does something primal to the body. It boils up inside you in an incensed rage, the unfairness searing every cell as it radiates outwards from the pit of your stomach. But when you're already angry at the person accusing you of something you know you didn't do, it feeds that rage with contempt and fuels it with self-right-eousness.

"And why would I do that?"

"Because you're petty? Because you want to hurt me? You tell me, Toby, you're the one who did it!"

"Oh, is the media being mean to you, Cole?" I said. "Now you know how it feels. I hope it hurts."

"So, it *was* you. Everyone said it had to be you, but I didn't want to believe it."

"Believe what you like," I said. "But this had nothing to do with me."

I ended the call.

When I stepped back into the salon, everyone was still looking at me.

"Did you do it, though, Tobes?" Mum asked. "I don't care what you told him, but you gotta be honest with me."

I shook my head. "It had nothing to do with me."

"So, who did it?"

It was a good question. Who had access to my phone? Did Elsa know my code? Had Aunty Cheryl decided to get revenge on Cole on my behalf? The whole situation was off.

"I have no idea. It wasn't me, I promise you."

Mrs Fitz stamped her walking stick against the floor, then waggled it at me.

"You need to step up and accept your responsibilities, young man," she said. "You're going to be a father!"

Part Two
AUNTY CHERYL'S SCRAPBOOK

British invasion!
Screaming fans greet Go Tos as U.S. tour kicks off

In scenes mirroring the Beatles' arrival in the U.S. in 1964, British pop stars the Go Tos landed at New York's JFK International Airport on Tuesday to scenes of pandemonium.

An estimated 6,000 of the boy band's American fans crowded the airport arrivals hall to await "the G2 five." The swarm of mostly teenage girls quickly overwhelmed JFK's seemingly unprepared security operation. Three girls fainted, and paramedics struggled to reach them.

The band's debut album, "Welcome to the Circus," has been a global smash hit, with five singles reaching number one in the U.S. Their latest single, "Why Don't You Call?," has been number one in the U.S. for six weeks.

The U.S. leg of the Welcome to the Circus Tour gets underway at New York's Radio City Music Hall on Thursday night...

One year after winning **Make Me a Pop Star**

Toby graduates in style!

Chloe, Cheryl and the team at Chloe's Hair & Beauty are proud to announce Toby has completed his apprenticeship with flying colours!

To book your cut and colour with the future star of Essex's hair and beauty scene, call the salon or visit our website. Bookings open now!

***Advertisement copy, two years after not winning* Make Me a Pop Star**

Which of these beauties is Cole's belle?

The Go Tos' Cole Kennedy took fellow "Make Me a Pop Star" legend Jocasta Rose to the BRIT Awards last night, sparking rumours the pair are dating.

While Rose looked at ease on Kennedy's arm in a black one-shouldered gown from Alexander McQueen, perhaps she shouldn't get too comfortable in the role? The pop heart-throb has been connected to a string of the world's most beautiful women in the past few years, including Truro-born Hollywood starlet Peggy Lambsley, British Nigerian model Aaliyah, and the socialite Miffy Beaumont-Flattery. But despite Kennedy being spotted in popular nightspots on both sides of the Atlantic and making red carpet appearances with each of these certified bombshells, none of them has been able to hold Kennedy's interest more than a few months.

It has been a remarkable transformation from mummy's boy to womaniser for the "Hold My Hand, Hold My Heart" singer. When the Go Tos attended their first BRIT Awards, three years ago, Kennedy took his mother, Orla, as his date. He took his sister, Fiona, to the Mercury Prize and the MOBO Awards and the Grammys the same year.

Will Jocasta Rose—at eight years Kennedy's senior—last the distance? Or will England's Rose find herself on Cole's compost heap with all the rest? At least his mum got a new house out of it...

Three years after winning Make Me a Pop Star

Pop star reveals beloved mother's devastating cancer diagnosis

Cole Kennedy's mum, Orla, has cancer.

Kennedy released a statement on behalf of his family last night, after an eagle-eyed reader of The Bulletin photographed Mrs Kennedy, 52, with family members outside Ipswich Hospital, Suffolk, on Thursday (pictured).

"My mother is being treated for ovarian cancer. There are around 7,500 diagnoses of this variety of cancer in the U.K. each year. If caught early, the prognosis is good.

"My mum is not a public figure, so I ask for privacy for her, and our family, while she gets the treatment she needs.

"Although we would not have asked for publicity around such a private matter, we hope Mum's diagnosis might encourage those at risk of ovarian cancer to have regular screening tests."

Four years after winning **Make Me a Pop Star**

"Cole's off the rails"
Friends worry following mum's tragic death

Concerned friends have spoken out about Cole Kennedy's increasingly erratic behaviour after the 21-year-old Go Tos singer was photographed snorting cocaine in a West Hollywood nightspot at the weekend.

It's unclear whether the pop heart-throb will face charges for his drug use, which could earn him a $1,000 fine or a year in a Californian slammer.

The pop star's behaviour has become more and more "rock and roll" since his mother died three months ago. In recent weeks Kennedy has been kicked out of a New York nightclub, started a brawl in a swanky Los Angeles restaurant, and appeared onstage in Chicago sporting a black eye and barely able to stand upright. Some American fans booed the previously untouchable "British prince of pop."

The Go Tos have been on tour in Asia and the U.S. since Orla Kennedy's death from aggressive ovarian cancer in March.

A friend told The Bulletin: "He is extremely vulnerable. He needs protecting. He needs rehab. He's not getting the support he needs from his record company. He's too much of a money-spinner to take off the tour. We're all incredibly worried about him."…

Four and a half years after winning Make Me a Pop Star

Boy band bloodbath!

Costumier gets 47 stitches after carve-up with rock and roll Cole

A member of the Go Tos' entourage was rushed to hospital and received 47 stitches after a drunken late-night brawl that saw a Florida hotel room trashed.

The band's costumier, Jasper Horner, was rushed to Miami's Mount Sinai Medical Center by ambulance yesterday at about 4 a.m., U.S. East Coast time, with extensive lacerations to his left arm (pictured).

It is understood the room at the centre of the brawl—at the swanky Bellhop Glades Hotel in Miami Beach—belonged to troubled Go Tos rabble-rouser Cole Kennedy. Sources at the hotel reported some £20,000 worth of destruction to the suite, including damage to walls, shattered windows, broken furniture, blood-splattered couches and wallpaper, and a £2,000 coffee maker that had been smashed into a bidet, "like something Tracey Emin would charge an absolute bomb for."

Hotel guests told The Bulletin they heard "crazed fighting" coming from an upstairs room at about 3 a.m. on Sunday, lasting at least 45 minutes. Although guests complained, the hotel did not manage to put a stop to the rock and roll fracas before the ambulance was called.

Horner, 28, is a long-time Totally Records employee, having worked with Jocasta Rose and Boy Treble. He is a graduate of the London College of Fashion.

Totally Records declined to comment.

***Almost five years after winning* Make Me a Pop Star**

Save Our Cole!
Rehabbed rocker in Paris sobriety summit

Has reformed rocker Robbie Johnswagger held a one-man intervention to save troubled pop star Cole Kennedy?

The pair were spotted in Paris yesterday having lunch al fresco (pictured) at the ritzy bistro Dupont's of St-Germain-des-Prés. While Johnswagger—famously once sacked from "Make Me a Pop Star" for drunkenness—stuck to water, the Go Tos' enfant terrible was drinking so heavily he knocked over an ice bucket and smashed a champagne bottle across the Rue de Buci.

The Go Tos are in Paris for the European leg of the band's Hot Gossip tour. It's understood Kennedy's former reality TV mentor flew in especially to meet with the young hellraiser, after friends and fans alike expressed concerns about Kennedy's increasingly erratic behaviour.

Is the former Buzzsaw frontman taking his young protégé under his wing to straighten him out? And, if so, is he doing it with or without the say-so of his former boss and co-host, Felicity Quant?

***Five years after winning* Make Me a Pop Star**

Cole checks into rehab!

Pop brat Cole Kennedy has finally checked into rehab.

Kennedy's management at Totally Records said the 22-year-old was being treated for drug and alcohol addiction and would be taking a break from touring and recording with the Go Tos.

Totally Records would not reveal where Kennedy was being treated, but The Bulletin understands that rather than a traditional detox clinic, he's attending the hippy-dippy "alternative" Pranayama Retreat in rural Derbyshire, where dozens of other clapped-out and drug-addled celebs have gone to dry out in recent years—most notably Kennedy's friend and mentor Robbie Johnswagger.

***Five years after winning* Make Me a Pop Star**

COLE LIKES POLE!

Britain's prince of pop Cole Kennedy is gay.

Kennedy released a short statement on his social media accounts overnight, announcing his new sexuality. It's unclear if Kennedy had been backed into a corner, but it appears the surprise announcement was the 22-year-old's own decision.

"Music is all about authenticity, and it's time to be honest with my fans—I am a gay man," he said.

"I'm choosing to come out now out of respect for our fans, respect for my art, and most of all, out of respect for myself.

"Most people know I've had a difficult time over the past year. I want to thank everyone for their support and understanding. Coming out is the next step in my journey, as I try to live authentically."

The shock news is sure to hit Kennedy's primarily female fan base hard. The Kenneddicts often turn up to Go Tos shows with placards declaring they're "marriage material." How will his female fans respond now Kennedy has gone from heart-throb to heartbreaker?

And how must the "marriage material" guy himself, Toby Lyngstad, be feeling right now? Could reality TV's ultimate long shot love declaration finally pay off for the Essex hairdresser?

Lyngstad wasn't in when The Bulletin stopped by his Colchester home last night to get his reaction, but a family member, Cheryl Hitchen, was on hand to shower our photographer with a glass of rosé (pictured).

Five and a half years after winning **Make Me a Pop Star**

"Marriage material" boy brawls outside Essex club

It took two grown women and a scantily clad go-go dancer to hold back Toby Lyngstad on Friday night, as the face of Britain's favourite meme lashed out at photographers and reporters outside popular Brentwood nightspot Luxxe.

The Bulletin was there to capture an apparently drunk Lyngstad stumbling out of the venue (pictured). A gaggle of reporters had gathered in the street, desperate to ask the question that has the whole internet talking—had Lyngstad always known Cole Kennedy was gay?

While Lyngstad brawled with the press, a member of his entourage, Cheryl Hitchen, told our photographer: "If you don't f*** off, I'm going to ram that camera so far down your f**ing throat, every time you fart you'll photograph your skid marks."

How times have changed for the cheeky Essex lad who found fame with a declaration of love!

***Five and a half years after not winning* Make Me a Pop Star**

"Marriage Material" Toby to enter "Celebrity Dorm Room"

Toby Lyngstad will enter the "Celebrity Dorm Room" house, Channel Three has announced.

Lyngstad has kept a low profile since his gaffe made him a national punchline, but Cole Kennedy coming out as gay two months ago has hauled him back into the spotlight.

The 22-year-old, who now goes by Tobias, had previously declined to comment on what he knew about Kennedy's sexuality. Surely, this means he's finally decided to spill all? What could have changed his mind, you ask? Sources close to the show say Lyngstad will get around £40,000 for the "Celebrity Dorm Room" appearance, whether he's the first "celebrity" evicted by public vote or he lasts the show's full four-week run.

Either way, it's a big payday for the Colchester hairdresser.

More than five and a half years after not winning Make Me a Pop Star

"Cole artpopped my cherry!"
Marriage Material Toby's shock confession!

TV's most famous unrequited crush wasn't so unrequited after all!

"Celebrity Dorm Room" contestant Tobias Lyngstad has spilt the tea about his torrid teenage love affair with the Go Tos' Cole Kennedy. On last night's post-watershed "Up Late" episode of the Channel Three show, where no topic is off limits, viewers were treated to the real story behind that infamous "marriage material" comment—and what happened next.

"He was my first love," said Lyngstad, who has clearly hit the gym and got a stylist in the years since "Make Me a Pop Star."

He was drinking homemade cocktails with fellow contestants Angela Guthrie, host of "The Renovation Repairers"; former test cricketer Hedley Rudloc; ex-Tory MP Honoria Reith and social media influencer Amber Light. The celebs were talking about losing their virginities.

"We did it on top of my ARTPOP bedspread while Mum was at the salon and Dad was out playing golf," Lyngstad said of his first sexual encounter with the future boy band icon. "It was awkward, fumbling, terrifying and incredibly sweet. That said, we soon got the hang of it. By the time he dumped me, he could play me like a guitar."

Lyngstad stopped short of sharing salacious details, despite being pressed by self-confessed Kenneddicts Light and Guthrie. It quickly became clear the teenage affair was more than puppy love.

Lyngstad said: "We just connected, you know? He would look at me like I was beautiful and, let's be honest, I weren't. He would listen to me like what I said mattered, like he was interested in what I had to say. Literally, no one had ever done that before. People think I'm thick because of how I speak and how I look, but I ain't. Cole saw that. And he was an open book, you know? Genuine, kind, loving, funny. What you saw was what you got. Who wouldn't fall in love with that?

"At the time, I would have done anything for him. Killed for him. Marched to the gates of hell for him. Got a spiral perm for him. I was 16 so I thought it was forever. It took me a long time to get over him."

Lyngstad revealed the break-up left him "depressed, non-functioning, and empty." He blamed the show's producers for orchestrating the split.

"A part of me will never forgive him being too weak to fight for us," he said.

Lyngstad said he had not spoken to Kennedy since their private text messages were published in this newspaper in the weeks after the Go Tos won "Make Me a Pop Star."

"I realise now our phones were probably hacked, but I spent a good year blaming friends and family for leaking the messages," he said. "That sort of thing can ruin relationships. I'm lucky my family are amazing."

The Bulletin strenuously denies that it has ever used phone hacking techniques.

Lyngstad revealed he decided to go on the show to talk about his relationship with Kennedy because he'd "spent six years being a joke, unable to fight back."

"Now Cole has come out, I can speak my truth without betraying either my word or my values," he said. "I'm here to reclaim my narrative. I'm here for my mental health. After this show, I never want to talk about Cole Kennedy ever again."

When Kennedy spectacularly revealed his homosexuality earlier this year, many media commentators and internet wagsters wondered whether Lyngstad might finally get his shot with Cole Kennedy. It turns out that while we were laughing at Lyngstad, the real joke was on us!

Almost six years after not winning Make Me a Pop Star

Tobias turns "Dorm Room" triumph into radio gig

"Celebrity Dorm Room" fan favourite Tobias Lyngstad will replace Raluca Albescu as the presenter of PureFM's "Pop Review."

Last month Lyngstad came third in the reality TV show, which locks has-beens, wannabes and internet-famous people no one over the age of 13 has heard of before into a room together and then broadcasts all the crap they say to one another.

Fans of "Celebrity Dorm Room"—an inexplicably enduring piece of television detritus—fell in love with the cheeky hairdresser from Colchester. Lyngstad spoke candidly about the humiliation his early "Make Me a Pop Star" fame caused him, his teenage relationship with the future Go Tos superstar and the time an unnamed Sugababe fell asleep on his waxing table.

In a statement, PureFM said: "Tobias's personality, his humour, his passion for pop music, are too fabulous to be contained to his mum's salon. The fans have spoken. They want more Tobias! We couldn't agree more. Join him every Saturday afternoon at midday for four hours of seriously entertaining pop music news, gossip, exclusives and waxing-table revelations."

Albescu announced last spring she was leaving "Pop Review" after five years in the hot seat to become a co-host of the new series of "Britain's Cake Off"—making her the primary reason men across Britain will join their families on the couch each Sunday night to watch it.

Almost six years after not winning Make Me a Pop Star

Part Three

TEN-AND-A-BIT YEARS AFTER MAKE ME A POP STAR

Chapter Sixteen

Tap. My microphone was live. The end of the potential next big hit for Manu Fernandez was fading out.

"What do we think, pop tarts? You know the drill."

I hit the button that fired off the sweeper giving the chatline number. I was riding the faders on the desk, playing with the levels. From the corner of my eye, I saw Nick glide into the news booth.

"Use the hashtag *Manu*. This is *Pop Review*. I'm Tobias Lyngstad. Coming up after the news at three, the new one from Jocasta Rose. Big day for new music. Don't go anywhere."

Tap. I fired off the ad break. *Tap.* My microphone was off. The promo was still telling the audience that *Pop Review* takes... pop... seriously, when there was a crackle in my ears.

"Tobes," Nick said. "It's dropped."

"Shit." I looked up, meeting my best friend's eyes on the other side of the glass. "Is it any good?"

"I don't know, it literally landed five minutes ago, but it's going to be bigger than Queen Victoria's knickers, obviously. They sent a whole PR package, with audio and everything. I barely had time to write the bulletin and clip it up. You might want to prepare yourself."

The news theme played out, and Nick's smooth Aberdonian voice told the listeners it was three o'clock.

"Cole Kennedy's highly anticipated first solo album since ditching the Go Tos three months ago has dropped," Nick said.

"Called *The Flame*, the album features twelve tracks, all written by Kennedy himself, and a new rock-influenced sound.

"Kennedy posted on his social media: 'I am reborn. I am free! Thank you so much to all my beautiful Kenneddicts for your love and support as we start this new adventure. This is for you.'"

I wanted to heave. His "beautiful Kenneddicts"? Cole's fans were terrorists in velour tracksuits, keyboard warriors for a toxic pop culture cult.

"The first single from the album is called 'Reborn,'" Nick said, firing off a clip of the track. I was hit by a wall of soaring strings and a solid rock beat. It was a sound to lift the soul. It was going to be a stone-cold hit, and I hated Cole for that.

"Former Buzzsaw frontman and *Make Me a Pop Star* judge Robbie Johnswagger has described *The Flame* as 'a love letter to real music from a soul set free.'"

Nick fired off a clip of Johnswagger speaking.

"*The Flame* is a soft rock / synth spectacle unlike anything we've heard from Cole since he stood on pop's most plastic stage and served us Nirvana's 'Smells Like Teen Spirit' with an authenticity that would have had Kurt Cobain weeping with joy. To all the 'Let Cole be Cole' campaigners of the past decade, this is your reward. This album vindicates your belief in him. Cole Kennedy is a true talent."

I put two fingers in my mouth and mimed vomiting. Nick, ever the professional, managed not to laugh as he finished reading his report.

"The pop star has also announced a worldwide tour, the Flame Tour, kicking off with a string of small UK shows in summer before heading to Europe, the US, and Asia, then coming home to close the tour with three big shows at Wembley Stadium in spring. Tickets go on sale on Monday.

"Kennedy has also signed a deal with WebFlix, giving the streaming service exclusive behind-the-scenes access to the tour, for a new documentary about the pop star set for release next year."

The chatline was refreshing so fast I thought the screen might melt. Yet another *Pop Review* had been derailed. Why did Cole always announce things while I was on air? It's like it was deliberate. I looked at my screen. Tarneesha had already dropped "Reborn" into the running order. As soon as I hit that button, straight after the news, I'd be playing Cole's new song. I wanted to scream.

* * *

Three days later I was at work pre-recording some promos for the next weekend's *Pop Review* when I was summoned by my boss. I made the grim trek along the threadbare carpet of the radio station's only corridor and knocked on Denzil's door. He was sitting behind his desk, reclined in a cheap Argos office chair that was definitely too rickety to hold his weight, with his feet up on the filing cabinet. The room smelt of Creed Aventus and Lucozade. His face was buried in a stapled bundle of A4 paper. Which surprised me, because who prints things anymore?

"You wanted to see me, babes?"

"Tobes, just the man!" Denzil swung his feet under his desk. "Come in, sit down."

I plonked myself on the chair opposite him. Denzil put the paper on the desk and took his glasses off. That always unnerved me. Without his Coke-bottle glasses, Denzil was a dead ringer for Stormzy, and it wasn't natural for your boss to make your knickers wet like that. He was well aware of the effect he had. There was a pause, heavy with the weight of expectation, and for a moment I thought he was going to sack me.

"Cole Kennedy," Denzil said.

My mouth went dry. This was worse than sacking. "What about him?"

"You're going on tour with him."

I stood bolt upright. It was a reflex action from the adrenaline hitting the bloodstream faster than the hit of poppers that got Aunty Cheryl kicked out of a Soho pub for making out with a hatstand.

"I most certainly am not."

Denzil threw the pile of papers over to me. They landed in a jumble against my stomach. "He's paying a lot of money to make sure you do."

"What are you talking about?" I found the staple and flicked the papers over.

"I'm talking about one million quid, baby!" Denzil shook his hand in a gesture I imagined was South London for making coin. "British. Pound. Sterling. Bruv."

"What?"

"It's all there in black and white." He pointed to the papers. "Cole Kennedy is paying us one million pounds for *Pop Review* to broadcast live from every night of the UK leg of his first solo tour."

I flicked through the paperwork, eyes scanning the words with growing horror. It *was* all there in black and white. Nightmare. This was Denzil's worst idea since he turned up to a Soho pub with a bottle of poppers.

"I can't have this," I said.

"You can. I've done it."

"No, you literally can't do this to me. It's in my contract. A contract you signed when I joined PureFM. I do not have to interview Cole Kennedy or any member of the Go Tos. If you want things in black and white, go look at *my* contract."

Denzil waved a hand at the chair behind me. "Sit down."

I sat. Heavily. The seat was hard, and it jarred right up the bit where only the best spray tans reach, but I managed not to wince.

"Do you like your job?" Denzil said.

"If you're threatening to fire me—"

He held his palms up towards me. "Whoa, calm down, Cardi B." He stood, his chino'ed groin now at my head height. He was so incredibly, dreamily tall. He walked around me to close the door, then perched himself on the edge of the desk, his knees inches from me, his crotch close enough to use as a microphone. He picked up the remote control from his desk and pointed it at the small TV in the corner.

"I'd like you to watch something," he said, pressing play. On the screen was a scene I instantly recognised—me, leaving the PureFM studios, through a clamouring scrum of reporters, photographers, and cameramen. It was filmed three months ago, on the day Cole Kennedy announced he was going solo.

"Any thoughts on your ex leaving the Go Tos?" a reporter shouted, microphone in my face.

I said nothing.

"Don't you even want to wish him well, Toby?" a photographer barked. And when I didn't reply, "That's not very nice. Fame's clearly changed you."

Having endured years of this, I knew he was trying to provoke a reaction, so I swallowed a reply. I doggedly tried to force my way through them, but they were blocking my path—another tactic meant to piss me off and lead to great pictures.

"Any advice for Felicity Quant about how to recover after getting dumped by Cole Kennedy?" a reporter asked.

Still, I said nothing, muscling through them.

"You're meant to be the country's top authority on pop music," another reporter said. "Don't you have anything to say about the biggest pop star in the world leaving the biggest boy band in the world?"

Denzil paused the footage. He looked down at me. I looked up at him.

"The board has come to the view that this situation is unsustainable, bruv," he said.

"What does that mean?"

"This is the biggest story in pop music right now, and you know the biggest pop star in the world. Intimately. It's our unique selling point, our competitive advantage, and you refuse to talk about him?"

"Yes," I said. "That was the deal. That's what the board signed up for."

"Well, I was hoping, under the circumstances, you might reconsider."

I laughed. "Why on earth would I do that?"

Denzil's hopeful smile fell from his face.

"Between you and me, bruv?" Shit. This sounded serious. "The station is in real trouble. The whole network is on the brink of going under. Both PureFM and TalkUK. The board is talking about cutting their losses and selling us off."

This conversation was well above my pay grade, but I couldn't see what it had to do with forcing me to hang out with an arsehole like Cole Kennedy—and I said so.

"Who do you think is going to buy us if we get sold, Tobes? Some cashed-up sheikh? Some neocon nightmare from the States? Some asset-stripping hedge fund?"

The idea made me feel ill.

"Whoever it is, Tobes, we'll all be out on our ears. Anyone who buys this place is going to slash costs, sack staff, and change the format completely. You think they give a shit about the R & B music that gives me life? You think they care about niche programming like *Pop Review*?"

"Niche? I'm the country's most popular pop music chat show!"

"Toby, you're the country's *only* pop music chat show. Every other station just plays the bloody music without yammering on about it. This is existential, little bro. Between streaming and podcasts, our entire business model is as fucked as... as fucked as..."

"My Aunty Cheryl?"

"Precisely, bruv."

"What has this got to do with breaking your word on Cole Kennedy?"

"Cole's money is a godsend. With that kind of swag, I can go to the board and say, 'Look, we're profitable, don't sell us.' That million quid keeps us in business, it keeps us on air. We can't look a gift horse in the mouth. All you have to do is follow Cole up and down the country in an outside broadcast van for a few weeks. You'll have to interview him a couple of times, there'll be a few publicity photos, but that's it. The rest of the time you'll be talking to fans, doing what you do best—making great radio. If you do every show and fulfil the terms of the contract, we get paid, everyone keeps their jobs."

I growled in frustration. I hated Denzil for doing this to me.

"Please, Toby?" He smiled that sexy, toothy grin that no doubt got him laid a lot. His eyes sparkled. He bounced one pec muscle. Then the other. Then he bounced them back and forth. He was like a bird on a nature documentary, hopping from foot to foot in front of a ladybird, trying to hypnotise me with his moves. I was glad we were back to the usual queerbaiting, but I would not be so easily blinded.

"Do you have any idea how miserable my life would be if I did this? It's literally why there is a clause in my contract."

"If there was any other way, Tobes. But we're on our knees here. Cole Kennedy has bought our arses, and every last one of us must bend over for him. He's got the cash, he gets to smash."

I flicked through the paperwork, feeling powerless, defeated. It was either do this and save the station, or refuse, and we all lost our jobs. I couldn't do that to Nick and Tarneesha. I reached the last page of the contract and stared at the signatures scrawled across it. Above Denzil's totally baller signature was the name of Cole Kennedy's lawyer: Fiona Kennedy, LIB.

Despite myself, I smiled.

"Oop, I see a smile," Denzil said. "I knew you wouldn't let everyone down."

"But—"

"We're sending out an embargoed press release tomorrow. You need to announce it and do your whole show about it on Saturday. You're a champion, Tobes."

Once again, I had lost control of my own narrative. Once again, Cole Kennedy was to blame. I was trapped.

"I want Nick as my producer." If I was doing this, I was at least having my best friend by my side.

"The outside broadcast van isn't modified for a wheelchair user to drive it, wouldn't Tarneesha be a bett—"

"Neesh can do the studio panelling back here. It's Nick or there's no deal."

Chapter Seventeen

Tap. I hit the button to fire off the ads leading up to the four o'clock news. I was off-air, and exhausted. I slumped back into my chair, leaned on the desk, and put my head in my hands. The news that *Pop Review* was "going on the road" with Cole Kennedy was irretrievably out in the world. "The genius was out of the brothel," as Aunty Cheryl liked to say about ex-Uncle Mike. Cole's team had supplied some specially recorded audio of Cole saying how excited he was about the whole thing, which, mercifully, meant I didn't have to interview him. Yet. The second we were on air, the studio phone lit up faster than a group of sixth-formers with a packet of newly nicked fags. I knew it would. Tarneesha had done a good job of weeding out any caller who even smelt like they might mention "marriage material," let alone indulge in the ludicrous fantasy that Cole Kennedy and I might become a thing. *Pop Review*'s fans weren't as obsessed as the diehard Kenneddicts, but they did seem to care about me. As the ads played out towards the news at the top of the hour, I heard Nick's voice in my headphones.

"You OK, pal?"

I lifted my head. He was smiling hopefully at me from the news booth. I gave him a thumbs up.

"If you're not doing anything, I'm meeting Dav and some of his pals for a drink at Miss Timmy's after this. Do you wanna come?"

I glanced at the clock on my screen. Thirty seconds before the news theme.

"Who's going to be there?"

"You know Sunny and Ludo."

"Sure."

"And I think maybe Petey Boy and Jumaane. I'm not sure. Depends whether GayHoller is in fruit today."

"What about the big Greek guy?"

"No, Stav's on his big Greek gap year. Come on, it'll be fun. Sandy Crotch is performing."

I weighed up my options. Taking the train home to Essex was now too risky. Someone might recognise me. My plan had been to take a taxi, but I'd only have spent the drive obsessively doomscrolling social media.

"Sure, I'm in," I said. The news theme started playing, and the red light went on in the newsroom, showering Nick in ruby hues. He gave me a thumbs up. His soft Aberdonian accent informed the Great British public they were listening to Nick Ross in the PureFM newsroom.

Ten minutes later, gagging for a restorative bevvie and looking forward to some top drag banter, Nick and I took the elevator down to reception. When the doors opened, all hell broke loose.

"Oh, holy shit!" Nick said.

Beyond the glass walls of the building were dozens of reporters, photographers, and camera operators. They were shouting my name, waving their arms and notepads, cameras clicking away madly, blocking my exit to Leicester Square. I turned my back to them while Nick frantically pressed the button to close the lift doors.

"What do we do?" My heart was racing. I felt a panic attack

coming on and tried to slow my breathing. This felt like Cole's coming out all over again. I was going to have to go into total lockdown. It was everything I knew would happen when Denzil insisted on this idiotic plan. The lift doors finally closed, and the elevator started going back up. It was only buying us time. Eventually, I *had* to go through that door.

"You're going to have to make a run for it," Nick said.

"On foot? Are you mad?"

"Some of us would love to be on foot, Tobias."

The elevator pinged, and the doors opened on the third floor.

"It's a joke, Toby. You can laugh." We stepped out into the radio station lobby.

"You think this is a time for jokes, babes?"

"It's always a time for jokes."

"Oh sure, when the garbage lorry hit your bike, were you laughing then?"

He stared at me, blinking.

"Steady on, Ricky Gervais."

"Sorry, babes. I'm a bit stressed, to be fair."

Nick raised an eyebrow. "No, Tobias, I didn't laugh when the bin lorry shattered my spine. But that *was* the day I learned the value of laughter in shitty situations."

"Sorry, I don't feel like laughing right now. I'm going to have to run the gauntlet with half of Britain's gutter press. They'll have mopeds, you know. Even if we get into a cab, they'll only follow us to Miss Timmy's and camp out there. There's literally no escape."

"There literally is."

"There isn't."

"Take the fire exit. It opens right out onto Charing Cross Road. You'll be on the far side of the building, and you can disappear into the crowd and weave your way up to Old Compton Street. Easy."

"What if they have someone posted on the back door?"

"They're not the Tactical Response Group, Tobes. Besides, you can't even tell it's a door to our building. You can barely tell it's a door. It's mostly a shelter for rough sleepers and a pitch for that terrible busker who only plays one song."

He had a point. "What about you? No man left behind and all that."

"I'll only slow you down," he said. "In the sense that you'll have to carry me down the stairs. And it's all uphill to Soho. And I don't fancy it. No, you go out the back and I'll go out the front and distract them."

"With what, babes? A puppet show?"

"I'll tell them you'll be down in ten minutes and you'll make a short statement. By the time they've worked out it's a ruse, you'll already be tucked up in Miss Timmy's, sticking a fork into a fat slice of Occasion Cake."

It was so cunning it might work. Nick ordered himself an accessible taxi. We waited until his phone pinged to say his driver was two minutes away; then he got back into the lift to face the media scrum, and I made my way down the fire stairs. As I circled down the floors, I wondered how the hell Nick would get out of the building in the event of a fire. He'd probably insist on a fireman's lift from Denzil. He'd have to fight me for it.

When I reached the fire escape door, my heart was thumping like it was attending an underground rave. I rested one hand on the door, putting my ear against it, as if I might be able to hear a photographer lurking on the other side. A deep breath to summon my courage, and I pressed the escape bar.

Pandemonium!

The fire alarm screeched through the building, into Leicester Square and beyond. I dashed out in the street in a panic and slammed into the back of a busker, sending him flying forwards into the road.

"Shit! Sorry, mate!"

"Dude!" he said.

I didn't even look at the guy. I was too busy scanning the street for photographers and reporters. The coast was clear, but it wouldn't be for long. The press would have known what was up immediately. They'd have taken one look at Nick's face when the alarm went off and hightailed it around the back of the building.

"You could have killed me," the busker said, holding his guitar protectively. "That's a busy road."

"I'm sorry! I have to go."

I made to run, but he grabbed my sleeve. It was so sudden and unexpected, it swung me around, making me lose my feet. My head whacked into the bins, and I landed awkwardly on the ground. Pain shot through my knee. My palms were grazed and already starting to sting. I was losing precious seconds.

"I could have been hit by a red bus, mate."

I rocked back, holding my knee, finding something soft to lean against—a rough sleeper's stashed sleeping bag. I looked up at the busker and apologised again. I peered around the bins and up the street.

"Shit."

Photographers.

It was too late. Short of a miracle, I'd been caught. This was going to make for an embarrassing front page.

Chapter Eighteen

I pushed open the door of Miss Timmy's to be assaulted by the reassuringly homosexual stench of roasting coffee, protein farts, and freshly laundered Calvin Kleins. I was greeted with kisses, and a slight frown, by Sandy Crotch—Miss Timmy's resident drag queen.

"Did you come straight from the urinal at Trough, dear?" she said, meaning the fetish club under the Vauxhall railway arches. "Or did you piss your knickers when you saw this cinch?" She turned so I could appreciate her waistline.

"Bit of an incident," I said, holding up my grazed palms instead. "I don't suppose you have some Dettol and wet wipes behind the bar?"

"It's a gay bar, dear," she said. "The council would shut us down if we didn't carry industrial-strength antiseptic."

When I reached the booth where Nick and his friends were sitting, I was greeted by silence and... more frowns.

"Hello, everybody," I said. That seemed to break the spell that was holding them. Dav, his best mate Sunny, and Sunny's boyfriend, Ludo, were all warm smiles and hellos. Then... back to frowns.

A waiter appeared. "What can I get you?"

"Two Essex Girl shots and a bottle of Krug, please," I said. The waiter nodded, frowned, and disappeared—not batting an eyelid at the fact I'd ordered a bottle of obscenely expensive champagne and two shots of a sickly vodka, peach schnapps, and cranberry juice concoction that had probably claimed more virginities across Essex than a busload of Premier League footballers.

It was Nick who spoke first. "You fucking reek, pal. What have you done to yourself?"

"I was escaping the press," I said, revealing my grazed palms to general gasps of horror.

"Via the sewers?" Dav asked. Sunny laughed.

"The fire alarm went off. I had to improvise. I spent twenty minutes hiding under a sleeping bag I found in the bins, pretending to be a rough sleeper. When the paparazzi finally cleared off, I had to pay Britain's most mediocre busker a bribe for not ratting me out."

Everyone was in fits of laughter—except for Ludo, who seemed distracted.

"The guy who only plays Bob Dylan?" Nick asked.

"His name's John, and he only knows 'The Times They Are a-Changin'.' I had to listen to it four times. And he demanded twenty quid."

"Good on him," Sunny said, lifting his cocktail to toast the entrepreneurial busker.

"He made me take him to a cash machine to get it," I said. "I had to make small chat with him all the way up to Cambridge Circus."

"Are you seeing him again?" Nick asked.

I scowled.

"You got his number at least, though, right?" Dav said.

"You lot are meant to be cheering me up," I said.

The waiter put my drinks down in front of me, and I knocked back one of the shots immediately, letting the alcohol heat my gullet and boil my stomach. As I lifted my champagne out of the ice bucket to pour myself a glass, Sandy appeared at the end of the table with antiseptic, wet wipes, and an airline-size bottle of Jean Paul Gaultier's Le Male (which, by the state of it, had been rolling around at the bottom of her handbag for at least four Pride seasons).

"I thought you might need some of this," she whispered softly into my ear. "Not being funny, love, but you smell like you've been fucked by a tramp."

As Sandy swanned off, the boys laughed uproariously. All except for Ludo, who was looking past me, over my shoulder, with concern on his face. I felt a twinge of worry.

"Did you not try the phone trick?" Sunny said, jogging me from my thoughts.

I opened the wet wipes. "What's that?"

"If you have no choice but to go through a scrum of reporters or photographers like that, put your phone to your ear and pretend to be on a call," he said. "Or better yet, *be* on a call."

"Sunny used to work for *The Bulletin*," Nick reminded me. How could I forget? Reporters from *The Bulletin* had been hounding me for a decade. So, when your best friend's boyfriend's best friend works for your tormentor, you tend to remember it. Not that Sunny had ever been on the hound-Toby-until-he-cracks beat. And he worked for the BBC now, anyway. As I reached for the antiseptic, I noticed Ludo typing a text into his phone.

"You can either pretend to be on an important call," Sunny said, "and keep marching through, completely ignoring the press pack. Or, better yet, you can smile and be friendly and apologetic, in a sorry-I-have-to-take-this kind of way. But whatever you do, keep on walking until you get into your car or whatever. Then speed off."

The antiseptic stung my palms. "They're all on mopeds. They follow you."

"Most of the time they just want their pics so they can make their money," Sunny said. "Give them something to photograph and they'll go away."

"Like what?"

"I mean, if you're a woman in a skirt, you might get into the car at a slightly risqué angle."

"Helpful. Thanks."

"Lift your T-shirt to scratch at your washboard stomach," Sunny said. "You can do anything. Be inventive. It has to be something they can write up, which is why 'accidentally sexy' is always a good option. You want it to be proper gossip fodder but still spin positively, so you don't hurt your brand. Worst-case scenario, go for relatable and goofy. Pretend to trip over your feet and laugh at your own clumsiness when you hit the deck. Something like that."

Sandy appeared at the end of the table again with a face like thunder. She leaned over to Ludo. "Which one is it, my dear?"

Ludo pointed, discreetly, and I turned my head to try to see what he was pointing at. "Shaved head."

"With the moustache and pink neck kerchief?"

Ludo nodded.

"Right you are, my darling." Sandy was off again.

"What's going on?" I asked.

Ludo put his elbows on the table and leaned forward. The four of us bent towards him like flowers towards the sun.

"The guy in the pink hanky was taking photographs."

"Of us?" Dav said.

"Of me?" I asked.

"I'm pretty certain you were the target, yeah," Ludo said.

There was a kerfuffle behind us as a group of drunk homosexuals was unceremoniously hauled from their table by a variety of staff members, including Sandy—who, it turned out, had a remarkably powerful full nelson.

"This is beautiful to watch," Dav said.

"Absolutely," Sunny added. "Drag queens doing what nature intended, keeping the gays in line."

"Isn't nature spectacular?"

"Notice how the female impersonator drags the sad little piece of shit towards the exit," Sunny said, mimicking David Attenborough's hushed, authoritative tones. "She is confident. She is strong. She is in six-inch bloody heels. He is powerless against her."

Dav joined in. "When she has finished playing with him, she will eat him. Then shit him out. And so, the circle of life is complete."

The boys laughed at themselves, and as the bell on Miss Timmy's door tinkled, announcing the eviction of my pursuer and his friends, the entire restaurant erupted into whoops of applause. Sandy reappeared at the end of the table, barely a sequin out of place.

"Sorry about that, boys," she said. "He took a few pictures, but they weren't much chop, and he hadn't posted them anywhere. I made him delete them, and he and his mates have all been barred for six months." She waved a perfectly manicured hand over the table. "And it's all on us today, OK? Order anything you like. But don't overdo it, because my OnlyFans is tanking, and if this place closes down, I'm all out of options."

She winked, and before I could thank her, she'd spun on her heel and was gone. I turned to Ludo. "Thank you."

"Don't mention it."

As I brought my champagne glass to my lips, I realised my hands were shaking.

"It's occurred to me," Nick said, "that there was an obvious problem with our escape plan."

"No kidding, babes."

"Not the fire alarm. Although I didn't know that even worked. Nothing else does in that building. No, I mean I had to go around the back of the building to get into the cab on Charing Cross Road in any case. You could have dashed straight out of the fire escape, into the waiting cab, and driven up here with me."

We sat there, blinking at each other. What a pair of absolute melts. I knocked back my second Essex Girl shot. The restaurant echoed with the sound of plastic fingernails tapping against a microphone. It was Sandy, taking her spot on the stage by the bar.

"When you fuckers came out for dinner and a floor show, I bet you didn't expect to see a drag queen wrestling a sad, faded twink, did you?" she said. "That wasn't on your bingo card for today, was it? Don't underestimate your Aunty Sandy, my dears. Not only am I an MDMA champion, I'm an MMA champion." Titters from the crowd. "While you lot spend your Saturday mornings getting fisted by drunk, closeted Australian backpackers under a railway arch, I'm down the dojo, fighting all comers, looking fabulous, as the UK's only fully sequined black belt. All so I can protect you lot of ungrateful mincing fuckers."

Applause, cheers, a wolf whistle.

"So, listen up, kiddies. This is a safe space. For all of us. Including celebrity members of our community, who have every right to come here and enjoy a glass of warm, heavily marked up Tesco Finest Pinot Grigio—and my glutes in this frock—all without being accosted."

The crowd cheered. Nick reached over and touched my arm.

"Are you OK, pal?"

I wasn't. Not really. I had no idea when I would feel safe out in public again. The chaos Cole Kennedy caused me usually lasted anywhere from a few weeks to a few months. But at least I felt supported in this moment. I nodded, grateful for Nick's concern.

"And that includes," Sandy continued, "taking photos of our famous guests to post on social media, to show your friends, or to sell to the fucking newspapers. Do I make myself clear?"

A murmur of laughter.

"I said, *do I make myself clear*? Everybody say 'Yes, Sandy.'"

A chorus of "Yes, Sandy" went up around the restaurant.

"Good girls. Now buckle up, because I've got a ten-minute Cher medley coming up, and my pill's just hit. Which will come first, 'The Shoop Shoop Song' or me shitting my knickers onstage? Let's find out. Place your bets, ladies."

* * *

Thanks to Sandy's generosity, we were on the table's third bottle of Krug, and the drinks were starting to make themselves known in both the conversation and the number of trips to the bathroom. Dav stood and announced he was going for a leak. Loosened by the booze, I was finally ready to vent about Denzil's stitch-up.

"So, why exactly are you doing this to yourself?" Sunny asked.

"Because a million pounds is a lot of money."

"Is it?" Ludo said.

I blinked at him.

"Ignore him," Sunny said. "Ludo has no concept of money. His family owns a media empire. His grandmother has an honest-to-God butler and lives in something his father legit calls a dower house."

"I have a jolly good concept of money, thank you," Ludo protested. "It's precisely because my family owns a media empire that I know a million pounds is a very small drop in a very leaky bucket."

"It's a lot to my network. And it might be enough to stop us being sold off to a hedge fund and losing our jobs."

"Is PureFM up for sale?" Ludo asked, eyebrows raised.

Nick and I exchanged glances. This definitely wasn't public information.

"Not officially, I don't think," Nick said carefully. "But the board has no appetite to fix what needs fixing, and it's been made clear they would offload us if they could."

Ludo nodded and plucked his phone off the table. Sunny asked his boyfriend what he was doing.

"Sending Father a message," he said. "The Sentinel Group is in acquisition mode. They might be looking to pick up an asset like Pure. I don't know."

"Um, the outcome we want is the company *not* being sold," Sunny said.

"Only because they think they'll lose their jobs. What if someone buys it and they get to *keep* their jobs?"

Nick and I looked at each other again. Nick shrugged.

"Does this mean I don't have to go on the road with Cole Kennedy?" I asked.

Ludo shook his head. "It's only a text. I'm not promising anything. Acquisitions can take years, and you could still get bought by the Nazi Party."

"Damn."

Dav came back from the toilet, wiping his wet hands on his jeans. "What did I miss?"

"Ludo's buying a radio station," Sunny said.

Dav nodded. "Sounds about right. Are we getting another round in?"

Breakfast TV bloodbath!
Krishnan's claws out for Cole in ex-lover showdown

What happens when you put two of Britain's most eligible homosexuals side by side on breakfast television's most famous yellow couch? A real catfight!

Sparks flew on the set of "Wake-Up Britain" this morning as host Krishnan Varma-Rajan interviewed pop star Cole Kennedy, whose sell-out world tour starts in Glasgow in three days' time.

You'd think the often-flirty Varma-Rajan might be keen to snag a date with the multimillionaire heart-throb, but all the TV hack seemed able to do was ask Kennedy about his ex, Tobias Lyngstad. The transcript is too deliciously uncomfortable not to share.

Kennedy: *I'm not here to talk about that. Let's talk about the album and my upcoming tour.*

KVR: *You're the one who invited Toby on tour. You must have known you'd be asked about it.*

Kennedy: *It's one small part of a big and really special show. This album is all about—*

KVR: *It's a publicity stunt. I'm giving you the publicity. Are you back together?*

Kennedy: *It's not a stunt. We haven't seen each other in ten years.*

KVR: *You haven't even spoken to him?*

Kennedy: *Not yet. I'm looking forward to it.*

KVR: *What are you hoping to get out of this? Why would Tobias agree to do this?*

Kennedy: *I'm looking forward to getting back out on the road, spending some time with my fans, and sharing what is an incredibly personal album for me.*

Varma-Rajan didn't get his answers, but they're good questions! They're also terrible dating form. Never ask about the ex on a first date, Krishnan. Scroll back through their Instagram like everyone else and save your ex-boyfriend questions for date number three.

Chapter Nineteen

The atmosphere in Glasgow was electric. Everything in the city was plastered with Cole's face, like he'd taken tips on how to run an effective outdoor advertising campaign from that bloke who runs North Korea. His face might have rolled past on a papier-mâché missile at any moment. Nick and I had spent the day getting the outside broadcast van set up and prepping for our first Pop Review Special. Cole's opening night show was still twenty-four hours away, but hundreds of people were milling about outside the Glasgow Arena. Every thirty seconds, a dozen gas cannons shot balls of flame high into the air—which certainly added to the sense that I was preparing to battle my demons.

"You need to scoot, pal," Nick said. "Got your backstage pass?"

I waved my lanyard at him. "Are you sure you don't need me to stick around and finish up here?"

"I've got a cassette lift to conquer the steps and a hot Latino security guard to protect me from the Kenneddicts; nothing can defeat me. Your services are no longer required. Go make your ex realise what he's missing."

I stopped to check my reflection in the window. In the ten years since I'd seen Cole, I'd rebuilt myself from the ground up. I had a personal trainer, a dietician, a naturopath, and a Harley Street dentist who'd installed a set of veneers so startlingly white that when I smiled, birds fell out of the sky. I was twenty-six, I had a good career, and if I did say so myself, I looked bloody gorgeous. Lean, toned, tanned. I'd have felt confident if my ex hadn't been a millionaire global superstar and beloved sex symbol.

"For Christ's sake, go!" Nick said.

At the stage door of the arena, I showed my pass to the security guy, who muttered into his walkie-talkie. The door eventually swung open to reveal Fiona Kennedy—still rocking her fabulous curves in a navy blue pantsuit, her hair tied back in a loose bun, still dyed the honey blond Aunty Cheryl had given her all those years ago.

"Toby! It's so bloody good to see you." She threw her arms around me and clutched me to her like a long-lost friend. "We're so glad you're here. Thank you for coming."

As we walked down a corridor underneath the arena, I could hear Cole and the band playing one of his new songs.

"Cole's still in tech rehearsal," Fiona said. "Would you like to come and watch?"

Obviously, I was tempted, but my legs were already so wobbly with adrenaline that I was walking like a toddler in roller skates, and to be honest, I didn't want Cole's first words to me in ten years to be "So what did you think?" because I'd be compelled to say something positive in return. When, in truth, I wanted to say something like "You broke my heart and ruined my life and I hate you with the kind of visceral hatred English football fans reserve for the England football team."

"I think I'll wait somewhere quiet, if you don't mind?"

We walked along a hallway lined with posters of famous acts that had performed in the venue. Taylor Swift. Beyoncé. Katy Perry. Fiona opened a door and deposited me in a green room.

"Can I get you anything while you wait?"

The rehearsals were so loud Cole's voice reverberated through my chest. "I'm fine, thanks."

"He won't be long. I know he's dying to see you." Fiona put a business card down on the table by the door. "My number's there if you need anything, but I'll come back with an ETA on Cole as soon as I can." She paused, holding the door open, looking back at me. She tapped her fingernails against the door and smiled. "It's so bloody good to see you."

As the door clicked shut behind her and I slumped onto a ratty couch, I couldn't help but wonder, given how badly things had ended between me and the Kennedys, why I was getting such VIP treatment.

* * *

After an hour, the green room door finally opened. I leapt to my feet, ready to see Cole. It was Fiona, popping back with an armful of snacks and a couple of bottles of water to keep me amused.

"He shouldn't be much longer. They've had a problem with the lighting rig."

Another hour passed before the door handle moved and the door opened. I jumped up again, prepared to finally face my famous ex. It was Fiona again, full of apologies.

"It's quite stuffy in here. Are you sure you don't want to come watch? Cole's got the encore to run through, then he'll be free."

"I'm fine," I said.

To be honest, I was bored, annoyed, and deflated, and I'd had enough of my makeshift prison. When Fiona disappeared again, I slipped out the door and tiptoed my way around the building until I found an entrance into the back of the auditorium. I opened the door. The change in air pressure and the cool of air conditioning hit me. I slunk down into a seat towards the rear of the dress circle, where the house lights were unlikely to catch me if they went up. The auditorium was dark, blue and purple lighting drenching the stage. A piano appeared to float in lingering mist from a smoke machine. In the centre of the stage, Cole Kennedy, dressed in a vest and jeans. He was maybe fifty metres in front of me, but I could feel the magnetic pull of him. He looked... godly. Sweaty. Tired. Sexy. I hated him, but I couldn't look away.

A dismembered voice came through a speaker. "OK, we're set. Whenever you're ready, Cole."

Cole grabbed the microphone, still in the stand, with both hands and looked out into the empty venue. It felt like he was looking directly at me.

"Do you want to hear 'Genevieve' the way I wrote it?" Cole asked.

One of his crew shouted "Yes"—a poor substitute for the screams of the Kenneddicts that question would get the following night. Cole counted the band in, and music filled the auditorium.

"*Waking up to your sad brown eyes,*" Cole sang. It was a more upbeat, more rock version of a song that was famous the world over. "*Making time for long goodbyes. Oh, Genevieve, oh, Genevieve...* Stop... Stop!"

The music stopped.

"This feels wrong. I feel naked. Can I get my guitar, please?"

A crew member grabbed the instrument and handed it to Cole.

"Let's go again. On four." He counted his band in again, this time playing along with them.

"*Oh, Genevieve, you know I have to leave. Oh, Genevieve, I wish I could stay. But life don't work that way. Oh, Genevieve, oh, Genevieve.*"

"That's much better!" Cole said when they hit the bridge of the song. "This feels right."

He was brilliant. A real showman. Everything a pop star should be. A professional. And in that moment, I hated him even more. I hated that he was living his dream, sharing his music with the world, being a famous pop star. I hated what he'd done to me, the cruel way he'd dropped me. I hated the way "marriage material" had haunted my entire adult life. I was furious that he'd engineered it so I had to be here, in the last place I would ever want to be—at one of his concerts, about to face him one-to-one. By the time the song finished, I'd worked myself up into a state, and I was ready for an encore of my own. If Cole was expecting a happy reunion, he was in for a shock. I was going to give him a rinsing. As Cole and his band hugged and congratulated each other, I sneaked out of the auditorium and crept back to the green room.

Chapter Twenty

Someone turned the handle to the green room door. This time, I knew it was Cole. If my heart beat any louder or faster, bird-watchers would turn up looking for a woodpecker. The door swung open, and in walked Cole Kennedy. He'd changed his clothes since rehearsals. Expensive Air Jordans, torn black jeans, a black linen shirt with very few buttons done up to reveal the clipped hair of his chest, the sleeves rolled up to reveal his tattoos. He was taller than I remember, his body thicker. The deep pools of his chestnut eyes met mine.

"Hey," he said. One syllable. His voice was deeper than it used to be, and soft and smooth as double cream. Something fluttered in my stomach. I felt sick.

"I'm sorry about the wait," he said. "Rehearsals ran over. You should have come and watched. Did Fiona look after you?"

Like television's bitterest prize girl, I waved my hand in the direction of a table filled with unopened drinks and snacks.

"Of course she has. She keeps this whole show on the road. Literally. I'd be lost without her."

A beat of silence.

"It's so good to see you," Cole said, pulling me uninvited into one of those big, smothering, arms-like-an-octopus hugs. He smelt of cinnamon and sweat. I patted his back, reluctantly. Cole's hair was damp against my cheek. He had managed a quick shower as well as a change of clothes. Great, so the smell of sweat was coming from me, not him. Cole finally released me and stood back.

"You look well, Toby. You look... amazing."

So did he, if I was being truthful. Cole's face had matured; his beard stubble was heavier. The boy was gone. The Cole who stood in front of me now was all man. But I still hated him, like I'd hated the boy who'd broken my heart.

"Thanks," I said, coldly.

"I can't believe you're here."

The long-lost-friends act was starting to do my nut. "You're literally paying me to be here. And, not being funny, that is the only reason I'm stood here right now. One hundred per cent."

I meant it to needle him, but Cole laughed. "Yeah, I know. That was Fiona's idea. She inherited Mum's cunning, and she's ruthless with it."

I'd been fit to erupt on him, but the mention of Orla dampened some of the fire inside me. Perhaps that's exactly why he'd mentioned her? Maybe Cole had inherited some of the Kennedy cunning too? Nevertheless, I behaved.

"I was really sorry about your mum," I said. "She was an amazing woman."

"Thank you. It's been five years, but we all miss her every single day. You didn't come to the funeral. We thought you might show up."

"Had the cops on standby, did you?" I felt guilty even as the words came out of my mouth. I hadn't gone to Orla's funeral because I didn't want to be anywhere near Cole. "Mum went to represent the family," I said, unable to meet his eyes.

Silence fell between us. I had no idea what to say next. I didn't want to be here. Denzil had insisted on this meeting to "clear the air" before tomorrow's live interview. Cole ran a hand through his hair, and it swished back into place.

"Hey, have you eaten?" he asked. "I'm starving. Do you wanna go and get some dinner?"

"As in, go out to a restaurant with you?"

"Can do, if you like."

"You must be mental, mate."

"Pardon?"

"I don't want to be seen in public with you."

Cole recoiled in what I took to be shock. "We could go back to mine, just the two of us," he said. "Come on, we haven't seen each other in years and—"

"Do you have any idea what you've done?" The words growled out of me like I was a cornered street dog. "The press has been having a field day with this for months. It's been unbearable, mate. I'm in *Make Me a Pop Star* hell all over again. So no, I don't want to be seen in public with you. It's bad enough I've got to interview you in the bloody street tomorrow, with cameras everywhere. I certainly ain't giving the paparazzi a free shot at humiliating me with 'marriage material' headlines by being seen in public with you tonight. And I definitely ain't going back to your gaff, because I can't bloody stand the sight of you!"

Could he have expected anything else? Cole perched on the edge of the table and folded his arms across his chest, looking crushed. I waited for him to speak. I was gagging for a fight, but he wasn't saying anything, and you can't have a duel if one bloke forgets to bring his pistol.

"I'm truly sorry," Cole said. "I had no idea this would raise so many negative feelings for you."

My eyebrows leapt so high off my forehead, the British Olympic pole-vaulting team would spend years studying the CCTV footage to work out how it was done.

"Are you winding me up? You cannot be serious right now."

Cole rocked from side to side, his top teeth chewing his bottom lip.

He shrugged. "We've got a lot of catching up to do."

"Catching up? For the past ten years there's been wall-to-wall coverage every time you've taken a shit. We don't need to catch up, Cole. Despite my best efforts, I have been kept relentlessly informed about your every move. I just want to be left alone to get on with my life."

"Wow, that's really a no, huh?" Cole said. "Look, clearly I've got some work to do to mend some bridges here—"

I picked up my blazer from the couch and put it over my arm, the universal gesture for *I'm out*.

"We've got a big day tomorrow," I said. "I should get some sleep. I will see you tomorrow for the interview."

"Please come. I've got this amazing house in Milngavie. You should see the record collection."

That pulled me up short. "You're staying in the West End, ain't you? There's a hotel currently surrounded by hundreds of screaming Kenneddicts and half the UK press."

"I thought you were relentlessly informed about my every move?" He cocked an eyebrow. "That's a decoy. I never stay centrally. You can't get any sleep with all that going on outside. Seriously, come back with me. I've got Marcel Dupont working the kitchen for the whole tour. He's a genius with—"

"The Michelin-star chef?"

"His mac and cheese is off the charts. You have to try it."

That was it. I was out. He had choked my chain long enough. "Pass. I'm going to Wagamama with my producer and his boyfriend."

"I like Wagamama," Cole said hopefully.

"Absolutely not. You're not invited."

"But Fiona said we're meant to be getting reacquainted."

"I'm going to dinner with my friends, not trying to make the front page." I stepped around Cole and opened the green room door.

"I'll see you tomorrow. Don't be late for your interview. Five o'clock. It's the caravan right out front. You can't miss it. It has the words 'Toby Lyngstad's a mug' written in big neon letters right above the door."

I marched out of the room.

"I'll be there," Cole called after me.

Chapter Twenty-One

We heard the screams first. From inside the broadcast van, Nick and I watched the stampede towards the arena's stage door. A horde of fans in pursuit of a pop star is truly a spectacle to rival wildebeest crossing the Serengeti.

"Our guest is on his way," I said as Kenneddicts swarmed Cole and his security detail. They were being followed by a camera crew. "Not sure how long it's going to take him to get here, mind you."

From the other side of the studio glass, Nick gave me a thumbs up. We were live on air. A package of interviews we'd recorded with fans in the street earlier in the day was playing out.

Nick's voice came through in my cans. "Let's play 'Genevieve.' If he's in the seat by the bridge, we'll go straight into the ninety-second career recap. If not, let's buy ourselves three minutes with 'Young, Dumb, and Numb.'"

It was my turn to give Nick a thumbs up.

Cole was signing autographs and posing for selfies, slowly but surely drifting towards us. He looked every bit the rock star. The swept-back hair, the sunglasses, the leather jacket over a vest. To be honest, he looked like he'd self-consciously dressed in exactly what he'd been wearing the first day we met. It felt like a power play, and I wasn't having it.

Cole's entourage arrived at the van door. I didn't move. Nick looked at me.

"Are you going to make Britain's prince of pop knock?"

I shrugged. In the end, Fiona did the knocking. I opened the door, and Fiona and Cole stepped inside.

"Where do you want me?" Cole asked. It was flirty and that annoyed me. I pointed to the empty seat. Cole sat down, grabbing his headphones. I sat opposite him, the studio desk between us. I put my cans on and fiddled with some knobs, giving him zero chat. On the other side of the glass partition, Nick was offering Fiona a seat. Outside, the WebFlix camera that had been following Cole around was pressed hard up against the glass of the van, filming. It was the only camera allowed inside the security cordon. I'd drawn the line at letting it inside the van, citing health and safety, as there was as serious risk I'd strangle Cole with the cable.

Cole was saying something. I pretended I hadn't noticed, which was incredibly petty but felt *so good*. He waved a hand in front of my face, and visibly annoyed, I slid one of my headphones slightly behind my ear.

"Just lining up the promo," I said. I wasn't.

"Doesn't the computer do all that for you?"

It did. I stumbled. "It's pretty old tech in here. I don't trust it. I like to double-check everything."

"Perfectionist, huh?" He grinned. "I guess you guys really do take... pop... seriously." Cole said it exactly how our promos say it— and I realised he must listen to the show. My body tingled with a numbness normally only achieved around forty seconds after a killer puts a plastic bag over your head. Outside, a ring of security guards held back Cole's fans. An enormous crowd had gathered. A gaggle of photographers and reporters leaned over the railings. They'd been salivating for this moment for a decade. This was the first time Cole and I had been seen together in public not just since *Make Me a Pop Star*, but since they knew our truth. My heart thumped so hard I could feel my butthole pulsing against the chair like it was trying to eat it. Teenage Toby and professional Tobias were crashing together irreparably, live on air, and I despised Cole for that.

I pressed play on the ninety-second promo. Cole and I listened to it go out—the early audio from *Make Me a Pop Star*, Dorinda Carter announcing the Go Tos winning the show, the chorus of their first single, "My Daydream Girl." Cole smiled, enjoying his trip down memory lane. Nick's pre-recorded voice-over shifted from the early hits and tours through to Cole's troubled years. I watched as the light faded from his eyes, disappearing into memory, and I knew in that instant that Cole had been to some dark places. Then, the gear shift. A grab of "Genevieve" and a voice-over about Cole coming out and becoming a successful songwriter. The smile returned. Then, finally, Cole going solo, and the release of "Reborn"—the soaring synthesised strings of the song creating a wall of sound in the studio.

"Good work," Cole said. He turned and gave Nick and Fiona a thumbs up. "Good work," he repeated.

I pointed at Nick, who leaned back and flung open the van door. "Let's have a bit of noise!" he shouted to the crowd. They obliged. *Tap.* I turned our microphones on and drifted up the fader on the external atmosphere mic, so the audience at home could hear the Kenneddicts going wild over the end of the promo.

"Cole Kennedy, welcome to *Pop Review*," I said over the crowd, putting a smile that wasn't there into my voice. Outside, the fans continued to go bananas.

"Thank you, it's special to be here. I've been looking forward to today for a long time."

"The start of your first solo tour?"

"Well, that, of course. But no, I mean coming on *Pop Review*."

That wrong-footed me for a second. "That's right, this is your first time on the show."

"It's amazing, when you think about it," Cole said. "I was in the biggest pop band in the world for ten years, and somehow, I haven't managed to get back on *Pop Review* since you took over as host."

Cole smirked. He was playing with me. Like a cat. In *my* studio. Oh, I wasn't having this.

"Well, you're a busy man with a busy schedule. We won't hold it against you. You're here now. And with a hit debut single, a bestselling album, and a sell-out world tour. You seem to have done OK without *Pop Review*'s help."

Nick glared at me through the glass. His voice came through my cans. "Play nice."

"Are you ready for tonight?" I asked Cole.

"Of course. The team and I have been working hard on this show for the fans, and I think—"

"You rehearsed much later than expected last night. Are you confident everything will come together? The bit I heard sounded well sketchy."

Cole raised his eyebrows. *Touché,* they said. And possibly *Game on.*

"Absolutely. We worked hard to get everything nailed down last night, to make sure the show is perfect for the fans. I wish you could have come along to watch the rehearsal. I think even the exacting Tobias Lyngstad would have been impressed."

Cole sipped from his cup of water, maintaining eye contact throughout.

"This is your first tour since going solo," I said. "How different is it this time, being on the road without your little friends?"

Cole spluttered into his water, and it dribbled down his chin. He wiped at it with the back of his hand. It was incredibly satisfying.

"I absolutely love Joey, Yosh, Taylz, and Chase. They're my best friends. I hope they'll get along to one of my gigs on this tour, but I know they're busy. Of course, it's different without them, and I miss them. We've been through a lot together. They've seen me at rock bottom. They supported me through everything. You don't forget how people treat you in important moments like that, Tobias. It's moments like that you know who your real friends are."

This was all-out war.

"You came out five years ago now. Why did you finally decide to stop lying to your fans?"

Nick was in my cans again. "For fuck's sake, behave, you daft bawbag."

"I owed a lot of people the truth," Cole said. "Including myself. I'd only begun to explore my sexuality when the Go Tos happened. I wasn't sure of who I was. But as time went on and I became more certain about who I was, I wanted to share that with the fans. I pulled the trigger on the truth gun, and I have no regrets. The fans have been super supportive."

Outside, the fans cheered. I cleared my throat to ask my next question, but Cole got in before me. "Some of them even think I'm still marriage material." He gave a thumbs up and a smile to the crowd outside. A scream went up. This was a drive-by shooting. An execution. My heart literally fell out of my arse and rolled across the floor in search of a place to hide.

I heard the click in my ears that told me Nick was about to speak. "You had that one coming, you nugget."

I returned to Cole. "Tell me about the album," I said, reading a question from the approved list to help get things back on track. "It's more of a rock sound than we're used to hearing from you."

"You've listened to it?" Cole's eyes lit up.

"I'm paid to listen to it."

"What did you think?" He looked like a kid seeking approval from the deadbeat dad he only sees every other weekend.

"I think this is probably what happens when you 'let Cole be Cole,'" I said. "I suspect this is the album you always wanted to make."

Cole smiled, his eyes alight. "It is. You know it is, Tobias. I always wanted to write my own songs and share them with the world. This album sounds like *me*, you know? I've been on a journey of self-discovery these past few years. Learning who I am. Coming out was a part of that story, and so is this album."

I couldn't stop myself. "Imagine the decade of music we could have had if you hadn't found yourself a part of the Totally Records sausage factory."

Nick glared at me. Fiona had her head in her hands. I'd so nearly got it right.

"I learned a lot with the Go Tos," Cole said. "I will always be enormously thankful to *Make Me a Pop Star* and Totally Records for the opportunity and for the platform they've given me. I wouldn't be the same artist without them. I wish them nothing but the best. And, Tobias, you love the sausage factory. Don't pretend. I listen to this show. You're as much a part of the sausage-making machine as I am. We're just a couple of silly little sausages, whether we admit it or not. And I think we've been very silly for a very long time."

It took me a second to recover my balance. "Nevertheless, 'Reborn' seems like a clear two fingers up to everything the sausage factory stands for."

"I think you've missed the point of the song. 'Reborn' is about freedom, about finding your voice. It's about self-expression. Identity."

"In which case I'm not sure I have missed the point of the song."

"It's a positive song. It's looking forward. Your interpretation is backward-looking and negative. You've got it turned about."

"How can you sit there and pretend the song isn't about escaping your contract with Felicity Quant?"

"Because I choose joy, Tobias. And if you're wallowing in the past, you'll never find it."

Our eyes were locked across the desk. A thousand things passing between us, unsaid.

Behind him, Nick gave me the wind-it-up gesture. I blinked, looked at my screen, and lifted a fader up.

"Well, good luck tonight," I said. "I'm sure it'll be a memorable gig for everybody here in Glasgow."

"You're coming along, yeah?"

"Of course."

Cole smiled. "Great!"

"I'm being paid to go." I couldn't help myself.

Cole rolled his eyes.

"Cole Kennedy, thank you for being our guest on *Pop Review.*"

"Taking... pop... *seriously*?" Cole said, sarcasm dripping off the last word.

Tap. I hit the button on a three-second sweeper that would play straight into "Reborn." I turned off our mics, and the red on-air light went dark. Fiona opened the studio door.

"I've half a mind to bang your bloody heads together," she said, sounding every bit as no-nonsense as Orla would have.

"That goes for me too," Nick added.

The light on the studio phone started flashing.

"I have to get this, I'm sorry," I said, picking up the receiver, my finger hovering over the button.

"Enjoy the show," Cole said. He looked deflated. Victory. As Britain's prince of pop and his sister walked out of the broadcast van, I pressed the phone line button. It was Denzil.

"What the fuck was that, bruv?"

Cole's Flame burns bright on opening night
Review by Davinder Singh

The venue plunges into darkness. The crowd in the Glasgow Arena erupts. Smoke creeps along the stage from the wings. The tension in the venue builds. It's visceral. The Kenneddict beside me is shaking so badly with anticipation that I can hear her teeth chattering. A spotlight sweeps over the crowd, circling around the 14,000 faces in the venue. "This is about you," it tells Kennedy's fans. "You are the stars of this show." The fans get the message. Women scream. The spotlight lands in the centre of the smoke-filled empty stage. There's one man missing, it tells us. It flicks off, plunging the entire auditorium into darkness. The crowd starts stamping and shouting for Kennedy. It goes on for a full minute, maybe two. When they finally get the message and quieten, a cello plays the six opening notes of "Reborn." It's a tease—a tease set to become a motif throughout the show, but we don't know that yet.

A flash of bluish-purple light as the cello strikes a solitary note, quick as a drumbeat. It's so loud, so unexpected, the audience is instantly silent. It's not "Reborn." It comes again—the note, the flash of purple light. Then darkness. The note comes one more time, this time followed by a couple of bars of music, and it's clear Kennedy is opening the show with the Eurythmics' iconic "Sweet Dreams (Are Made of This)." The crowd cheers in recognition. They've been wrong-footed. It's created a tension. Then the same few bars, now accompanied by a swirl of lights. Then silence and darkness. What is the message here? Not the tease; that's good showmanship. But why open with this song? Kennedy has twelve tracks on *The Flame*, and he has five old Go Tos songs he's allowed to sing—the ones he originally wrote for the band. There are enough hits among them for a crowd-pleasing concert. Why the cover? Why *this* cover?

The cello plays the same few bars again, and finally we get to see the cellist. He's high up on a platform above the stage, gently backlit with LEDs in the same soft bluey-purple light. He's barely a silhouette. After the same few bars cycle one more time, the spotlight finally goes on. It's Kennedy. He's shirtless. It looks like he's only wearing underwear. The knees straddling the instrument are bare. The crowd goes absolutely wild, but Kennedy doesn't stop playing. Who knew he could play the cello? This is new information for the fans—obsessed fans, Kenneddicts, who thought they knew every minute detail about their hero's life. It's the first clue that we're in for a special night. On the big screens, we see a tear form in Kennedy's near side eye. It's not CGI. It's real. It falls, and suddenly there's not a dry eye in the house. Fans are screaming their love. Finally, he sings the famous opening chorus of Annie Lennox's song. It's just Kennedy and the cello. It's stunning. There's not a noise from the audience. He sings the first verse, and the meaning of this opening number becomes clear. Kennedy is telling us he has been used and abused. Tonight, he's baring his soul. This is his therapy. We are his therapists. The lights go out for a split second, and the crowd is hit by a wall of sound. An entire orchestra is now backing Kennedy's vocals. They're not onstage —there's no orchestra pit. It's a backing track, recorded by the London Philharmonic last month. Kennedy sings the bridge, then he's plunged into darkness as the orchestra plays what was originally a keyboard solo. His voice returns for the next verse, but where's

Kennedy? Out of nowhere, we hear an electric guitar. Kennedy emerges from beneath the stage, guitar in hand, wearing what looks like it might be the leather jacket he wore to the "Make Me a Pop Star" auditions a decade ago, and he's giving the crowd a sexy, growly, rock and roll rendition of the chorus. For the rest of the song he's Mick Jagger, he's Freddie Mercury, he's Ozzy Osbourne. He's a long way from the safe, sweet, plastic boy band heart-throb we're used to. The Kenneddicts are eating it up. Then, *slam!* A cold ending. The music stops. There's a spotlight on Kennedy. His guitar is gone. We never even saw him get rid of it. He's gripping the microphone stand. Is this the moment he stops to talk to the crowd? No, a synthesiser strikes up in the background, playing the unmistakable first six notes of "Reborn." Again, it's a tease. He gives us "Battle Cry."

What follows is a two-hour synthesised, orchestrated soft rock spectacle. Kennedy gives the crowd everything they're aching for and so much more they didn't even know they wanted. It's a musical feast.

"This is for you," he tells the crowd when he finally speaks. "It's always been for you."

He gives us "Sidestepper," "Gaslight Tonight" and "The Whole of Me" from his solo album, before bursting into a fully orchestrated version of the Go Tos' biggest hit, "Genevieve." The crowd practically sighs with relief—the tension of not knowing whether we were going to get any of the songs he wrote for the Go Tos dissipating.

I wonder if we might get more covers. Perhaps Roy Orbison's "You Got It." Erasure's "A Little Respect." Nirvana's "Smells Like Teen Spirit," or any of the other tracks Kennedy covered on "Make Me a Pop Star." He swerves them. When he finally dips into his bag of covers, he chooses a slowed-down, string-heavy rendition of Metallica's "Nothing Else Matters." We're deep in the mellow part of the second half now, the six "Reborn" notes now an obvious motif, creatively woven into almost every other song. Musically, it's exquisite. The level of artistry is nothing short of genius.

There's a pause. It looks like Kennedy is going to speak, but he changes his mind. He goes directly into "The Flame." Everyone around me is crying. Tears are streaming down Kennedy's face.

"Enough wallowing," he says when he's done. A hi-hat. A steady drumbeat. Smoke billows across the stage. A bright, warm yellow light fills the auditorium as a piano comes up through the middle of the stage. The crowd cheers. Cole stands at it and gives us the first six notes of "Reborn" again. We're all so thirsty for it by now. He turns to the camera, the big screens showing that famous cheeky grin. "Do you want it?" he's saying. Screams of "yes" from the audience. He shakes his head, then casually taps out the Beatles' "Here Comes the Sun." From there, track by track, the tempo increases until Cole ditches the piano and a synthesiser plays the first six notes of "Reborn." It's finally here. The audience roars their appreciation. It's the perfect way to end an unforgettable gig. But, of course, Kennedy doesn't end there. Having accepted his applause, he gifts us his encore.

"Hey, do you guys wanna hear 'Genevieve' again, but this time, the way I wrote it?"

He didn't need to ask.

What follows is vindication. The Kenneddicts were right all along. Felicity Quant should have "let Cole be Cole." The Totally Records pop factory had one of our generation's greatest musical geniuses in their hands, and they squandered him. They should have taken him out of the plastic wrapper and let him play, because unleashed from the shackles of manufactured pop, Kennedy's talent is breathtaking. His stage presence, his musicality, his charm, his energy, his passion, his talent combine to create a spectacle that is without a doubt the best concert this country has seen this century. Do *not* miss this gig.

The Flame Tour has upcoming dates in Manchester, Cardiff, Birmingham, Leeds, and London before heading to Europe, Australia, Asia, the U.S., and beyond. It returns to London for three final dates at Wembley Stadium next spring.

Chapter Twenty-Two

I hated that I couldn't fault Cole's show. But I had no time to process it anyway. As soon as it ended, Nick and I dashed around, recording reaction interviews with fans outside the arena. The audio would be sent back to Tarneesha in London to package up, ready for us to play during the next night's Pop Review Special from Manchester. We were sitting in the outside broadcast van getting ready to send the files when I got a text.

Denzil: *Kennedy's team are sending a car. Get in it.*

Toby: *U must b joking.*

Denzil: *You two need to sort this out. We can't afford a repeat of tonight's Joan Crawford v Bette Davis pissing contest. Disaster bruv!*

Toby: *No way u know who those 2 women R!*

Denzil: *Googled 'Cardi v Nicki but super gay' to find beef you would understand.*

Denzil: *Listen fam, if the Kennedys pull their sponsorship, whatever happens with the board is all on YOU. Our jobs are on the line here. Real deal. You got that?*

Denzil: *FIX IT!*

I had told Denzil about Ludo's efforts to convince his dad to buy the Pure Network. As he'd pointed out, it was an outrageous long shot—the kind of thing drunk people say to each other in a pub. And we couldn't even be sure that if the Sentinel Group did buy us, we'd all keep our jobs. The best thing to do, he said, was to put the whole idea out of my head and focus on ensuring the board didn't put the station up for sale in the first place. Annoyingly, that meant playing nice with Cole Kennedy.

A black SUV with heavily tinted windows rolled up. It was well intimidating. Nick and I stared at it, not moving. A massive security guy, built like a Navy SEAL who'd been created Transformers-style using eight other Navy SEALs, got out of the driver's door. He had black aviator sunglasses on, even though it was nearly eleven at night.

"If I never see you again, it's been great, pal," Nick said.

My legs were jelly. "Come with me?"

"Absolutely not. Dav is back at the hotel. If he's finished writing his review, I'm going to bury my face between his sweet brown arse cheeks and devour him like a pair of Tunnock's Teacakes."

"That's... a lot of information, Nicholas."

"To be clear, I will not be taking calls, answering text messages, or rescuing your useless orange bahookie. I have had enough Toby time for today."

"You think about the colour of people's butts a lot, do you know that?"

"Go!"

* * *

It was a mansion. There was, thankfully, not a paparazzo in sight. Fiona ushered me in, deposited me in a sitting room, and left. Between her coolness, Nick's annoyance, and Denzil's "fix it," I really was in the naughty corner. The room was colour-drenched in a deep blue, with tan leather couches, dark wood furniture, and brass lamps. It felt like one of those high street barbershops that look flash through the window but, when you get inside, smell like toxic masculinity and aggressively stale smegma. I could hear Cole's voice up the corridor but had no idea who he was talking to. Security, maybe? Smart to keep them around. There was less chance of me murdering him with witnesses about. Especially given his driver and security guy, Mitch, was built like a bomb shelter. I checked my reflection in the mirror above the fireplace and realised my hands were shaking. I'd spent a decade imagining what I'd say to Cole if I ever got him alone again. Having missed my chance to go for his throat in the green room the day before, it felt like the moment was finally here. But not only was I required to be on my best behaviour, I was trembling so much my voice had all the resonance and authority of Tiny Tim singing "Tiptoe Through the Tulips" after half an hour trapped in an industrial freezer.

The door opened, and Cole stuck his head through. I spun around to face him.

"Hey," he said.

"Hey," I squeaked, and cleared my throat. "Hey."

For a moment I thought Cole was going to hug me again, but he must have thought better of it.

"Thanks for coming."

"Of course."

The tension in the air was so thick, it got held back a year and its parents had to cough up for a tutor. My heart was thudding. A wave of emotions washed through me—hate, fear, residual first-love vibes, contempt, awe.

"Can I get you a drink?" Cole asked. "Are you hungry? Marcel is doing his mac and cheese if—"

"Mac and cheese again? The guy has a Michelin star."

"I know, but it's, like, really good."

It was on the tip of my tongue to ask "Does Marcel also say 'Here comes the aeroplane,' or are you old enough to shovel it in for yourself now?" but I stopped myself. I was under strict instructions to fix things. And I was hungry.

"Sure, why not?"

Cole smiled and shouted up the hallway for Marcel to bring two servings. He offered me a drink. My choices were water or a zero per cent IPA. I took a sparkling water. Cole indicated for me to sit, and I sank, gratefully, into the tan leather armchair. It had the patina of age and smelt the way cologne ads tell you real men should smell—like dead cow. Cole drifted over with our drinks and sat down on the end of the couch nearest my armchair, under a massive painting I suddenly realised was an actual Hockney.

"Who are you renting this place from, Noël Coward?"

He passed me my water. "Isn't it cool?"

"Great show tonight," I said. "Genuinely." If I was there to fix things, a complimentary truth was a good place to start. Star pupil, me.

Cole's face lit up. "Really?"

"I can't fault it. It was everything the fans deserved."

"Thank you, that means a lot to me. I know you take this stuff as seriously as I do. It makes your praise more worth earning."

I rolled my eyes and leaned back in the chair. "Fame has made you a smarmy creep, I see."

Cole edged forward, elbows on his knees, looking earnest. "Listen, could we start over? Clear the air, at least, before we head to Manchester in the morning? I don't want this energy hanging over us the whole tour."

"I'm more than happy to leave the tour right here and now, mate, I ain't bothered," I snapped. "I didn't ask for this. I don't even know why I'm here."

Denzil was going to kill me. Cole didn't rise to it.

"You're here because I wanted you to be here. I asked for you, specifically. You must have seen the contract. You must know I set this whole thing up."

I leaned forward, putting my water down heavily on the coffee table. "Why, though? Is it revenge? Because you're petty? Do you want to hurt me?"

"It's because I've spent a long time wishing you were still in my life," Cole said.

I scoffed. "That explains all the missed calls on my phone, the birthday party invitations, the Christmas cards." I slumped back into the armchair. "You must think I'm an idiot, mate."

Cole had the grace to look sheepish. "I was scared to call. I thought you hated me."

"Did you work that out all by yourself, Poirot? Well, hold on to your knickers because, you ain't gonna believe this, I still hate you."

"We were kids, Toby."

I spluttered, struggling to find the words. "Are you joking me? You abandoned me to become a national punchline while you went off to live my dream."

"But look at you," Cole said. "You wanted to be famous, and you *are* famous. You're part of the cultural fabric of this country now. People love you. You leveraged it, like you always said you would. You made it happen."

I was fuming. "Famous? Do you know what I've been through? Did you hear the 'marriage material' jokes? Read the articles? Did you even know your 'beautiful Kenneddicts' graffitied the salon in homophobic slurs? Do you have any idea how traumatic that was? I dropped out of school. I lost all my mates. It ruined my life. Mum had me on suicide watch."

"Toby, I'm so sorry, I—"

I got to my feet, finger pointed squarely at Cole's face. "Over and over again, I was humiliated. Every time you hit the headlines, they'd drag the pathetic 'marriage material' kid into the story for another kicking. It never ended. My whole life since I met you has been a cheap punchline."

"Toby, I'm so sorry." Cole's brown eyes looked sad and sincere. "I didn't realise. But... I want to hear about it."

Something hot was burning my face, and I realised it was tears. I wiped my cheeks on my sleeve. Cole grabbed a box of tissues from the mantelpiece and handed it to me.

"Please, Tobes, sit down."

I sat, plucking half a dozen tissues from the box.

"When you came out, it all went into overdrive," I continued. "Photographers outside my house. Abuse from strangers in the street. You know there are entire subreddits devoted to how I turned you gay. Like I'm an infectious disease. Like being gay is contagious."

"The fans do get a bit wild sometimes," Cole said. "Teenagers can be... intense. I'm sorry." He reached across and squeezed my knee, and I ripped it out of his hand.

"That's bang out of order, mate."

Cole held up his hands in surrender. "I can see this has all had a negative impact on you, and I want to say I'm genuinely sorry about that. If I could go back and change it, I would. It sounds like you had all the downside of fame without any of the advantages, and that's shitty. Please, give me a chance to make it up to you. I want us to be friends."

I laughed. "We are never going to be friends."

For a moment, Cole looked crushed. Then he seemed to rally, like he didn't believe that was possible.

"Fine, we don't have to be friends, although I think that would be sad."

"Boo-fucking-hoo."

"I see age has made you rich with maturity."

I opened my mouth to fight back.

"Sorry!" Cole said. "I didn't mean that. Old habits. Turns out spending a decade in the sausage factory makes you incredibly sarcastic. It's something I'm working on with my therapist."

"Is that what this is about?" I asked. "Am I here because your therapist says you need some kind of closure?"

"Closure? No. But Summer—that's my therapist—has taught me a lot about healing, and about the energy we choose to carry. She's helped me let go of a lot of stuff and tune in to a more positive energy."

"How lovely for you."

"You know, I was angry with you for a long time," Cole said.

"You were angry at *me*?"

"Yes. Unfairly. And I owe you an apology for that. I should have trusted you. But I was lied to, very convincingly, by the label. And I held on to that energy for far too long—"

It twigged. "Is this about our texts?"

Cole looked uncomfortable. He ran his fingers through his hair.

"I never leaked them!"

"I know that *now*," he said—and our eyes met. "But at the time, as far as we knew, no one else had those messages. You were the obvious suspect."

"Well, *The Bulletin* was hacking everyone back then—"

"We weren't hacked," Cole said, certainty in his voice. "If we'd been hacked, they'd have printed the whole conversation. But they didn't. Did you never notice they left out the fact that I was gay? If *The Bulletin* had the complete messages, they'd have known that, and there's no doubt that would have been the headline."

He was right. But in all this time, I'd never noticed it. The leaked texts were so obviously our texts, I'd never thought to check how accurate they were.

"Which means I'm in the clear, because if I was out for revenge, surely I'd have included that detail."

Cole shook his head. "That was the bit that convinced me it was you. Queer Code 101, remember? You promised me you'd never out me."

"So, who leaked it, then?"

Cole sighed. "Felicity Quant."

"Are you joking me?" You could have knocked me over with the Wi-Fi signal. "How did she even get hold of them?"

"You remember they took our phones off us and gave us new ones? Turns out they went through our old phones looking for kompromat to use whenever it was convenient."

"And you stayed in the band after she did that to you?"

"It was years before I found out," Cole said.

"What did she have to gain from throwing you under the bus like that?"

"Huge wave of free publicity. Lots of sympathy for me. Plenty of juicy detail for the fans. Tabloids onside. Most importantly, she knew I'd think it was you. She did it to keep us apart, Toby. She didn't want us finding our way back to each other."

I was shaking, again. Cole reached over and held my fingertips in his—despite the snotty tissues in my hand. The warmth of his touch was instantly familiar, like slipping on a favourite old hoodie when the evening chill comes in. This time, I didn't pull away.

"Why?"

Cole smiled. "You were a threat to the band."

I laughed.

"You were. You were a threat to me and my bankability. You had a gun held to my head, remember? You wouldn't sign the NDAs. Felicity needed girls screaming for me, dreaming about marrying me."

I let Cole's fingers drop, putting my head in my hands. "How'd you find out it was her?"

"Robbie Johnswagger." Cole sipped his water. "He told me about it over lunch one day. I was going through a rough patch. Truthfully, I was off the rails. This was ages after he'd been sacked from *Pop Star*. He'd cleaned up his act by this point. He was worried about me. He pulled me aside and explained a few things, and this was one of the things he told me. It made me so sad because I'd been angry at you for so long. And I was so upset that Mum had died thinking you'd done that to me, to her, to all of us."

We sat in silence for a moment. When you spend a decade of your life living with an injustice, it coils around your gut like a rope, tying in all this rage. When the truth comes out, the ropes are cut, and suddenly, you're freed from the tension, and it's a physical relief. I felt like I could breathe, finally. But while I knew an injustice had been done to me, and what I'd been through because of it, I'd been so angry I never stopped to think about what it had done to Cole. If his boss could do something so evil to him, what had he gone through during the past ten years? Even thinking about it wound me up.

The door opened, and Marcel Dupont walked in. I recognised him from the telly. He put a silver tray on the coffee table.

"Macaroni au gratin, messieurs," he said, lifting the silver lid with a flourish. There were a few green things on the side, and he ran through them, pointing his finger at each in turn, announcing something in French. I didn't understand a word, but I know asparagus when I see it. We thanked him. He waved a hand and disappeared back out of the room.

"Don't let it get cold," Cole said, grabbing a bowl. "It's best piping hot." He sat back, cross-legged on the sofa, put a big cushion between his thighs to use as a table, and began to eat.

"Ooh, ibs hob!" he said, trying not to burn the roof of his mouth. "So, wob dib you thin ob the new Zara Larssob albub?"

* * *

For two hours Cole and I chatted about music—who we liked, who was overrated, who was the next big thing. It felt like old times, like the kinds of conversations we used to have late into the night, chatting on our phones in our bedrooms, or at the cheap motorway hotel where the *Make Me a Pop Star* producers had put us up. We dissected lyrics, compositions, and production choices. For ages, we talked about the healing nature of music. It was the most stimulating discussion about pop music I'd had in years. It felt good. I was disappointed when there was a knock at the door and Fiona stuck her head in.

"I'm sorry, Cole. It's America."

"Jerry?" he said.

She nodded. "I know you said no calls. I tried to put him off."

"It's fine. I'll be right there."

Fiona disappeared up the hall. Cole turned back to me and apologised.

"This call might take a while," he said. "Will you wait for me?"

I looked at the time on my phone. It was after two in the morning.

"I should get going. We've got the drive down to Manchester in the morning."

Cole looked disappointed. "OK," he said. "Mitch will drop you back at your hotel."

I smiled my thanks.

"Hey, I know this is late notice, but I have a thing at eight tomorrow morning, and I'd love it if you would come with me."

"Like a public engagement? Absolutely not."

"Why not?"

"Did you listen to anything I said tonight? I can't be seen with you in public. My life would be hell."

"We were seen in public together this afternoon. Photographed. Filmed, even."

"That was an interview. I'm not going with you to whatever breakfast TV interview you've got. The press will think we're dating, and I'll be hounded by paparazzi for months."

"It's not an interview. It's a private engagement, and Fiona's already had everyone sign an NDA. No one will even know we're there."

Exhaustion was starting to wash through my body. It was late. I wanted my bed, and I needed a sleep-in. "Nick and I have got to hit the road by ten, so—"

"I'll have you back by ten, I promise. Please say you'll come."

Cole looked at me with those soulful puppy-dog eyes. For a moment, I was sixteen again, falling hopelessly in love with the first boy who'd ever flashed me a bit of ankle. I could feel myself caving.

"What is it, though?"

"It's a surprise," Cole said. "I don't want to spoil it."

My curiosity was piqued, and I felt my resistance wavering.

"Cole!" Fiona's voice echoed up the hallway.

"There'll be no press, no photographers, no waitstaff sneaking pics on their iPhones?"

Cole smiled. "Promise. It's all totally on the down-low."

"Fine," I said. Cole fist pumped the air. "Do I need to dress up?"

"Come as yourself. You're perfect as you are." He wrapped me up in a farewell hug that smelt of cinnamon and leather. "It's been so good to see you. We'll pick you up at seven forty-five."

With a trademark smile, a cheesy double finger point, and a theatrical swivel on his heel, Cole was gone.

Chapter Twenty-Three

The SUV pulled into the car park for the Gartnavel General Hospital.

"If you're going to make me watch some old creep in a white lab coat dissect a body or something, I will absolutely do my nut," I said.

"Shhh. I told you, you'll love it."

Mitch popped the door and held it open. "Perimeter is secure, Mr Kennedy. No scrum."

"Scrum?" I asked.

"There's no press," Cole explained. "See, told you."

Five minutes later we were walking around the gynaecological oncology ward, still without a photographer or reporter in sight, just a lot of patients and nurses with smiles wider than their faces. A member of the hospital administration staff was introducing Cole to the patients—some who'd come in for surgery the night before, others who were recovering from earlier surgery, and some who'd come in for chemotherapy. Fiona and I hung discreetly back.

"Does he do this often?" I asked.

"Everywhere we go," Fiona said. "Without fail."

Cole was posing for a selfie with a woman who was rigged up for her treatment. She must have been about my age. Mid, maybe late, twenties. No older. She had no eyebrows and had a bandana wound around her head. She was wearing what looked like a homemade crocheted cardigan in extremely cheerful rainbow colours. She looked so sick and *so* tired but thrilled to be meeting Cole Kennedy.

"Isn't it painful?" I asked. "To be reminded all the time?"

"It makes him feel close to Mum," Fiona said.

"That's so sad."

"He was on tour most of the time Mum was ill. He didn't get to be there for it. I don't think he's ever forgiven himself."

I stepped further into the room, closer to Cole and the woman, hoping to catch a bit of their conversation. Cole's arm was around her shoulder. At first, I thought they were taking more selfies. Then I realised a child's voice was coming out of the phone. They were on a video call.

"Do you know who this is?" the woman said. There was an indecipherable noise from the child. "Genevieve, this is Cole Kennedy. He's come to visit Mummy in the hospital."

The little girl began singing "*Oh, Genevieve, oh, Genevieve.*"

"That's right!" the woman said. "Cole is the man who wrote your special song!" The woman had tears in her eyes. So did Cole. My heart nearly broke.

"Would you like to sing your special song with me, Genevieve?" Cole asked, his face wide-eyed and goofy, in that way adults ham it up for children.

Cole started singing. "*Oh, Genevieve, you know I have to leave...*"

Cole's beautiful baritone echoed through the hospital a capella, drawing nurses and patients like moths to a flame. A good-looking lad —the woman's husband, I guessed—took out his phone and recorded the moment. His eyes were wet, and his hand was trembling. A nurse took the phone from him, volunteering to film. The woman, singing along with her idol, serenading her daughter through the phone, reached for her husband's hand. He grabbed it and held it like it might be the last time. Still, they sang—through smiles and tears.

"*Will you wait for me, Genevieve, with your sad brown eyes? Will you forgive me, Genevieve, for all these goodbyes? Oh, Genevieve, oh, Genevieve, I wish I could stay. But life don't work out that way. Oh, Genevieve.*"

I'd heard that song a thousand times. I had never realised it was *so* sad. How had Cole written a song like that? What had he been going through? By the time the song was done, there must have been about twenty people hanging around. Everyone was crying.

* * *

Back in the SUV, I stared down at the door handle, rubbing the back of a fingernail across the fabric of the door, letting the weight of what I'd witnessed settle over me.

"Her name's Iona," Cole said. "The cancer is in her abdominal cavity. Stage four. Just like Mum."

Fiona looked up and reached a hand behind her seat. Cole grabbed it and held it.

"She's twenty-six, Fi. Same as me. Genevieve is four. Four!"

Why had he done this to himself? Was he punishing himself for not being there when Orla died? I wasn't sure this was healthy.

"The husband was a wreck," Cole said.

I looked over at him. He was still staring out the window. Glasgow was going past, but he wasn't looking at it, not taking it in.

"Iona's mum was lovely. Genevieve's grandma. She was looking after Genevieve. She said Iona was 'an OG Kenneddict.' *OG.* She actually said *OG.* Like, how old must she be? Sixty-something?"

Fiona didn't speak but let Cole hold her hand. I followed her lead and said nothing. If Cole did this everywhere, Fiona and Mitch must have been through this dozens of times. I figured they knew what he needed in this moment. He seemed childlike. Not only because he was holding his sister's hand but because there was something childlike about the way he was grappling with the idea of mortality. This was so uncomfortable. I was totally baffled about why I was here.

We pulled up outside the Glasgow Arena slightly before ten, as Cole had promised. Nick was already there.

"Thank you for coming," Cole said. "It means a lot to me that you did."

I stuck my finger into the door handle and turned to look directly into Cole's eyes for the first time since we'd left the hospital. "Why did you ask me to come this morning?"

Cole looked surprised. "Did... did you not have a good time?"

"You took me to an oncology department to have *a good time*?"

"No! It's... I thought... I mean, we'd been talking about the healing power of music, and—"

My door swung open without me lifting the handle. Mitch stood on the other side, holding it for me to get out. The sun glinted off something, and I noticed he was wearing a trans flag lapel pin.

"I should go," I said. "Nick and I have got a four-hour drive ahead of us."

"No, don't go!" Cole said. "Come with us in the jet instead. There's a lot I want to tell you."

"You're taking a jet from Glasgow to Manchester?"

"Um... yeah."

"We will discuss your reckless carbon footprint later," I said. "But I can't. The van isn't modified for Nick to drive."

"Both come in the jet, then! Pleeeeease." Cole's eyes were pleading.

"You're missing the point. We need to get the van to Manchester for tonight's show. No van, no show. And if there's no show, there's no million quid. Your rules, not mine."

"Stay right there," Cole said, opening his car door. "I have an idea."

Chapter Twenty-Four

Twenty-four hours earlier, if you'd have asked me for the definition of hell, this would have been it. I was bombing down the M74 towards Manchester at fifty miles an hour in PureFM's knackered old broadcast van, trying not to get blown off the road by crosswinds, with Cole Kennedy sitting beside me in the passenger seat. Cole was bouncing around like a kid on Christmas morning, excited for what he kept calling "our road trip." I hadn't wanted to agree to this, but how could I say no to Cole after what I'd witnessed that morning? I had one condition—that he travel incognito.

"Will you pull that hat over your face a bit more," I said, reaching over and yanking the peak down.

"Stop it!" Cole batted my arm away. "You're in the slow lane, no one is going to recognise me all the way over here."

"This isn't one of your SUVs with blacked-out windows." Even I could hear the frustration in my voice. "This is an ancient mobile home, it's ninety per cent glass, and it's covered from arsehole to breakfast in the *Pop Review* logo. People are going to stare. Everyone stares."

I knocked the cap down further over Cole's face.

"Careful, this is a new hat!"

"I know, I dug it out of the merch bag and gave it to you less than five minutes ago."

Cole pulled out his phone to take a selfie.

"Woah, what are you doing?"

"Posting an Insta story in my snazzy new hat."

"Oh no you don't!" I tried to snatch Cole's phone, the van swerved, and the front wheel went over the rumble strip. I grabbed the wheel and nearly over-corrected, swerving back into the inside lane. Shrieking tyres and honks pierced the air.

"Jesus, Toby! OK, no selfie. Just... don't get us killed, will you?"

In the wing mirror, I could see the three black SUVs of Cole's security team behind us. Mitch was flashing his headlights at me. I hit the hazard lights, letting him know everything was OK. The last thing I needed was to piss off a guy whose pronouns were speed, surprise, and violence.

Cole laughed at a message on his phone.

"Look at this," he said, holding the screen up for me to see. It was a selfie of Nick and Fiona, sipping champagne in Cole's private jet. It seemed Nick had adapted to the high life quickly. And here I was, getting high on diesel fumes and babysitting my ex for the next four hours. A lorry thrummed up beside us, overtaking.

"Selfie for Fiona," Cole said, shifting around so we were both in the frame.

"No selfies!" I was concentrating on not getting blown off the road as the lorry passed us.

"Smile!" *Click*. "Wait, you can't see my snazzy new *Pop Review* hat."

"Stop saying *snazzy*."

"Let's go again."

"Cole!"

"Smile!" *Click*.

"Aw, you look grumpy in this one." Cole flashed me the pic, but I was too focused on the road. "Hat looks great, though," he said. "Very snazzy." *Swoosh!* The image had been sent.

"Don't post that!"

"I didn't. It's for Fi only, I promise. And for me. A memento of our road trip... and this magical time we're spending together."

He was boiling my piss now. "Reborn" came on the radio, and I reached over and switched it off.

"Hey, I love that song."

"What is this all about, Cole? Why are we here?"

"Because the M74 is the best route to Manchester."

"You know what I mean. Why did you pay a million quid for *Pop Review* to come on this tour? Why take me to the hospital this morning? Why are you in my shitty van instead of twenty thousand feet above my head in your private jet, getting wanked off by Hire-a-Twinks, or whatever it is you do up there? Is this genuinely all because you found out Felicity Quant lied to you? Because, if so, this feels like an apology that could have been an email."

Cole pointed at a sign up ahead.

"Ooh, there's a motorway services. Can we stop and get some snacks?"

"Stop avoiding the question!"

Cole went quiet. When I looked over at him, he'd finally pulled the hat down but was staring doggedly out the side window, avoiding eye contact. I swear I could feel his heartbeat through the van's bench seat. We sailed past the exit for the services. Cole's shoulders slumped.

"Do you know the day we met was the best day of my life?" he said.

"Well, you aced your audition. The judges loved you. Even the woodlice eating the floorboards knew you were going to be a star. So, that's hardly a surprise."

"You know that's not what I mean," he said, turning to face me. I glanced over at him. His eyes were red.

"You better not have the audacity to cry right now—"

"You were smart, funny, confident—"

"Shut your lying mouth, Cole Kennedy. I was none of those things. I was a fat, spotty, awkward, orange—"

"Orange, I will concede, but you weren't even remotely fat. That was all in your head. You still had a bit of puppy fat in the face, that's all."

"Puppy fat? Mum once said I was 'cherubic,' and Aunty Cheryl asked how many cherubs I ate in an average sitting."

Cole laughed. "Do you think Aunty Cheryl might have been responsible for some of your body image issues? Everyone has puppy fat at sixteen."

"Why are we talking about puppy fat?"

"I wasn't. You were. I was talking about the fact I met this amazing boy who charmed me with his brains and his wit, and who saved me from the Hallelujah Curse, and who filled a pair of skinny jeans in the most... *delicious*... way possible."

I roared in frustration. "You're doing my nut, Cole."

"You wore your sexuality loud and proud at a time when I was still coming to terms with mine. That was so sexy. The instant I laid eyes on you, I knew I wanted you. Within half an hour, I swear, I thought, 'I could fall in love with this guy.'"

I closed my eyes, blinking away the frustration, hurt, and rage, giving myself a moment to find the right words. But when I opened my eyes, the tail lights on the lorry in front of me were shining bright red, and we were speeding towards them way too fast. I slammed on the brakes. We lurched forward. Cole put his arms out to avoid smashing into the dashboard. The tyres squealed. I closed my eyes, waiting for the sound of crunching metal and shattering glass.

We stopped just in time.

"Jesus, are you OK?" I said, my heart thumping like a coked-up jackrabbit having a wank.

"I'm fine," Cole said. He put his hands on his head. "The hat's OK. We're fine over here. Are you OK?"

"I'm OK." I looked in the mirror. Cole's fleet of SUVs, no doubt with better brakes than the van's, had safely stopped. I craned to look up the road ahead. The traffic was at a standstill, with red tail lights as far as I could see. "I think there might be an accident. I don't think we're going anywhere for a while."

"I knew we should have got snacks. How amazing would a doughnut be right now?"

I looked out the window at the vehicle directly to the right of us. It was a minibus full of teenage girls. They were jumping about excitably and pointing at the van and the *Pop Review* signage. One girl mouthed the words "taking... pop... seriously."

"Get down!" I said, hitting Cole on the arm. "For God's sake, keep your hat down." I slapped it over his face. "Here, lie down. Do *not* look out the driver's side window." I explained about the bus and the girls. Cole was calm. He appeared used to this sort of situation. He lay down along the bench seat of the van.

"This is cramped," he said after a minute. His legs were folded hard up against the passenger door. He shuffled back, resting his head on my lap. "That's better."

"That's assault," I replied. But he didn't move.

I sat there in disbelief. Cole's head was warm against my leg, the smell of cinnamon and hair shampoo filling the air. His face was right by my dick. Like, if he turned his head to the left, his lips would brush the zip of my jeans and I'd feel the warmth of his breath against my groin. And for all I hated him, all my cock knew was that there was a fit guy with his face in my lap, and it would not ask my brain for permission to launch. This was too intimate, too uncomfortable. But I had no choice but to put up with it because the alternative was a busload of schoolgirls recognising one of the most famous pop stars in the world and then *bedlam*. We were trapped. Trapped by the traffic, by a busload of teenagers, and by the things we used to feel for one another. I looked down at him. Cole smiled.

"This, by the way, is why I always take the jet."

Twat. "I didn't ask you to be here."

"I wouldn't have missed our road trip for the world."

"Because you fell in love with me instantly?" My words were ripe with disdain. "When we were kids?"

"To be fair, that's not quite what I said. The only person I fell in love with instantly that day was Gaston."

I rolled my eyes.

"How is Gaston, by the way?"

"Barking at the great postman in the sky."

"I'm sorry to hear that."

Cole's phone beeped. "That's Mitch, asking if we're OK." Cole texted something back. "I've asked him to send the chopper for me. You'll be OK if I bail, won't you?"

"Are you serious?"

Cole laughed. "Of course not. But I find it reassuring that apparently you *don't* want me to leave. Because, honestly, you were giving off some pretty frosty vibes."

"You don't say?" Cole was buried in his phone. I reached over and turned on the radio. It was a Jocasta Rose track. "Oh, it's your ex-girlfriend," I said. "Is this too painful for you? Do you want me to turn it off?"

"She was never my girlfriend. We're mates." Cole pointed at his face. "Big homo, remember?"

How could I forget?

"You know we had the paparazzi camped out in our street for a month when you came out," I said. "Outside both the house and the salon. I couldn't open a door without reporters asking me if we were getting together."

Cole didn't look up but stayed buried in his phone. "Sorry about that. It's the price of fame, I'm afraid."

"I wasn't famous. I was a hairstylist who'd said something stupid on the telly once."

"I'm sorry." He looked up. I glanced down, caught his eye, and looked away again.

"To be honest with you, it was the first time I truly understood I couldn't control my fame. That I would never escape it."

"You finally decided to leverage it, like you always said you would," Cole said, his eyes finally meeting and holding mine.

"You know what, I bloody did. And I ain't sorry about it."

"Yeah, I was dead proud of you for that."

Cole smiled, returning to his phone. His head was hot on my thigh, and I could feel sweat soaking into my jeans. Jocasta started singing the chorus, and Cole joined her. His voice was deep and mellow and beautiful, and it vibrated through my leg like he was trying to rouse me. I was transported back a decade, to moments like this—lying on each other's laps at the *Pop Star* hotel, debating which nineties boy band had the most cultural impact, or singing along with the radio, harmonising with each other, playing with our musicality. As Cole sang, I started to sing, too—playing with the harmony, as I'd always done, while Cole sang the lyrics. It had been a long ten years since we'd heard our voices together. His baritone was richer, more mellow. My tenor was rusty, out of practice. Our voices weren't the same anymore, but then, we weren't the same boys we'd been back then either. There was too much water under the bridge for whatever this was. I stopped singing.

"Why *did* you come out, in the end?" I asked, when the song finished.

Cole paused. "It was when Mum got sick." He moved his phone to look up at me. "She told me life was short and I had to live my truth."

I met his eyes. "And Felicity let you do it?"

"Oh, not for ages, and she didn't want to," Cole said, disappearing back behind his phone. "Things might have turned out very different if she had. But eventually it was contract renewal time. And I'd been so, so unhappy. I said I'd leave the band unless I was allowed to come out."

"That was ballsy."

"Thank you. I also told them I wanted to write a song for the next album."

"How'd you swing that? I thought everything was focus-grouped by the sausage factory."

"Fiona," he said. It was all the answer I needed. "It still got sausage-factoried, though."

I thought about hearing Cole sing "Genevieve" "the way I wrote it."

"I prefer your version," I said.

"Thank you."

The driver of the lorry in front of us got out of his cab and went for a piss in the bushes. The busload of girls whooped, hollered, and catcalled.

"So, Jocasta was never your girlfriend," I said. "But did you ever have any boyfriends?"

Another silence. Cole's face stayed hidden behind his phone.

"One," he said, and something in his voice sounded broken. "I don't want to talk about it. Can't, in fact. NDA. Pop star stuff. You know how it is." He emerged from under his phone, his big chestnut eyes searching mine.

"What about you? Have you had any boyfriends?" He waggled his perfectly trimmed eyebrows.

"Since you?"

"Yeah."

"No, I've been sitting out on my widow's walk this entire time, quietly stitching my hymen back together and waiting for you to return from the sea."

Cole snorted. "Come on, there must have been someone special. You can't have been single this whole time. Look at you. You're still gorgeous, even without the puppy fat."

I rolled my eyes and looked away but felt the rush of heat go to my face like mission control had fired up all burners and was preparing for lift-off.

"No one serious," I said, watching a random stranger shake off his drips. "I've been going solo for a decade."

I could have told him about the hook-ups and the endless arrangements with various "down-low" lads who had more to lose than I did, but why should I? I didn't owe him that.

Cole looked baffled. "Was I your last boyfriend?"

"You try sitting in a bar or going on GayHoller when you're me," I said, annoyed. "Every arsehole thinks he's the first guy to ask if he's 'marriage material.'"

Cole burst into laughter.

"It ain't funny," I said, shifting my leg to make his head accidentally-on-purpose bump into the steering wheel.

"Ow!"

"And those are only the ones who didn't straight-up rinse me for ever thinking I was good enough for you in the first place."

"Come off it, no one does that."

"A lot of people hate me because of you, Cole."

Cole's thumb was scrolling urgently through his phone. "Not everyone hates you. I know for a fact plenty of fans were desperate for us to get together. Did you never read any Colby fan fiction?"

"Someone wrote fan fiction about us?"

"A *lot* of people wrote fan fiction about us." Cole was still scrolling. "Wattpad is a wild place."

"When do you get the time to read fanfiction?"

"Seventy-five per cent of being a pop star is sitting around bored out of your mind, waiting for something to happen. People don't appreciate that," he said. "Anyway, a lot of the stories are quite good. You should definitely read some. In fact, we should read some now."

"I don't think—"

"*Toby stood naked before him.*" Cole was reading, his voice breathy and mocking. "*As naked as the day he was born. Only six shades more orange. Exactly how Cole liked him.*"

"Wait, did you already have that open in your phone?"

"*Toby was as hard as notorious East End gangster Reggie Kray (or whichever one was the gay one) after a particularly satisfying kill.*"

"You cannot be serious."

"*Cole beckoned him over, eyes devouring him. His hole burned with desire to feel Toby inside him—burned with an intensity he hadn't known since that time he accidentally got Veet up there—*"

I laughed. "You're making this up!" I said, pushing Cole off my leg, so he had to sit up.

Cole shook his head. "I swear to you, every word is real. It's right here." As he held up his phone for me to see, the busload of schoolgirls began to scream—and my worst nightmare was realised.

"Get down!" I tried to push Cole back onto the seat, but he was already waving at the girls.

"It's too late, they've seen me," he said, trying not to move his lips. "Stay calm."

Not only had they seen him, but they were also now hanging out the windows with their phones out, filming him.

"I do *not* want to be seen with you!" I snatched the hat off Cole's head, put it on, and lay down across the seat—unavoidably, right across Cole's lap. My chest was tight. I couldn't catch my breath. I felt the familiar fear grip my body. "Oh God."

"Relax," Cole said, lips still taut. "Mitch is already on it. The footage will all be deleted. No one will ever see it."

"I can't breathe."

Cole looked down at me, his eyes wide with concern.

"Toby? What is it?"

"Panic attack," I choked out.

"What can I do? How do I help?"

I shook my head. Cole put a hand on my chest, firmly, and looked into my eyes.

"Toby, you're safe. Nothing is going to happen to us. This is a standard Code Blue. Look, Mitch is offering them all free backstage tickets to tonight's concert and the meet-and-greet afterwards on the condition they delete everything. It's going to be fine."

"What if they don't delete it?"

"Would you argue with Mitch?"

I closed my eyes and focused on my breathing, trying to calm my body. After a few minutes, Mitch knocked on the van window to give us the all-clear. The girls would cooperate.

Ten minutes later, my panic attack had subsided and traffic started moving. The girls in the bus waved. Cole smiled and waved back. "See you tonight!" he called out, nearly deafening me in the process. I pulled the hat further down over my face.

"So, I'm sensing you really don't want to be seen with me, huh?"

"You think?" I turned on the ignition, and the van rumbled into life.

"Do those... happen a lot?"

"Not as often as they used to."

Cole was quiet for a moment. "They're my fault, aren't they?" he said softly. "I'm sorry."

I remembered my first ever panic attack, the day I ran home from school. There had been so many more over the years. Always to do with Cole. I put the van in gear, checked the mirrors, and slowly moved off.

"This is incredibly stressful for me," I said.

"I see that now. That was scary. I'm sorry."

I changed gear.

"I've spent ten years trying to separate my narrative from yours. It feels like you're unpicking all that hard work. Stitch by stitch. Deliberately."

"Well, yeah," Cole said. "Of course."

"Are you serious?" I looked over at him in disbelief.

"That's... why I'm here."

"To ruin my life?"

Cole's eyes glowed with sincerity. "To heal."

Chapter Twenty-Five

Cole's security team decided it was too risky for Cole to drive into central Manchester in the van, so we pulled into a motorway lay-by outside the city to "make the exchange." To my surprise, I was kind of sad to see the back of him. Once we'd settled into singing along to the radio, "our road trip" was quite good fun.

By the time I got to the Manchester Arena and met Nick, we had less than two hours to set up the van before we were on air. Thankfully, Tarneesha had done a lot of the heavy lifting from London, but Nick and I had to plug in cables, do mic checks, and test the line to the station. Obviously, we were busy gossiping instead.

"We were in the air less than half an hour, Tobes," Nick said, his voice coming through my headphones. "It takes me longer than that to get out of Covent Garden Tube station most days. You should have seen the wee bitty snacks they put on. Did you know Cole's got a Michelin-star chef on that plane?"

"I know."

"The one off the telly," Nick clarified. "The silver fox."

"Marcel Dupont. Did he make mac and cheese by any chance?"

"Sushi, sashimi, a whole charcuterie board with prosciutto, chorizo—"

"Beats paying fifteen quid for a pack of Pringles on easyJet."

"And oysters!"

"Does he ever cook anything, or just wait until the animals have been dead long enough to serve?"

Nick opened the van door and ducked his head out to test the exterior mic we used to pick up atmosphere, like cheering crowds and the sound of fainting Kenneddicts smacking their heads on the pavement. Nick's voice came through my headphones slightly quieter than before.

"Have you ever had oysters, Tobes?" Nick said. I watched the needle bounce on the screen and lifted the level a smidge. Nick pulled himself back inside the van. "It's like having a mouthful of superthick, salty spunk. But like, if spunk was chewy."

"I've had them, and I'll stick to Pringles, thanks."

Nick shrugged. "How was the drive down with the people's prince of pop?"

"Like being trapped in a small cage with a relentless Labrador."

"But are you getting on? Have you done enough to be civil when you interview him in Cardiff next week?"

A burst of heat radiated out from my stomach, and I felt my face redden. I hid behind my microphone, but it was too late. Nick had already seen my guilty blush.

"I know that face, Tobias Lyngstad," he said. Sweat burst from my palms. Nick was practically vibrating with excitement. "The last time I saw that look on your face, you were coming home drunk from the BRIT Awards with Krishnan Varma-Rajan's TV make-up on your trousers."

"Stop right there," I said, holding up both hands. "Nothing happened with Cole. Nothing is going to happen with Cole."

Nick scoffed. "I can see it in your face. You've gone from hating Cole Kennedy to picking at his knicker elastic in less than twenty-four hours. Bloody hell, this is the biggest thaw since the last ice age, Toby. Any minute now a woolly mammoth is going to stride into a barbershop and ask for a short back and sides."

"Nothing happened!" I protested, standing up with a jolt and sending my chair crashing into the wall behind me. "All right?"

"Maybe it didn't, but you're catching old feelings. It's in your face."

"He sang 'Genevieve' to a four-year-old girl called Genevieve whose mother's dying of cancer," I said, the words falling out of me in a rush. "You try staying angry at someone after you've seen them do that."

Nick eyeballed me. "What. Happened. In. That. Van?" He jabbed a finger into the desk on each word.

"We talked!"

"Good. Talking is good. What did he have to say for himself?"

I slumped back into my chair, rested my head in my hand, and looked at my best friend through the studio glass.

"He said he wants us to heal."

I told Nick everything Cole had said, including Felicity's trick with the text messages.

"Cole says a lot was stolen from us and he wants the friend back that he lost. He said he wants to make up for lost time."

"And how do you feel about that?"

"He ruined my life, Nick. He can't smile and flirt and sing songs to adorable toddlers and expect that all is forgiven. I've got *trauma*."

"You have trauma?" Nick said. "Toby, a garbage lorry slammed into my bicycle and snapped my spine like a KitKat, but I still have to take the bins out every Tuesday night."

"Wow. Feel free to bring a gun to a knife fight, Nick."

"My point is, life goes on. OK? You got hurt. You're still alive. Look at you. You're thriving. If you've got unresolved issues, then healing is exactly what you need. And that's what Cole wants too. So far, I don't see the problem."

"I can't switch off everything I feel."

"I know," Nick said. "But we choose how we react to situations in life. You can choose to start to forgive."

I stood up, walked around the glass partition, and put my arms around Nick's shoulders. "Sorry, I didn't mean to get aggie with you, babes."

"I know, you daft bawbag."

The clock said half an hour until showtime.

"I need to pee," I said.

"Go for me, too, will you?"

I laughed at the vintage dad joke, but then Nick slipped a water bottle into my hand. It was warm and filled with yellow liquid.

"Is this?"

"Yeah."

"When did you—"

"While you were blethering on back there like Meryl Streep. Drop it in the bin for us, will you?"

"You're disgusting, babes, you know that?"

As I grabbed the van's door handle, Nick reached out to stop me.

"Hey, have you listened to Cole's album?"

"You know I have. What are you on about?"

"But have you actually *listened* to it?"

"Nick, I need to pee."

"I was talking to Fiona on the plane. When you interview Cole next week, I think you should ask him why he named the tour *The Flame*."

I shrugged. "It's the name of the album. What else would he call it?"

"But *Reborn* would be a much better name for the album and the tour, don't you think?"

I pushed down on the door handle, and a rush of cool air and street noise flooded in. "Haven't thought about it."

"I think you should ask him," Nick said.

Chapter Twenty-Six

It had been a long week. For the third night in a row—one night in Glasgow and two in Manchester—I'd done two hours of live radio surrounded by thousands of Kenneddicts. I'd seen Cole's concert three times. Although it did not get old, I was as mentally, emotionally, and physically exhausted as a police sniffer dog who'd done double shifts all Glastonbury weekend. A late-night call from Denzil had informed me the board had "received overtures from an interested party." I felt like the station's entire survival was in my hands.

I'd got out of the shower and was ready to fall into bed when my phone pinged.

Fiona Kennedy: *We're in the car park under your hotel. Can you come down?*

I groaned. The Kennedys had monopolised every waking hour of the last week. I wanted to sleep. Still, my curiosity switch had tripped. I replied saying I'd be right down. I ran a brush through my hair and threw on my boysenberry puddy-cat velour onesie and my fluffy slippers. I was way too tired to make an effort. If Cole wanted to see me at one in the morning, he could take me as he found me. It was only going down in the lift that I remembered the paparazzi might be lurking about. I looked at my reflection in the elevator mirror. I looked like someone had tried to recreate *Weekend at Bernie's* with a dead Pink Panther. The press would have a field day if they saw me like this. I popped the hood up over my head. One puddy-cat ear stood upright, the other flopped down. At least if I got papped with Cole now, there was a chance I wouldn't be recognised and the tabloids might take him for a fetishist.

The elevator chimed, and the silver doors shuddered open. Cole was nowhere to be seen. I don't know why I expected a global super-star to be standing in the middle of an underground car park in a hotel that was teeming with fans who'd been to his concert. A pair of head-lights flashed, and a big black SUV rumbled up and stopped right in front of me. A door opened, and Fiona's face appeared. She waved a hand, urging me to get in.

"What's going on?" I asked as she climbed out of the car.

"We need your help to bury a body," she said, rolling her eyes—a good reminder that no one's patience is at its best at one in the morn-ing. "What do you think? Cole wants to speak to you."

I peered in. Cole was seated in the back of the car. He waved at me like Forrest Gump. I climbed in.

"What's new, pussycat?" he said. Two car doors slammed. Mitch had joined Fiona outside.

"Am I the body you're going to bury? Is that what this is? Because if I'd known, I'd have blow-dried my hair."

Cole reached across and felt the fabric of my ears. "I was going to bury you, obviously, but this is so super cute, I'm going to have to reconsider."

"I believe bundling me into a hessian sack and throwing me into the canal is the traditional way to deal with unwanted cats."

Cole's eyes met mine and locked. I could feel the heat of his hand through the velour hood of my onesie. "But that assumes the kitty cat concerned is unwanted," he said.

I slapped his hand away and pushed the hood down.

"Speaking of wanting things, it's late, what do you want?"

Cole shrugged. "To thank you. For this week. For giving me a chance to clear the air a bit. It's felt good to hang out, you know?"

Despite myself, I did know. "It's not every day someone drops a million quid to hang out with me. The least I could do was put on my party dress and show up."

"I'm glad you did. It means a lot to me that you agreed to it."

"To be clear, I was not given a choice."

"Of course you had a choice."

"Ah, no, I didn't. Denzil made that crystal clear. The station needs that swag or the board is going to sell us to some soulless hedge fund who'll strip our assets and kick our arses onto the street. I'm literally here because Denzil didn't give me a choice."

Cole looked crushed. "It wasn't meant to..." I could see his mind processing what I'd said. "Is that genuinely the only reason you're here?"

"If I'm being honest with you, yes." And there was a part of me, the part of me that had spent ten years hating Cole Kennedy, that enjoyed watching the words sink into his chest like the blade of a stiletto piercing his heart. But there was another part of me, the part buried deep inside me that was forever sixteen, the part that felt like the last few days had been a gift from the universe, that felt more than a little guilty.

"But I'm glad I'm here," I said, letting my better angel win. "It feels good to talk."

Cole's face brightened. "Good. And we've got plenty of time to talk." Our eyes met again—and I felt the old attraction tug in my chest. I fought it, dropping my gaze to my lap.

"Anyway, I wanted to pop by and say goodbye," Cole said. "I'm off in the morning for a four-day promo tour for the US shows, so I won't be around."

"Oh." I felt a little deflated. I had no right to. I hadn't been expecting to spend time with Cole between gigs. Nick and I were driving down to Cardiff in the morning and leaving the van in a lock-up, then catching the train home for a few days. Yet, in that moment, I felt like I was going to miss Cole, and I wasn't quite ready to say good-bye. We had more things to talk about, process, and catch up on. Talking to Cole had been therapeutic. I felt like I was starting to let go of a lot of anger, disappointment, and hate.

"Hey." I felt awkward, like a teenager summoning the courage to ask his crush out on a date. "Are you free now?"

Cole's smile was all teeth and cheeks, but it quickly morphed into an apologetic grimace.

"I'm sorry. I've got a round of radio interviews in the US to do. East Coast, then West Coast. Then I've got a Zoom call with my US tour team. Then it's straight to the airport."

"When do you sleep?"

"Rock and roll, baby!" he said. I felt tired on his behalf.

I looked down, not wanting Cole to see the weird disappointment I was feeling. I pulled at a thread on my onesie. Cole's finger found my chin, and my heart flipped. I looked up into his soulful eyes.

"I'll see you on Thursday, though, in Wales," he said, letting his hand fall. "Chase is coming to the show. He's looking forward to seeing you."

"Oh," I said, returning my gaze to my lap. I wasn't sure if I was ready to see any of Cole's old bandmates again. I hadn't seen any of them since my last day on *Make Me a Pop Star*.

I wound the loose thread around my finger and tugged at it, but instead of it snapping, a heap of stitches pulled loose, making a great big hole up the length of my leg.

"Bollocks!"

Suddenly, I felt like I was going to cry. Call it stress, call it chronic sleep deprivation, call it being trapped in the back of a car with your ex-boyfriend. But I was literally and metaphorically coming undone.

"Tobias Lyngstad, are you undressing in the back seat of my car?"

Cole said. "I don't know what you think this is, but I'm not that kind of girl."

"I have to go," I said. I scrambled for the door handle, flooded with embarrassment—about not only the hole in my onesie but this unshakeable feeling I'd been rejected again. All these old feelings were bubbling up inside me, and I felt a panic attack coming on. I opened the door and made a dash for the elevator. Which, as escape plans go, was not the smartest. I slammed my finger into the button, then had to wait ten seconds for the damn thing to open. Why hadn't I taken the fire stairs? The doors were right there. My chest tightened. When the lift finally opened, I leapt inside, too terrified to turn around in case Cole was watching me. I flicked my hood up and cast my eyes to the floor, not wanting to catch a glimpse of Cole in the mirror—knowing he must be staring at me. I grabbed at the seam of my onesie, holding it together so my knob didn't fall out through the hole. My heart was thumping in my chest. After what felt like forever, the doors began to rattle to a close.

"Wait!" I heard Cole shout. I looked up, instinctively, to see the reflection of Cole diving between the closing doors and into the lift. At almost the same instant, I felt his body crash into mine. I lurched forward, into the mirror, and turned to find Cole standing inches away from me, his eyes wide and pleading, his warm, minty breath on my skin. His mouth was moving, but he wasn't saying anything—nothing I could hear, at least. It was like a fever dream. Everything was in slow motion, fuzzy. Then Cole's hands—warm, strong, beautiful hands—were sliding inside my hood, cradling my jaw, his fingers trembling as they grazed the hair behind my ears. I was frozen. Then his lips were on mine.

Everything around us dissolved. In an instant, with the warmth of his breath in my mouth, the taste of him on my tongue, we were Cole and Toby again. We were sixteen again. Two young boys, lost in lust and love and wonder. His kiss was a time machine, and we hurtled back to a place before all the hurt, the pain, the monster of fame.

I sank into his body, felt him press against me. Then I pulled myself free and slapped him. A decade's worth of trauma, of anger, of hate, flooding back.

He put his hand to his face. His eyes met mine, full of confusion. The elevator door opened. I had no idea what floor we were on, who might spring us in here. A photographer? A dozen bloodthirsty Kenneddicts ready to sacrifice me to save their idol? We both spontaneously straightened—stiff-backed like naughty boys, pretending nothing had happened. Fiona was standing there, hands on her hips, looking well annoyed. We hadn't gone anywhere at all. We were still in the basement. The whole interlude—the kiss, the slap, reliving an entire decade of pain—must have lasted only a matter of seconds. Cole's eyes were fixed on me. I looked at the floor, my heart pounding in my throat, adrenaline coursing through my body—confusion blurring my thoughts. I was definitely going to cry.

"Cole, you've got a pre-record with Seacrest in five," Fiona said. "I'm sorry, I know this is important. But we have to go."

Cole nodded. I kept staring at the floor, my fist gripping at the hole in my onesie, unable to leave it alone.

"I'll see you Thursday," Cole said, "and we can talk." I didn't look up, but I nodded. Cole stepped out of the lift to stand with Fiona. I hit the button for my floor. When I finally looked up, Cole was staring at me.

"Keep pulling at that thread, Toby. Promise me you'll keep pulling at that thread."

The doors rattled closed, the ground beneath me shifted, and the elevator started to rise.

Chapter Twenty-Seven

Nick and I were sitting at a grimy service station picnic table beside a plastic children's playground that was so sunbleached it looked like it was haunted by the ghosts of other dead playgrounds. We were tucking into Greggs vegan sausage rolls and trying not to think about how much diesel particulate we were ingesting. It had been a quiet journey to Cardiff so far.

"This mood you're in," Nick said, licking ketchup off his finger, "I'm guessing it's about your sexy squillionaire ex?"

I picked a flake of pastry off my sausage roll and let it crumble between my fingers. Since Cole had kissed me in the lift the night before, I had been going over and over it in my mind. What did it mean? Why did he do it? It had sent a million conflicting emotions bubbling up to the surface, and I felt overwhelmed.

"I'm fine," I said. It wasn't convincing even to me. There was no way Nick was buying it.

"Are you sure? Because, genuinely, for a while there I thought I'd accidentally climbed into a van with Sally Field. I thought someone's kidney transplant had failed."

"Huh?"

Nick looked appalled. "Don't tell me you've never seen *Steel Magnolias*? It's literally set in a salon."

I shook my head.

"Right, well, we'll be fixing that little oversight in your cultural education as soon as we get back to London." He took a bite of sausage roll, and we sat in silence, listening to the rumble of motorway traffic while he chewed. "You know what I think?" he said, finally. I looked up at him. "I think you've got quite used to having your sexy, rich, famous ex chasing you around these past few days, and you've liked it. Now he's gone and you won't see him for four or five days, and you"—he pointed his sausage roll at me—"don't know how to handle it."

"Oh, fuck off," I said. "That's not it."

"No?"

"No."

"Then tell me what's up."

I picked up my sausage roll and took a bite, avoiding eye contact with Nick.

"Toby, you insisted I come on this tour with you, despite it being diabolically wheelchair inaccessible at every turn. You wanted me here for a reason, and I hope it wasn't so I could sit on the side of a motorway while car fumes smoked my lungs to pastrami, because very little of my body operates optimally as it is—"

"Cole kissed me," I blurted. "All right? He kissed me. Now you know." I looked over at Nick. He raised his eyebrows.

"Is that all?"

"Isn't it enough?"

"Depends. How do you feel about it?"

"I don't know."

"Did you kiss him back?"

"I slapped him across the face."

"That seems definitive." Nick licked a bit of pastry off the back of his hand. "So why are we moping, then?"

"Because before I slapped him, I *might* have kissed him back." I put my head in my hands.

"This is a roller coaster ride."

"If you're going to judge me—"

"Don't be stupid. I've paid my penny, I've got my ticket, and I'm already sitting in a stranger's vomit. So, why'd you hit him?"

"Because I hate him."

"Do you really, though?" Nick let the last of his vegan sausage roll slide back into the bag and put it down. He reached a hand across the table to me, and I grabbed it. "Or are you in the habit of hating him?"

"He ruined my life," I said. "It took me years to get over all that crap, I've finally got my life sorted, and it feels like he's come back to screw it all up again, you know what I'm saying?"

"You think he's back to deliberately ruin your life?"

"In the van the other day, he said this was about healing. I thought he meant he wanted to be friends. But if he wanted to be friends, why the kiss? Why disrespect me like that?"

"Maybe he's doing it because he's still in love with you, you absolute roaster."

I pulled my hand away. "Don't be stupid."

"Have you listened to *The Flame* yet, Toby?"

I groaned in frustration. "This again? What is it with you—"

"Don't you think this whole 'reborn' thing of Cole's is him pressing the reset button?" Nick said. "That guy has been through some shit. Can you imagine having Felicity Quant controlling your life for ten years? You saw what it was like for a few weeks. He's finally escaped. You remember all the 'let Cole be Cole' stuff back when the Go Tos formed? What if he feels like he's lost track of who he is and this whole thing is him pressing a great big reset button and going back to where he was the last time he truly felt like himself?"

I stared at Nick, my jaw slack, mouth open. "You've put a lot of thought into this."

"I've had a lot of thinking time on this tour because my best friend keeps ditching me to hang out with his ex."

I rolled my eyes. Nick fished the last of his sausage roll out of the paper bag.

"It's Fiona's theory, not mine," he added, sinking his teeth into the pastry.

"Maybe us being together *was* the last time he was happy. But he doesn't get to rewind the tape. Life doesn't give us do-overs. He hurt me. I can't forget everything that's happened."

"No one's asking you to," Nick said, mouth full, pastry falling from his lips. "It's about what you do next. We get to choose how we react to situations, remember."

Sentinel Group in talks to acquire Pure radio network for £120M

The Sentinel Group, owner of this newspaper, is in advanced negotiations to buy the Pure network of radio stations.

Pure Group owns a network of 36 broadcast licences across mainland U.K., including both the music format PureFM and local talkback stations TalkUK, and the flagship TalkLondon station. The business has an estimated value of £120 million but has suffered from falling listenership and a lack of investment.

As a listed company, Pure Group was required to reveal the intended takeover to the market yesterday under the Financial Conduct Authority's Disclosure Guidance and Transparency Rules.

If the Sentinel Group's acquisition is successful, it would take the Pure Group into private ownership for the first time since 1983. The Sentinel Group has been owned by the Cardle and Boche Families Trust since 1927.

Chapter Twenty-Eight

Denzil drained the last of his Lucozade, screwed the cap back onto the bottle, and flung it into the bin by his desk. Nothing but net. It was only Monday morning, but there were about five other bottles in there. Denzil consumed so much sugar that when he opened his mouth, I could hear his teeth screaming to be released.

"Early ratings are in, you smashed it," Denzil said, leaning back in his chair with his hands behind his head, showing the full width of his back and the sheer bulk of his biceps. That the fabric of his Oxford shirt hadn't burst open at every seam defied the laws of physics. Whoever made it had to be a Time Lord, because that shirt was definitely bigger on the inside.

"Thank you," Nick and I said in unison.

"How did you go with Cole? Have you fixed it?"

I stumbled over my reply. "There's been some defrosting."

"Defrosting?" Nick said. "If things defrosted any faster, the pair of them would be surrounded by a gaggle of concerned climate scientists."

I glared at Nick.

"Good," Denzil said, "because the Cardiff interview on Thursday *cannot* be a repeat of Glasgow. We clear, my brothers?"

We nodded.

"We've got the board and the big swinging dicks from *The Sentinel* landing on us this Friday to talk about the takeover. Now that the board has definitely decided to sell us, the last thing I need is grief because Toby's picked a fight with the guy whose cheque is the only thing keeping us on air. Capisce?"

"*The Sentinel* ain't going to shut us down, are they, Denz?" I asked, suddenly worried I'd set in train our own destruction.

"No idea. I'll know more on Friday. But, one, they're a media company, and, two, they're British—which is about as good as we can hope for. Speaking straight, I think they're mostly interested in TalkUK, so they might even leave us alone to get on with it. But I wouldn't swear on a souvenir pair of Cardi B's knickers that that's what'll happen."

"I'm not sure Cardi B wear—"

Nick cut me off. "If they wanted to spend some money, I wouldn't complain. This place is falling apart."

"It's not that bad." Denzil looked affronted.

"Every time I flush the disabled toilet, I get an electric shock."

"That's to stop you doing coke off the toilet seat," I said.

"Can we stay on track, please?" Denzil looked frustrated. "Between us, since the takeover hit the news, other potential buyers have been sniffing around. And believe me, they're not the sorts of motherfuckers we want buying the network. We can't give *The Sentinel* any excuse to think we're a bad investment. I can do without any hint of scandal. This thing needs to be a hit. We need the good publicity, the credibility, the cultural clout, and Cole's million quid to grease the wheels of this deal."

"So, I need to cosy up to my ex, or we're still all out on our arses?" I summarised. "No pressure, then."

"How are you holding up, Tobes?" Denzil asked. "It must be mad weird."

"I'm not gonna lie to you, it's been an emotional week."

"Bringing back a lot of old feelings, I bet."

"Nothing I can't handle."

"Toby's absolutely fine," Nick said. "No meltdowns at all. We've started calling him the Iron Homosexual."

I slapped him on the arm. "Quit it."

Denzil looked at us suspiciously. "Is there something you aren't telling me?"

"Only that I will not fail in my mission," I said. "Nothing will pierce my resolve."

"It's not your resolve he'll be piercing," Nick said.

I slapped his arm again. "I'll slash your tyres in a minute."

"Any hope of..." Denzil waggled his finger in the air, hopefully.

"I'm not getting back together with my ex so you can sell a radio station."

"Fair enough, bruv." Denzil spun around, plucked a bottle of Lucozade out of his bar fridge, cracked the lid, and took a swig. "But do you think you could see your way clear to maybe being photographed together, at least?"

"There'll be publicity shots from the interview," I said, blood pressure rising.

"Yeah, but I mean, like, if you *happened* to get photographed going into a restaurant together or something..." Denzil waved a hand around casually. "Nothing untoward. Maybe a hug? Within range of the paparazzi."

"I'm not doing it, Denz."

"No, of course not. But, if you *did*, for example, happen to get photographed walking down the street with Cole's arm around your shoulder. I'm just saying, I would not be upset about it. So we're clear."

"Are you having a laugh?"

"I'm saying we'd have your back, that's all. It would be OK with us. With Pure. And with the board. During this difficult time."

Denzil smiled.

"Are you ordering me to get photographed with Cole Kennedy?"

"Of course not." Denzil raised his hands. "I'm certainly not suggesting that you fake date a pop star to save the network. I'm saying if you *happened* to start dating a pop star, or if the public somehow got the impression you were, it wouldn't hurt our figures. The network would support you, and we'd find a way to deal with all the amazing publicity."

Nick laughed. I was speechless. Denzil unscrewed the cap of his Lucozade and took a swig, all without dropping eye contact. As he screwed the lid back on, he popped one pec muscle, then the other, then both pecs back and forth in quick succession. The Lucozade people were missing a trick not using him in their advertising.

I stood and stabbed my finger into his desk. "It's too much, Denz. I'm not doing it. Interviewing Cole in a professional setting is one thing. But I would never put myself in a situation where his fans, or the press, might think for even a millisecond that there's anything personal going on between Cole and me."

Denzil leaned back in his chair.

"Because that is the fastest way I know to ruin every single part of my life," I said. "And I might love this station, but I won't destroy my life to save it."

"Tobes, I hear you. I'm not asking you to do anything you're uncomfortable with."

"Good."

"But if you *do* do something you're uncomfortable with, just make sure it's on camera."

I roared in frustration, turned on my heels, and stormed out of the building.

Chapter Twenty-Nine

The next day, I was in my happy place, Chloe's Hair and Beauty in the Colchester high street, making the most of my time off in lieu. Mum had given me a trim, and I was waiting for Aunty Cheryl to give me one of her Lad's Deluxe Manicures. I hadn't heard from Cole since that kiss. Not a phone call, not a text.

"Wonderwall" came on the radio.

"Tune!" Aunty Cheryl called out across the salon. Someone pumped up the volume, and everyone started to sing the opening lyrics.

"Did I ever tell you about the time I shagged one of the Gallaghers backstage after an Oasis concert?" Aunty Cheryl said.

"Yes," everyone said. We'd all heard the story a hundred times before—all of us except a woman who was getting her hair foiled.

"You never! Which one was it, babes?"

"Well, I thought it was Noel, because he was quite sweet and cerebral in the way he fished around in my knickers," Aunty Cheryl said. "But halfway through he opened a fridge and cracked a can of Carlsberg, and I thought, no, this is Liam."

The woman was absolutely living for the gossip. "So, which one was it?"

"Neither!" the whole salon said, in chorus.

"Turned out he was a crafty drunk who'd managed to get his hands on a backstage pass. But, in my defence, he did have a northern accent and a mod cut."

My phone rang, and I almost jumped out of my skin. Who calls people? Withheld numbers, that's who calls people. I thought about letting it go to voicemail, but when you work in the media, you never know when a withheld number might be a life-changing opportunity. The call from *Celebrity Dorm Room* had come exactly like this. I pressed the green button.

"I can't stop thinking about that kiss."

My heart stopped. "Cole?"

"Not sure I like the question mark on the end of that. Who else have you been kissing?"

I looked around the salon, making sure no one had heard me say his name, and ducked behind the curtain into the back room.

"Why are you calling me?"

"I just told you. Listen, it's about to get quite noisy here. Can you stay on the phone with me? I might not be able to hear you, but please, keep talking."

"What are you on about?" I heard a heavy door open, then there were screams and shouting coming down the phone line, like Cole was calling from inside one of his own concerts.

"I'm not sure if you can hear me," he said. "I've been on breakfast TV, and it seems while I was on air, half of New York made its way down to the studio."

Apparently, Sunny's technique for dealing with an unwanted media scrum was well known. Was that the real reason for the call? The excitement at hearing his voice left me. In the background, I could hear Mitch asking the photographers to clear a path.

"So, you thought you'd call the ex you recently assaulted in a lift?"

Cole laughed. "Yeah. First person I thought of. Truthfully, you're the only thing I've thought about in days."

Aunty Cheryl screeched across the salon that she was ready for me. I popped my head through the curtains and waved that I was on the phone. She huffed.

"They've got mopeds," Cole said. "Damn, with the traffic in this city, they're going to be impossible to shake."

"Fall over," I said. "But make it sexy. And laugh at your clumsiness."

"What?"

I explained the second part of Sunny's technique: Give them a good photo, and they'll leave you alone. Five seconds later, I heard a thud, followed by another thud, followed by a thousand shutters clicking, followed by Cole's deep throaty laugh. Then the call dropped out.

It's His Royal Heinie!

He might be British rock royalty, but the Prince of Pop Cole Kennedy has come crashing down to earth!

The former Go Tos singer was knocked flat on his keister in the middle of Fifth Avenue Tuesday after walking smack-dab into a New York City lamppost.

Kennedy (26) had appeared on "Sunshine Daily with Matt and Miley" and was apparently so engrossed in a phone call as he left the NYBC studios he didn't see the 20-foot-tall streetlamp. The force of his shoulder slamming into the pole seems to have spun Kennedy around and knocked him off balance. Gravity did the rest.

"You know we put these on the other side of the street in England," Kennedy quipped as his security detail helped him to his feet.

"I bet that's going to bruise," he added, lifting up his shirt and pulling down the waistband of his jeans to inspect the damage.

While our photographers saw no sign of that bruise yet, Kennedy's cell phone was a goner. We hope he carries travel insurance!

Chapter Thirty

Nick and I were holed up in the broadcast van in the car park out the back of the Cardiff International Arena, doing our live show. Outside, hundreds of *Pop Review* fans and Kenneddicts milled about. So did the paparazzi. My hands shook like that glass of water in *Jurassic Park*. I'd thought about nothing but Cole and that bloody kiss for days.

"Showtime," Nick said.

A string of black SUVs rolled up into the arena car park. My T-Rex had arrived. The fans went wild. As the cars stopped, photographers shouldered and elbowed each other to get the best shot. The crowd mobbed Cole's vehicle. Mitch's spectacular bulk emerged from the car, pushing the fans and photographers back. I could hear the screams, even through my headphones and the van's soundproofing. I couldn't see Cole—just the swirling, chanting crowd, and a placard that read: "I'm not a nurse but I'll check that bruise for you!" As the mob lurched and surged, the sign spun around. On the other side, it said: "I'm marriage material!" I stared at it. The words seemed to drown out all the noise, and I felt myself get smaller, folding in on myself, shrinking.

"You OK, pal?" Nick's voice in my headphones shook me out of my stupor.

"Fine," I lied. I checked the clock—a DJ's reflex.

Then suddenly Cole's tall, confident figure—dressed all in black, swoopy hair flicked back—leapt over the barrier and strode across the car park towards the broadcast van with a wide smile across his face. The fans screamed. Cameras clicked and flashed, sparkling like stars. I couldn't take my eyes off him. In the mellow early-evening sunlight, Cole was absolutely stunning. But then, Cole would be stunning in no light at all. You could blindfold someone, stick them in the back of a wardrobe in a house with no electricity in the middle of the woods in the middle of the night, and their head would still turn if Cole Kennedy walked past. Twenty seconds later, he was standing in the doorway of my studio, eyes twinkling. His fingertips held the door frame above his head, and the angle lifted his shirt to expose a sliver of honeyed flesh above his beltline. A vein divided the taut skin of his obliques and plunged down into his jeans.

"Hey," he said through plump lips that, last time I'd seen him, had been pressed against mine. "Something smells incredible in here, is that you?" He swooped into the room, reached across to rest a hand on my shoulder, and pulled his face close to mine. I recoiled.

"Cameras!" I said. Cole stopped, nodded, and let his hand drop. His chestnut eyes, glinting with flecks of amber, betrayed disappointment.

"Not even a peck on the cheek?"

I shook my head. "Not even."

"Brutal."

Cole sat in the guest chair to the side of the desk. This allowed him to stretch his right leg down the gap between my desk and the wall—blocking my exit from the doughnut of my desk. I'd set up everything expecting him to sit opposite me, as he had before. I swung the microphone around and asked him to speak into it so I could check the audio level.

"I still can't stop thinking about that kiss, about how good it was to taste you again," Cole said.

My heart spluttered and misfired like a clapped-out motorcycle. "OK, level's fine. Thank you."

"You..." Cole paused. "Kissed me back, Toby. Right up until you slapped me, you kissed me back. And it gave me so much hope."

"I did not!" I glanced through the glass at Nick and Fiona, who were pretending they weren't listening in. Every microphone is a live microphone, if your producer knows what they're doing—and Nick absolutely knew what he was doing. Cole brushed his foot playfully against my outer thigh, and I swivelled my chair out of his reach, scanning the windows to make sure no photographers were close enough to see what was happening.

"Quit it!"

Cole withdrew his foot, and as the relief washed over me, so did a feeling of something else: regret. I *wanted* his foot there. I wanted to feel Cole's body against mine. I wanted his playful touch. I wanted to feel connected to him like that again, the way we used to be. I wanted to launch myself over the desk and wrap my arms around him and feel his body underneath mine and his hot breath in my mouth. I wanted Cole Kennedy. And that terrified me. I was clenched like clenching was the only thing holding in my internal organs.

"Thirty seconds," Nick said through the studio speaker, rousing me from my thoughts. I slipped my headphones back on. Cole sat up straight, and I did the same. Then he leaned forward and gently slid the can back off my right ear, as tenderly as a lover tucking in a lock of stray hair. The intimacy of it took my breath away.

"I forgot to say thank you," he said.

"What for?"

Twenty seconds on the clock.

"Your advice for dealing with the paps was... awesome."

"I saw the photos. You really committed to the bit."

"Oh no, that wasn't acting. I absolutely slammed into that lamp post. I was too busy talking to a cute boy on the phone and wasn't looking where I was going."

I blushed with the intensity of a steam burn. Why was it so hot in here? Was my skin falling away in sheets?

Ten seconds.

"And the fall was real," Cole went on. "The damage to my phone was *very* real. But getting my arse out... That wasn't for the cameras. Not really. Although it made great press. No, that was all for you." He winked and unleashed that trademark sexy smirk. "Because... it's *all* yours, Toby. Whenever you want it."

On the other side of the glass, Nick's jaw was on the floor. Fiona's eyes were as wide as the eyes of an owl that had done a line of cocaine shortly before receiving a nasty surprise.

Zero seconds.

Silence.

Nick wound his finger in the air frantically, pleading with me to start talking, but I couldn't speak.

"Toby!" Nick's voice barked in my cans. The fog lifted. *Tap.* Our microphones were live.

"Cole Kennedy, welcome to *Pop Review*!"

The list of questions Nick and I had prepared for the interview were up on the screen, and for the first few minutes, I worked my way through them. As we chatted, Cole's foot found its way around the desk and pressed against mine. With every new question, he pressed a little closer to me—first his foot, then his ankle, then our calves pressed against each other. Despite this—or because of it, I don't know—the conversation was flowing. We were deep into a discussion about Cole's music, and soon the list of official questions had been abandoned and Cole and I were doing the exact thing that had brought us together in the first place: talking about music.

"This is essentially a soft rock album," I said. "Why the orchestra?"

Cole's eyes lit up. "Don't you love the richness? The strings make the music soar." Cole was in his element. Journalists never asked him this stuff, yet this was his genius. "I was listening to *Revolver*, the Beatles album, and I had this epiphany..."

Nick's voice came through my cans. We had two minutes left with Cole. I gave him a thumbs up. Nick's voice came again. "Go back to the list of questions, you daft bawbag."

I waved him off. I was letting Cole be Cole. The heat of Cole's calf muscle was electric against my leg.

"There's no doubt the orchestra elevates the sound—" I said.

"Right? Imagine 'Eleanor Rigby' without the strings. Make it a straight pop song, or rock song, and it's got nowhere near the drama or the urgency—"

"But 'Eleanor Rigby' has no traditional rock instrumentation at all. That's not the approach you took for 'The Flame.' You mixed the two..."

Nick was waving frantically on the other side of the studio glass, pointing at the screen.

Cole continued. "No, that's right, the cello, double bass, viola, and violin provide the dramatic sweep you might expect from keys, but in 'Reborn'..."

Nick was in my ears again. "For fucksake. Ask him why he called the album *The Flame!*"

I waved Nick away. Cole was effusive, gesturing wildly. The passion was dripping from him, and I wasn't going to interrupt. This was what the fans wanted. This was *Pop Review* taking pop seriously. But, more than anything, there was an intensity in Cole's eyes that I recognised from the sixteen-year-old boy I had loved—and it filled my soul to the brim, the way a gospel choir fills a church until the roof lifts. All the while, Cole's leg was against mine, the heat of him travelling up my body. Occasionally, his hand would reach across and rest on my knee or cup the underside of my thigh, and I never wanted it to end.

"The theme of the album is the idea of being reborn," Cole said.

"I wanted to give the music a feeling of taking off, you know? This sense of a grand arrival, or of your spirit being lifted by angels..."

Nick was pointing doggedly at my computer screen. He mouthed the words: "Ask him, you melt."

Again, I ignored him. I turned to look out the window at the hundreds of fans watching our interview. *Tap.* I faded up the outside mic. "What do we think, guys, does the album feel like being lifted by angels?" I gestured for them to make some noise, and they roared. Cole waved at the crowd and clapped his hands together in a gesture of prayer and gratitude. He tapped his chest over his heart and blew the Kenneddicts a kiss. They went wild. I slowly faded the exterior mic back down. One minute left. Nick's eyes were pleading. I looked down at the screen. Oh, yeah, that question. Sure, why not?

"If being reborn is the theme of the album," I said, "why did you call the album and the tour *The Flame*? Isn't 'Reborn' the perfect name?"

Nick looked to the heavens and threw his hands up into the air.

Cole's hand tightened on my thigh. That famous smirk lit his face, and his eyes sparked with mischief. I knew that spark. It was the spark he got when he teased me.

"Why do you think, Tobias?"

"Um..." I was stumped. "Has it got something to do with fire being cleansing? Perhaps it still represents a fresh start but with less, um, placenta?"

Cole laughed. "Tobias, have you even listened to the song?"

"Of course I have."

"What's it about?"

"It's a break-up song..."

Nick was in my ear. "Twenty seconds. Wrap it up."

"Tell you what," Cole said. "You go away and listen to the lyrics. I think if you listen a little more closely, it'll all become clear."

Nick's finger was giving me the wind-up. He was shaking his head, like he was disappointed in me. I wrapped up the interview.

Outside, the Kenneddicts cheered, and I fed the audio through before hitting the button to fire off "Reborn." *Tap.* Our microphones were off. The interview was over. Cole sat there, leaning towards me. His shirt billowed open, and I could see the neatly clipped hair of his chest and the tattoos he'd acquired in the years since we'd been together. A gold pendant swung hypnotically from a chain around his neck.

"Did I muck that up?" I asked, confused.

Cole reached a hand over and grabbed mine. "That was the best interview I've done in years."

"So, why do I feel like I've failed a test?"

"You didn't fail anything," Cole said. His finger brushed along the seam of my jeans. "Keep pulling at that thread, Toby."

Fiona's head popped through the door. "We gotta scoot."

Cole let me go and stood up. I felt his absence, the warmth of his body leaving my personal space. I wanted to rush towards it, cling to it, follow it.

"You're still coming to the show tonight, right?" he asked, tucking his hands into the back pockets of his jeans.

"Of course."

"Come backstage afterwards?"

I couldn't say yes quickly enough. The chance to spend more time alone with Cole was suddenly the thing I wanted most in the whole world. Fiona handed me a backstage pass, then grabbed my neck and pulled me down to her for what I thought was going to be a peck on the cheek.

"Much better," she whispered in my ear. "Thank you."

As she turned and left, Cole pointed a finger back and forth between his sister and me.

"No kiss for me, though, right?"

"Absolutely not," I said. There were at least two dozen photographers outside with their lenses trained on us.

"See you tonight."

"Of course," I said, knowing every second until I could get him alone was going to be agony.

"Good. I've got a surprise for you."

"Last time you said that, you took me to an oncology department."

And with that, Cole turned and disappeared from the studio and into a swarm of security guards.

My phone pinged.

Denzil: *Much better bruv.*

Chapter Thirty-One

After the show, Fiona took me down to Cole's dressing room to wait while he did a meet-and-greet with his fans. Nick had bailed on me to go back to the hotel to sext with Dav. At least that's what he told me. I suspected he wanted to play *Mario Kart* without Princess Peach annoying him the whole time. The room was drab and soulless, with dirty white walls and sticks of charity shop furniture. I sat on the couch for half an hour, scrolling my phone. When I got bored with that, I decided to snoop. With its being a dressing room, I'd expected racks of costumes, bottles of hairspray, and tubs of greasepaint, but Cole's "people" must have already cleared all that away—the show was on the road again in the morning, headed to Birmingham for two more gigs. All that remained, sitting on the table in front of the mirror, was a brown leather overnight bag with three little initials, *C.J.K.*, in gilt. I ran my fingers over the stitching and the embossed lettering. Quality. I leaned closer and breathed in the leather. The latch was undone, and the bag was unlocked. Something glittered, catching my eye. Carefully, I slid my hand in and fished it out. A small black bottle with a gold cap. *Oajan*, the script across the front read, then the words *Parfums de Marly*. I sprayed it into the air and let the scent wash over me. *This*. This was the smell of Cole Kennedy. This was where that note of cinnamon that followed him everywhere came from. And citrus. Honey. Vanilla. This was why Cole Kennedy smelt like a pastry shop. I felt my pants tighten as my body responded to the thought of Cole, the smell of him. I slipped the bottle back into the bag, and my fingers brushed a piece of soft fabric. It was the shirt Cole had been wearing earlier. Gently, I plucked it from the bag and buried my face in it—sucking in the smell. I was rigid now. I adjusted myself into a more comfortable position. As I slipped the shirt back into the bag, I spotted Cole's underpants, neatly folded, down the end of the bag. My cock pulsed, urgently. I pulled the underpants out of the bag, held them up in front of the light, and stuck my other hand inside my jeans to double-check I hadn't spectacularly soiled my own pants. *Click*. The door opened. I spun around, quick as lightning, whipping my hands behind my back. As I waited for Cole to emerge through the door—a split second that felt like an eternity—I wiped my fingers on the only thing I had to hand, Cole's underpants.

"Toby Lyngstad, as I live and breathe!" It wasn't Cole. It was the wrong Go To altogether. Behind my back, I rolled the underpants up and dropped them into Cole's bag.

"Chase!" I said. "What are you doing here?"

The muscular frame of my former *Make Me a Pop Star* roommate moved across the room towards me like he was breaking free of a rugby scrum with the ball. Chase's hand was outstretched. I shook it without even thinking. My hand was more, er, *moist,* than I'd have liked it to be. I saw it register on Chase's face. When the handshake was over, Chase tucked his hands into his armpits and discreetly wiped the moisture on his shirt.

Five minutes later, we had raided the non-alcoholic minibar and were sitting on the couch, fast running out of pleasantries.

"It's good to see you, boyo," Chase said for the tenth time. Cole aside, I hadn't seen any of the Go Tos since *Pop Star*. Chase had always been lovely, but I didn't have much to say to him. And his presence bothered me, because I'd thought Cole was mine alone for the evening.

"Are the others here?" I asked, worried Taylor, Joey, and Yoshi might be about to waltz through the door to make my nightmare complete.

"Fear not," Chase said. "Joey is in the States somewhere, probably shouting at Republicans online and telling people he's working class because he mines Bitcoin. Yoshi will be cross-legged in a forest somewhere, meditating on the meaning of life and only eating things that fall from the tree directly in front of him. And Taylor is in South America somewhere, spreading super gonorrhoea and life lessons in disappointment to unsuspecting women."

Chase sucked on his bottle of water. Of all the Go Tos, he was the most normal. Chase had met a fan in Australia, married her in secret in Thailand three weeks later, and for the past five years, had been dragging his wife and an ever-growing brood of small children around on tour.

"So, are you and Cole back together, then?" Chase asked. The bluntness of the question winded me.

"No," I said—because we weren't.

"He used to mope around after you something terrible," Chase said.

"That's ancient history."

Chase shook his head. "Cole was such a misery after you got kicked off the show. Felicity nearly booted him out of the band."

"What?" This was new information.

"It was only after the thing with the text messages that he finally settled down. But he was miserable for ages. We all were. Can you imagine what it's like, waking up every morning with Felicity Quant's fingers wrapped around your balls?"

I shuddered.

"Not literally, you understand," Chase added. "Metaphorically.

Do you know, I didn't see my parents for six whole months after *Pop Star*? They had no idea where I was until they'd see on the TV that I'd been on breakfast television in California or done a gig in Zagreb or appeared at a shopping mall in Tokyo. I've had ten years of this shit. We're not people to her, we're a commodity. A product. I don't decide when I wake up, let alone what city I'm going to wake up in. I don't get to decide what clothes I'm wearing. I don't even get to decide where I stand in a line-up. Everything is planned. No wonder the boys are all a bit fucked in the head. I'm a twenty-eight-year-old man, Toby, whose phone is currently turned off because when Felicity sees the posts on social media of me at Cole's gig, she's going to lose her shit at me. You had a lucky escape, boyo."

I thought of all the crap I'd dealt with over the past decade and wasn't so sure.

"And I got lucky, too, of course," Chase said. "I met Hannah. She keeps me on the straight and narrow. But the only person Cole had on tour was Jasper, and that was always going to be a disaster."

"Jasper?" I asked. "Is that the ex?"

Chase looked surprised. "You know about Jasper?"

I shook my head. "Not much. I know there was an ex. And I know when Cole mentioned him, he sounded sort of broken."

Chase nodded slowly, his bright blue eyes meeting mine. "Jasper was a costume designer for the band and one of Felicity's flunkies. He was stuck to her side for years, feeding off her like a tick. I don't know if she got bored with him and wanted to pass her parasite onto a new host, or whether it was the need to keep Cole in the closet, or to try to cheer him up because he was always so miserable, or because Jasper was a gay she could trust to be discreet and because he was *there*, but Felicity threw them into the path of each other."

"Like a set-up?" I asked.

"More like Jasper was on a pre-approved list of potential boyfriends. Unfortunately, Jasper was also both a massive sociopath and the Totally Records in-house drug dealer, so that ended the way it was always going to end. Cole didn't stand a chance—"

The door flung open, and I looked up, expecting to see Cole, but instead, a camera crew burst into the dressing room. My heart plummeted, carried away in an avalanche of fear to the pit of my stomach. This was a trap.

"We'll set up over here," a woman with a clipboard and a pen stuck in her long curly hair said. "Cole will come in this way, so set camera one up to capture his entrance." She looked around the room, unimpressed. "Christ, it's drab in here. Kirsty, can you grab some set dressing and make this space look more intimate, more rock star, but also low-key homely?" The woman I took to be Kirsty shot back out the door. "Where's that bloody genealogist got to? Someone find her..." As more instructions were barked, I felt the quickening beat of my pulse through my body. My fight or flight response was wound so tight my whole body risked spontaneously combusting into a misty puff of blood. The woman looked at me for the first time, and as our eyes connected, I saw the look of recognition on her face. My chest tightened, the air left my lungs, and I felt an overwhelming wave of nausea. She was *not* going to get me on film.

"Camera two!" she shouted, eyes never leaving me. "Where's Phil? I need camera two, *now*."

With that, I stood and ran for the door.

"Camera two!" I heard the woman shout as I rounded the door frame. I looked back, catching Chase's piercing blue eyes and the look of concern on his face, before I bolted up the corridor, out of the arena, and into the street.

Chapter Thirty-Two

At quarter past ten the next morning I was sitting in the driver's seat of the van—the GPS set, my hands on the steering wheel, desperate to hit the road. Where was Nick? Not only did we need to make tracks, I was in urgent need of a debrief about the night before. I honked the horn. My phone pinged.

Nick: *Sorry, he called shotgun.*

The passenger door opened, and Cole Kennedy jumped in, wearing his *Pop Review* baseball cap. He held up a bag of sweets.

"I come bearing the Haribos of apology." He pushed the peak of his cap back so I could see his eyes. Nick, I guessed, was in the jet again. "I'm sorry about last night. I had no idea that was going to happen."

"Really?" I was gripping the steering wheel as intensely as Aunty Cheryl gripped the off-duty Magic Mike dancer she found in the bar on our Royal Caribbean cruise last winter. "So that little stunt wasn't the 'surprise' you promised me?"

"No!" Cole held up his hands in surrender. "Chase was the surprise. I thought you'd like to see him. You two always got on. I practically had to sneak him in. Felicity has been reading him the Riot Act all morning, apparently."

"You know the press can *never* see us together!" I said, feeling the heat rise in my face. Dammit, I was going to cry. I fought it. "Why would you let an entire TV crew anywhere near your dressing room, when you knew I was in there? It ain't right."

"They weren't the press," Cole said. "They're the WebFlix crew that's following me around. They're making my documentary. I get final say on the edit. Even if they film you, it wouldn't go out unless I gave approval."

It wasn't enough. Hot tears welled, and I turned to look straight out the windscreen so Cole couldn't see them.

"Did you, or Fiona, or anyone on your team, tell them to film me?"

"Absolutely not," Cole said.

"Because they seemed pretty determined to film me."

"I think when they saw you in my dressing room, they got a bit overexcited. Journalistic instinct, or whatever. I'm sorry. I know that must have been triggering for you. But I promise, I didn't know they were going to be there. They were there to film me, not you."

"The stupid thing is," I said, "I thought we were going to hang out last night, the two of us. And all along you'd planned to film your ego project and spend time with your mate."

"Toby, please look at me." I felt the warmth of Cole's finger against my chin, gently pulling me to face him. My eyes met his. "Toby, they wanted to film me last night because they've found my birth mum."

My anger evaporated. "What?"

"The producers have been looking for my birth family, and they've found my mum. She's alive. She's living in New Zealand. I'm going to go out there next month to meet her. I'd go sooner but... schedules."

"Cole, that's amazing." I slid my hands into his. There were tears in Cole's eyes now too.

"The crew had just found out and wanted to film my reaction when Fiona told me. They had no idea you were in my dressing room."

"I ain't bothered about that now," I said. "Tell me about your mum. What do you know about her?"

"No, come on. We need to scoot, I'll tell you on the drive. But… can I have a hug first?"

I shuffled across the bench seat and put my arms around him. I felt like an absolute melt. Cole's arms slid around my body and held me tight, his cheeks damp against mine. He smelt of cinnamon and citrus, and I breathed it in like a drug. What must he be feeling? I wondered. I should have been there for him last night.

"I'm sorry I ran off. I thought you'd stitched me up."

"No, I'm sorry you were alone in my dressing room for so long. I hope you weren't too bored before Chase arrived." He looked over at me with an eyebrow cocked.

Oh God. Please. No…

"Not at all," I said, cautiously. "Whyyyy do you ask?"

"Left my pants in a right old state."

I shrieked and tried to pull away, but Cole's arms gripped me tighter, and his hand wove up into my hair and held my head firm against his. Cole's breath was hot against my ear. "I loved it. I haven't taken them off since I found them."

I shrieked again. "You're winding me up?"

Cole's shoulders started to shake, and a laugh rumbled up from his belly. "Maybe. Maybe not. If you behave, you'll find out. Come on, start the van. We've got places to be."

* * *

As we drove up the M4 towards the bridge over the River Severn, which would take us up to Birmingham, Cole told me how the WebFlix producers had followed a paper trail through local councils, fostering agencies, social services, and emigration records to track down his birth parents. His birth mum's name was Marie Everest. She came from Ipswich.

"She was seventeen when she fell pregnant," Cole said. "Her parents wouldn't let her keep me."

"Were they religious?"

"I don't know. I think it might also have been about my dad."

Cole scratched at the thick black hair on his forearms.

"You mean his skin colour?" I asked.

"The producers said I'd have to ask Marie for the details when we met in person. But they did tell me that he was Turkish. He was also seventeen, and they met at the local kebab shop where he worked."

"So, you're Turkish?"

"According to the DNA test I did, I'm Turkish, Iranian, Syrian, Georgian, you name it."

"Your birth dad, do they know what happened to him?"

Cole went quiet. "I don't have all the details. They've confirmed he died, though. A motorcycle accident. Before I was born. I don't even know if he knew he was going to be a dad. I wondered if that might be why Marie decided to give me up."

I reached over a hand, and Cole grabbed it, squeezing it.

"How do you feel about it all?"

Cole shrugged. "It is what it is. I can't change the fact he's dead or that my mother put me up for adoption. I had a brilliant childhood. I love my parents. There's no space for regret, you know?"

"But you must be feeling something."

"I am, obviously," he said. "But my therapist, Summer, says we can't change the past, so have to learn to sit with the discomfort the past has left us. If we let it weigh us down, it'll only make us unhappy in the moment we're in. And every moment is a new moment. So, while you should acknowledge the discomfort, you have to live in the moment. That's the only thing that's real. The past, the future, they're not real. All we have is this moment."

I'd never thought of the world like that before. All the countless hours I'd wasted worrying over everything that had gone down, or what the future might hold. If someone had taught me years ago to see the world like this, I might not have spent so much of my life doing my own head in. That said, I was willing to bet living in the moment was harder than it sounded.

"I'm sorry I wasn't there for you last night," I said, glancing across at Cole.

"It's OK," he said. "Last night is also in the past. Fi was there. And Chase. I was well looked after."

"All the same, I'm sorry."

We drove across the Prince of Wales Bridge, and a comfortable silence fell between us. The sun was shining, the sky was blue, the wide silver ribbon of the River Severn shimmered to the north and to the south of us. Behind us, a string of black SUVs shadowed us. As we came off the bridge, a sign said it was forty-seven miles to Stonehenge. Cole practically bounced out of his seat.

"Oh my God, we have got to go to Stonehenge."

I glanced over at him. "It's a hundred miles out of our way."

"Live in the moment, Toby! Come on!"

"You're onstage in nine hours."

"That's plenty of time."

"And I'm on air in five. In *this* van. I can't afford to miss a show, because someone put a condition in my contract that says if I miss a show, my network doesn't get our million quid."

"That was Fiona," Cole said. "It's a gorgeous day. Come on. I want to feel the sun on my face and the grass under my feet."

But I loyally followed the GPS, taking the turn-off for the M5 up to Birmingham. Cole pulled his cap down over his face, folded his arms, and put his bare feet up on the dashboard.

"That's sad, Tobias."

"Oh, I'm back to Tobias, I see."

"Today would have been the perfect day to see an ancient historic monument."

"What happened to sitting with the discomfort?" I asked. "How does sulking like a five-year-old fit in with that?"

"I didn't say I was perfect. It takes practice."

"So, practise."

"Can't we call in for a little bit?"

"Imagine the chaos it would cause if Cole Kennedy rocked up unannounced at Stonehenge."

"We could go in disguise!"

"Did you bring a spare Druid costume, babes? Only mine's being dry-cleaned."

"Fine," Cole said, kicking his legs down and opening the packet of Haribo. "But I haven't given up on feeling the grass under my feet today. It's a gorgeous day. I spend way too much time surrounded by air-conditioned concrete. I'm a farm boy. I need grass and dirt and..."

"Cow poo?"

"Cow poo is a remarkably underappreciated commodity."

Five minutes later Cole was plugging in his phone to share a playlist of obscure Estonian pop he thought I would like when he started tapping wildly at the GPS screen.

"Hetty Pegler's Tump!" he said.

"Are you having a stroke?"

"Hetty Pegler's Tump," Cole repeated, frantically pointing at the screen. "It's a historic ancient monument. And we're driving right past. Can we go? Just for half an hour. Please? Let's sit in the long grass and enjoy the sun."

I looked at the GPS. Sure enough, there were the words *Hetty Pegler's Tump* right underneath the words *Uley Long Barrow*. A barrow is an ancient burial ground. I knew that because there were heaps of them around Colchester. We'd gone to one called Lexden Tumulus when we were doing the Romans in school, but I didn't remember too much about it. All I could remember was we had this lush tour guide who wore a centurion uniform. He had thighs like the trunks of horse chestnut trees, and when he bent over to fix his sandal, I copped an eyeful of both of his chestnuts and the horse they rode in on. Come to think of it, I'm not sure he should have been working with children. Anyway, I'd never heard of Uley Long Barrow, so I didn't think it was famous. If it was anything like the barrows at home, there'd probably be no one there. If Cole wanted grass under his feet, Hetty Pegler's Tump seemed like a safe, Kenneddict-free option.

"Sure," I said.

"Get in!" Cole pumped his fist and lobbed a Haribo into his gob.

It was almost midday, and the summer sun was high in the sky. Cole Kennedy and I lay flat on our backs in the tall grass with our shoes off. Above us, a vivid blue expanse and dots of fluffy white clouds. Beneath us, the skeletons of a bunch of people who, according to the interpretive sign, died more than five thousand years ago. There was absolutely no one around—just us, some deceased ancestors, and four of Cole's Jack Reacher–fied security detail. It was almost romantic.

"You know those texts?" I asked.

"*Those* texts?"

"The one where you said you felt like you'd grown up in the wrong country, the wrong culture, and the wrong religion."

Cole picked a stalk of grass and rolled it between his fingers. "Of course."

"So, now, knowing you've got Turkish heritage, I was wondering if you finally felt like you belonged somewhere? Like, has it helped?"

"It certainly explains my fetish for watching big hairy guys wrestling in olive oil."

I laughed. "You don't have to be Turkish to enjoy that. That's universal."

"Oh. That's disappointing," Cole said. "I thought I was connecting with my culture."

"Besides, I thought you liked your boys fat and synthetically orange."

"Someone once told me the correct term was cherubic." Cole rolled onto his side, facing me, and propped his head up on his hand. "I like that too. But then, I think we always have a thing for guys who remind us of our first love. Subconsciously, at least."

"I remind you of your first love?" I frowned, pretending to be confused.

Cole smiled and flicked me with his stalk of grass. I pushed it away, playfully, hamming it up a bit because, well, I was lying in a wildflower meadow with the most beautiful man in the world and he was flirting with me like we were sixteen again.

"Can I play you a song?" he said.

"You're not getting a guitar out, are you?"

"Oh God, no! I'd never serenade anyone."

"Thank goodness for that, babes. Because, to be honest with you, people think things like that are romantic, but it makes the person playing the guitar look like a divvie, and it's dead uncomfortable for the person forced to listen to it."

"Noted," Cole said, with a wry smile. "I was planning to play you something from my phone, if that's OK?"

"Sure," I said, still uncertain. Cole scrolled through his phone, then laid it on the grass between us. It started playing "The Flame." When the words kicked in, Cole sang softly along with them, his eyes never leaving mine.

"*You lit a fire inside me that burned like the sun. You lit the way forward. You were the one. How did it burn out? Please, baby, explain why the fire died inside you. And I'm still holding the flame. It burns and it burns and it burns. You turn and I yearn and you burn—me.*"

I lay in the grass, stunned. Nick had been right. I'd never truly listened to the lyrics before. The song finished, and we lay there for a moment, looking at each other. Cole's mahogany eyes searched mine, begging me to say something.

"Did you write that about me?"

"I wrote it *for* you," Cole said. "It's about us."

"But it's a song about unrequited love."

"You know, you're very deep into mansplaining territory at this point."

I rolled onto my side, leaning on my elbow.

"I wrote it one night after watching you on *Celebrity Dorm Room*."

"Not the—"

"The drunken night on the couch?" Cole chortled. "Yeah, that episode."

I cringed. "I'm sorry for anything I said that upset you. I didn't mean to tell your business. I went on that show wanting to reclaim my narrative. I only meant to tell enough to exorcise the 'marriage material' demon."

"I don't think you can exorcise it, Toby," Cole said. "That meme is bigger than either you or me. It belongs to the culture now."

I hadn't thought of it that way, but I supposed he was right.

"Anyway, I didn't mean to tell the whole country about losing our virginity. In my defence, I was terribly drunk."

Cole laughed. "Don't be silly. That conversation gave me hope. I sat up all night, pouring out my heart onto the page the way you'd poured yours out on that couch."

A dragonfly hovered between us for a moment, then zipped away.

"That was five years ago. Why did you only reach out now?"

"Felicity. The band. The rules. I'm sorry."

"The album..." I said, recalling what Nick had said to me. "Everyone reckons it should be called 'Reborn,' but you called it 'The Flame.' That's for me too?"

"You're on your second warning, soldier," Cole said. "Three strikes and I'm going to have to kiss you." His trademark smirk lit up his face, and his eyes sparkled. My heart was pounding so loudly in my chest, the ancient bones in the dirt beneath us would have been within their rights to complain to the council.

"Was... this whole album... for *me*?"

Cole laughed gently. "Not quite," he said, leaning towards me. "You're getting closer, though." He bopped my nose with the soft, bristly end of the grass. My mind raced, putting the pieces together.

"Calling it the Flame Tour, dragging *Pop Review* along, that was all because, what? You've loved me all this time?"

Cole leaned in closer, his lips almost touching mine. His breath was sweet, like berry-flavoured Haribo. His leg hooked over mine, rolling my hip towards his. He was so near now, so inside my personal space, that I could see the thousand ways the sunlight caught the amber in his eyes. He was *so* beautiful.

"That's three strikes. Would you like to collect your prize now, Tobias?" Cole's eyes glimmered with mischief, lust, and hope, and I could resist him no longer.

"Yes, please."

Before I could close my eyes, the heat of Cole's lips found mine. He kissed me tenderly at first—delicately, like he was savouring this thing he had yearned for, like this kiss was a precious gift and he meant to unwrap it slowly. His hand slid around my waist and pulled me towards him, closing the gap between our bodies. A lock of Cole's hair fell against my cheek, tickling it. I flicked it back for him, gently raking my fingers through his thick black hair. The tenderness of the gesture seemed to awaken something in us both, and we kissed deeply, passionately, urgently. I held Cole's jaw in my hand, the bristles of his stubble rough against the soft flesh of my palm. Cole rolled me back onto the grass, letting me feel the weight of him on top of me. Breathlessly, he pulled away, stopping only to look at me, like he was seeing me for the first time, like he was drinking me in. It was how he used to look at me, all those years ago. Cole said more with the hungry flickering of his gaze in that moment than we'd ever managed with words.

He ran his thumb gently across my lips, tenderly cupping my jaw with his fingertips, before weaving them up into the blond tangle of my hair.

"I've wanted to do that for so l—"

A heavy shadow blocked our sunlight, cutting Cole off mid-sentence.

Mitch cleared his throat. "I'm sorry, Mr Kennedy, Miss Kennedy says to tell you playtime is over and you're needed in Birmingham."

Cole sighed. "Oh, all right."

"Estimated time of departure, twelve twenty-three. Two minutes' time," Mitch said. "Travelling in delta formation, as before." Mitch nodded, turned, and walked down the barrow towards the cars.

"You make your security guys call you Mr Kennedy?" I asked.

Cole rolled his eyes. "It's not my rule, it's theirs. Something to do with their union, supposedly. Truthfully, I think they find it funny."

Cole got to his feet, brushed himself off, and reached a hand down to pull me up. We walked back to the van hand in hand.

Chapter Thirty-Three

The air sizzled with anticipation as the opening notes of "Sweet Dreams (Are Made of This)" reverberated around the Arena Birmingham. The crowd screamed. The hairs on the back of my neck would have been standing on end, if I hadn't made certain there weren't any. I'd seen Cole's gig half a dozen times now, but never from the wings of the stage. Nick whacked me on the leg and offered up his beer bottle for me to cheers. High above us, Cole was dressed only in his underpants, his legs straddling a cello. I felt jealous of it, to be honest.

"I can see right up your boyfriend's arse," Nick said, looking skyward.

"He's not my boyfriend," I protested for the hundredth time. Since the moment we'd arrived, Nick had been relentlessly pumping me to explain why Cole and I had been so late getting the van up to Birmingham.

"He's got glutes like two baseballs in a sock," Nick mused, still looking up. "But you probably noticed that while you were banging him in a lay-by on the M5."

"I keep telling you, nothing happ—"

The full orchestration of the opening number filled the auditorium, making it impossible for Nick to hear my response. Suddenly, Cole was right beside us, untangling himself from the rope he'd used to fly down from the rafters. He was stunning, wearing nothing more than tiny black briefs, a microphone pack, and mascara.

"Jesus, he's got the bat tucked in at the front, as well," Nick said. I slapped his shoulder in warning. Cole's eyes found mine. A team of three women bustled around him, fabric flying everywhere, but his eyes never left mine. Ten seconds later, Cole Kennedy was completely dressed and ready to get back out onstage to sing the verse. He had maybe eight seconds. Nine max. But he strode towards me with determination on his face, scooped me up in his arms, and kissed me like he wanted his Haribo back. Before I even knew what was happening, he was gone, but his voice was singing the next verse. A few moments later, he came up through a trapdoor in the centre of the stage with his guitar, his vocals drowned out by nearly sixteen thousand screaming fans. Nick glared at me, eyebrows raised—proving it's possible to call out someone's bullshit in at least three Scots dialects using only the top half of your face.

"Nothing happened, my aunt Fanny."

"Shut up, will you? If the press gets a whiff of this—"

Nick rolled his eyes. "Oh, I wish you'd said something sooner, I've already faxed Rupert Murdoch. You daft bawbag."

An hour or so later, Nick went off in search of an accessible loo. I needed to go, too, but I knew Cole was coming up to "The Flame," and call me sentimental, but now that I knew it was "our song," I wanted to hear him sing it. In fact, it had become a bit of an earworm since Cole sang it to me in the field. I'd found myself humming it quietly as we drove up the motorway, and when Cole heard me, he'd looked over, smiled, put his hand on my leg, and joined me in singing it. Soon, he was singing the verses and I was joining him for the chorus. Then we started playing around. He'd sing the chorus and I'd harmonise, or I'd sing a verse and he'd riff off the melody with vocal interpretations. We must have spent half an hour mucking around with the musicality of the song—singing to each other, singing *with* each other, playing together, pushing each other, experimenting, learning, and falling deeper, and deeper, and deeper into whatever this was.

The music had stopped, waking me from my thoughts. Onstage, Cole was standing at the microphone. He looked like he was going to speak. I'd seen every single show of this tour, and Cole had never spoken before singing "The Flame."

"Who here has ever been in love?" Cole asked the crowd.

Panic began to rise inside me.

"I love you, Cole!" a woman shouted. Thousands of Kenneddicts cheered.

"I love you too," he said. More screams. He waited for them to die down. "Who here has lost someone they should have held on to?" he asked the crowd. Another cheer, more subdued than the last. That's when I realised Cole was going to tell our story onstage. This would fire our fledgling flirtation out of a cannon and onto the front page of every newspaper across the country. I waved frantically, trying to get Cole's attention. My heart rate climbed rapidly up through its gears. I couldn't breathe. Tremors made it hard to stand upright. I willed Cole to hear my thoughts, willed him to look in my direction.

"Some people think this is a song about unrequited love," he said. "But this is a song about hope."

Finally, Cole looked over at me. He smiled that trademark smirk, winked, and played the opening notes of our song. Relief washed through my body like that first, glorious colonic irrigation after Christmas. Nick rolled up silently beside me and hit me on the leg, nearly making me jump out of my skin.

"You OK, pal? You look like you've passed a kidney stone."

At the end of the show, after the "Genevieve" encore and five curtain calls, Cole ran off the stage and scooped me up into his arms. He spun me around, his lips finding mine.

"What are you boys doing now?" he said, putting me down. "Do you want to come back to the house for a bite?" His eyes looked hopeful.

"Are you including me in this invitation?" Nick asked.

"Of course," Cole replied.

Nick shook his head. "That's very nice of you, but Friday night is date night, and I'm FaceTiming my husband in half an hour. Tonight, he's recreating the scene in *True Lies* where Jamie Lee Curtis strips for Arnold Schwarzenegger. He's spent all week learning the choreography. I cannot let him down."

Cole spluttered.

"I'm sorry, he says things like this sometimes," I said.

"I'll leave you two to your baseball game." Nick winked and unhooked the brakes on his wheels. "Don't forget we've got a production meeting at ten, Tobes." He spun around and rolled away.

"Two for dinner, then?" Cole asked, putting an arm around my shoulder. "I have to go do the meet-and-greet, but Mitch will stop by your hotel and pick you up in an hour—"

"No," I said, surprising myself almost as much as Cole. "Not tonight. It's been a big day. I need to sleep."

Cole frowned. "Have I done something wrong?"

No, but he nearly had—and I hadn't liked it. Not one bit.

"Tell me," he said.

"Fine. I thought you were about to tell sixteen thousand strangers our business, and it scared the hell out of me."

Cole looked worried. "Did it happen again?"

I nodded.

Out of nowhere, Cole yelled, "Clear the stage!"

Somewhere, someone repeated his order, and people scurried away like mice. Within seconds, the backstage area was quiet except for the distant sounds of the last Kenneddicts shuffling out of the auditorium.

"Toby, I am so sorry," Cole said. "I didn't think. I should have. I feel terrible. Now I've caused a second panic attack. Please, forgive me."

"Two?" I scoffed. "You've caused hundreds, mate."

Something seemed to click in Cole's brain, finally. I could see it in his face.

"I promise I'll do better," he said, reaching for my hands. "The last one you had scared the hell out of me. I didn't know what to do. Tell me what you need from me. I'll do anything."

"You can start by not telling sixteen thousand strangers about us."

Cole nodded. "I hear you. I got carried away, and I'm genuinely sorry. It's just... I'm so happy, I want to shout about it from the rooftops. I want to run up to strangers in the street and tell them I've won the golden ticket. I want to pay Russian hackers to spam people's social media accounts with the news that Cole Kennedy has convinced the most amazing guy in the world to at least give him a shot." Cole's hands held my shoulders, his eyes pleading. "I get that you're not ready. I can wait."

"Cole, I'm not gonna lie, I'm *never* going to be ready for that."

"*Never*?"

Cole looked crushed.

"This thing, between us, it has to remain a secret."

Cole let his hands drop. "For how long?"

"I told you, the minute there's any link between you and me, my life becomes hell. Not only mine, my family's too. I can't go through all that again. And my family shouldn't have to."

Cole leaned back against the amplifier tower and let his head roll back, looking skywards. He buried his hands in his pockets and let loose a long, sad sigh. I wasn't sure whether to leave, to speak, or to hold him. It must have been a full minute before he spoke.

"You know, I wouldn't tell anyone about Jasper," he said, finally. "For the whole eighteen months we were together. I wouldn't let him tell anyone about us."

"You weren't out," I said.

Cole rolled his head sideways, his eyes meeting mine. "I mean, *no one*. The band knew, obviously, and all the crew. But no one else. He never met my family. I never met his. He always complained about how shit that made him feel, but I never listened. I didn't care."

"Why not?"

"Jasper said I was ashamed of him."

"I'm not ashamed of you," I said.

"He was right. I *was* ashamed of him."

Cole wasn't listening. He didn't need my response. He needed to say what was on his mind. I sensed he'd been carrying this around for a long time.

"He was a shit boyfriend," Cole said. "He had a lot of jealousy issues. He was incredibly controlling, and not letting him meet my family became the one little bit of control I felt I had over him. We were both taking a lot of drugs, which doesn't help rational decision-making. It was a completely toxic relationship."

I put my arm around Cole's waist to coax him into a hug. His arms wound around my shoulders, enveloping me in his warmth, the smell of sweat and cinnamon.

"One night a photographer snapped us together on a beach in Florida, and we got into a huge fight because I got Totally Records to pay for exclusive rights to the photos to stop them being published. I wasn't publicly out yet, but Jasper knew how much I wanted to be out. It was the perfect opportunity to do it. Once the photos were out, what could Felicity do? But I didn't want people to know about Jasper. I couldn't go on TV and say 'Yes, I'm gay, and this is the man I love,' which is Crisis Comms 101. Because I didn't love him. Jasper was furious. We were both high. He started smashing up the hotel room, saying he was sick of being my dirty little secret. He slammed a champagne bottle through a glass coffee table. Then he tripped over a cord and fell straight into it. He ended up in the emergency department. I refused to go with him."

I recognised this as the famous incident that led to a £20,000 hotel bill and, eventually, to Robbie Johnswagger's intervention.

"He was so angry about that, he told the team I'd thrown him through the table and threatened to go to the press."

"He never!"

"Thankfully, Jasper's cuts and all the evidence supported my version of events, not his. Totally Records paid him a heap of hush money, made him sign an NDA, and at the end of the US tour he went off into the sunset, never to be heard from again. And I was finally allowed to check into rehab."

"Cole, I'm so sorry. That must have been awful."

"Rock and roll, baby," he said, and kissed me on the forehead. "My point is, I feel like I've earned this karmic energy. If you're not ready for the world to know about us yet, Tobes, that's OK. But if this... thing... between us becomes a capital-*T Thing*—and I genuinely hope it does—then I don't want it to be a secret. I want the whole world to know."

Cole's eyes searched mine. He brushed his fingers through my hair and cradled my head in his hand.

"I don't think I can give you that," I said.

Cole's thumb stroked slowly back and forth behind my ear, making my whole body tingle.

"I've waited a long time for you, Toby," Cole said. "Precisely because I know you're worth waiting for. It's going to be torture, but I respect your wish."

There was an explosion of relief in my gut, and the heat rose through my body in a mushroom cloud, destroying everything in its path.

"Thank you," I said.

Cole pressed a hand against the small of my back, pulling me into him. The baseball bat dug into my stomach as he kissed me, and I leaned into him to make sure he knew I still wanted this.

"But I reserve the right to make it my full-time job to convince you otherwise," he said as we pulled apart.

Ugh.

I was too tired to argue the point.

"I have to go to the meet-and-greet," he said. "Sure I can't persuade you to hang out later?"

"Not tonight," I said. "Tomorrow, maybe."

Cole shook his head. "I'm going to Melbourne to see my therapist."

"Australia?"

"Derbyshire." Cole laughed. "It's like fifty miles up the road. I can't be this close to Summer and not see her. Besides, I have a lot to talk to her about."

"Fair enough," I said, knowing he meant me—and literally this conversation. If it helped him get it, that was fine by me. "I'll see you at showtime tomorrow night, then?"

"It's a date."

Chapter Thirty-Four

The next night Nick and I went along to Cole's meet-and-greet to interview some dedicated Kenneddicts and get some audio to use during the following week's *Pop Review Specials* in Leeds and London. It was a Saturday night, the crowds had left, and Nick and I were packing up our equipment when Cole drifted over, looking sheepish. His hand went up into his hair, swooping it back.

"So, this might sound a bit forward, but I was thinking, I have a plane to catch now. Why don't you catch it with me?"

"Now?"

"Yeah. Why not?"

"Because I have work to do."

"I think I can clear this with your boss," Cole said. "I have some sway there."

"But Nick can't drive the van—"

"We're not driving the van up to Leeds until Thursday," Nick said. He turned to Cole. "When will you be back?"

Cole smiled. "I'll have him back by Thursday, I promise."

"But the show—"

Nick wasn't having it. "You've got nothing to do until ten o'clock Thursday morning. Go!"

"Good," Cole said. "Because I want to take you somewhere special."

"Is it up the arse?" Nick said.

Cole laughed. "It's a place I've always wanted to show you."

"Is it the bit between your hole and your balls?"

"Nick!"

"Close," Cole said. "It's definitely a little slice of heaven. Will you come?"

I heard myself say "OK" and felt my heart do a triple-twisting double back salto that would have made Simone Biles feel like she wasn't trying hard enough.

* * *

Ninety minutes later, we landed at some random airfield somewhere in the UK and transferred into a black SUV that had been waiting for us. Neither Cole nor Fiona would tell me where we were going. We drove through countryside and small villages for about fifteen minutes before the vehicle indicated and we turned into a gravel driveway with a sign that read *Dollops Wood Farm*.

"No way!"

Cole grabbed my hand and held it. "Welcome home," he said, smiling broadly.

I'd never been to Cole's family farm before. It felt intimate, somehow. The SUV pulled up in front of a new-build mansion. Fiona and Mitch opened their doors and got out. I grabbed the door handle, but Cole squeezed my hand.

"This isn't us," he said. The back of the car opened, and Mitch removed Fiona's luggage. Fiona appeared at Cole's window, and he wound it down.

"You coming in to say hi to Dad?"

"No, don't wake them all up. I'll see them in the morning. *After* milking, to be clear. Tell the kids Uncle Cole can't wait to give them great big smooshy hugs."

Fiona said goodnight, and Mitch, having deposited Fiona's case on the doorstep, jumped back in the car. We drove off along another gravel track.

"Does Fiona have kids?" I asked, confused.

"No, my brother Tully does. Twin girls. I built this house for Mum and Dad, but after Mum died it felt a bit small, so Tully and his wife, June, moved in. Then the girls came along."

"So, where do you live, then?"

"You'll see."

We drove around a hill and down a gully, then through a patch of trees, before pulling up in front of a small, ramshackle, single-storey flint stone cottage.

"This is where you grew up, isn't it?"

"It's a bit cosy," Cole said. "But it's filled with good memories."

The house had been opened up for Cole's arrival, and while he went around closing windows against the cool night air, I had a shower to freshen up. While Cole took his turn in the bathroom, I padded around the house in my underpants, snooping. Children's paintings covered the fridge door. In the living room, Orla stared back at me from inside a photo frame, and I wondered how she would feel about me being here. In the corner, I spotted Cole's old guitar, the one he'd been carrying the day I met him, the one that made him look so effortlessly cool, the one he'd serenaded me with. I strummed my thumb across the strings, and Cole appeared in the doorway, as if the sound had summoned him. He looked breathtakingly beautiful, wearing only his pants, his olive skin glowing in the warm honeyed light of the lamp's flickering bulb. His muscles were lean and defined, his legs and arms dark with hair and tattoos. Stray drips of water caught in the neatly clipped hair of his chest and glistened in the light. I was staring.

"Play something for me?" I said.

"Nah, people think things like that are romantic, but it makes the person playing the guitar look like a divvie, and it's dead uncomfortable for the person forced to listen to it."

I laughed. "Whoever told you that is an arsehole without a romantic bone in their body."

"True," Cole said. "But he's going to have a romantic bone in his body any minute now, so—"

"Oh, you did not!" I picked a cushion off the armchair and whacked him with it. Cole batted it away.

"I have a better idea," he said, giggling. "Amuse yourself for a second. You'll know when to come through."

"What are you up to?"

Cole waggled his finger. "Curiosity killed the cat." He turned and walked away, the round muscles of his bum stretching the limits of Calvin Klein's seam construction.

"Fine!" I called after him. "But if I walk in there to find you wearing whiskers and squatting over a litter tray or something, I am out of here!"

Cole's laugh echoed up the hallway. "Who told you about the litter tray?"

A moment later, I heard a piano strike C. As it struck two D-sharps and two more C's, recognition dawned. It was "Firework." As the A-sharps and G-sharps followed, I headed up the hall towards the sound. When I reached the room, Cole's bedroom, he was sitting at a small upright piano, lit only by the moonlight streaming in through the open window. The net curtains flapped gently in the cool night breeze. Under the window, there was a large bed covered in an old patchwork quilt. As Cole continued to play the song I had once been so passionate about but had long since come to dread hearing, I stood behind him and put my arms around his shoulders. His body was warm and damp from the shower. His hair was wet against my stomach. I wound my arms down around his chest, playing with the graze of hair, feeling his nipples harden under my fingertips. Cole stopped playing, one hand reaching up, his fingers weaving through mine. Our eyes met, and he pulled me down onto the stool beside him, budging over so we each had one bum cheek on the seat. Cole started playing again, his eyes never leaving mine. He got as far as the bit about the Fourth of July before I couldn't take it anymore. My lips found his. Fireworks seemed to explode around us. I kissed him hungrily. Cole was all heat and lust and minty freshness. I traced my hand from his chest and down the firm central line of his stomach to his waist, and teased the elastic of his pants. He groaned into my mouth. His hand found my hip, urging me onto him. I twisted around to straddle him, but we were too close to the piano, and I overbalanced the stool, sending us both crashing onto the rug. We didn't even stop to check the other was OK. We kept kissing. Urgently. Passionately. Our hands scrambling, exploring each other's bodies, clawing away the tiny garments that were all that stood between us and pure, glorious, skin-on-skin nakedness. We kissed breathlessly, sighing into each other's mouths, our chests rising and falling with furious exertion. Every cell in my body ached for Cole, yearned to feel the weight of his body bearing down on mine. I was desperate to feel the warmth of his flesh, his skin, his muscles, pressed against my body. The funky smell of arousal thickened the air. Sweat beaded on Cole's lip, and I licked at the saltiness. As the amber of his chestnut eyes sparkled in the moonlight, as I held his silky firmness in my hands and drew him into me, it felt like coming home. This was what belonging felt like. I had missed this. I had missed *him*. We had missed so much.

Out from under Cole's shadow

The Go Tos start anew with fresh "Californian" sound

In a surprise music drop, the Go Tos last night released their first album since Cole Kennedy's unexpected exit.

The band announced the release of "Sunkissed and Barefoot" on social media at midnight U.K. time, causing a frenzy of excitement amongst the band's loyal fans, the Extremes. By midnight West Coast U.S. time, the album had been streamed forty-nine million times.

It is the band's ninth album, and the first in four years without any songs written by Kennedy.

Band member Yoshi Kawaguchi said on social media: "This album has been a real labour of love for the four of us. We're so happy to share it with you. It might be our best work yet! If a Californian summer was a sound, 'Sunkissed and Barefoot' would be it. Peace out."

The band's label, Totally Records, said the album was recorded at the famous Sound City Studios in Los Angeles this spring and embraced "a more trans-Atlantic vibe" than previous musical outings.

The real question on every music fan's lips now is, Will the Go Tos knock Cole Kennedy's "The Flame" off the top of the charts?

Davinder Singh

Chapter Thirty-Five

Something wet and slimy landed on my face, waking me from a deep and restful sleep. I slapped my hand to my cheek, wiping away some kind of goo. Confused, I opened my eyes slowly against the blistering white light of the morning.

"Holy shit, that's a cow!" I said, scrambling across to the far end of the bed. The huge caramel-coloured animal had stuck its entire head through the open window above the bed and was stood there, chewing and drooling and having a good peek. Cole's bare round arse, uncovered when I took the bedding with me, slowly disappeared underneath him as he rolled over. The splendid nakedness of him was breathtaking. You could have painted this scene, stuck it on the wall in the National Gallery, and claimed it was some obscure Greek myth.

"Morning, Genevieve," Cole said, reaching a hand up and scratching the gigantic beast under its chin.

"*This* is Genevieve?"

"She most certainly is." Cole stretched himself out, letting every muscle in his body tense, his plump morning cock rolling from side to side as he yawned.

"You wrote that whole song about a *cow*?"

"I'll have you know, she's an incredibly special cow."

"How?"

"For starters, she could have paid for the big house ten times over." Cole reached a hand down to scoop up his underpants. "She's the second-richest cow in England."

"Second?"

"After Felicity."

"Fair."

"And I raised Genevieve myself," he said, hooking the pants over his feet and sliding them up his legs. "Her mum died when she was born, and I bottle-fed her from day one."

Cole tucked everything neatly away, then got up onto his knees and buried his face in the cow's neck, scratching her all over her head. I don't speak cow, but I knew exactly what it felt like to have Cole Kennedy's hands all over your body. Genevieve's head whipped around in ecstasy, her horns slicing through the air. I was well beyond their reach, but I crept further back. Cole didn't seem bothered at all. Slobber flew everywhere. I grabbed my underpants from the floor and put them on before drool could land on them.

"*Waking up to your sad brown eyes,*" I said, recalling the lyrics to Cole's biggest hit. "*Making time for long goodbyes. Oh, Genevieve, you know I have to leave. Oh, Genevieve, you know I have to leave. Oh, Genevieve, I wish I could stay. But life don't work that way.*" I laughed. "I can't believe you wrote that song about leaving your cow!"

"Don't listen to him, Genevieve, he's jealous."

"How have you never told this story in public before? All those chat shows. This never came up."

"I would never kiss and tell," Cole said.

I shook my head. "Even Graham Norton didn't get this story out of you."

"That song means too much to too many people."

I thought of Iona, in hospital in Glasgow, and wondered how she was doing.

"I'm going to make coffee now, Genevieve," Cole said. "It's lovely to see you. Thanks for coming to say hello. I love you!"

The cow shuffled her rear end around to the side, swung her head out of the window, and walked away. Cole shut the windows and tottered across the bed towards me on his knees.

"Shall I make coffee?" he said, reaching his arms out to wrap me up in a hug. "Or do you have something else you need besides caffeine?"

My hand found his chest, stopping him in his tracks. "Not until you've had a shower."

Twenty minutes later, I was wandering around Cole's kitchen in someone else's terry bathrobe, fighting with the Nespresso machine, when Cole wandered in, still towelling water out of his hair. He wore nothing but old torn jeans, steam still rising from his skin.

"Good morning, beautiful," he said, pulling me into him and planting a kiss on my lips. "Are you ready for the invasion?"

"Invasion?"

Two tiny raven-haired children burst into the kitchen, screaming for their Uncle Cole. A minute later—as Cole stomped around the kitchen pretending to be a giant, with one niece wrapped around his leg and the other around his arm, to squeals of delight—the front door opened again and their mother, a petite Filipina woman, stumbled in.

"Sorry, Cole," she said, out of breath. "I told them not until ten o'clock because Uncle Cole is sleeping. One minute they were hypnotised by Peppa Pig, the next the little fuckers had made a bid for freed —" She noticed me and stopped mid-sentence, wide-eyed. "Fuck me with a banister brush, it really is you. Fiona said you were here, but I didn't belie—"

"Juney, this is Toby," Cole said, still stomping around with children dripping off him. "Tobes, this is my sister-in-law, June. Tully's wife. And these brave, giant-slaying Lilliputians are Althea"—he shook his arm—"and Andrea"—he shook his leg. The children squealed and giggled.

June threw her arms around me. "You took your bloody time, but we're glad to finally have you here." Then she squeezed me tight and whispered in my ear, so Cole couldn't hear. "He is a very gentle boy, and he's been through a lot. If you hurt him, I will gut you like a pig. If you try to hide, I will track you down. I will find you. I will stop at nothing. Nowhere will be safe. Are we clear?"

I choked on my reply. "Clear."

"Good boy." She patted my back and released me, smiling like she *wasn't* a trained assassin.

"Coffee?" I offered.

Over the course of the day, I met Cole's brother, Tully, and his dad, Andy. After June, I hadn't been sure what to expect. These people must have hated me for years, thinking I'd betrayed Cole's confidence and leaked our texts. But their welcome was warm and unconditional. I felt not only like I was being adopted into the family, but like they already considered me a part of it.

At lunch, June made a stack of cold sandwiches, Tully and Andy came in from the fields, and everyone sat around the table, catching up on everyone's news. Andy had been asked to stand for the district council. June had been co-opted onto the committee of the twins' playgroup. Tully was having trouble fixing "the big windmill" and had to go into town for parts. Cole listened intently to all of it and, when June asked him how the tour was going, volunteered a summary as casual as if she'd asked him how his studies were going. I waited for Cole to tell his family the producers had located his birth mother, but he said nothing. I exchanged glances with him, mouthing the word "WebFlix," but Cole shook his head.

Cole offered to help Tully fix the windmill, so when he came back from town, we went with him to the dam. It was a glorious, sunny afternoon. Cole was in his element—shoes off, stripped to the waist, climbing up and down the tower, shouting instructions back and forth to Tully. I lay in the long grass, wishing my phone had reception and sneaking photos of the world's sexiest windmill mechanic. When the windmill was finally fixed and the tether released to let the blades turn, the water started pumping, and the brothers high-fived like teenage boys.

"You coming?" Tully asked, when the tools were packed up in the truck.

"I think we'll hang here for a bit," Cole said. "Might have a swim."

Tully's eyebrows went up. "No shagging in the water. Some of us have to drink that."

Cole laughed. I blushed. As he took off, Tully shouted back: "Don't forget you're on dairy duty this afternoon. Bring the girls up with you for five o'clock."

"The girls?" I said as the truck kicked up dust. "Aren't the twins a bit young to—"

"The cows," Cole said.

* * *

We lay back in the grass, exhausted, our bodies tangled up in each other, naked as the day we were born. Insects hopped, flitted, and buzzed around us. The breeze tickled our skin, drying the stickiness that was slicked across our stomachs. I gently ran my fingers through Cole's hair, brushing it back behind his ear.

"Why didn't you tell everyone you've found your birth mum?" I asked.

Cole sighed and nodded towards the water. "We should rinse off."

Clearly, I wasn't getting an answer.

Cole stood, the sun shining on the magnificent nakedness of his taut, lean muscles. He held out a hand for me.

"Come on. Wash with me."

"I thought Tully said—"

"It's fine! Do you know what the ducks do in that water?"

Cole waggled his hand. I shook my head. "Not until I know what the ducks do in that water."

Cole laughed, turned around, and walked into the water. His arse was spectacular in the sunlight. His buttocks bobbed against the surface like a sexy floatation device, and I wanted to cling onto it like I was Kate Winslet and in *Titanic*. I watched Cole washing himself, rinsing away the evidence of the afternoon's exertions. The water glistened as it ran down his body. You could paint this and hang it in the National Gallery, too, I thought. But the real prize was not the aesthetic beauty of the man in front of me but the privilege of seeing *this* version of him. This wasn't Cole the pop star, Cole the showman, or even the Cole that secretly visited hospitals in his spare time. This farm was the one place where even Cole let Cole be Cole. This was his happy place, the place he knew he absolutely belonged. I recognised it because the salon was that place for me. It was the place where I grew up, where I was most comfortable, my most complete self, my most honest self. I understood why Cole had done so much to keep the farm private and to cling to his childhood home. I was honoured to be here. I stood and joined him in the water.

Cole started singing "The Flame." Softly, at first, but as I added the harmonies, he grew louder. He stood in the shallows, water up to his thighs, sun shining on his magnificent body. He held out a hand, encouraging me to come deeper. I reached for it, and he guided me towards him. We held each other, naked in the water, with the summer sun beating down on us.

* * *

The dairy smelt like someone had made a smoothie using yogurt that had been left in the fridge for a week too long, and poop that had been left in the cow for a week too long. Cole told me the cows that looked like Genevieve were Jerseys and the black-and-white ones were Holsteins. Andy opened the dairy gate, and the cows wandered in. A dozen at a time would line up along each side of the shed and put their heads down to enjoy their dinner. Cole ran up and down the lines, washing the cows' udders with a rag, and Andy ran along after him, putting on the "teat cups" that would extract the milk. I'm not going to lie, they looked like four Fleshlights strapped to a Pokémon ball by hosepipe. They bounced up and down on the cows' nipples as the suction turned on and off, and you could watch the milk spurt into the Pokémon ball through the little round window. How had no one told the enterprising filmmakers from Raging Stallion about this?

After a while, Andy started singing "Hit the Road Jack," the old Ray Charles song. It was wonderful to watch Cole and his dad, bouncing on their heels to the music in their heads. It took me a shamefully long time to realise it, but the percussive sound of the milking machine provided the perfect beat for the song. I pointed this out to Cole.

"Eighty-six beats per minute, but with the suction cycle it sounds like a hundred and seventy-two beats," he said, over the sound of the machine. "Watch this." Cole stuck a finger in the air and said loudly: "One shot!"

Andy replied, call-and-response-style, with the opening lines to Eminem's "Lose Yourself"—and father and son bounced around the dairy in perfect unison, rapping together. I couldn't believe it. I'd expect it from Cole, maybe, but Andy knew every word to the whole song. I sat on a stool in the corner, watching father and son singing and working together, absolutely in sync. I wondered how Cole's news would change their relationship and, suddenly, understood why Cole hadn't said anything at lunch. He needed this—this touchstone moment that symbolised being at home. He needed this time with his dad. One more afternoon of togetherness before sharing the news that he'd always feared might upset his parents and change his relationship with them forever.

That evening, Cole and I had dinner with the family up the big house. June put the kids to bed, and we all sat on the couch watching *Britain's Cake Off*, which was always a bit weird for me because the host, Raluca, had hosted *Pop Review* before me. The judges were sampling the contestant's Battenbergs when Cole lifted my hand to his mouth, kissed it, stood up, and disappeared from the room. I looked at Fiona, wondering what was going on. She shook her head gently. A moment later, Cole reappeared in the doorway with a bottle of liquor. I looked at Fiona again, more panicked this time. She shook her head again.

"Dad," Cole said. "You got a minute?"

Everyone looked at Andy. Andy looked up at his son, then at the bottle. He took a deep breath, but his eyes shone with nothing but love and compassion.

"Bad enough to pull out your mum's bottle of Teeling single malt," Andy said, leveraging himself out of his armchair. "It must be serious."

Cole turned and walked up the hall. As Andy followed him, he said: "If you've got that boy pregnant, Cole, so help me God..."

They'd been gone about half an hour when my phone pinged.

Denzil: *Hey lovebirds. Deal with Sentinel looking shaky. Could use your help.*

Toby: *If this is wot I think it is the answer is no! We r not going public. Eva.*

Denzil: *Just one little picture together. Come on. He's right there. Your phone is already in your hand. We need the publicity, bruv.*

Toby: *U dont own my private life. Im doing my bit.*

Denzil: *Big talk from an employee who's currently absent without leave, Toby. Help a brother out?*

I turned my phone off. I was starting to prefer being out in the fields, where there was no phone reception and Denzil couldn't find me.

It was another hour and a half before Andy and Cole reappeared in the living room doorway, both red-eyed, Andy swaying lightly on his feet.

Later that night, back at the cottage, Cole snuggled in beside me in the bed and coiled his body around mine. There was no smell of alcohol on him.

"I take it you told him they found your birth parents," I said.

I felt Cole nod against the pillow.

"How'd it go?"

"Surprisingly well." Cole stifled a yawn. "He didn't even bat an eyelid."

I kissed him on the forehead. "You were gone a long time. I was worried."

"We had a lot to talk about," Cole said, one finger circling my nipple absently.

"Orla?"

"Mum. You. My birth parents. We had a lot to say. Maybe we should have said some of those things to each other many years ago. But I..." Cole drifted off. I squeezed him tight. He turned his head, looking up at the ceiling. I kissed his ear and his jaw, the stubble of the day's beard prickling my lips.

"But he was fine with it?" I asked. "He's OK with you meeting your birth mum?"

"He said he always knew the day would come." Cole turned to face me, his soulful eyes glistening with water. "And he was glad that day was finally here, and he hoped it would fill the hole in my heart and answer all my questions. But he said to remember that no matter what I might discover, I'd always be a Kennedy, this would always be my home." Cole deepened his voice and pretended to be his father: "*Remember, son, we are family, and we always will be. Every soul under this roof loves the bones of you, and always will. And don't you bloody forget it.*"

A lonely tear ran down Cole's cheek, and as I wiped it away with my thumb, it occurred to me that I had been a soul under that roof when Andy had spoken those words. I smiled to myself. Whether he knew it or not, Andy had been speaking for me too.

Secret ex-lover to dish dirt on pop king Cole in tell-all memoir

Cole Kennedy's top-secret gay lover during his Go Tos heyday has written a scathing, no-holds-barred memoir about his eighteen-month relationship with the one-time hellraiser.

Jasper Horner, 32, was the band's costume designer at the height of Kennedy's drunken, drug-fuelled rabble-rousing period, which saw the one-time teen heart-throb fall from grace. It was during this period that Kennedy and Horner carried out their illicit affair.

A statement from Horner's publishers said: "There's a dark side to Britain's prince of pop, and the world deserves to know about it. The real Cole Kennedy is not the fun-loving boy bander the Kenneddicts think he is. In this gripping, breathtakingly candid memoir, we hear first-hand from the man who knows Kennedy better than anybody else—the man who loved him, lived with him, worked with him, travelled with him, and secretly shared his bed for a year and a half. You think you know the story of Cole Kennedy. 'Dirty Little Secret' will shatter those illusions."

It turns out pop king Cole was a dirty old Cole, and a dirty old Cole was he!

"Dirty Little Secret" is out later this month and will be serialised in The Bulletin in the week leading up to publication.

Chapter Thirty-Six

I woke to a fist banging angrily against the bedroom door.

"Fucksake, Cole, don't you answer your texts anymore?" It was Fiona, and she sounded mad.

We got up and scrambled for our clothes. We were at Cole's London house, on a hill near Hampstead Heath. It was a Sunday—the morning of the last of Cole's three shows at the capital's famous Millennium Dome. Cole and I had spent a full, glorious week together, hanging out whenever we could, sneaking around on the down-low in both Leeds and London. We did normal, couple-y stuff. We watched TV on the couch. I cooked him my grandmother's traditional Swedish meatballs. He showed me seven new ways to find my prostate. The press hadn't cottoned on to our affair and didn't seem to suspect a thing.

Fiona pounded at the door. "Cole, let me in."

"I'm coming. Geez." He muttered something under his breath. "Is this about the Go Tos knocking us off number one?" he called out. "I was thinking about that. Should we bring forward the release of—"

"It's not about the bloody Go Tos. Open up!"

On his way to the door, Cole slapped me on the arse and clicked his tongue, like he was geeing up a horse. The moment the door handle was down, Fiona burst into the room, absolutely raging mad. She held out her phone, and we read the headline.

"Jasper can write?" Cole said.

"It's not funny," Fiona said. "It's a big fucking problem."

"Should I..." I pointed a thumb at the door.

"No, stay," Cole said, grabbing my hand. He sat on the edge of the bed and pulled me down beside him. Fiona started reading the article aloud. With every sentence, Cole shrunk a little, his happiness leaving him in column inches.

"Why would he do this?" Cole asked, his head in his hands.

"I'm no Sherlock, but money seems like an obvious motive," Fiona said. "Revenge, maybe? Attention? A spot on *Celebrity Dorm Room*, who knows?"

Those last words popped like a bubble, and an awkward silence fell between us all.

"Sorry, Tobes," Fiona said. "I wasn't thinking. You were in a completely different situation."

Was I, though? I was an ex who used his connection to Cole for profit. That's exactly what Jasper was doing. What conversations had Fiona and Cole had about me back then? Cole rubbed his eyes with the palms of his hands.

"But Jasper already got a ton of money."

"Be real, Cole." Fiona was pacing around the room. "He'll have blown through all that on drugs or rent boys ages ago. What didn't go up his nose will have gone up his arse."

Fiona was shaking her phone like she wanted to snap its neck.

"But he signed NDAs," Cole said. "Legally, surely, he doesn't have a leg to stand on."

Fiona pressed her hand to her forehead. "They're not *our* NDAs, Cole. They were Totally Records' NDAs."

"He still signed them."

Fiona threw out her hands in exasperation. "Catch up, Cole!

Felicity Quant can release Jasper from those NDAs at any time. Who the fuck do you think is behind this book? Jasper doesn't have the brains or the contacts to pull off a stunt like this. This is all Felicity."

Cole looked worried, realisation dawning. "Do we know what he's going to say?"

"What *could* he say?" Fiona said. "I've organised a crisis comms strategy meeting for nine o'clock. Angie, Carmel, Winslow are all on their way. We need to go through every single claim Jasper could possibly make."

"Everything?"

"Absolutely every last thing. We can't afford any surprises. We have to work out an initial public response, and we need to work out a legal response. Then we need to work out the long-term comms strategy. This is a fucking mess."

Cole looked shocked. I couldn't imagine how he felt. Not only had his ex written a tell-all book, but now he had to tell his sister everything they got up to when they were together? I wouldn't tell Elsa one-tenth of what Cole and I had got up to, and the most perverted thing we'd done was get a bit handsy in the cabin of his old man's tractor. Fiona wrapped her arm around Cole's shoulder and rested her forehead against his.

"We're going to fix this, OK?" she said, almost whispering it into his ear. "I promise." She kissed the top of his head. "Do you need to do the mantra?" she whispered. "Come on, let's do Summer's mantra. I can handle what comes my way."

Cole mumbled the words.

She stroked his hair. "Happiness is always available to me."

Cole muttered something.

"No, say it for me. It doesn't work if you don't say it."

"Happiness is always available to me," Cole murmured.

Fiona closed her eyes and spoke into the mess of Cole's hair. "I am unaffected by the judgement of others."

Cole parroted the words.

"The best is yet to come," Fiona said.

"The best is yet to come," he repeated.

Fiona kissed him on the head and went back to pacing. I'd never seen Cole's demons up close like this before. He was always so happy, so glib. Seeing him like this scared me. I put my arm around him. He rested his head against mine. Something deep inside me, something primal and male, made me want to *fix* this for him.

"I need an advanced copy of that book," Fiona said. "Do we know anyone in publishing?"

Cole shook his head. Suddenly, I realised I might literally be able to help.

"So, I don't know if this is useful, but my best friend's boyfriend's best friend works for the BBC's *Compass Point*, and he used to work at *The Bulletin*, so he probably still has contacts there. And my best friend's boyfriend's best friend's boyfriend's family actually owns *The Sentinel*, if that's any use?"

Fiona stared at me, slack-jawed.

"The fucking gays, man," she said. "They run the whole world. How you people have been so oppressed for so long is nothing short of baffling."

"Do you want me to try to get a copy of the book?" I asked.

Fiona threw her phone into her bag and slumped into the chair.

"Toby, the only thing I've ever wanted in my life more than a copy of that book is Felicity Quant's head on a pike by Southwark Bridge. Well, that and Kevin Jonas. If you can get me that book, I'll seriously owe you one."

There was a moment of silence, while I took on board the seriousness of the situation.

"Kevin Jonas?" I shook my head. "*Kevin*?"

"I know, right?" Cole said. "Like, Joe is right there."

"Right?"

"Oi!" Fiona said. "Stick to the point. Do you think you can get that book?"

I shrugged. "I have absolutely no idea, babes. But I will certainly try."

"Thank you, Toby. If you can pull this off, I might be able to swing you a knighthood." Fiona stood up and put her bag over her shoulder. "The PM owes me a favour or two." She put her hand under Cole's chin and lifted his face to hers. "We're going to fix this, OK? Shower, put on your game face, and meet everyone downstairs in twenty."

Fiona marched out the door. Cole and I sat there in silence for a moment, Cole's head on my shoulder. He smelt of sleep and morning and boy.

"Do you genuinely think you can get a copy of the book?"

I combed my fingers through his hair. "I have no idea."

"Promise me something?"

"Sure."

"Don't read it."

How bad was this book? What did Jasper have to say that was so terrible Cole didn't want me to read it?

"Of course not," I said, and kissed him on the head.

Neither of us made to move.

"What are you thinking?" Cole asked.

I shook my head. "Why would you choose Kevin?"

Chapter Thirty-Seven

It took longer than I imagined. But on a warm, drizzly evening, I found myself on Shaftesbury Avenue in London's West End. Among the theatregoers, tourists, and Friday-night revellers, I spotted Ludo Boche standing outside the Gielgud Theatre, deep in conversation with a middle-aged woman with fabulous teased-back 1980s hair. Tucked under his arm was a neat brown paper parcel. I scooted across the road to meet him.

"Both cheeks!" he said as we kissed hello. "You're in theatreland now. Best look like a total lovey, so you don't blow your cover."

"My cover?"

Ludo discreetly pointed to the book under his arm.

"Oh! I see, the book."

"Ixnay on the booknay," he said, tapping the side of his nose with his finger, before introducing me to Wilhelmina. "Willy is an old friend. She's the theatre critic for *The Sentinel*."

"Delighted to meet you," Wilhelmina said. "Slightly disappointed we didn't get to deliver the merchandise using a dead letter drop in Saint James's Park."

"Oh, that would have been much more fun," Ludo said. "Or we

could have met on a mist-covered bridge at midnight. Much more cinematic."

"Or we could have shoved it down the back of a radiator in the men's WC at the British Museum," Wilhelmina suggested.

"That's much *less* cinematic, though," Ludo said.

"Depends who else is in there," Wilhelmina said, digging Ludo in the ribs.

Ludo slapped a palm to his head. "Wait, should I have photographed each page and sent this to you on microfilm?"

I hadn't heard anyone laugh at their own jokes like that since Aunty Cheryl knocked back a balloon of nitrous oxide in a Benidorm backstreet and tried to get sassy with a street lamp. When they noticed I wasn't laughing, they straightened themselves up.

"Sorry," Ludo said, handing me the book. "Got a bit carried away."

Wilhelmina joined in the apology. "It's been such an enjoyable mission."

"Mission?" I was confused.

"Stealing the book," Ludo said.

"You *stole* it?"

"Not me," Ludo said. "Wilhelmina 'Quick Fingers' Post here swiped it off the desk of *The Sentinel*'s music reviewer."

"Oh my God! Won't you get in trouble?" I asked.

"She won't even notice it's missing," Wilhelmina said. "She reviews music for *The Sentinel*. Musicians only appear on her radar after they've been dead for two hundred years. Minimum. There's no way she's heard of Cole Kennedy, let alone plans to write about him."

Ludo tapped the top of the book. "Besides, by the time the embargo lifts, *The Bulletin* will have printed all the juiciest bits already, and all that'll be left for everyone else to write about is how jolly terrible the syntax is."

"Have you read it?" I asked. "Is it bad?"

"The syntax?"

"The things Jasper has said."

Ludo grimaced. "I've skimmed it."

"And?"

Ludo fished around, looking for the right words. "Look, I guess it's a bit 'rock and roll.' But who among us hasn't made the odd youthful mistake?"

Wilhelmina's pin-thin eyebrows leapt so high they risked catching a breeze and taking flight.

"Who among us hasn't been shagged in a toilet on a four-day cocaine bender?" she said.

The words twisted in my heart.

"Oh, come on, Willy, that's a British rite of passage," Ludo said. "Do you think people go to Ascot for the horse racing? No, they go to snort fat lines of dirty drugs off grubby Portaloo seats and get buggered senseless by the hot older brothers of the chaps who bullied them at Eton."

Wilhelmina squinted. "That was oddly specific, Ludo."

Ludo's eyebrows went up. "Not me. I didn't go to Eton." He quickly turned his attention back to me. "Bad news on the acquisition."

"Acquisition?"

"Of the Pure Network. By *The Sentinel*."

"What do you mean? What's happened?"

Ludo shrugged. "Bit of a wrinkle, I'm afraid—"

The bells started to ring, calling the audience into the theatre. The poster on the wall showed it was preview night of a new production of Arthur Miller's *The Crucible*.

"That's us," Ludo said. "Listen, Sunny is stuck at work, so I have a spare ticket, if you'd like to see the show? Then we're meeting my brother at Maxime's afterwards, if you fancy it?"

The book was itching in my hands. I'd delayed too long as it was. I needed to get this contraband copy of *Dirty Little Secret* to Fiona so she could start working her way through it. The first serialisation would appear in *The Bulletin* in the morning.

"I better go," I said. "But, quickly, *The Sentinel's* still buying Pure, yeah?"

"If they can, yes." Ludo glanced at the crowds disappearing inside. "Must dash, dear fellow."

I thanked them both, and we said our goodbyes.

As I jogged towards Piccadilly Circus, weaving through crowds of pedestrians with the book buried safely under my arm to keep it dry, it started to speak to me, to tempt me. Like Gollum with the One Ring in *Lord of the Rings*, now that I possessed it, I couldn't give it up. I *had* to know what was in it. I abandoned the Tube and turned up Regent Street to find a bus stop. The bus would give me a lot more reading time.

From Dirty Little Secret, by Jasper Horner

New York might be the city that never sleeps, but Cole physically could not sleep. He had been on a four-day cocaine bender. He was jittery, and his eyes were so dark and bloodshot, he looked like a corpse. I was sleepless, too, terrified that if this continued, a corpse was exactly what I'd wake up next to.

Cole couldn't perform. He was useless onstage. Chase and Joey were carrying his parts. The management team travelling with us had confiscated and flushed his drugs at least five times on the US tour up to this point. The thing about addicts is, they're resourceful and they're sneaky. They always seem to know where to get more gear. Cole never went without. No sooner had one lot been flushed than another little baggie would appear out of a pocket or a satchel or a pair of socks. For illegal drugs, it was mostly coke. For the legal (but illegally obtained) it was a predictable cocktail of uppers and downers. Adderall. Dexedrine. Xanax. Ambien. Except for the night we went to Punk, the infamous New York club, well known for its free-for-all orgies. That night, someone sold, or gave, Cole a tab of Ecstasy.

"I'm going to Punk," he'd announced, standing in the bathroom door of our hotel room, in his pants.

"You're not going to Punk," I said, patiently. He'd come offstage two hours earlier, skipped the meet-and-greet, and because it was a Friday night, wanted to go blow off some steam in a club. That's a normal thing for a guy in his twenties to want to do, and we had security with us, but Cole was in no fit state to go out in public—and Punk is no ordinary club.

"A guy on GayHoller is picking me up," Cole said. "He's going to be downstairs in five minutes. I need to get ready."

He held up his phone and showed me a picture of a blond beefcake with shoulders like motorcycle helmets. He looked like a Viking.

Needless to say, I was not having Cole go clubbing with a random from a hook-up app. We argued about it for five, ten, fifteen minutes —I have no idea. What I remember is, he was so belligerent I finally agreed to let him go, as long as I went with him and Totally Records' security drove us there. In truth, I doubted the venue would let him in. He was way too out of it. I thought we'd be back at the hotel inside half an hour.

"We need to think about the paps," I said. "You can't be seen going into a sex dungeon. It'd be the end of the band."

"You do costumes, make me a disguise!" he said, waving his arms in the air like I could magic up an outfit out of nothing. In the end, that's exactly what I did. Punk is avant-garde and post-gender—I could dress him up in almost anything. The key was he couldn't be recognisably Cole. I borrowed a blond wig and a silver sequined dress from the backup singers' wardrobe, put him in false eyelashes and some heavy make-up to disguise his face, and away we went.

Forty minutes later, we were in a grimy warehouse nightclub. Two storeys were dance floors, but the basement was strewn with mattresses and filled with groups of naked, sweaty men indulging in the kinds of sex I'd only heard about in theory. Our security detail— Anton, Dexter, and Michelle, all ex-military—waited outside. A chain of communication had been arranged with the club's bouncers. If we got into trouble, our security team would be inside in a flash. For our guys, it was as much as their union would let them do—and more than they should have had to put up with. While I went to the bar and got us both some water, Cole took a pill. MDMA always made Cole incredibly horny. I returned to see him disappearing into the crowded dance floor. I lost him for maybe five or ten minutes. When I found him again, he was in a toilet cubicle with a broken door, the dress hitched up around his waist, with a huge Viking bent over him—and a queue of half-naked men lined up to take their turn. My heart was broken. I loved Cole. I had given him everything of me. I was torn between fury and eviscerating pain. But I had to protect him.

"That's my boyfriend," I shouted. "Get away from him."

The men laughed. The Viking roared and spent himself, and I screamed for security. But two of the other men grabbed me, covered my mouth, and held me back. I was forced to watch, helpless, as the Viking pulled his jockstrap back up, and the next man took his place. And Cole? When he finally looked back and I caught his eye, all I got was a stupid gurning smile, and a thumbs up.

Chapter Thirty-Eight

An hour later, I got off the bus at Golders Green in shock from the claims in Jasper's book. I found Mitch waiting for me. When we got to the house, the SUV pulled into the garage, and I waited for the door to come down completely before I got out of the car, making absolutely sure none of the paparazzi gathered outside Cole's Hampstead compound got a photo. My whole body was shaking.

"Have you got it?" Fiona said, as I walked into the large open-plan kitchen and living room. Cole was dressed in slouchy pyjamas and was buried so deep in the brown leather couch it looked like a gigantic fungus was swallowing him.

"Hello to you, too, babes," I said, my head still spinning. I handed her the book. It looked decidedly well-thumbed from where I had skimmed through it with all the forensic precision of a panicked squirrel.

"Sorry," she said, kissing me on the cheek. "Thank you." Fiona dropped the book into her bag and shovelled in assorted notepads and scraps of paper. "Cole, I'm taking this back to mine. If Winslow, Carmel, Angie, and I pull an all-nighter, we might have something by morning. Stay by your phone, please." She swung her bag over her shoulder. "Love you," she said to her brother. "Don't let him leave the house!" she said to me, before bouncing out the door, keys jangling.

"Hey," Cole said. He looked childlike, broken, swamped by his couch, surrounded by empty crisp packets, water bottles, and disintegrating balls of tissue. He stood, put his arms around me, and pulled me into a hug. "I missed you. I'm glad you're here." His eyes were puffy and red. I returned the hug, but I could feel myself holding back. If even half of what I'd read in Jasper's book was true—the drug taking, the sex parties, the violence, the infidelities, the self-entitled douchebagginess—I wasn't sure I knew who Cole was at all.

* * *

"You read it," Cole said as I sat down beside him with a freshly made pot of peppermint tea. I paused, unsure whether to admit it. "I can tell. You're looking at me differently now."

I shook my head. "Don't be silly."

"I knew you would."

I poured the tea, grateful to have something to do. "Has there been any news?"

"Fiona spoke with someone from Totally Records this afternoon. They deny they're behind the book."

"So, they'll be suing him for breaching his NDA, then?" I handed Cole a mug of tea.

"You'd think that. But no, it's 'not in their interests to invest capital in protecting an asset they no longer own.' That's a direct quote, by the way. If you ever wondered how they viewed us, there's your answer."

"Wow." I sat back with my tea.

"If nothing else, it confirms Totally Records is behind this book."

"But why are they doing it?"

"Because FQ doesn't like to lose."

Silence fell between us.

"How bad is it?" he asked.

I sighed, not wanting to have this conversation but wanting answers. I told him about "the Viking."

"Is that how he says that night went down?" Cole scoffed and shook his head, then let it drop towards his lap like he was a condemned man. "Do you want to know the truth?"

I nodded.

"I'd just come offstage. The show had been terrible. I'd been high for days. A week maybe, I don't know. I desperately needed sleep, so I said I was going to take a couple of downers and go to bed. But Jasper wanted to go out. 'But it's New York,' he said. So, he swapped out one of my bennies with a tab of E, and before I knew it, I was flying. Funnily enough, suddenly I felt like going out." Cole stood and started pacing around the room. "Jasper puts me in like a wig or some disguise, and we go to Punk. Then he abandons me on the dance floor to go who knows where and do God knows what. I could have died that night, Toby. In fact, I almost did." Cole knelt beside me on the couch, the veins in his neck and his arms pulsing with anger. "It was one pill too many. That 'Viking' was an off-duty paramedic who broke down the toilet door to make sure I was OK. The only thing he put inside me that night was his finger—to make sure my airways were clear. The guys standing around? Regular concerned dudes. They had to hold Jasper back because he was hysterical. He'd fucked up, and he knew it. He was more worried about Felicity's reaction than what might happen to me."

I pulled Cole up onto the couch, and he curled up beside me like a child.

"I was lucky I didn't have to go to hospital. Jasper nearly killed me that night."

It was such a different version of events, it sat uncomfortably with me.

"Why go for such a big lie, though? Isn't choking on your own vomit enough drama? Why make up the whole Viking-sex thing?"

"That's easy," Cole said. "Vomiting only makes me look stupid. Fucking strangers in a filthy nightclub toilet turns me into a cheat and makes him look hard done by."

I grimaced. Cole caught it.

"You don't believe him?" he said. He sat up. "Come on, Toby, you know me. Do I *seem* like a 'let's go to an orgy' kind of guy?"

Well, no, he didn't. And from what I'd read of it, the book couldn't have made Jasper sound more squeaky-clean if he'd been fired out of an autoclave machine into a paddling pool of bleach. And Chase had made it clear that's not who Jasper was. They were both probably on so many drugs, neither description of that night could be entirely believed. But, on balance, Jasper's story didn't ring true.

"I don't believe him," I said. Cole's eyes flickered with relief. "But from tomorrow morning, *The Bulletin* is running bits of that book every day, and what I believe won't matter one bit. It's what the public believes. And they're going to want to believe it all."

"It's so unfair," Cole said. "I'd finally got control of my own narrative. My own life. I was *free!*"

"Sue him into financial Armageddon, babes," I said. "Get the truth out of him in court. It'll be the trial of the year."

Cole shook his head. "Jasper's fighting his own demons. We have to focus on the real enemy in this situation."

My phone pinged.

Ludo Boche: *You'll never believe who's sitting across from me in Maxime's.*

Chapter Thirty-Nine

Despite Fiona's explicit instructions not to leave the house, we left the house. I tried to talk Cole out of it, but he wasn't having it. When he told Mitch where we were going, Mitch tried to talk him out of it. No luck. And full credit to him, because I wouldn't say no to Mitch for love nor money nor access to Shawn Mendes's private hard drive. Mitch was terrifying. But Cole paid his wages. So, that's how we found ourselves parked up opposite Maxime's in a big black SUV. Maxime's was a ritzy members' club for creative types that took up two floors of a renovated Victorian hospital on a quiet back street on the Saint Giles side of Soho.

"There she is," Cole said, throwing open the door and bounding across the street to confront Felicity Quant.

Felicity wore a beaded, champagne-coloured minidress that glittered in the streetlights. Her oversized sunglasses were staked through her severe bob. A small handbag hung from one skinny arm, while the other skinny arm flew up in the air in search of a black cab. As Cole reached her, she looked startled.

Mitch opened his door. "Stay in the car."

Thanks to the SUV's soundproofing, I missed the first volley of exchanges. But I didn't miss the look on Felicity's face. Her initial shock dissipated, and she seemed to grow in height and confidence—like a cobra rising in warning above a threat. As I lowered the electric window, I could hear Cole shouting.

"Why are you doing this to me?"

Felicity maintained her poise. "Have you been drinking again, Cole? Are you high? Why must you throw your life away like this?"

Cole stepped forward, fists at his side, and I was horrified by the thought that he might be violent. That wasn't the Cole I knew, but this woman had been his captor and torturer for a decade—who knew what that might drive him to? Mitch stepped in, putting a hand on Cole's chest. Felicity looked at him like she'd only now noticed him.

"Michelle?" she said. "Oh my God, I hardly recognised you. Those in—"

"Don't you dare use his dead name!" Cole yelled, arms flailing wildly.

I certainly hadn't seen that coming.

"I suggest you calm down, Cole," Felicity said. "You're embarrassing yourself with this childish display." She was looking around distractedly—possibly searching for that cab, maybe a police officer, perhaps even her own security detail. Why didn't she have one?

"I know you're behind Jasper's book," Cole spat.

Felicity shook her head. "Is that what this is about? If your ex wants to tell the world you're a terrible shag, that's up to him. Nothing to do with me."

"Liar!"

"Be careful, Cole," she said, looking dead at him. "A word like that has consequences."

"You vindictive bitch."

"Ah, name-calling. I think this conversation is done, don't you?"

Felicity turned to look up the street, raising her arm again. A black cab flashed its lights. But Cole wasn't finished.

"You've made your money off me, why can't you leave me in peace?"

She swung around to face him. "I think you'll find that you made your money off *me*. If it weren't for me, you'd be up to your armpits in cow shit right now. A little gratitude wouldn't go amiss."

"Gratitude?" Cole's arms were thrashing. "After everything you've put me through? After everything you put Toby through?" He swung an arm around and pointed to me sitting in the car. The gorgon's eyes met mine, and my body turned to stone. The leaden weight started in my stomach and radiated out until I was frozen solid, unable to move. Felicity slowly turned her gaze back towards Cole, a smile cracking across her face.

"Marriage material?" She laughed, almost uncontrollably. "This is too much! You're even more tragic than I thought." She looked over at me again. "The pair of you."

"Toby is the best thing that ever happened to me," Cole said. "And you've tried to ruin it twice."

"Twice?" Felicity said—and her smile grew even wider. The black cab rolled up to the kerb, blocking my view. When it was gone, so was she. Cole stood there, under the brightly lit awning of Maxime's, looking shattered. Fiona was going to kill him—and she was the least of our worries.

Cocaine Cole caught in clandestine clinch with Marriage Material Toby!

It seems Cole Kennedy is such damaged goods, he's finally caved in and given long-time stalker Toby Lyngstad the chance he's been waiting for.

Still reeling from the shocking allegations made about his drug taking, alcoholism, and sexual excess in ex-squeeze Jasper Horner's sensational tell-all memoir, a defiant Kennedy was photographed kissing the "marriage material boy" outside the pop star's posh north London home this morning.

With Kennedy's reputation in tatters, this newspaper can't help but feel sorry for the radio DJ, who finally gets his man, only to discover he's no longer worth the cost of the ink to print the wedding invitations. Marriage material? We wouldn't clean our boots with it...

Chapter Forty

It was Denzil who broke the news, in the most Denzil way
possible. I was on air at the time.

Denzil: *You proper came through for me, bruv! I knew you
wouldn't let the team down.*

The small skittish ape that lives in the primitive part of my brain
smashed its fist repeatedly against the big red button marked
Panic Now.

Denzil: *The board is thrilled. This is exactly the shot in the arm we
needed. Get in, my son! I won't forget this, you beautiful homosexual.*

Now I *was* seriously frantic. I googled myself and found the
photograph. It was Cole and me kissing on his back patio earlier that
morning. He'd told me it was safe from the paparazzi, and I'd let my
guard down. I threw my headphones off in disgust. They slid over the
end of the desk and swung from the cord like a hanged man. Nick and
Tarneesha stared back at me in astonishment through the glass.

"You OK, pal?"

I wasn't. My whole life felt like it was unravelling. Since that
moment in the car park under the hotel in Manchester, this had been
inevitable. If you keep pulling at the thread that's keeping everything

together, what do you expect? I held my phone up to the glass, showing Nick the *Bulletin* article and the carousel of images of me making out with a shirtless Cole, in the glorious morning sunshine, not three hours earlier. Nick's voice came through the studio speaker. "Well, that was a bit careless, you walloper. How'd you let them get that?"

"Helpful, thanks," I said, pressing the button to speak to the booth. "It's meant to be a private forest behind Cole's house, but someone must have let them in. Apparently, there's no honour among the mega rich."

Nick rolled his eyes. "What's this country coming to when you can't even trust hedge fund managers, commercial barristers, and the chinless fuckers who hide their intergenerational wealth from His Majesty's Revenue and Customs inside dodgy family trusts not to sell you out to the paparazzi?"

"Is this really the time for a lecture on this country's gross inequality, Nick?"

But he had a point. Someone had let the photographers in—and I realised the chance of Felicity knowing someone who lived in Cole's enclave was, let's be real, incredibly high. With the first instalment of *Dirty Little Secret* in that morning's *Bulletin*, interest in Cole was fever-pitched. We'd been reckless. Stupid. And we were paying the price.

Tarneesha hit the button to speak to me. "Track's ending, Tobes. Fifteen seconds."

We limped through the show, neglecting the phones and filling the airtime with music and pre-recorded interviews. The chatline screen spun like a dentist's drill the whole four hours. When the on-air light finally plunged into darkness for the last time at the end of the show, Tarneesha made a dash for the exit, claiming she had to help her mum with a church thing. Nick's voice came through my headphones.

"Miss Timmy's?"

I shook my head. "Can't risk it."

"Of course you can, you dafty. We've refined our escape plan now. You're not going home with a face like a slapped arse. Come on, you're coming out with the boys."

I wavered. I was lugging a suitcase of dirty clothes around with me. Who knew what the press would make of that? *Cole turfs Toby out into the street!* Or *Toby dumps cocaine Cole!* But to be honest, a drink and a laugh was exactly the distraction I needed. The risk, though…

My phone pinged.

Tarneesha: *Bedlam out the front. At least a dozen photogs. xx*

I pressed the button to speak to Nick. "Haven't got any cash on you, have you babes?"

"What for?"

"In case I need to bribe John again."

Twenty minutes later, I burst through the station's back door onto Charing Cross Road—the fire alarm wailing into life—dashed past our resident busker, and flung my suitcase in the back of the waiting accessible taxi.

I lobbed a crumpled twenty into John's open guitar case. "That's to keep shtum, OK? Maybe spend it on the Bob Dylan songbook? Expand your repertoire with a second song."

John looked at the note, then back to me. "The price has gone up for keeping shtum."

"Jesus." I'd done this to myself. Why did I have to be a smart-arse? I flicked my gaze up to the street corner to check for paps and frantically fished another crumpled twenty out of my pocket. "That's all I've got, OK? Do me a solid, will you?"

John pointed up Charing Cross Road. "There's a cashpoint up by—"

But my time had run out. I leapt into the idling cab, where Nick was already waiting for me. As the taxi drove off, a disorganised gaggle of photographers came screaming around the corner of the building. I ducked my head down as the cab rumbled past them and off up the street.

* * *

I pushed against the door for Miss Timmy's and let Nick enter first. As I stepped in behind him, dragging my suitcase, the whole venue went quiet. At the far end of the restaurant, Sandy Crotch appeared from behind two green velvet curtains and made a beeline towards us.

"That'd be right," she called out across the room, loud enough for everyone to hear. "When I want a bit of hush to sing Barbra Streisand, I can't shut you fuckers up. But the minute someone a bit famous walks through the door, suddenly I can't get a peep out of you. You're sat there like stunned mullets, drooling into your foreskins like my grandad in his final week at the hospice."

"Married him yet, Toby?" someone called out.

Sandy clapped her hands together, pointed at the lad, and stared him down. "One more word out of you, Jeremy Arkwright, and you'll be drinking that salad through a fucking straw down Saint Thomas' A&E. Are we clear?"

The colour drained from Jeremy Arkwright's face faster than a British water company can drain sewage into a river.

"This is a safe space for everyone in our community," Sandy told the room. "Unless you fuck me off. In which case you'll learn precisely how unsafe this community space can become, because these fists have seen more action than Jeremy Arkwright's internet-famous arsehole. And I'm fast. I could be pounding you before you even realise I've moved. So, don't try me."

The crowd laughed. Sandy grabbed me by the elbow and leaned into my ear. "I've put the lads out the back in one of the curtained booths. Give you a bit of privacy."

Nick rolled off ahead of us. Sandy threaded her arm through mine. We walked up the aisle between the tables, the punters watching us as intently as if we were underwear models at a Calvin Klein catwalk show.

"Don't mind them all staring, Toby darling," Sandy said, in a stage whisper. "This dress is vintage Schiaparelli, and you *know* how Italian haute couture attracts the gays like flies on shit."

Two-thirds of the way up the room, I spotted a lad filming us on his phone. I tried to hide my face, but one arm was trapped in Sandy's and the other was dragging the suitcase. As we walked past him, there was a flash of magenta fingernails as Sandy whipped the phone out of the guy's hand.

"Naughty, naughty, Derek. If you want this back, come and see me after class." Then, as we walked by the next table, Sandy dropped it into a jug of water. "Bring a bag of rice."

The room burst into applause. Sandy pushed me through the velvet curtains into the back room, where all the boys were waiting for me. She pulled the curtains to a dramatic close behind us both, then stuck her head back through it, into the restaurant.

"Have I made myself abundantly clear?"

"Yes, Sandy," came the chorus from the queers.

I flopped down onto the banquette seat beside Nick, Dav, Sunny, and Ludo, and let my head fall onto the table.

"Drink?" Sunny asked.

* * *

Sandy brought me two Essex Girls, on the house. I knocked both shots straight back. The alcohol burnt through my stomach hot and slow, the way a fire moves through a peat bog. As I put the second glass down, I noticed my hand was shaking.

"You OK, pal?" Nick asked.

"No."

My phone vibrated. The caller ID said it was Mum. I had a sick feeling in the pit of my stomach.

"Bubby, we're in chaos here," Mum said. "Are you orright?"

"What's happening?"

"There's a heap of reporters out the front of the salon, and they won't leave. They keep shouting things and harassing customers. Your Aunty Cheryl threw a box of penises over them and told them to piss off, but now they keep goading her to see what else she'll do. The salon phone's been ringing hot with reporters all day. We've had to unplug it. We close in half an hour, but your sister says they're camped out the front of the house as well. What should I do?"

I looked at Sunny and Ludo for advice.

"Paps?" Sunny asked. I nodded. He waved for me to give him the phone.

"Hello, Mrs Lyngstad, this is Sunny Miller. Let's see if we can find a way to get the wolves from your door. What have you told them so far?" Sunny nodded as he listened to my mother. "Are you certain you've given them no reason to think Toby's heading back to Essex any time soon?" A pause. "OK, great." Sunny's green eyes flashed back towards me. "Toby, can I check. Do you have any photos from a holiday abroad that you've never posted on your socials? Preferably somewhere remote. Lying on a beach somewhere, or better yet on a cruise, or trekking up a mountain."

Nick laughed. "You won't get Toby up a mountain unless he's carried up there in a sedan chair with a Hemsworth on each corner."

Dav whacked his husband on the arm.

Sunny's green eyes were still on me. "It's vital it's something you've not posted anywhere on social media. And nothing that looks like anything else you've posted. And you must have the same haircut."

"Probably," I said. "I've got heaps of pics from Gran Canaria."

Sunny gave me a thumbs up.

"OK, Mrs Lyngstad, we're going to try a diversion. It probably won't last long, but it might buy you some time until things have died down. Tomorrow lunchtime, we're going to post a picture on Instagram that makes it look like Toby's skipped the country. Once it has been posted, there's a chance some reporters will notice it and drift away. Others either won't see it or will be suspicious and will stick around. Give it a couple of hours, then we need to plant the idea that Toby is genuinely abroad."

This could not have sounded madder to me if Sunny were sitting there with visible signs of mercury poisoning while pouring tea for an impatient rabbit, but the other boys were smiling like Sunny was a ginger genius.

"It's absolutely vital you don't say it like it's an announcement," Sunny said. "Don't throw open the salon door and say 'Toby's in Gran Canaria,' or they'll be proper suspicious. You need to mention it in passing. In fact, it's best if it comes from someone else entirely. Is there someone you could get to walk past the salon, ask what all the commotion is about, and then get them to say something like 'but Toby's in Gran Canaria.' Can you do that?"

Sunny smiled. "Mrs Fitz sounds perfect."

With the plan in place and my phone back in my hands, I started absently scrolling through my photos, looking for the perfect image.

"Do you want to stay at ours until this blows over?" Nick asked.

"Jolly good idea," Ludo said. "Rather ruins the ruse if you're spotted taking the bins out in your jimmy jams."

"You'd be very welcome," Dav added.

I smiled, grateful to have such wonderful friends. Sandy popped her head through the velvet curtain and plonked a bottle of champagne down on the table. "I don't mean to alarm you, my darling, but there's a swarm of photographers turned up out the front."

My heart sank.

"How did they find you so quickly?" Ludo said.

Sandy picked at the foil on the bottle. "If it was one of the punters, they'll soon discover six inches up the arse is more than enough when it's a rhinestoned stiletto."

I shook my head. "John will have sold me out. Serves me right for being chippy with him."

"John?" Ludo asked.

"PureFM's entrepreneurial resident busker," Nick said. "It's amazing he doesn't have his own house by now, the way he shakes everyone down."

The champagne cork popped, and Sandy began pouring out the fizzing golden liquid. "What do you want me to do about the photographers?" she asked.

Sunny answered for me. "Nothing at all." He pointed at my suitcase. "When you're ready to leave, Toby, you're going to march out of here with that suitcase and get straight into a taxi. The last thing you're going to let the photographers hear you say before you shut the door is 'Airport, please, driver.' Make sure you don't say which one."

"But they'll have mopeds," I said. "They'll follow us."

"Up the motorway?"

Maybe Sunny *was* a ginger genius? I smiled and raised my champagne flute. We might even get away with this, I thought.

As we all clinked our glasses, a text pinged my phone.

Mum: *Elsa says someone's up the side of the house going through the bins. What should we do?*

The 7 best hot takes on "marriage material" finally landing Cole Kennedy

@exkennedictabbey: *Toby did the smart thing and patiently bided his time until Cole was in the bargain bin. Never pay full price for damaged goods, y'all! #discountcole*

@ronsonnicola28: *Imagine having so little self-worth that you let the guy who turned you into an internet meme use you as a plot twist in his ill-advised redemption arc. Who is writing @TobyLyngstad's story, Colleen Hoover?*

@sandwichf1lla: *He might not be marriage material but Cole K sure is desperately-snog-my-way-to-good-press material. #popreview #thegotos*

@OctimusTate: *Give Cole a break. Dude's a player. All us players got that one ex who's both still in love with us and so insecure that when we snap our fingers, their legs open right up.*

@LadyAndreaG25: *So what if he might throw you through a glass table from time to time, Cole Kennedy's hot. Amirite?*

@HannahW99: *Self-respect is the most valuable commodity we all have. It costs nothing. Don't trade it for a lump of Cole. #respect #colekennedy*

@Cole4Eva: *This whole situation is desperately sad. Cole's reputation is being trashed by someone who clearly bears him a huge grudge. Imagine if your ex wrote a tell-all book about your time together. I bet you wouldn't like what you read. Jasper Horner is a bitter, evil creep. #teamcolby #kennedictforlife*

Chapter Forty-One

Three days later, I found myself sitting in Nick's car in the car park under his building, waiting for Cole to arrive. It was the morning Cole was due to fly to Stockholm and the first time I'd left Nick and Dav's apartment since arriving there direct from Miss Timmy's. I had cabin fever. Now, finally having stepped out the front door, I was terrified someone was going to rumble me. The press seemed to have bought the big lie that I was in Gran Canaria, but that hadn't stopped them finding new angles to fill the paper every day. I wore my purple onesie, partly so I could throw up the hood if anyone came by, and partly because I hadn't taken it off since I'd moved in. Dav had volunteered to sew up the leg the evening I arrived because, and I quote, "I've just seen how impressively thorough your spray tan is, and that's more information than I needed at dinner."

Cole's big black SUV rumbled up to the gate. As I pressed the button to let him in, I felt both excited to see him and annoyed that all this cloak-and-dagger stuff was necessary. Cole climbed out of the car with a cheeky smile on his face.

"Is this for me?" He batted the velvety ears of my hood, pulled me into a hug, and kissed me. "You can tell me if this is your kink, Tobes.

Purple kitty cats in underground car parks is incredibly niche, but... I can work with it."

I buried my face into his shoulder, sucking in the smell of him. He ran his hands up into my hair, letting the hood drop down.

"I've missed you," I said.

"I've missed you too."

Fiona got out of the SUV and coughed politely. "Before you boys get too carried away, can I borrow Toby for a second?" She was holding a pile of papers and a pen. Cole released me.

"I'm sorry, Toby," she said, "but with everything that's going on, we've had to beef up our insurance. We need you to sign a new NDA. We also need you to sign a release form for some incidental footage WebFlix might want to use."

This was a punch to the stomach.

"I already signed an NDA and a release form when I did all the paperwork for *Pop Review* joining the tour."

"I know, but this one covers..." She searched for the right words. "All the personal stuff that wasn't covered by the original NDA."

I shook my head in disbelief. Cole reached for my hand and pulled me towards him. "I'm sorry, I know it's a pain. It's j—"

I pulled my hand away. The annoyance that had been bubbling below the surface—my frustration at being cooped up like a prisoner, of not being able to go to my own home, of my face and name being dragged through the mud in the papers every day—began to fizzle and pop. Steam and smoke began to billow from the top of my metaphorical mountain.

"Let me guess, you feel like I've got a gun pointed at your head?" I said.

Cole seemed to shrink at that.

"Tobes, don't be lik—"

Fiona raised a hand between us. "I'm sorry, Toby, after Jasper—"

"You're comparing me to *Jasper*?"

"We know you're nothing like Jasper," she said.

"Ten years," I said, starting to pace. "In ten years, I've never said a word against you. Not a single social media post. I kept your secret. I never outed you. I certainly never wrote a fucking book. The one time I spoke about you publicly, I did so with kindness and love and reverence. *Despite* the fact my association with you ruined my life, my reputation, my mental health—"

"Tobes, be fair," Cole said. "It's admin. It's not about you."

A car door closed. Fiona had got back inside the SUV—leaving the paperwork on the bonnet and leaving Cole and me to our fight.

"You seriously think I'm going to go to the press about you? I hate the press. Do you have any idea what I'm going through, what my family is going through? And it's all your fault."

Cole tried to pull me into a hug, but I shrugged him off. "It's tough on all of us right now, but it'll blow over," he said. "It always does."

"That's fine for you to say, with your blacked-out windows and Jack Reacher in your back pocket. You're leaving the country in an hour. I'm *literally* hiding out at my best friend's gaff because someone was going through my mum's bins."

"Always put rat traps in your bins," Cole said.

"I don't have rats, I have reporters!"

"That's why you put rat traps in your bins. Old trick of Robbie's."

"Arghhhh!" My cry of frustration echoed through the concrete car park.

Cole held up his hands. "Look, we don't think you're going to go sell us out. We know that's not who you are. Fiona's being extra cautious. After everything that's happened. It would mean a lot to me if you would sign it. It's meaningless. It's basically symbolic."

Finally, Cole had said something I agreed with. I looked him directly in the eye. "You're right, babes. One hundred per cent. It's symbolic of the fact you don't trust me. It's symbolic of the fact you think I'm here to profit off my association with you."

"Profit off your association?"

I'd finally hit a nerve. Good. I wanted a fight. I wanted to see a bit of mongrel burst through the sweetness. I wanted to have this out. "Toby, you don't even want to be seen in public with me. This whole past month you've been behaving like I'm a—"

"Dirty little secret?" I said.

Cole looked wounded. "You wouldn't even go to Stonehenge with me because people would see us."

"Look at what happens to my life when people see us together!"

"Do you know how it feels to think I'm only good enough for you in private?"

"Shall I ask Jasper how it feels?"

I was like a sniper. You could almost see Cole recoil from where the bullet entered his heart.

"Are you ashamed of me?" he pleaded. "Do I embarrass you? Or is it that you want all the good stuff that comes with being with a celebrity—the money, the private jets—but not the hard work of dealing with the price of fame?"

The volcano finally erupted. "Oh my God, you so nearly had it, babes. You were *so* close. But you can't open your eyes wide enough to see the world outside your own narrow experience. This is about protecting myself."

"From me!" It was a statement. There was no question mark in the way he said it.

"From the circus that comes with you."

"The circus is a part of my life," Cole said, hitting his chest with his finger, tears welling in his eyes. "You don't get to have me without it."

"Can you hear yourself?"

"You think I don't know how hard the circus is? It's been my life for a decade. But it won't always be this way, Toby. In a few years, no one will care. You know as well as anyone pop music moves on. I've got what, five years, and I'll be forgotten. But right now, the circus is a big part of my life. I hate it as much as you do, but it's part of the deal." He was pleading with me now. "I need someone who'll walk tall and proud by my side, who'll be there for me when it all gets tough, who'll be there to tell me it'll all be OK."

I looked Cole square in the eye. "I'm sorry, but that person was never going to be me."

"That person *is* you, Toby," Cole said. "I know that person is you. You're stronger than you think you are. Together, I genuinely believe there's nothing we can't do. The press will get bored with us in a few days anyway."

My tears burnt my cheeks. "I've been 'marriage material boy' for ten years, Cole. The press *never* gets bored. I'm sorry, I'm not built for this."

Cole's arms reached out for me, then fell back to his sides. We stood there, both in tears, three feet apart, neither of us able to close the gap.

"Are you breaking up with me?" Cole's chestnut eyes pleaded for me to give the answer he wanted to hear.

I wavered, unsure what I wanted. If I was honest with myself, what I wanted was what we had together when the rest of the world wasn't watching, when no one else got to have opinions about us. But that wasn't on offer anymore. If I thought about it, I'd been lucky to have what we'd had for so long. It was always going to end. But did I want to lose Cole from my life completely? I thought of the hours in the broadcast van, getting to know each other again, and the amazing week on the farm, falling in love with each other again. Was all that over? I wasn't ready to make that decision.

"No." I shook my head. "No, I'm not breaking up with you."

Cole leapt forward and folded me up in a hug. "Thank you." He kissed my neck, my cheek, my ear. His face was wet against mine. "Thank you, so much. We can make this work. I promise. I know we can."

I held him in my arms, not feeling at all sure that we could make this work. I couldn't be the guy who broke up with Cole Kennedy right before he left the country on an eight-month-long world tour. But the fight had opened a wound that needed time to heal.

"You don't have to sign the NDA," Cole said. "I trust you."

"I think Fiona—"

"Fiona is being a big sister. And a lawyer. Will you come to Stockholm for Friday night's show?" Cole's eyes looked hopeful.

I wiped my face on my sleeve. "If you're inviting me because you need a translator, they speak better English there than we do in Essex."

"Please say you'll come."

I shook my head. "I have a job to do."

"I can fly you out Friday afternoon and get you back in time for your show Saturday lunchtime. Come on, it'll be fun. And the world already knows about you now. The sooner I start showing you off, the sooner the press will get bored with us."

The thought turned my bowels to water. I tapped my hand against Cole's chest. "I'll think about it."

"Let me know, yeah?"

"Of course." But something inside me had curdled. Being a dirty little secret had suited me fine. Cole's plan would turn us into public property. What was a nice thing for him would be a nightmare for me —and I felt like I had very little control over any of it. But what choice did I have? I spotted the pile of papers on the bonnet of the SUV where Fiona had left them and, in a fit of self-destructiveness, decided to do something symbolic of my helplessness. I picked up the pen and signed them.

Cole's TV love confession: Toby is my flame!

It's official! Britain's bad boy prince of pop has been banging DJ Toby Lyngstad all over the U.K. for the past month.

In an interview that quickly went viral on social media, Cole Kennedy confessed his love for DJ Toby Lyngstad on a Swedish television chat show last night, and admitted he wrote "The Flame" while pining over Lyngstad during their years apart.

Asked by TV host Nils Nilsson about being caught kissing the "Pop Review" presenter, Kennedy was effusive about his love for "marriage material boy."

"Toby is the best thing that's happened to me in years, and I'm so happy we've found each other again," he said. "We have an incredible connection. He knew me before the rest of the world did. He knows the real me. Not many people do."

Lyngstad is of Swedish heritage, and Nilsson asked the singer if his boyfriend had taught him anything about Swedish culture.

"Not much, but I've tasted his meatballs," Kennedy replied...

Chapter Forty-Two

The internet had exploded. I could almost about forgive Cole for the meatballs comment. He meant it innocently enough, even though a naked mole rat trapped in a Pringles tube at the back of the pantry could have seen the jokes coming. What I couldn't forgive him for was baring his soul about our relationship. Why had he done it? He hadn't listened to a thing I'd said. I'd spent a week in hiding, waiting for things to cool down, and he went and threw gas on the fire. By Thursday night I was well annoyed and determined to get my life back. Before I could even consider flying to Stockholm for Cole's gig, I needed some time in my happy place, surrounded by the people I loved and trusted. I called Mum and arranged to head into the salon in the morning for a trim, an eyebrow threading, and a facial. But when Friday morning came, I was woken by a text.

Mum: *Please don't worry bubby, but it's best you don't come into the salon this morning. Probably a good idea to stay off your socials and the news sites, too. Have a safe trip and give all our love to your grandparents if you get to see them. Xxx*

As far as messages designed to not invoke panic go, that was right up there with "I don't mean to alarm you, Captain Smith, but I *think* that was an iceberg." And, like the *Titanic*, I had a terrible sinking feeling. I tried to call Mum immediately, but she didn't answer. So, I did the thing she had expressly told me not to do and checked social media. That's when I saw it: a photo of Chloe's Hair and Beauty in the Colchester high street—or what was left of it. Someone had smashed the windows, trashed the inside, and tried to burn it down. Spray-painted across the wall in big red letters were the words *UR 2 UGLY 4 COLE!!!*

My heart broke. I burst into tears. This wasn't simple wanton vandalism, this was a deliberate desecration. It was a hate crime, and it was directed at me, but it was my family who were paying the price. Shock took hold of my body. I began to shake. I grabbed Nick's keys, got straight in the car, and—after ten frustrating minutes pissing about trying to work out the hand controls—drove towards Essex.

* * *

An ambulance was driving away as I pulled up to the salon. There was glass everywhere. The press had long since beaten me there and were waiting—the whirring and snapping of digital cameras announcing my arrival. Mum flung open the salon door and ushered me in.

"I told you not to come, bubby."

"The ambulance. Is everyone OK?"

"The photographers were getting a bit up in your Aunty Cheryl's face, so she took a swing at one of them."

"Oh my God."

"With a bottle of rosé."

"Wait, she had wine?"

"Only she missed him, went tits up, and landed flat on her arse on all that broken glass."

"Is she OK?"

"She was flirting with the paramedic, so I think she'll be fine. But they'll be pulling bits of window out of her bum for weeks, I reckon. That's the thing about a G-string, it don't offer you much protection in an emergency situation."

I looked around the salon. They'd tried to set fire to the reception desk, burning piles of paperwork and foam from the chair, melting the computer screen, and scorching up the wall. The graffiti was three feet high in blood red. It was over the mirrors—which were all smashed—the brickwork, the art. Products and glass were strewn all over the floor. All four of the sinks were smashed. The curtains to the back room had been yanked down and lay trampled on the floor.

"I'm so sorry, Mum," I said, choking on my tears.

Mum had built this business up from nothing. She didn't deserve this. This salon had paid for my school fees, it had trained me in my first profession, it had given me countless hours of joy and friendship. This salon was more than somewhere to get your hair or nails done: It was a home from home, a sanctuary of respite and relaxation and rejuvenation for hundreds of people in our community. It was my happy place, and someone had violated it. I stood there, surrounded by the shattered remains of the salon, unable to shake one clear, resounding thought: This had happened because of my relationship with Cole Kennedy. All the horrendous things that had happened to me since I was sixteen had happened because of Cole Kennedy. My family was suffering because of Cole Kennedy. I was miserable *because of Cole Kennedy*.

Absolutely miserable.

And I could not see how my life would get better as long as Cole Kennedy was in it. This chaos—this circus—came with him.

I stayed to help Mum clean up the salon. Dad arrived with some of the boys from the construction company, and they set about repainting and replacing broken and burnt fixtures. By six o'clock that evening, thanks to a massive team effort, the salon was almost restored. Mum had lost a day's trade, and goodness knew what the day had cost Dad, let alone Aunty Cheryl's buttocks, but the salon was back to something like normal. As Mum folded the last of the clean towels, I knew normal was *exactly* what I wanted. And I could have either normal or Cole Kennedy, but not both.

"I'll put those away," I said. "I need to make a call. I'll lock up. You go home."

With nothing of interest left to photograph, the press had gone home. They had their story for tomorrow. I pulled the new curtains across the rail and sat on the floor in the back room with my back against the cupboard. The air was warm and damp from the dryer, but I found myself shivering. The place smelt like fresh paint. I pulled out my phone and considered sending a text but decided Cole deserved better than that. He picked up on the first ring.

"There's my beautiful boy," he said. "Are you here? I'll send Fiona to go get you."

I couldn't speak. The words had left me completely.

"Tobes?"

"I..."

"Are you OK? What's up?"

"I'm at the salon," I said, and I told him what had happened.

"Toby, I'm *so* sorry. Look, I'm onstage in like an hour's time, but I can fly home right after the show. Stockholm's not that far. I can be with you by about one o'clock. Sooner if Mitch will let me parachute out over Colchester."

"No!" I said, a little too forcefully. "Don't do that."

"I'm happy to do it. I've got the WebFlix camera crew here filming the show and tonight's meet-and-greet, so I can't bail on that, but I'm happy to come if you need me."

"Cole, I can't do this." It spilt out of me, and the overwhelming feeling was relief.

"What?"

"I'm sorry. I should have said so the other day, but you looked so sad and I couldn't, but... I can't do this."

"Nooo, no, no, no. Please don't do this—"

"I'm a normal person, Cole. I want a normal life. I don't want fame. Not on this scale. I don't want to date a pop star. This circus, it's not for me."

"Toby, what are you saying? Don't be sill—"

"This isn't only about me. This is about my family. The people and places I care about."

"Are you at home? I'll be right there. It'll take me like two or three hours. Don't move."

"Don't you dare!" I said. "Your fans have paid to see a show. My cousins are in that audience, and they'll be devastated if you cancel. So will thousands of other people. So will your insurance company. And Fiona would kill us both. Please, do your job. Do the show."

"Do the show." Cole laughed. It was hollow. He sounded completely deflated. I felt terrible, but I had done the right thing. All I had to do now was stick to my guns.

"I'm sorry," I said. "You deserve so much better. You deserve someone who can handle being seen in public with you. You deserve that person who can ride the waves and show the world they're proud of you. I'm sorry that person isn't me."

"But... I *love* you," Cole said.

"I know. I love you too."

And I hung up the phone.

I reached up to the benchtop, pulled down the stack of warm, freshly folded towels onto the floor, curled myself up in them, and burst into tears.

Where's Toby, Cole?

Has Cole Kennedy already been dumped by on-again, off-again squeeze DJ Tobias Lyngstad?

The pair hasn't been seen in public together since being caught canoodling in the pop star's garden.

It's the latest evidence the scandal-plagued recovering drug addict is struggling to get back on the straight and narrow, despite his publicity machine pumping out a stream of positive stories.

As the European leg of Kennedy's tour gets under way, his controversial lifestyle has seen the former pop wunderkind tumble from the charts—and his old bandmates take number one with their new single, "Earthquake Woman"...

U.S. media giant YMC outbids Sentinel Group for Pure Network

A bid by the Sentinel Group (owners of this newspaper) to buy the Pure Network, owners of PureFM and TalkUK, has been gazumped by an offer from U.S.-based ultraconservative media group Ypsilanti Media Corporation (YMC).

The offer, understood to be in excess of £200 million, is not subject to foreign ownership of media laws, despite TalkUK being one of the most influential talkback radio networks in the country. The laws apply only to newspapers.

Representatives of YMC declined to comment on the offer and what it would mean for the format of either radio network if the deal was approved by Pure's board. However, in the U.S., YMC runs a string of hard-right-leaning talkback and Christian rock music radio stations, leading to criticism by media commentators that YMC is trying to buy power and influence in the U.K.'s democracy.

Part Four

EIGHT MONTHS LATER

PRESS RELEASE

WebFlix exclusive behind-the-scenes documentary reveals the real Cole Kennedy

WEBFLIX

For Immediate Release

Think you know Cole Kennedy's story? Think again.

A new fly-on-the-wall documentary produced by Cuckoo's Nest Films for WebFlix, "A Fire Inside Me: The Real Cole Kennedy Story," reveals the man behind the headlines—and fans will be shocked by what they discover.

Cuckoo's Nest followed Kennedy for the first year after he left the Go Tos, the "Make Me a Pop Star" sausage-factory boy band that made him a household name. The documentary covers recording "The Flame," his sell-out debut solo global tour, controversy, scandal, heartbreak and solving the mystery that has haunted him his whole life —the truth about his birth family.

Cuckoo's Nest executive producer Valerie Lee said viewers will get to follow Kennedy on an emotional visit to New Zealand, where he meets his birth mother for the first time, and to Istanbul, where he meets his birth grandmother. She said viewers will go backstage with Kennedy on the Flame Tour and get exclusive access to some of the pop star's most private thoughts and moments in what was "undoubtedly one of the most momentous years of his life."

"Fans will also learn the truth about the experience of pop stardom from someone who spent a decade inside the machine. I think viewers will be surprised how much of a sweatshop pop really is. The truth is nothing short of scandalous," Lee said.

"A Fire Inside Me" drops on 16 April. Running time: 180 minutes (3 × 60-minute episodes).

Chapter Forty-Three

A Friday morning found Tarneesha, Nick, and me sitting around the table in our production office, planning the last ever episode of *Pop Review*. Well, Neesh and Nick and were planning it while I watched Instagram videos of Cole rehearsing for that night's big gig—the first of his three final shows at Wembley Stadium.

Tarneesha threw a highlighter at my head. It glanced off my temple and hit the wall.

"I *said* we've got Jocasta Rose as our final guest in the two thirty-five slot."

"Good, I like Jocasta," I said, not taking my eyes off my phone.

Instead of using a backing track, a live philharmonic orchestra would be joining Cole onstage for the stadium shows. It must have cost a bomb. But, even on Instagram, the sound was incredible.

"We've got her for twenty-five minutes, so I'll make a couple of packages—one looking back at her early career and one about the last couple of years," Tarneesha said.

Nick tapped his finger on the desk. "What if we made the second one clips from her interviews in the studio over the years? Not just with this deaf bawbag, but with Raluca as well?"

"Sounds great," Tarneesha said. "What do you think, Tobes?"

I was only vaguely aware of this conversation going on. I'd scrolled to another video. Cole was in a costume I hadn't seen before. Apparently, he'd switched up his outfits for his stadium shows. He wore black leather boots, black leather trousers that looked remarkably like they were designed for Turkish oil wrestling, and a billowing puffy shirt laced up with rope in the front. He looked like a pirate. A sexy pirate. Stunning.

"This is a song about hope," Cole said on the video, and my heart twinged. Great balls of orange-and-golden flame burst high into the air, swirling into the sky in boiling mushroom clouds. The orchestra struck up the opening notes of "The Flame." I was shaking like Aunty Cheryl that time she tried to cure her hangover with two unmarked white well-they-look-like-paracetamol-to-me tablets she found on the pavement outside Sticky Vicky's in Benidorm.

"Tobes!" A pocket calculator glanced off the side of my head.

"Ouch!" I checked my face for blood. "Where did you even get that from, babes?"

"I have a fax machine down here as well. I'll throw that next."

Nick looked exasperated. "Neesh was saying we'll open the phone lines for the last hour and give the show over to the fans to share their memories and stories about what *Pop Review* means to them. What do you reckon?"

"Sounds good," I said.

"Unless..." Nick said. I waited for him to finish, but the words didn't come.

"Unless?"

Nick hesitated. "Unless, maybe, you wanted to do something about the fact Cole's stadium sho—"

"No, not that. It's in my contract. No Cole."

"But it's all anyone is talking about," Tarneesha said. "You've been ignoring to watch rehearsal clips. You're as obsessed as everyone else."

"No," Nick said. "Toby is obsessed with his ex. And he's been watching clips of his shows and endlessly cyberstalking him like a desperate mooning saddo for the past eight months. Because..." Nick slapped me across the back of the head. "He..." He slapped me again. "Should never..." *Slap*. "Have broken up with him." *Slap*.

Denzil popped his head through the door, and we all sat upright like naughty schoolkids caught misbehaving.

"Guys, let me introduce you to the new owners," Denzil said. "This is Harland, from YMC."

A guy who looked like the baddie in every single Muppets movie stepped into the room, followed by three other men who looked like they were assembled in the same factory. They all had names straight from *The Dukes of Hazzard*. Denzil introduced us, and we nodded politely. We'd been sacked by email three weeks earlier. From Monday morning, PureFM would be a Christian rock music station. The signage for Hallelujah Radio had already gone up outside. It's the sort of thing that happens in the media. It's a brutal industry. We had accepted our fates. But they hadn't even kept Tarneesha on staff, and her mother was a Pentecostal minister, so our goodwill for these arse-holes was non-existent.

"Nice to meet y'all," Harland the cartoon villain said. All he was missing was a big hat and a horse. His existence was undoing the hard-wiring in my brain. Hollywood had mistakenly led me to believe Texans were all hot as hell.

"Orright?" I said, trying to give these gentlemen the right amount of sneer.

The men were all Southern politeness but dead behind the eyes. Being stuck in a room making small chat with a Black woman, a homosexual, and a homosexual in a wheelchair had clearly tripped the diversity switch in their brains, and they'd powered down for safety reasons.

"I hear one of you is off to the BBC," Harland said.

Nick raised his hand. "Guilty as charged."

"I've never met a commie in a wheelchair before," he said.

My jaw was on the floor. Nick opened his mouth to speak.

Harland burst into laughter. "I'm just messin' with ya. Everyone in merry old England seems so quick to believe we're all rednecks, it's hard not to have fun with it. No, I'm glad to hear you've landed on your feet."

I looked at Nick, fizzing with anticipation for his reply. But he smiled and said nothing.

"Shall I take you through to see the studio?" Denzil said, breaking the uncomfortable silence.

"Why, I'd like that, Denzeel." He turned to the three of us. "Nice to meet y'all. God bless you—and good luck with whatever comes next in life's journey."

With that, they left. "Sorry," Denzil mouthed as he closed the door behind him. It was Nick who broke the silence.

"Do you think it's the circumcision that makes them such insensitive pricks?"

Tarneesha laughed. "Honestly, thought you was gonna shiv him for a sec."

"Not like you to hold your tongue, babes," I said.

Nick smiled. "Always be gracious in victory."

"Victory?" Tarneesha said. "He's sacked us."

"Not sacked, Neesh," Nick said. "Made redundant. It's an important difference. I've got twenty-five grand of that arsehole's money landing in my bank account on Monday. All because he has made me redundant. What he doesn't know, and I have no intention of telling him, is that I'd lined up the gig at the BBC two months ago, and I've only been hanging around for my payout."

"Sneaky bastard!" Tarneesha offered her fist, and Nick bumped it. "And the BBC was happy to wait two months?"

"Neesh, I'm a gay man in a wheelchair with a Sikh husband. The

BBC would have given me David Attenborough's pelt to wear as a raincoat if I'd asked for it."

"You're the best in the business," I said. "They're lucky to have you. And they know it."

It was Tarneesha who got our meeting back on track.

"So, to be clear, despite this show's deep involvement in the Flame Tour and Cole Kennedy being the biggest pop star in the world, we're *not* including him in *Pop Review*'s final ever show?"

"Correct," I said.

I unlocked my phone, and the tinny sound of Cole singing "The Flame" filled the room.

"OK. Good decision," she said.

"Super healthy," Nick added.

I turned up the volume and felt my heart vibrate to the sounds of Cole's voice singing our song, backed by a full orchestra. My whole body ached to hold him, though I knew I never would again.

Chapter Forty-Four

ap, tap. Our microphones were live. The last notes of the song played out.

"That's 'Not Pretty' by Jocasta Rose—and Jocasta is my guest in the studio today for this final ever *Pop Review*. Jocasta, we're nearly out of time, but before I let you go, what's next for you?"

"Well, I'll have a new album coming out in the summer—I can't tell you much about that—"

"Come on, babes, it's my last show! Give us a little exclusive. Go on."

"I couldn't. I'll get in trouble!"

"With who? Come on. Give us a treat."

"Well, I will say my new album will have a couple of duets," she said coyly.

I hammed up my excitement. We had forty seconds left until we hit the ad break. "Tell me who you're singing with? Spill it! Loyal fans need to know."

Jocasta flushed bright red. "So, I was touring the US recently, and I bumped into an old friend, and we decided to do some writing together.

We locked ourselves in a hotel for a few days and listened to some great old music—you know, the Stones, Queen, even some Dolly Parton—and we chatted and wrote and made music, and, yeah, we came up with some beautiful stuff. I can't wait to share it with the world."

The counter on my screen showed I still had twenty seconds to fill. On the screen beside it, the chatline was refreshing so fast the words were an indecipherable blur. I had no idea what they said, but that didn't stop me saying, "Judging by the chatline, I'd say your fans want to know who it is!"

Jocasta rolled her eyes, and through gritted teeth, she said, "It's Cole Kennedy."

Of course it was.

Fifteen seconds left.

"Jocasta, it's wonderful to see you, as always. Thank you so much for being a part of our final show. And in the words of Sweden's second-greatest export—after my dad, obviously—thank you for the music."

"You're so welcome, thank you so much for having me."

Tap. Jocasta's mic was off. "Coming up after the news, the last goodbye. Send your memories through to the chatline or give us a call. In the final hour of *Pop Review*, we throw open the airwaves to the most important part of the show—you."

Tap. I fired off the ad break. *Tap.* My mic was off. The second the on-air light went dark, Jocasta said, "I'm so sorry! I was trying to avoid mentioning Cole, but—"

The studio door opened, and Jocasta's manager walked in. "Jay, we have to scoot."

Jocasta stood. "I'm sorry. Are you OK?"

"I'm fine."

Jocasta leaned over the desk and kissed me on both cheeks. "Sorry, I gotta run. But... he misses you, you know."

And with that, she disappeared.

Nick's voice came through my cans. "Tobes, have you checked your socials in the last fifteen?"

I caught his eye through the glass and shook my head. I pressed the button to speak to him. "Course not, babes, I was interviewing Jocasta."

"Check your phone."

I pulled my headphones down around my neck and grabbed my mobile. A message from Nick linked through to Instagram. A video started to play automatically. Cole Kennedy was shirtless, dressed only in his pants. My heart skipped at the sight of his muscular body. He was backstage somewhere, and in floods of tears. I pumped up the volume as loud as I could.

"I can't do it," he said. "Please, don't make me do it."

"Do it for the fans," said Fiona's voice. The footage cut to a crowded auditorium, fans stamping their feet and screaming "We want Cole!" The audio of Cole and Fiona's conversation continued over the top.

"I can't."

"You can. Say it with me: Happiness is always available to me."

"I don't want to."

"You do. You know you do. You'll feel better if you do."

"I don't want to feel better. I want to die."

"You don't want to die."

The video cut back to Cole. "I've lost him forever this time." Cole cried in a choking, mournful wail. I burst into tears. He was crying about *me*. This must have been filmed in Stockholm, right after we broke up. I felt intense, searing guilt—and so much regret. The video showed Cole hugging Fiona, his eyes puffy, his face a mess of stage make-up.

"What you're missing is his love, and that's OK," Fiona said. "I know it's not the same, but there are twenty thousand people out there who love you too. If you want to feel loved, then go out there and give them a show. Can you do that for me?"

Cole sobbed but slowly nodded. "OK."

The camera cut to Cole sitting at his cello, bow in hand. A voice told him they were ready. Cole's shoulders started bouncing up and down as more tears came, but he collected himself, took a deep breath, put his shoulders back, lifted his bow, and struck the first note of "Sweet Dreams (Are Made of This)." A wall of screaming fans. Then it cut to Cole rising up through the centre of the stage, thrashing at his guitar, tears streaming down his face. A montage played out under the song, running through the highs and lows of Cole's long year since going solo. Newspaper headlines flashed up, showing all Cole's controversies, then footage of him pacing around a hotel room and smacking a newspaper against a table, then at the farm, with his family. The music switched to "The Flame," and the video showed me interviewing Cole in the outside broadcast van, Cole meeting fans in the street, Cole and me backstage somewhere sitting opposite each other on a couch, laughing and looking longingly at each other. Where had they got that footage? It cut to a shot of Cole and me lying in the grass at Hetty Pegler's Tump. Who'd filmed that? Mitch?

"Toby wasn't 'marriage material boy' to me; he was simply... marriage material," Cole's voice-over said. "And I lost him because of the circus that book created."

The video cut to us dancing around in the dairy together, singing and laughing and joking. Andy must have filmed that. Or maybe Tully. There was footage of us kissing, looking very much in love in the summer sunshine, completely oblivious to the camera. I should have been angry. I should have felt violated. But my heart ached. This felt like a love letter to our relationship, and I missed Cole so much it hurt.

The music transitioned to "Reborn," and Cole was on a plane, graphics showing a cartoon jet landing in New Zealand and Istanbul, then footage of Cole hugging a couple of women I took to be his mother and grandmother.

"I've felt lost my whole life," Cole said in the voice-over. "All my life I've been searching for something. My music is how I process it, make sense of it. My music is my gift to the world. But this is, now, a gift to me. I know who I am, finally. I know what I want. It's time to take control of my narrative. It's time to tell *my* story."

As a fully orchestrated version of "Reborn" hit its soaring heights, Cole stood in the spotlight on a darkened stage, taking his applause, arms raised in the air, hands in fists of defiance, sweat dripping off him, his face a beaming smile. He looked triumphant, reborn. The video cut to a black screen, then the words *A Fire Inside Me* appeared, followed by *The Real Cole Kennedy Story*, then the WebFlix logo and "all episodes, April 16."

The door to the studio burst open, and Tarneesha looked at me with eyes of fury.

"Will you put your bloody cans on, we're on in fifteen seconds. The chatline and switchboard are in absolute meltdown." She disappeared back out the door into the production booth. I scrambled to put my headphones on.

The promo finished playing out: "Taking. Pop. *Seriously*."

Tap. My microphone was live. It took a second for the words to come, and when they came, I sounded shell-shocked.

"This is the last ever *Pop Review*, I'm Tobias Lyngstad, and thank you for being with me. Let's take a quick look at the chatline before we get to the fresh new track from Swedish wunderkind Felix Sandman."

The chatline was still spinning, so I hit the space bar to pause it. Always dangerous, going live without pre-reading the messages—but I was flying by the seat of my pants, and it was the best I could do.

"Marsha P says, 'I've been listening to *Pop Review* since I was twelve and I've been team Colby since day one.'" I coughed. "OK. Thank you, Marsha. We've got a voice note here. Let's hear from Medhat." Tap. I hit play on the voice note.

"Oh my God, Toby, are you mad? You're like, *soooo* cute together.

For God's sake, go out there and get your man. We're all rooting for you!"

I looked at Tarneesha, who was meant to screen these notes before they went to air. She shrugged.

"Let's hear a track," I said, pressing the button to fire off the song. *Tap*. I switched my microphone off. I punched at the button that allowed me to speak directly to Tarneesha.

"What are you playing at?"

"It's not me," she protested. "It's been non-stop since WebFlix dropped their promo. It's all anyone wants to talk about."

"It's our last show, babes, can we talk about *Pop Review* please?"

"The listeners want to talk about you and Cole."

"Absolutely not."

But for the next three-quarters of an hour, every caller and every message to the chat line was about the same topic: People were suddenly invested in a Cole and Toby love story they had barely known was happening.

Tammy F: *You're so cute together! OMG! #teamcolby*

Yara A: *I can't believe he wrote The Flame for you and you still let him go a second time! Are you mad, Toby? Go fix this, immediately!*

Tim L: *My boyfriend and I have a spare front row ticket to tonight's show at Wembley. For the love of all that is holy, please come with us. You have to get back together with Cole.*

Ravi D: *Don't listen to the haters! Love is love. You two belong together!*

A message from Tarneesha flashed up on the screen: "Robbie from Leeds is on line one." *Tap*. My microphone was on. I back-announced the song and hit the button that put line one live to air.

"Robbie from Leeds has called into the show," I said. "Robbie, what has *Pop Review* meant to you?" I lifted the fader to hear Robbie speak.

"Well, I'm more of an old rock and roller, me," he said, and I recognised the voice immediately.

"Is that... Robbie Johnswagger... of Buzzsaw fame?"

I looked at my team through the glass. Tarneesha shrugged again, but Nick couldn't hide his smirk.

"The one and the same, young lad," Robbie said. "Long time, no speak."

In fact, I hadn't spoken to Robbie since that fateful day by the pool on *Make Me a Pop Star* when I was swapped out for Taylor Knight.

"I wanted to wish you all the best for your final show and thank you for your contribution to the music industry," he said. "It might not have been the role you thought you'd play, but I want you to know we all respect the way you talk about music. You bring real intellect to the conversation, and we'll miss you doing what you do, because you're bloody good at it."

My throat felt like it was trying to swallow a snooker ball. "Thank you," I squeaked out. "That means a lot, coming from a legend of the industry."

"I do think you've been a bloody bellend about Cole, though, to be blunt."

Sideswiped at a thousand miles an hour. My whiplash had whiplash.

"If he was good enough to be considered marriage material twelve years ago, he's certainly good enough to be marriage material now. Helen Keller could see you two love each other and belong together, and she's been dead for sixty years. Pull your bloody finger out."

I couldn't form words. I flailed about, trying to find something to say.

"You do love him, don't you, Toby?" Robbie asked.

I nodded until my vocal cords caught up with my head.

"Yes, of course," I said defensively. "I think I've probably loved him since the day we met."

"There we go, doesn't that feel better?"

It did.

"So, why aren't you together? Everyone thinks you belong together. I do. His family does. He does. The listeners of *Pop Review* obviously do."

I sighed. "That's the problem, isn't it? Everyone has an opinion. It doesn't matter that I will probably love him until the day I die. When the public has no idea about us, things are great, but the second they know we exist, they have opinions—sometimes they express those opinions by smashing windows, spraying nasty things on walls, and trying to burn down a salon. I can only take so much. One way or another, the opinions of other people have kept us apart for twelve years. And, I'm gonna say it like it is, you were a part of that."

"Not me," Robbie said.

"You were part of *Make Me a Pop Star*."

"And I have to hold my hands up to that and own it. That show has caused a lot of people a lot of pain, and I was a part of that. But it was also me who pulled Cole aside and told him to take care of what you two had. I thought he'd regret it if he lost it. I could see what was coming. I knew what the producers were doing. I should have done more to protect you both, and I'm sorry. I've only ever wanted what's best for Cole. And aside from his music career, Cole has only ever wanted you. If anyone should know that, it's me—because he and I have been through some shit together."

Tears were streaming down my face. I looked through the glass to the production booth, where Tarneesha was also in tears and Nick was in whatever is Scottish for tears.

"Do you think I should call him?" I asked. Nick mouthed the words "thank you" and theatrically bowed. Neesh was nodding like a plastic dog on the dashboard of a Ford Fiesta.

Robbie laughed. "Call him? It's a bit late for that."

It was a punch to the gut.

"You need to show him. Do something to make sure Cole sees how you *really* feel about him."

The chatline was whizzing so fast it risked melting the screen. I hit pause to stop it refreshing.

Bernard V: *Rock and roll Santa delivering real talk.*

"What should I do?"

"That's up to you," Robbie said. "Cole wrote you a love song. Go write him a love story. Give it a happily ever after. He's a good kid. You boys deserve forever."

* * *

The post-show plan had been to join the gang at Miss Timmy's for a celebratory dinner in Soho, but as we waited for the lift with our little boxes of personal belongings, all I could think about was Robbie Johnswagger's advice.

"You should go out the fire escape one last time," Nick said.

I shook my head. "I'm unemployed now. I can't afford John's fees."

"John's gone," Tarneesha said.

"What?" Nick and I said in unison.

"The council banned him from busking anywhere in the entire City of Westminster."

"Brutal," Nick said.

"When did that happen?" I asked.

"Like, two months ago."

The lift chimed, and the doors opened. Nick and Tarneesha got in. I didn't move.

"Are you coming?" Nick asked.

"I think I *will* take the fire escape," I said. "For old times' sake."

Nick nodded. "We'll hail a cab and meet you round the back."

A few minutes later I burst out of the fire escape onto a wet Charing Cross Road, setting the alarm wailing and nearly slamming into a street mime dressed in a Breton striped shirt and white gloves.

"Sorry, mate!" I said, then did a double take. "John?"

John pointed an index finger to each corner of his mouth and smiled.

"I thought you weren't allowed to busk anymore?"

John's face transformed into a sorrowful frown, fists kneading the corners of his eyes as he pretended to cry.

"Is this because the council banned you from busking?"

John held an index finger aloft, smiled, and tapped his head, like he'd outwitted the bastards.

"Good for you, mate," I said as the accessible taxi carrying Nick and Tarneesha pulled up beside us. I turned to climb in but was stopped by a tap on the shoulder. It was John, obviously. He mimed unzipping his mouth.

"You need to sort your life out, mate," he said.

"Pardon?"

"Who in their right mind gives up a sweet piece of arse like Cole Kennedy? You need your head read!"

His gloved hand zipped his mouth back up—to cheers of applause from Tarneesha and Nick. The whole world genuinely did have an opinion about my business. But John was right.

"Look after yourself, babes," I said, climbing into the taxi. As I took my seat, I pulled out my phone and scrolled through my contacts until I found the number I needed and hit call.

"Fiona? I've been really, *really* stupid, and I need your help."

Stars align for Kennedy's final gig at Wembley

After two nights with the roof on, it appears Cole Kennedy's third and final Wembley Stadium show tonight will take place under the stars.

The Flame Tour has been a global sell-out, and Kennedy has packed capacity crowds of 90,000 into all three Wembley shows, having previously sold out three London gigs at the Millennium Dome.

Though the show was billed as an "open-air spectacular," crowds at Friday and Saturday nights' shows missed out on some of the planned full pyrotechnics displays because rain meant the stadium's roof was closed. While many artists prefer to keep the roof open and risk the rain, Kennedy is performing with a full live orchestra—and when a hundred members of the London Philharmonic tell you they don't want to get their instruments wet, even a superstar like Kennedy has to listen.

It's understood the filmmakers of the much-anticipated Cole Kennedy documentary *A Fire Inside Me* will be recording some closing sequences for the programme at tonight's show, so if you're one of the lucky fans who'll be there, make a lot of noise!

Chapter Forty-Five

Wembley Stadium was buzzing. It did not get bigger than this—the largest venue in music in the UK. Live Aid 1985 was held here (well, sort of—in the old stadium). Adele, Taylor Swift, the Spice Girls, George Michael, and Take That had all played here. Now, the stadium was hosting the biggest pop star Britain had produced in a generation: Cole Kennedy. Ninety thousand Kenneddicts screamed their appreciation. Cole had ramped up the showmanship for his farewell gig. Not only a live orchestra sitting onstage, but a full choir—at least forty voices. The costumes were more lavish, the pyrotechnics more spectacular, the energy beyond anything I'd ever seen at a live gig. The crowd looked blissed out, high on the level of artistry Cole was delivering. And I was sitting in my seat, shitting my knickers like clinical dysentery was the colour of the season. In the seat next to me, Aunty Cheryl opened her leather jacket to reveal a smuggled hip flask.

"Dutch courage?"

I shook my head. She shrugged, opened it, and downed a swig.

Nick leaned over. "You OK, pal?"

I nodded. But I wasn't OK. Not really. We were deep in the

mellow part of the second half of the show. Cole was singing his moody, spooky rendition of Metallica's "Nothing Else Matters." It was nearly time. My hands were so wet with sweat I had to keep wiping them on my jeans. "The Flame" came next on the set list, but Fiona had warned me of a change-up for the final show—a two-minute gospel spectacular version of Metallica's big hit. The choir kicked in, and the sound soared. The crowd erupted, unable to believe the musicality they were hearing—the experimentation, the raw talent it took to create this wall of sound in a football stadium, the audacity required to take Metallica to church like this. This performance was iconic. When it ended, ninety thousand people burst into rapturous applause. Cole stood centre stage, leather-booted feet together, arms outstretched, pirate sleeves billowing, face looking up to the stars, soaking in the love. He turned to blow kisses to the choir, to the orchestra, to his band. The WebFlix camera crews captured it all. When the crowd finally hushed, Cole stood at the microphone.

"This is a song about hope." He stamped his foot, and flames burst from the stage and spiralled up into the sky.

A voice came through my headset. "Whenever you're ready, Toby."

Cole started to sing "The Flame."

"You lit a fire inside me that burned like the sun. You lit the way forward. You were the one."

I stood, took a couple of deep breaths, and nodded to Nick, who twisted the knob on the battery pack in my back pocket. The stadium was alive with music—the orchestra, the choir, Cole's rich, resonant voice. When he reached the chorus, I started singing the harmony.

Cole put a hand to his earpiece, confusion flashing over his face. It was enough that I knew he was hearing me, that the sound tech was feeding my audio through to him.

"It burns and it burns and it burns," Cole sang. But he was distracted. He looked around madly. A spotlight landed on me from

high above, like a spacecraft beaming me up. Through the bright white haze of the light, I saw Cole look up.

"Toby?"

The crowd exploded. I held my arm out towards Cole, reaching for him.

Cole pointed. He laughed. He fell to his knees. "Toby!"

The strings of the orchestra and the angelic voices of the choir soared, and Cole Kennedy burst into tears. I dashed out of my row, down the stairs, and out of the gate into the standing-room-only area —the spotlight following my every move. The Kenneddicts parted for me as I ran across the field. They were screaming my name, wishing me good luck, slapping me on the back. Cole got to his feet and started singing the second verse. He couldn't take his eyes off me, nor I off him. His arms were outstretched towards me, tears streaming down his face as he sang. The choir took over the harmonies, and I ran faster. Behind the crush barriers, the massive imposing edifice of Mitch guarded the stage. I barely had time to notice Mitch's cheeks were wet before he picked me up like a rag doll and deposited me on the stage. When the chorus hit, I was centre stage at Wembley Stadium, standing in front of the man of my dreams, the man I had loved since I was sixteen years old, singing to him, singing *with* him, singing a love song he'd written for me. And an orchestra and a choir and ninety thousand Kenneddicts joined in.

As we sang, I understood, as I'd never truly understood before, why this was a song about hope. I was *so* full of hope. Cole squeezed my hands as we sang. The choir and the orchestra built an earth-shaking crescendo. The sound was visceral, it felt like my body had become the music, and as the final notes played out, as our shoulders shook with grief and relief and love, Cole threw his arms around me, and the fireworks exploded around us. A stadium full of Kenneddicts went absolutely nuts. Cole buried his face in my neck, kissing me. I breathed in the familiar smell of him, the cinnamon and the citrus and the sweat. I tasted the saltiness of him on my lips and gripped him tight in my arms. It was a promise that I would never let him go again.

"I'm sorry," I said. "I love you. I love you so much. I've always loved you."

"I know, baby," Cole said. "I know. And I love you too."

Then Cole's lips found mine and we kissed, and the stadium erupted into chaos. Flames burst out of the stage and soared into the night sky above. And when it had all died down, I stood onstage in Cole Kennedy's arms, and from the orchestra, a piano started to tinkle the opening bars of the Beatles' "Here Comes the Sun."

"The Flame" goes to number one!

A year after it was released, Cole Kennedy's "The Flame" has hit number one on the U.K. charts, knocking off the Go Tos' "Sweet Cherry Cola" after a three-week run at the top.

The track rocketed up the charts this week after a video of Kennedy singing the song live onstage at Wembley Stadium with on-again-off-again boyfriend radio DJ Tobias Lyngstad went viral on social media...

Chapter Forty-Six

I woke to huffing and snorting and opened one eye.

"Good morning, Genevieve," I said, reaching a hand up to scratch under her chin. The air was cold against my skin, and the breeze was making the curtains billow. I snuggled deeper under the quilts.

"You're up," Cole said, padding in from the kitchen wearing nothing but underpants, a mug of steaming-hot tea in each hand. He bent over to kiss me and deposited my tea on the bedside table. "Good morning, beautiful."

"Are you talking to me or Genevieve?"

Cole laughed. "Both?" He threw a leg over me, straddling me, and reached over to put his tea down on his side of the bed. "OK, girl, time to go. I'll see you this afternoon." Genevieve huffed and kicked her head back. "Good girl." Cole edged forward up the bed to close the windows, his crotch resting on my chin. My arms were trapped under the blankets, but I felt playful, so I buried my face in his junk and showered it with kisses.

"No, don't wake him up," Cole said. "We have half an hour, at most, before the girls come running in here." He shuffled back down the bed and leaned over me so I was pinned by his knees and his elbows. "They'll have heard the chopper bring us in last night. They'll be bugging Juney to come over by now."

"We can achieve a lot in half an hour," I said, winking mischievously.

Cole smiled and leaned back, releasing my arms from their quilt cocoon. He stretched out the lean muscles of his body, giving me a show.

"You want to touch this?" he said, with a cheeky grin.

"Please," I said, putting my hands against his neatly clipped chest. I could feel his heart beating beneath my palm.

"It's yours," he said. "I am *all* yours."

I ran my hands down his stomach to his waist and held his hips.

"Forever?"

"Forever."

I reached up, threw my arm around his neck, and pulled him onto me. He kissed me softly.

"It's funny, you know," he said, lips against mine. "I spent all those years worrying that I didn't belong anywhere, and all this time the place I belonged was right in front of me."

"The farm?" I frowned. "You knew you belonged here?"

Cole rolled his eyes. "With you, you numbskull."

"Ooooohhh, yeah. Smooth. I like it."

"Shhh. You're ruining it."

"Sorry, I really trod on your moment there, didn't I?"

The sound of small children squealing in delight signalled the end of our peace and quiet. Cole leapt up. "Clothes on, mister. The invasion has begun."

POP STAR SHOCKER!
Cole blows the lid on TV show's dark secrets

Cole Kennedy's WebFlix documentary, "A Fire Inside Me," has revealed a cornucopia of scandalous abuses at the heart of the TV show that made him famous.

Kennedy and other celebrities interviewed for the show—including former judge Robbie Johnswagger and series one winner Jocasta Rose—levelled a plethora of disturbing accusations at Felicity Quant's Totally Television and the producers of "Make Me a Pop Star."

Revelations include contestants being forced to sign complicated contracts after days with little sleep, often without parental or independent legal advice, "gruelling" sixteen-hour rehearsal sessions, the exploitation of mentally and emotionally vulnerable people for entertainment purposes and contestants being sent home from the show with absolutely no aftercare.

Kennedy revealed how producers forced him back into the closet and booted his teenage sweetheart, now boyfriend, Tobias Lyngstad off the show so female fans wouldn't realise he was gay. He alleged producers deliberately humiliated Lyngstad by turning "marriage material" into a phenomenon, then stole and leaked their private messages to the press to drive a wedge between the young lovers.

The documentary also cast doubt on the explosive claims made by Kennedy's ex, Jasper Horner, in his tell-all memoir, with a series of witnesses, including a New York paramedic, giving versions of events markedly different to Horner's.

Backing up Kennedy's scandalous claims about Totally Records' business practices, singer Jocasta Rose revealed Quant had subjected her to "routine body-shaming, crash diets and dangerous weight loss."

Rose split with Totally Records a decade ago and said Quant "has done everything in her power to try to tie me up in legal disputes over my music, including songs I wrote, for years."

"I wouldn't let anyone I know or love sign a contract with Totally Records," Rose said. "It's an abusive relationship, and you'll spend years trying to escape it."

Rose yesterday released a funk version of Dolly Parton's "Jolene," arranged by Kennedy. Rose has previously revealed that she and Kennedy have written and will perform several duets on her next album.

The documentary also revealed Johnswagger was sacked from "Pop Star" not for drinking, as Totally Television claimed, but for standing up to Quant and the show's producers over the treatment of contestants and Totally Records' signed artists.

Quant has been contacted for comment.

BOMBSHELL BACKTRACK!

Kennedy's ex claims Quant "made me lie" in £2M book deal

Cole Kennedy's disgruntled ex is backing away from the scandalous allegations he made about the pop star in his tell-all memoir.

Jasper Horner's claims of Kennedy's drug abuse, sexual proclivities and rock and roll lifestyle put the skids under the pop star's career when it was released last summer. But now Horner claims he "feels used" by Felicity Quant.

"She offered me two million quid to tell my story," he said. "She tore up all the NDAs and contracts I'd signed. I didn't even have to write the book, just sign the deal. She arranged the ghostwriter, all I had to do was tell him my story.

"But what's in that book is not what I said. Felicity didn't let me see it until it was already printed and on its way to bookstores. By then it was too late. When I told her I wanted nothing to do with the claims in the book, she waved my contract in my face and told me I had no choice but to stick to 'my' story."

Horner said he was speaking out now because he wanted to add his voice to the flood of stories about Quant's business practices that have emerged since Kennedy's WebFlix documentary was released.

"I'm genuinely sorry to Cole for the hurt all this must have caused," he said. "I was a terrible person when we were dating. I was struggling with addiction. Like Cole, I'm clean now. I can't put right what I did back then, but I can set the record straight about our relationship and the rubbish that was written in that book."

Quant could not be contacted for comment.

COMMENT

The Last Hallelujah: Why we won't miss "Make Me a Pop Star"

If all good things must come to an end, then so, presumably, must all rubbish. Finally, after polluting our airwaves for 17 years, Channel Three has pulled the plug on the toxic cavalcade of shattered dreams that was "Make Me a Pop Star."

It may have given the world some of the biggest names in music, but it also humiliated innocents, exploited the vulnerable and forced us to listen to depressed teenagers sing "Hallelujah" more times than human endurance can bear. For that alone, it should be fired out of a cannon, directly into the sun, where it can burn for a million years in a billion nuclear explosions. The boil has been lanced, the cancer has been cut out. The downfall of Felicity Quant's toxic empire was a long time coming, but at last we are all free.

Nothing can stop the rivers of cash that flow into the pockets of Quant's famous miniskirts—she owns too much of our music industry for that. But the scandal that surrounds her means her brand is now as publicly toxic as it has been privately toxic for many years. If that's enough to stop more talented young hopefuls wasting their best years being milked dry to the point of desiccation by Quant's plastic pop factory, then perhaps, one last time, we should all sing "Hallelujah"?

Lyngstad launches YouTube channel for pop

Tobias Lyngstad has launched a YouTube channel, Seriously Pop, which the former PureFM presenter says aims to "be the place pop fans gather to discuss music."

Lyngstad's partner, the former Go Tos singer Cole Kennedy, has been promoting the venture on his social media, helping the channel clock up close to five million followers already…

Cole to release tell-all book

Fresh from the success of his WebFlix documentary, Cole Kennedy has signed a book deal with Proud Marlee Press to publish an authorised biography of his life.

In a statement, the publisher said journalist Ludo Boche had been engaged to write the as-yet untitled book, in close collaboration with Kennedy.

Boche has a biography of the late Sentinel theatre critic and icon of London's West End Ben Diamond coming out this summer.

"YES, CHEF!"
Marcel Dupont to wed Cole Kennedy's sister

Cole Kennedy's manager and big sister Fiona looks set to beat her famous brother up the aisle, announcing her engagement to Michelin-starred celebrity chef Marcel Dupont.

Don't expect a fancy society wedding—the couple are famously private. So private, in fact, this gossip column had no idea they were dating. Whenever the wedding is, you can guarantee the catering will be top shelf. All they need now is a wedding singer...

Epilogue
THREE MONTHS LATER

The sky was grey, and the wind blustering through the ancient rocks of Stonehenge was chilly. The joys of summer in England. I tucked my hands into my armpits, but the synthetic fabric of my waterproof jacket completely failed to provide any warmth. Cole kicked his shoes off.

"Are you mad? It's absolutely bitter. You'll catch your death, babes."

"I want to feel the grass under my feet," he said. "Can you believe we've come all this way and they don't even let you touch the rocks?"

"Nope, no rock touching," I confirmed.

"Like, I've wanted to see Stonehenge all my life, and now I'm *so* close. I can see it. It's *right there*. But I don't feel like it will be real until I can actually touch it. I need to put skin to stone, you know?"

The wind whipped around us, lashing drizzle against my face. I put up my hood.

"Can you hold me? I'm bloody freezing."

Cole slid his arms around me, his oversized loose-knit jumper making him as soft and warm as a teddy bear. I leaned into him, stealing his heat. I closed my eyes, pretending I hadn't seen a group of teenage girls walking towards us.

"Can we please get a picture with you?" one of them asked.

"Of course!" Cole said cheerily, and the girls squealed in delight.

I opened my eyes and reached out a hand for their phone. "Here, let me take that for you."

"Would you be in the picture, too, please, Tobias? If you don't mind?"

I smiled. "Of course not." I waved them in. "A selfie, then."

Taking photos with Cole's fans, I had discovered, was a bit like going for a leak at the pub. You can drink pint after pint and not need the loo. But the second you do, the moment you break that seal, it's a never-ending flood, and you're off to the toilet every five seconds. Once we had taken a selfie with these girls, the floodgates would open, and everyone would be queuing up to meet Cole and take a picture. He loved every minute of it. I was still getting used to it.

"So, is he marriage material, then, Cole?" an older man shouted across the field. His teenage daughter looked mortified.

"I'd marry him in a heartbeat," Cole said. And for the first time on that blustery Wiltshire hilltop, I felt warm. Not only flush with love and gratitude, but with a rush of self-satisfaction—and with the realisation that being "marriage material boy" no longer carried any weight. It couldn't hurt me. I felt unburdened. I was comfortable in myself, so I was finally free to leave it behind, to move on.

We spent an hour meeting fans, taking photos, in the freezing cold afternoon. The five-thousand-year-old ancient monument we had come to see was being almost completely ignored by everyone. Everyone except Cole, that is.

"Fuck it, I'm doing it," he said, a look of steely determination on his face.

"Doing what?"

"Are you coming with me?" Cole turned to me with a massive grin. He grabbed my hand and looked across to the stones.

"Oh no, we can't, babes, we'll get in trouble."

Cole could not have cared less. Before I knew it, we were under the rope, our arms wrapped around the ancient granite pillars. Cole's eyes were closed, his face pressed against the rock, a smile on his face as broad as the landscape around us. Someone blew a whistle and shouted for us to get back.

"I told you we'd get in trouble," I said.

"Rock and roll, baby," he said, squeezing my hand.

Sometimes the headlines write themselves. And we were definitely going to make headlines.

THE END.

Author's Note

Thank you for reading *Going Solo*. I hope you enjoyed your time with Toby and Cole. If you've previously read *The Paper Boys*, I hope you enjoyed catching up with some familiar faces and places.

When I started planning *Going Solo*, I wanted to write a book set in radio—the industry where I started my media career. Although I knew I wanted a DJ and a pop star to get together, I didn't quite intend for this book to become such a commentary on reality television and the way it treats people and the effects it has on people's lives. But once I came up with the idea of the boys meeting at the *Make Me a Pop Star* audition, the die was cast. I'm a reality television survivor (no pun intended), having taken part in a show that aired some twenty years ago. So, in this book, I drew on some of my real experiences and those of my friends. I experienced first-hand the manipulation of producers, other contestants trying to throw me under a bus, the horrors of a media pile on, and a string of super nasty comments on the kind of discussion boards that existed online in the days before Twitter/X and Facebook. I felt shame, embarrassment, humiliation, depression and regret. I still don't talk about that experience fondly. Unlike Toby, I've never leveraged it. Perhaps until this book.

Make Me a Pop Star is obviously entirely fictional, but I read and watched a lot of interviews with people who had been on shows like it in real life, including the wonderful Rylan Clark—who, in some ways, was probably an early, unconscious inspiration for Toby. To be clear, I adore Rylan, and Toby is *not* Rylan. As part of my research, I watched the BBC's fantastic documentary *Boybands Forever*. It charts the rise of boybands in the 1990s—including the ones I grew up with and loved: Take That, East17, Boyzone, Five, Westlife and Blue. The show is an alarming insight into "the sausage factory" and the reality of being in one of those bands. I recommend you seek it out and watch it, if you can.

I also listened to the BBC's fabulous podcast *Offstage: Inside the X Factor*, which told the stories of those who took part in, and worked on, the most famous music audition reality show of all—the one that gave us One Direction, Leona Lewis, and Little Mix, among so many others. Some of those stories are tough to listen to. Some of the elements I've included in this book are based on common experiences of people who took part in similar programs.

In 2021, the UK Parliament held an enquiry into the treatment of reality television contestants and introduced new rules through the industry regulator, Ofcom. Under the rules, broadcasters are required to take due care of the welfare of anyone who might be at risk of harm as a result of taking part in a reality TV show, including providing aftercare. Hopefully, this is making a difference.

As I had in *The Paper Boys*, in this book I wanted to explore the role the media plays in our society—this time from the point of view of those who are on the receiving end of the media's treatment. I was a reporter for a long time and, although I've never actually gone through anyone's bins, I have been asked to do a lot of things I'm not proud of—including trespassing not just on private property, but on private grief. Most relevant to this story, at one point in my career my newspaper editors had me chasing, day after day, a sporting hero whose career had descended into scandal and drug addiction. So, I've seen this from both sides. Cole and Toby spend a decade apart and, in that time, everything they learned about each other was through the media—which is, by definition, a distorted filter. What do we really know about the lives of the people we read about in the media? We should always question the narratives we consume. (Including the narratives they feed us themselves, about themselves, on social media. That, too, is a distorted filter.)

To be clear, the Go Tos and Cole Kennedy aren't based on any particular artists. But, as Jen, one of my amazing beta reader team, said: "this is very One Direction coded". The route to fame and the fact I chose five lads makes the comparisons easy, but it wasn't deliberate. I was a bit old to be a Directioner and I never really followed the band beyond enjoying their songs. Liam Payne died while I was editing this book and that tragedy, among other emotions, reinforced for me just how deeply we love our pop stars. Those crushes we develop on our favourite boybanders as teenagers never really leave us. (In my case, I was incredibly white-bread and was in love with Boyzone's Ronan Keating, and if he knocked on my front door today and confessed his undying love for me, I'd have to have a very uncomfortable conversation with my husband.)

Like any romance, the true theme of this book is "love conquers all". But I also wanted *Going Solo* to explore themes of identity and belonging, of control—having agency over our own lives, decisions and narratives—and of the idea of 'home'—what it is, what it represents, who we are there, and who we let in. These are all fundamental to our feeling of security, our health and our happiness and I wanted to see what happened to these characters when those things were changed, taken away, threatened or invaded.

A note on Katy Perry, who attempted a comeback during the writing of this book and found controversy left and right. I chose 'Firework' for Toby not only because it was the biggest song around in the years before the early part of this book is set, but because I remember watching *Katy Perry: Part of Me* and seeing her get up on stage right after being dumped by her husband, Russell Brand. This provided the inspiration for the scene before Cole's Stockholm show.

You may have noticed some familiar surnames in this book. Fashion icon Dame Mary Quant also died while I was writing this book. I gave Felicity Mary's look and her surname. In my defence, when I started writing her, Felicity wasn't going to be the baddie. My apologies to the late Dame Mary. Meanwhile, Toby's name, Lyngstad, was chosen because I love ABBA and its Anni-Frid's surname. Devotees will note I've made Toby's family of Swedish heritage, while Lyngstad is generally considered of Norwegian origin (as is Anni-Frid). If you spotted that and tut-tutted, please note you're my kind of nerd and you are welcome here. By the way, Toby mentions a couple of real artists, whom I love: Metteson is a real Norwegian artist producing fabulous pop music right now. Felix Sandman is a Swedish artist and a bit more established. His track 'Miss You Like Crazy' is the real theme song to this book.

Finally, *Going Solo* is a fantasy. It's the fantasy so many of us have as teenagers—that the pop star on the poster on our bedroom wall is going to spot us in the crowd, recognise how special we are, and choose us. I hope this book gave you some of those old teenage flutters and that, despite the passage of time, you still have the bladder control to enjoy them. Thank you again for reading.

Be queer and mighty, always,

D.P. Clarence

10 April 2025

Acknowledgments

Thanks first and always to a dear friend, the writer and critic Beejay Silcox, whose tireless belief that writing books is what I'm meant to be doing with my life is sometimes the only thing that gets me back to my computer. Every writer needs a Beejay and I'm incredibly blessed to have found mine twenty-nine years ago, sitting beside me at the front of class, delivering withering and unsolicited critiques of all my high school enemies—and then cheering me on as I delivered "an incredibly subversive" oral presentation to our English class on my chosen text, Dolly Parton's 'Jolene'.

Mahoosive thanks to the wonderful team of professionals who helped me tell Toby and Cole's story: my tireless cover designer, Bailey McGinn; my peerless development editor, Natasha Bell; my fabulous copy editor and proofreader, Elyse Lyon; my other proofreader-for-life and good friend, Wendy Wood; and fellow author and awesome hooman Valerie Gomez (@valeriegomez_writes, author of *Cover Story*), who once again created the beautiful chapter illustrations.

Huge thanks to my team of #bookstagram beta readers for their invaluable insights and advice, including Andrea (@ladypenelopeslibrary), Jen (@fae_princess_in_space), Rose (@bookspines.and.roses), Mitch (@born_this_way2), my dear friend and author Kate (@kemery82, you must read her YA mystery, *My Family and Other Suspects*), Bernard (@_veelox, who was my eyes and ears on the realities of being a wheelchair user).

As ever, thank you to my amazing chums from the "Nashers" writing group—Yvette, Nia, Dervla, Derek, Ann, and Lou—for beta reading, endless advice, continued inspiration and friendship. (Lou's book, *The World Happiness Organisation*, is out now! You can find it on Amazon.)

Thank you to Allie, for helping me consider the finer points of trans representation.

Big sticky love and endless thank yous to my husband, Luke, who continues to believe the lie that if he leaves me alone to write, I might eventually earn £30,000 a month doing this.

And, as ever, the biggest thanks of all goes to you for reading. I continue to be astounded by the amount of love I get from total strangers who read *The Paper Boys* and reached out to tell me how much they enjoyed it. I hope you enjoyed your time with Toby and Cole. If you did, please consider leaving a review or telling a friend about *Going Solo*. It's a huge help for independent authors like me, and I appreciate it more than Aunty Cheryl appreciates blackout curtains and Berocca after a big night on the town.

Be queer and mighty, always,

Dan

D.P. Clarence

P.S. Sign up to my newsletter at www.dpclarence.com for occasional freebies!

About the Author

About the Author

D.P. Clarence (Dan to his friends—including you, dear reader) was a journalist for a long, long time before finally deciding to bite the bullet and do the thing he always wanted to do—write books about boys kissing other boys.

His debut novel was The Paper Boys, the first book in the Brent Boys series, starring Sunny and Ludo. The free novella, *The Silly Season*, follows what happens to Sunny and Ludo next. *Going Solo* is the second full novel in the series.

Dan is an avid reader of everything from rom-coms to literary fiction—but he especially loves LGBTQ+ fiction. You can see what he's been reading lately, on Instagram and Goodreads.

Originally from Australia, Dan lives in London with his husband and their very smiley corgi.